Sharing Shane

Hannah Murray

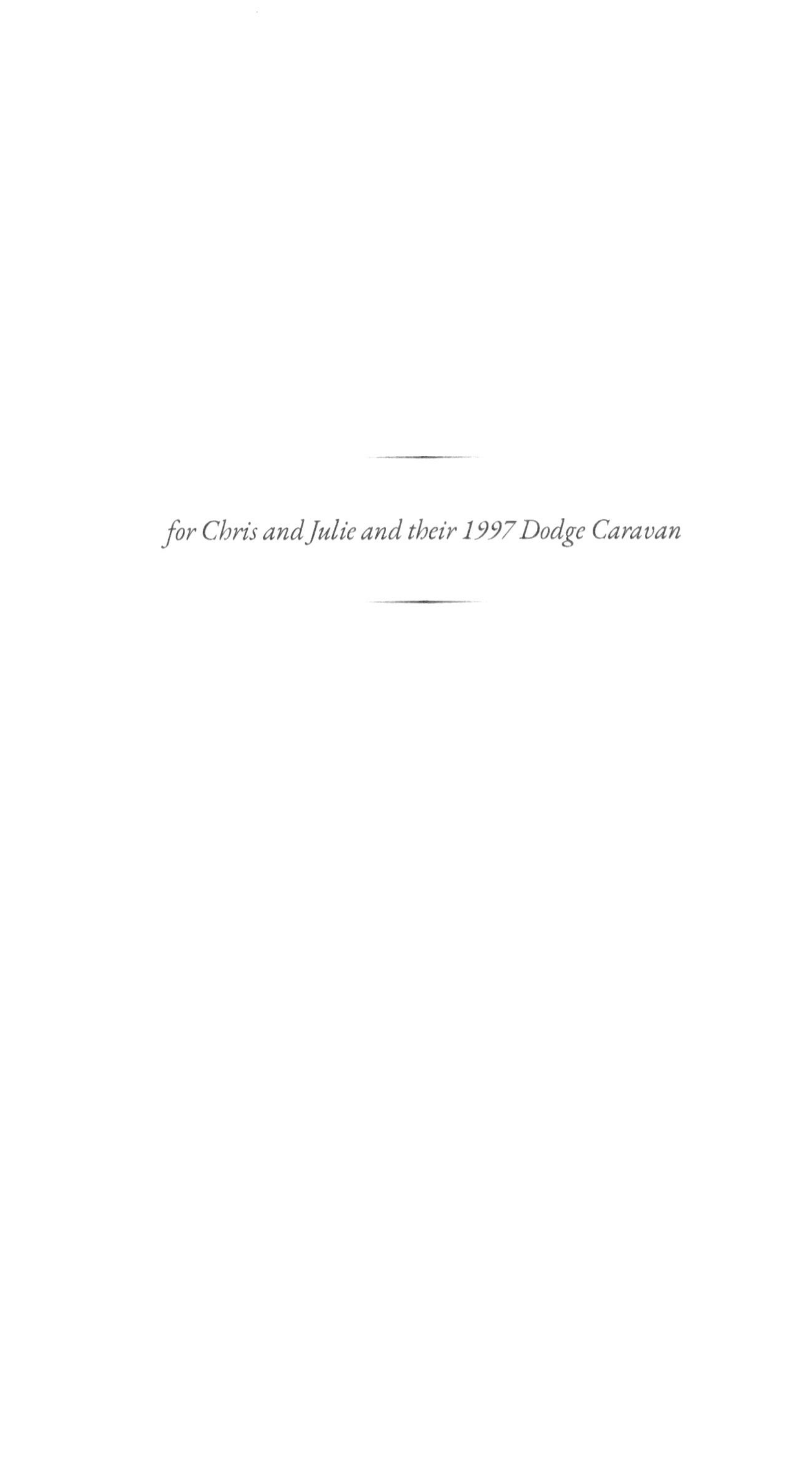

for Chris and Julie and their 1997 Dodge Caravan

"Nobody has ever measured, not even poets, how much the heart can hold."

— ZELDA FITZGERALD

thing he did whenever he was agitated, and seeing it only added to her sense of baffled guilt. "I'm sorry, honey, but this call is crucial. I want to go over my notes, make sure I'm prepared."

She nodded. "Okay, bad timing. It's just...well, it's been a while."

His gaze was puzzled. "Been a while?"

"Since we've been together," she told him, huffing out a breath when he continued to look blank. "Had sex, Derek. It's been a while since we had sex."

He shrugged, unconcerned. "Not so long."

"Yes, so long," she corrected him, determined to have this conversation once and for all. "I mean, you spent the night last night and you barely even spoke to me before you went to sleep."

"Baby, I was beat. My boss is up my ass on this marketing campaign, and you know my promotion is riding on it."

"I know." She took a breath and made a conscious effort to unclench. "I just miss you."

"I miss you too, babe." He smiled, making his blue eyes crinkle. "But it won't be forever. Besides, you can't blame it all on me. Your schedule has been insane lately, too."

That was true enough. She'd finished her master's degree last fall and had been working as a speech therapist in a clinical fellowship since January. The work was challenging and often frustrating, and she often found herself at the office well into the evening. She was so happy to be in a job where she felt like she was making a difference in the lives of the kids she worked with, she hardly noticed the long hours and time spent away from home.

But she at least tried to make time for Derek, and lately it didn't feel reciprocal.

"I know the promotion is important to you. I do," she

One

"Babe, c'mon. I'm going to be late."

Veronica Black tamped down on a surge of impatience and danced her tongue over her boyfriend's earlobe, following it up with a skim of her teeth. He loved having his ears nibbled, and could usually be counted on to throw her down on the closest flat surface and plow her like an Iowa cornfield whenever she did it.

Except this morning, apparently, because he jerked his head away. "Roni. I told you, I have a conference call."

"Not for twenty minutes." She shoved aside her annoyance at the nickname and focused on making *something* happen, even if it was just a make-out session with a side of heavy petting. She slid her tongue down the side of his throat, grimacing at the bitter taste of the cologne he'd slapped on. "We can do a lot in twenty minutes."

"Dammit, I said no," he snapped, and pushed her away.

Stung, she took a step back. "Okay. Sorry."

Derek signed, long-suffering and annoyed, and strok hand down his silk tie. It was his calming down gesture, s insisted when he looked skeptical. "And I'm proud of you for working so hard for it."

He smiled at her now, a slight quirk of his mouth that showed just a hint of teeth. "Thanks, babe."

"I just want to spend some time with you," she continued. She laid a hand on his chest and looked up at him. "Just the two of us."

"And we will," he promised. He leaned down to press a kiss to her forehead, patting her hand at the same time, then smoothly stepped away. "We have that vacation coming up. When is it, three weeks?"

"A week and a half," she corrected.

He took out his phone and frowned at the screen. "That can't be right."

"It's a week and a half away, Derek," she said and the bite in her voice had him lifting his head again. "We've been planning it for months, and I know it's on your calendar because I put it there myself."

"It's there, don't worry," he said, his tone soothing once again.

"Okay." Mollified, she smiled. "Though I hope we'll be able to connect before then."

"Depends on how this campaign goes," he said absently, already back in his phone. He tapped away on the screen for a minute, then glanced up. "Don't you have to go?"

"Hmm? Oh." She glanced at the clock on the wall. "I'm not meeting with my boss until eight-thirty, and my first client isn't until ten. I have plenty of time."

"Maybe, but you should get going. Traffic is a bear around campus this time of day."

"Which is why I walk to work," she reminded him, perplexed. "What's with you this morning?"

He sighed, another long-suffering sound that threatened

to set her teeth on edge. "I'm sorry, Veronica, but I have to prepare for this call."

"You're kicking me out?" She blinked. "Derek, this is *my* apartment."

"Believe me, if I had enough time before the call I'd go back home." He glanced around her living room, with its clutter of books and furnishings, no doubt comparing it to his minimalist, grey-walled condo and finding it wanting, as usual. He shook his head. "Can you head out early, stop for a coffee along the way or something?"

"If you need the time," she began.

He gave her a relieved smile. "Thank you."

"Hey." She took his face in her hands. "You're really anxious about this call, aren't you?"

His expression twisted with embarrassment, a flush blooming under his self-tanner, and he gave her a sheepish smile. "It's just important, that's all. If I nail the campaign, I get the promotion. And if I get the promotion, I can start looking at some of the bigger marketing firms. It's my future. Our future."

"You got this," she told him and pressed a firm kiss to his lips. "And I'll get out of your way so you can do what you need to do."

"Thank you." He gave her a genuine smile that lit up his handsome face, and most of her resentment at being booted out of the apartment faded away.

"Do you want to have lunch today?" she asked, crossing to the front door. She grabbed her messenger bag off the coat hook and glanced over her shoulder in time to catch his frown. "I mean, if you have time."

"You don't have to work this afternoon?" he asked, his frown deepening.

She hooked the bag over her head, the strap across her chest. "Nope. The office is closed this afternoon because they're doing some scheduled building maintenance, so I'm all clear after twelve-thirty."

"I'll see how the morning goes and call you, all right?"

She beamed at him and opened the door. "Sounds great. Knock 'em dead."

"I'll do my best," he promised, and with one last kiss, nudged her out the door.

She was smiling as she jogged down the steps of her building, and bounced out onto the sidewalk in a good mood. The early May sunshine was struggling through the few lingering clouds from last night's thunderstorm, and she had a moment's regret that she hadn't grabbed her sunglasses.

She was half thinking of going back for them when the phone she'd tucked into her pocket jangled the ringtone she'd assigned to her best friend. She winced, tempted not to pick up, but knew if she didn't Delia would just keep calling.

She dug into her pocket and swiped to answer. "Hang on, Delia. Let me get my earpiece in."

It took her a second to fumble the little device out of her bag, and another few to connect the call. "You there?"

"Hell must have frozen over, you figured out your Bluetooth." came the sardonic reply.

Veronica rolled her eyes and stuffed her phone back in her pocket. "Don't bust my balls, I've had a weird morning."

"Speaking of balls," Delia went on cheerfully, "how'd things go with Dead Dick Derek last night?"

Veronica swallowed a snort. "You're not seriously calling him that."

"The man hasn't fucked you in over a month, so yes, that's his name now."

"It's as much my fault as his," Veronica protested.

"That's bullshit, and we both know it. I have it on good authority that you're a firecracker in bed."

Veronica shoved at the hair blowing in her face. "You've been talking to your cousin again."

"Yes, because you blocked him on social media, and now he's asking me for your number. I didn't give it to him," she went on before Veronica could panic, "because you're more family to me than he is. But he's getting annoying."

"One drunken night freshman year," Veronica muttered, "and I'm still paying for it."

"Joel will get over it. He only gets weepy over you when he drinks. Which, come to think of it, is pretty much all the time."

"And you know this how?"

"His mother told me. He's in Oklahoma now, living in her basement."

Veronica stopped at the end of the block, glanced both ways, then stepped out into the street. "I don't need to know this."

"Knowledge is power, Veronica."

"Thank you, Francis Bacon."

"Who?"

"Francis Bacon. He's the one who said knowledge is power. Thomas Jefferson said it a bunch of times too, but Bacon said it first. I mean, we think. It was 1597, so the records are kind of sketchy."

"Nobody cares, V."

Veronica rolled her eyes. "Did you have an actual reason for calling, or did you just want to torture me?"

"Of course, I have a reason, and you haven't answered the question yet."

"I've forgotten what it was, since you insisted on reminding me of younger Veronica's poor decision-making skills."

"How did last night go?" Delia repeated.

Veronica sighed. "He fell asleep."

Delia's gasp was sharp in her ear. "He fell asleep?"

"He's been working long hours on this marketing campaign," Veronica said, her voice trailing off weakly.

"Oh, honey."

"I know." Veronica slowed as she approached the coffee shop. "Something's up."

"Something is *definitely* up," Delia agreed.

"He's just busy." Veronica reached for the door handle, then stepped back. There were way too many people in there, and none of them needed to hear this conversation. "We've both been busy. We just need to find some time to be together, that's all."

"That's all?"

"That's all," Veronica said firmly. "We've got Bermuda coming up, and we'll have a whole week where it's just the two of us, with plenty of time to have sex, and it'll be great."

"I'm willing to believe that if you are."

Veronica decided to ignore that. "And thank you, by the way, for the hookup on the resort. I would never have been able to afford this without your discount voucher."

"We can't use it before it expires, so it was just going to waste. Besides, we'll probably get another one. Julian is in charge of coordinating next year's surgical conference, and the resort is schmoozing him hard to hold it there."

"Well, thank you anyway."

"Anything for you, sugar tits. Dead Dick Derek, on the other hand..."

"Shut up," Veronica laughed. "You can't keep calling him that."

"Oh, but I can. Where are you, anyway? You want to get breakfast?"

"Can't. I have a meeting with my supervisor in an hour."

"So? That's plenty of time. Let's go to Frank's Diner."

"That's all the way across town," Veronica protested. "This is my mid-fellowship review, and I—oh, shit."

"What?"

"Shit!" Veronica stepped out of the flow of pedestrian traffic to dig through her messenger bag. "I left the folder with all my notes for this meeting in my desk at home."

"So? Go get it. You can't be more than what, four blocks away? And you just said you had an hour before your meeting."

"I know, but Derek is back at the apartment, and he had an important conference call this morning."

"You can't go back to your apartment to pick up a folder with important papers in it—papers that are vital to your career as a speech therapist, something you've been working your ass off to accomplish ever since you left teaching three years ago—because your boyfriend is on the phone."

"Anything can sound silly when you put it that way."

"Yeah, silly is the word I was thinking of."

"Okay, I'm walking back."

"Congratulations on being a grown-up."

Veronica weaved her way through the people crowding the sidewalk. "You're such a shit."

"It's part of my charm," Delia reminded her. "Hey, have you gone shopping for your trip yet?"

"Not really. I mean, I bought a new bathing suit online, but that's it."

"Then we should go this weekend," Delia said immediately. "You need fun beach clothes."

"I have summer clothes, Delia."

"You have summer work clothes," Delia corrected, "because all you do is work. You need fun play clothes."

"So, I'll pick out a few sundresses online."

"Amateur," Delia chided. "Come on, go shopping with

me. We can go to the outlet mall in Birch Run and I promise not to push you to go outside your budget."

Veronica snorted in disbelief.

"Okay, I won't push much. And I'll only sneak one or two things in. We never have any fun anymore."

"Okay, okay." Veronica hurried across the street, racing to beat the light. "How about Saturday? Or today, actually. The office is closed this afternoon, so I'm free after lunch."

"Ooh, we can have lunch at Frank's Diner."

"Sorry," Veronica said, walking into her building. "I'm going to have lunch with Derek if he's free. But I can meet you after."

"Fine." Delia's voice held an annoyed grumble. "Playing second fiddle to Dead Dick is getting kind of old."

"I can't tell if you're joking or not," Veronica said, panting a little as she hurried up the stairs.

"Mostly joking," Delia answered. "But I do miss you."

"We'll do a girl's night soon, I promise." Veronica tiptoed up to her front door, digging out her key. "But I'm here, so I have to go."

"No, wait. I wanted to talk to you about something else."

"Can't it wait?"

"Well, it *could*, but we're on the phone now. It's about your trip."

"I need to get my paperwork, and I need to be quiet so I don't screw with Derek's conference call."

"Fine, I'll hold. Should I hum some annoying music?"

Veronica stifled a snicker and carefully turned her key in the lock. "You're such a jackass."

"That's why you love me," Delia said and began to hum.

Veronica had to stifle another snicker when she recognized an extremely slow—and yes, annoying—version of Shake It Off. She quietly pushed the door open, wincing when it creaked. She kept meaning to ask the building manager to take a look at that, but like everything else it had taken a back seat to her schedule.

She left the door ajar, not wanting to make it squeak again, and crept on her toes to the small desk she kept in the corner of her living room.

"God, you sound like a herd of elephants," Delia said in her ear. "I thought you were trying to be quiet."

Veronica rolled her eyes and hissed, hoping her friend would take the hint and shut up.

"I will not shut up," Delia said with a laugh. "Triple D can't hear me, and you can't talk back, so I'm going to get in as many words as I can."

Veronica bit her lip to hold back the retort and carefully slid the drawer of the small desk open. The red folder sat in the center, right where she'd thought it would be. She scooped it up and tucked it in her bag, eager to get out of the apartment before she alerted Derek to her presence.

She crept back to the door, her steps slow and exaggerated, and she was just laying a hand on the knob when she heard it.

Delia, who had been in mid-rant about some movie that wasn't nearly as funny as it was supposed to be, asked, "Was that a moan?"

It had certainly sounded like one, coming from the direction of her bedroom. She frowned, then shook her head. "Derek's on his conference call," she whispered. "I'm sure it was just—"

She broke off at another sound, this one distinctly *not* mistakable for anything that might occur over a conference call about a marketing campaign.

"Okay, that was a squeal." Delia's voice had gone dark with suspicion. "A sex squeal. What is he doing, watching porn while you're at work?"

Unlikely, considering the conversation they'd had a couple of months ago about incorporating some sexy movie-watching into their love life. Derek had been appalled at the thought, and though he'd been adamant that he wasn't judging her, Veronica had still been left with the distinct impression that he'd thought there was something wrong with her for suggesting it.

Which was a problem for another time, because the latest noise to drift down the hall hadn't come from some random porn star—it had come from Derek.

"That's Derek," she whispered. "That's his 'oh baby, right there' moan."

"He fucking better be jerking off."

Veronica wasn't sure exactly which emotions were tangled up in the ball of lead that had taken up residence in her gut, and she didn't want to take the time to parse it out at the moment. But she definitely recognized the beginnings of rage as she tiptoed down the hallway to the open bedroom door.

He wasn't jerking off.

Time seemed to freeze as she took in the details. There was her brass bed, the one she'd found at the Ann Arbor flea market two summers ago and spent the better part of a month restoring to a mirror gleam. The jumble of clothes she'd left piled across the quilt her grandmother had made for her when she'd graduated from high school was still there, evidence of her early morning scramble to find something to wear. Her books still sat on the windowsill and bedside tables, her plants still hung from their baskets by the windows. And that was her boyfriend standing with his back to her, half bent over the gleaming footboard.

The naked woman bent over in front of him? That was new.

Veronica recognized her next-door neighbor right away, though Cami was usually a little more put together when they ran into each other by the mailboxes. Her red hair was tangled around her head instead of in the sleek braid she usually favored, and her porcelain skin held a distinct flush.

It looked like they'd been going at it for a while, she noted dispassionately. Cami was covered in a light sheen of sweat, and there was a line of damp down the back of the dress shirt Derek still wore.

Which was still tucked neatly into his slacks, she noted, and had to stifle a bark of hysterical laughter.

If the moans were anything to go by, they seemed to be enjoying themselves. She could hear them clearly now, standing mere feet away, breathy pants and muffled squeaks from Cami and the heavy moans from Derek that told her he was nearing his big finish.

She almost walked away and left them to it, but then he shifted slightly, angling to the side just enough for her to see his cock withdraw, then plunge back inside.

His bare, uncovered cock.

"Are you fucking kidding me?" she demanded as the bubbling rage spilled over, and had the grim satisfaction of seeing them leap apart as though someone had set fire to the air between them.

Derek's eyes were wide with shock, and she was pretty sure his face would've been dead white if not for the self-tanner. "Roni! What are you doing here?"

"Seriously?" Veronica ground out while Delia cackled gleefully in her ear. "That's what you're going to say to me?"

"What...I mean...you..."

"I came home to get the paperwork for my meeting," she informed him icily. "Which I forgot because you hustled me out the door this morning so you could prep for your 'conference call'." Her eyes raked over him, still fully dressed except for his wet dick poking out of his pants. "What exactly is this marketing campaign, anyway?"

"Baby, I can explain," he began.

"Really?" She folded her arms across her chest, raising a brow when he flushed. "You can explain why you were balls deep in my next-door neighbor without a condom?"

"I...I..."

She nodded. "That's what I thought."

Veronica spared a glance for Cami, who was scrambling into her clothes. "And you," she said, her voice filled with disappointment. "I thought better of you."

Half into her pants, the redhead flushed a bright cherry red from her nipples to her hairline. "Veronica, I just—"

"How long?" Veronica demanded.

Cami blinked. "What?"

Veronica jerked her head towards Derek, who was gaping like a fish with his wet dick hanging out of his open fly. "How long have you been fucking my boyfriend?"

Cami's gaze darted to Derek, then back to Veronica. She swallowed hard. "About two months."

"And how long without condoms?"

Cami swallowed again. "The...the whole time. I'm allergic to latex."

"You've never heard of a non-latex condom?"

"Veronica, I'm really—"

"Oh, shut up." Veronica cut her off and turned back to Derek. "Give me my key."

He held up his hands, palms out in a classic *hey, I'm harmless* gesture. His expression had gone from shocked dismay to calculated charm—she could actually *see* him trying to think his way out of the mess he'd fucked his way into. "Veronica, let's talk about this."

She had to fight to keep her hand open instead of curling it into a fist to punch his smug, cheating face. "Give. Me. My. Key."

He shoved a hand into his pocket. "You're overreacting."

"Am I," she said coldly, not a hint of question in her tone, and Delia cackled again.

His face twisted, anger and annoyance flitting through his expression before he smoothed it out again. He pulled her apartment key off his key ring and laid it in her palm, then clamped his hand over hers before she could pull away.

"Baby, come on. You don't want to do this."

"Let go, Derek."

His fingers tightened. "We can talk about this."

"The only thing we can talk about right now is what's going to happen to your kneecaps if you don't let go of my hand and get the fuck out of my apartment." She forced her lips to peel back in a smile. His face blanched, his fingers slackening, and she pulled free.

She slid the key into the pocket of her slacks, then stepped back. "Get out."

"You have to let me explain," he insisted. "You owe me that much."

"Oh, shit, he did not just say that," Delia muttered in her ear.

"Owe you?" Veronica sucked in a breath. *Don't kill him, you can't kill him. "Owe you?"*

Out of the corner of her eye she saw Cami start to slink out of the room, her shirt clutched to her chest. Deciding to keep her focus on the person who deserved her wrath, she ignored her neighbor.

"If you don't leave now," she told Derek, her voice utterly calm, "I will break your nose, stomp your knee, and twist your penis off and feed it to you."

"Nice one," Delia said approvingly as Derek's mouth dropped open in shock.

"And since you've conveniently left it out for me," Veronica went on with a pointed glance at the penis in question, which didn't look nearly as happy as it had a few moments ago, "I can start there.

"Although if you're still here, Cami," she called out, raising her voice slightly, "I'll feed it to you instead."

A high-pitched squeak sounded in the hallway, followed by running footsteps and the slamming of her front door. Veronica quirked a brow at Derek. "Looks like that snack is all yours, pal."

That got him moving. He hastily tucked his pride and joy away—still wet, *ew*—and zipped his fly. He'd recovered somewhat, and his face was now twisted into what she'd always privately thought of as his *I'm-very-disappointed* face. "Clearly, you're not ready to be reasonable."

"Clearly," she replied drily as Delia snorted in her ear.

He shrugged into his suit jacket and gathered his briefcase. "I'll call you tonight, after you've had a chance to calm down."

She started to tell him she wouldn't answer, then shrugged. He'd find out soon enough.

Taking her shrug for assent, he smiled. "We'll get past this. You'll see."

"This motherfucker is delusional," Delia muttered, and Veronica said nothing. She watched him straighten his tie and started for the door, briefcase in hand. He slowed as he drew near her, raising his hand as though he wanted to touch her, then thought better of it. He gave her one last smile—a combination of compassion, reassurance, and confidence that made her blood boil all over again—and slipped out the door.

Veronica waited until she heard the front door click shut behind him, then let out the breath that she'd been holding in a string of curses.

"And then some," Delia agreed when she'd wound down. "Was he really standing there with his dick out?"

"His bare dick," Veronica confirmed, disgust coloring her voice. "No condom."

"Dumbass," was Delia's succinct opinion. "What are you going to do?"

"Get an STI test." Veronica concentrated on breathing, willing the haze of rage away. "Then I'm having the quilt dry-cleaned."

"Oh, your grandmother's quilt?" Delia asked in dismay.

"Yeah." Veronica frowned at it. It was probably mostly protected by her pile of discarded clothes, which she was also going to have to have cleaned. Shit. "I'll have to do that later. And I need to call a locksmith, too. I got Derek's key back, but..."

"Better safe than sorry," Delia agreed. "Won't your building take care of that?"

"It'll take them too long. I want it done now."

"Want me to call my guy?"

"Yeah. Yeah, I do." Veronica blew out a breath. "Shit, I'm pissed."

"No kidding."

"No, I mean *pissed*. I have to calm down before my meeting."

"I'd offer to get you high, but I'm out of edibles and you probably don't want to do that before work, anyway."

"I really don't."

"Why don't I come over to your place right now, and I'll hang out until you get back. We can order lunch, get the locks changed, gather up all of Dead Dick Derek's stuff and set it on fire. Then we can get nice and loaded."

"I thought you said you were out of edibles."

"I am," Delia said mournfully. "And my weed guy is in Florida visiting his mother."

"You know marijuana is legal in Michigan now," Veronica reminded her. "You can just go to the dispensary."

"Gary's been my guy since college, he'd be crushed if I went somewhere else," Delia said. "But it may come to that, because I don't know if I can handle life without THC right now."

"You're independently wealthy, your husband adores you, and your most pressing problem on any given day is which restaurant to have lunch at. What's to handle?"

"Julian's mother is in town," Delia said darkly.

"I stand corrected," Veronica said with a laugh. "Is she still leaning on you to have kids?"

"She's not getting any younger, Julian is her only son, the name will die out if we don't have babies," Delia parroted. "It doesn't matter how many times we both tell her we're not interested in procreating, she just keeps singing the same tune. And he's no fucking help. 'Got rounds, babe', he says, then goes to the hospital and leaves me with his rabidly baby-hungry mother all day long."

"Yeah, you need weed for that." Veronica glanced at the clock and winced. "Shit, I'm going to be late."

"Am I coming over or not?" Delia demanded.

"Yes, come over." Veronica walked out of the bedroom and headed for the front door. "I'll be done with work by twelve-thirty, then I'm going to get tested. I'll pick up some lunch on the way back."

"I'll order something," Delia countered. "You'll bring back some fast-food horror, and I want real food."

"Fine." Veronica scanned the apartment as she walked through, making sure no cheating boyfriends or half-naked neighbors lingered. "If you want to drink, you'll have to bring booze, too. I'm all out."

"I don't know why we're friends," Delia groused.

"I'll let you set fire to all Derek's stuff."

"That's why we're friends."

Veronica opened the front door. "You're on your way?"

"Yeah. I'll call the locksmith when I get there."

Veronica closed the door behind her, testing the knob to be certain it was secure. "Have him bring a deadbolt, too."

"You got it. See you later."

"Bye."

Veronica fumbled the earpiece off, then shoved it into the messenger bag with the fateful paperwork. She hurried down the stairs and out of the building, quickening her pace towards campus. She'd get through her meeting and her morning clients, then worry about what to do about Derek.

And whether or not it would include the need to post bail.

Two

By one-thirty she was stretched out on her living room couch, a taco in one hand and a glass of wine in the other. The wine had a bendy straw in it so she could drink it lying down.

"You're so fucking classy," Delia told her.

Veronica let go of the straw just long enough to say, "I know," then clamped her mouth around it again and sucked up more wine.

When the glass was empty, she set it on the floor and turned her attention to the taco. "You should talk, you're the one who ordered street tacos." She bit into it with undisguised glee, then mumbled around it, "I thought you were going to order up some fancy pants rich lady food."

"Cheating boyfriends deserve tacos," Delia said, then frowned. "Well, the cheating boyfriend doesn't deserve tacos, but when you find your boyfriend cheating on you, you deserve tacos."

Veronica mumbled her agreement around a mouthful of her well-earned lunch.

"And anyway, I was craving meat. Judith," she said with a

sneer for her mother-in-law, "has decided to go gluten-free and vegan."

Veronica paused with the taco halfway to her mouth. "Why?"

"She says she's trying to be healthier." Delia bit into her own taco and chewed. "Which would be fine if that were true, and she wasn't doing it just to fuck with me."

"Hand me a salsa packet, would you?"

From her cross-legged perch on the other side of the coffee table, Delia dug through the pile of food cartons, napkins, and condiment packets. "Green salsa or regular?"

"Regular. Thanks." Veronica caught the tossed packet one-handed, tore it open with her teeth, and squeezed the contents onto her taco. "Why do you think she's fucking with you?"

"Because she was eating a BLT on sourdough in the butler's pantry at two o'clock this morning, that's why."

"What were you doing up at two o'clock in the morning?"

"I wasn't. Julian put cameras in the kitchen. Caught her red-handed."

Veronica blinked. "You have video cameras in your kitchen?"

"Judith demanded Julian put them there, so she could make sure the housekeeper wasn't slipping anything non-vegan or gluteney into her food. I didn't know anything about it until Cora spotted them and asked me." Delia shook her head. "She thought we were spying on her, that we thought she was stealing or something. Julian came clean when she threatened to quit."

"Wait, wait, wait." Veronica made the effort to shove herself into a seated position, holding the taco aloft so none of the salsa would spill. "She asked Julian to spy on your housekeeper?"

"Yep."

"Because she thought she'd try to sneak her some dairy or eggs or pasta or something?"

"Yep."

"And those are the cameras that caught her eating bacon."

"You see why I need weed?"

Veronica snorted and salsa dripped out of the taco and onto her hand. She licked it off. "What did she say when you called her out?"

"I didn't." Delia looked smug. "I told Julian he had to do it, or I'd tell her about his vasectomy. Then I told Cora to make prime rib for dinner. With French bread."

"Nice."

"I know. I can't wait to see the look on her face."

"You rich people have weird problems," Veronica said and bit into her taco.

Delia thought for a moment, then shrugged. "You're not wrong."

Veronica's phone, lying face down on the coffee table, began to ring.

"Is that him again?"

"Yes." Veronica set her taco down and reached for the wine bottle. "He's called eight times since this morning. Four while I was in my meeting. Thank God I'd turned my phone off."

"Does he think you're going to talk to him?"

"No, he thinks I'm going to take him back."

"How could he possibly think that?"

Veronica shrugged and filled her wine glass. "My guess? He doesn't hear the word 'no' very often. And when he does, he can usually talk his way out of it. He's a born used car salesman."

"You caught him balls deep in your neighbor," Delia pointed out.

"Like I said, he doesn't hear 'no' a lot." Veronica passed the bottle, already half depleted, across the coffee table. "And I haven't answered any of his calls or texts, which is pissing him off."

"Good." Delia filled her glass. "What are you going to do about the trip?"

"The trip?" Veronica's eyes went wide over her wine glass. "Oh, shit. The trip. It's already paid for."

"By you," Delia reminded her.

"Yeah, but he gave me the money for his half." She frowned, then reached for her phone with a sigh. "I guess I have to send it back to him."

"The hell you do." Delia snatched the phone off the table before Veronica could. "Keep the money. Compensation for your pain and suffering."

"I can't do that, Delia," Veronica told her. "He paid me using a money transfer app, I'll just send it back the same way."

"He fucked your neighbor on your grandmother's quilt."

"Okay, maybe I'll let him sweat it a while."

"That's my girl," Delia cheered, and held up the bag of takeout. "More?"

Because it was as good an idea as any, Veronica held out her hand.

"Remind me to call the airline," she said, carefully squeezing salsa onto her fresh taco. "I bought Derek's plane ticket with my miles, so I can probably cancel it."

"You bought his plane ticket?"

"With miles," Veronica repeated defensively. "I didn't spend any money."

"Miles *are* money," Delia said, exasperated. "You cancel the ticket, and I'll call the resort."

Veronica chewed her taco thoughtfully. "What can they do?"

"They can get his name off the reservation, at least." Delia dug her phone out of her bag, then stared pointedly at Veronica. "What are you waiting for?"

Veronica sighed and set down her taco and wine. She didn't want to deal with this right now. Getting drunk was a much better idea, and she wasn't even halfway there. Tipsy, she concluded as she stood. The room only tilted a little before righting itself, and she was able to walk a reasonably straight line across the living room to the desk. She dug out the confirmation email from the airline, the one she'd dutifully printed and placed in her desk drawer at Derek's hyper-organized insistence, and made her way back to the couch.

It took all of ten minutes to cancel the reservation, though they charged her a cancellation fee. She figured she could afford it, since Derek's money was still sitting in her bank account. By the time she gave it back to him, she would've gotten paid again. And they were going to refund her miles, so all in all, it was much less painful than it could have been.

Task accomplished, she set her phone down and refilled her wine. Delia was talking to someone, presumably at the resort. She wasn't saying much, just a lot of agreeable humming and the occasional "I see" or "of course". It didn't look like the conversation was winding down anytime soon, so Veronica set her wine glass on the arm of the sofa where she could easily reach the straw and picked up her phone.

She'd lost two rounds of Candy Crush and was working on a third when Delia hung up. "Well, the good news is they can take his name off the reservation."

Veronica set the phone aside and leaned over to suck up more wine. "What's the bad news?"

"You can't go by yourself."

"What do you mean?" she mumbled around the wine straw.

Delia's lips twisted into a grimace. "The discount voucher

stipulates double occupancy. There have to be two people or the whole thing gets canceled without a refund."

Veronica's mouth dropped open and her wine straw fell out. "Seriously? I have to find someone else to come with me?"

Delia nodded. "They'll put down whoever. The reservation's in your name, and you can bring whoever you like as a guest. You just have to bring *someone*."

"You."

"Huh?"

"You can come with me." Energized by the idea, Veronica leaned forward. "We'll hang out on the beach, drink fruity umbrella drinks, get spa treatments. It'll be so much fun, Dee."

"I'd love to, sweetie," Delia began. "But I've got the hospital fundraiser that week. Julian's giving the keynote, and he's so nervous. I can't ditch him."

Veronica scowled. "Dammit. I liked you better before you got married and devoted to someone else."

"You could take your sister," Delia suggested.

"Oh, no." Veronica shook her head vehemently, sending her short swing of dark hair dancing. "I'm not asking Gwen. She'll spend the entire week telling me about her latest fad diet, she won't want to drink because 'empty calories', and every time I eat something that's not a raw vegetable, she makes this noise." She sucked air through her teeth to demonstrate. "Plus, last time I talked to her she was raving about some vagina exercises she was into."

Delia blinked. "Vagina exercises? You mean Kegels?"

"No, I mean like actual weight lifting. She saw some woman on Instagram doing it, and now she's obsessed."

"How do you lift weights with your pussy?"

"I have no idea, but if you want to find out, call Gwen. She'll tell you all about it."

"No, thanks." Delia gave an exaggerated shudder. "What about some of your friends from school?"

"I doubt it, not on short notice." Veronica drained her wine and reached for the bottle. "Are you sure you can't ditch Julian? I knew you first."

"Yes, but he gives me orgasms and pays for all my marijuana."

"Hell, I can't compete with that."

"Hang on, hang on." Delia picked up her phone. "I might know someone."

"Not cousin Joel," Veronica said with sudden horror.

Delia laughed. "No, not cousin Joel."

"Not one of your ooh-la-la rich friends, either. I can't handle the Ladies Who Lunch."

"Snob," Delia said absently, still scrolling through her phone.

"Well, yeah." Veronica leaned back into the sofa, snuggling into the piles of pillows, and tried not to spill her now straw-less wine. "I only put up with you because I knew you when you were dirt poor."

"So, I'm what? Your token rich friend?"

"Pretty much." Veronica laid her head back against the cushions and stared at the ceiling. "You know what?"

"Shh, I'm on the phone."

"I'm not that sad," Veronica said, ignoring the directive. "I mean, I'm pissed. My grandmother's quilt, for God's sake."

"Wyatt, it's Delia Bell. How are you?"

"And without a condom, so I had to go get tested, and you know I hate getting blood drawn." She could hear Delia talking to someone on the phone, a buzz of sound in the background. "But I'm not sad."

She lifted her head to look at her friend. "Why is that, do you think?"

Delia tilted her phone away from her mouth. "Because

you recognize that he's a cheating piece of shit who doesn't deserve your sadness. Now shut up, I'm on the phone."

"Yeah, but you'd think I'd be a little sad," Veronica protested, frowning at the ceiling. "I mean, we were together for two years. We were practically living together."

"No, you weren't. Yes, that's her," Delia said into the phone. "She's drunk."

"I am not drunk," Veronica said with dignity. "I've had two glasses of wine, for God's sake. I'm…"

"Relaxed?" Delia offered.

Veronica pointed at her. "Exactly. I'm relaxed. And I'm entitled to be as relaxed as I want because my boyfriend is a cheating dick with a dead dick."

Delia snickered into the phone. "Anyway, do you think he'd be interested? Yeah, talk it out and call me back. Sure, no problem. Bye."

Delia set her phone down with a grin. "I may have just sold Triple D's half of the vacation."

Veronica blinked. "To whom?"

"To Wyatt." Delia frowned at the coffee table. "Did you eat the last taco?"

"Probably," Veronica said and belched.

"So classy."

"Thank you. Who is Wyatt, and why did you sell him my vacation?"

"Wyatt is a friend of Julian's. He's a pediatric nurse at the hospital. His husband is a lawyer at some law firm I can never remember the name of, but the firm is holding their annual retreat at the resort the same week you're going."

Veronica nodded. "So, he wants to go with him?"

"He's already going with him."

"Then why does he need Derek's half of my vacation?"

"He doesn't. Shane does."

"I'm confused."

"That's because you're drunk," Delia told her and poured the last of the wine into her own glass.

"Relaxed," Veronica corrected haughtily, then burped again. "'Scuse me. Explain this, please."

"Shane is Wyatt's partner. He's a woodworker."

"What's a woodworker?"

"Shane is."

Veronica rolled her eyes. "I mean, what does being a woodworker mean?"

Delia shrugged. "In Shane's case, it means he makes custom wooden furniture pieces, like tables and chairs, cabinets, beds. He made the mahogany sideboard in our formal dining room."

"Really? I love that piece. It's gorgeous."

"I know. It was hideously expensive and worth every penny. Judith even complimented me on it."

"So, Shane is Wyatt's husband?"

Delia sipped her wine. "No, Seth is Wyatt's husband."

"Then who's Shane?"

"Wyatt's partner."

"I swear to God, Delia," Veronica began.

Delia laughed. "Sorry. That had the makings of a great bit, I just wanted to see how far I could take it. Shane is Wyatt's *other* partner."

"Other partner?"

Delia nodded. "Wyatt and Seth are married, but they have a polyamorous relationship."

"Which means..." Veronica prompted.

"It means they both have relationships outside of their marriage. I don't think Seth is seeing anyone else at the moment, though, and anyway, from what Wyatt's said he prefers casual hookups to relationships outside his primary. But Shane and Wyatt have been together for a couple of years."

Veronica rolled that around in her mind. "Maybe I am drunk because this makes no sense to me."

"It's kind of hard to wrap your head around at first."

"No kidding." Veronica frowned. "So, Shane is the one who'd be buying Derek's half of the vacation?"

Delia nodded. "Seth and Wyatt are already going for the firm's retreat. Wyatt said he's been bugging Shane to join them, because he's been buried in work and Wyatt thinks he needs a break, but the place is sold out."

"Oh. So would Shane be staying in my room with me, or would he be bunking with Seth and Wyatt?"

Delia shrugged. "When Wyatt calls me back, I'll ask him. Are you okay if he stays with you?"

"I guess. There's plenty of room, right?"

"I honestly don't know." Delia looked thoughtful. "I mean, it's supposed to be for a couple, even with the upgrade."

"What upgrade?"

"Oh right, I forgot to tell you. That's what I called about this morning. I got you upgraded to a beachfront condo instead of just a room in the main hotel."

"How?"

"It was being renovated, and it was finished ahead of schedule. And they were overbooked on the hotel end, so they called to ask if you could take the condo instead, and I told them yes."

"I forgive you for being rich," Veronica said solemnly.

Delia rolled her eyes. "Can we set fire to Dead Dick's stuff now?"

"Okay." Veronica pushed herself off the couch and started for the bedroom. "I have to gather it all up. Want to help?"

Delia started to answer, then turned to her phone when it buzzed. "That's Wyatt."

Veronica waved a hand. "Talk to him, then find me in the bedroom."

"Okay. Hey, Wyatt."

Veronica moved down the hall, Delia's voice fading away as she stepped into her bedroom. She went right to the dresser in the corner, and the second drawer from the top that she'd cleared out for Derek's use. Yanking it open, she eyed the contents with satisfaction. A couple of T-shirts, a pair of jeans, two pairs of the silk boxers he liked so much. Dress socks, a sweater, and three silk ties, neatly rolled.

She dumped the drawer out onto the floor and moved to the closet.

His gray suit hung there, still in its dry-cleaning bag. She tossed it onto the pile. Two dress shirts, one white and one in a pretty blue that Derek liked because it brought out the color of his eyes. She tossed the shirts on top of the suit. A pair of running shoes, practically brand new, and his beloved Ferragamo loafers joined the pile.

She'd moved on to the bathroom by the time Delia joined her.

"Okay, so Wyatt said—" She broke off when she saw the plastic shopping bag in Veronica's hands. "What's all that?"

"Derek's grooming products."

Delia peered into the bag. "He keeps all that here?"

"Not usually, but he went shopping yesterday. Nordstrom's had a sale, and he likes to stock up." Veronica shook the shopping bag. "I didn't give him a chance to gather it up when I booted him out. What did Wyatt say?"

"Huh? Oh. He said Shane is in, so I called the resort and switched the names."

"Cool. What about the sleeping arrangements?"

Delia pulled a jar of moisturizing cream out of the bag. "I should take this for Julian. He needs to start taking care of his skin."

"With my blessing." Veronica pulled a half-full tube of eye

cream from the cabinet. "The sleeping arrangements?" she prompted. "Me or the boyfriends?"

"Boyfriend," Delia corrected. "Shane and Wyatt are in a relationship, Shane and Seth aren't."

"Okay, then is he sleeping with me, or with his boyfriend and his boyfriend's husband?"

"You." Delia glanced up. "Is that okay?"

"Is he an asshole?"

"No." Delia frowned. "Kind of quiet, and he communicates mostly in grunts, but he's nice. At least he was when he was working on my sideboard."

"A nice grunter." Veronica thought for a moment, then shrugged. "I'll be spending most of my time at the beach anyway, so we probably won't run into each other that much."

"Cool," Delia said. "Can I have this eye cream, too?"

"Take whatever you want, it's all going in the trash."

Delia frowned. "Are you sure? Some of this is expensive. You could probably return the stuff that's still in the package."

"I'm sure I could return it. The receipt is still in the bag." Veronica pursed her lips. "I could use a little extra cash to buy vacation clothes."

"Awesome. We can do that after we burn the rest of his stuff."

"Yeah, about that. I don't think we should."

"What?" Delia's pretty face moved into a pout. "Why not?"

"Because someone should get some use out of them. That's a practically brand-new suit, and I bet someone could use it. Besides, I'm not sure my landlord would appreciate me having a bonfire on the balcony. They won't even let me have a grill out there."

"Good point." Delia chewed her lip for a moment, considering. "I know an organization that works with recently released prisoners. They help with resume writing, interviewing skills, give them something nice to wear on job interviews. We could try there."

"Perfect. And the stuff they can't use can go to the thrift store."

"I was really looking forward to burning them," Delia said with a sigh.

"I know, honey." Veronica patted her friend on the shoulder. "To make it up to you, I'll let you pick out at least two outfits for me."

Delia's face brightened. "Deal. You separate the returnable face goop from the non-returnable face goop, and I'll grab the clothes. My driver can pick us up in about fifteen minutes, I told him to stick close by."

"Rich bitch," Veronica called after her.

"Snobby bitch," Delia called back.

Veronica snorted out a laugh and started sorting. She had a nice little buzz on from the wine and a whole afternoon of shopping with Derek's money to look forward to. And best of all, she was getting revenge without having to post bail.

"That's a win," she decided and started mentally shopping for a new bikini.

<hr>

Shane eyed his lover with a combination of amusement, affection, and resignation. Or rather, the back of his lover's head. His surfer boy blond locks were currently sporting a raging case of fuck-hair, courtesy of their mid-day romp and Wyatt's win of the who-gets-to-bottom coin toss. "Are we really doing this?"

Wyatt put his phone down on the nightstand and rolled over so they lay face to face in the big bed. "We're doing this, babe. You need the break."

Wyatt had that determined look in his pretty blue eyes, the

one that told Shane he'd dug in and wasn't going to budge. "You know how I feel about horning in on your time with Seth."

"I told you, Seth agrees with me," Wyatt told him patiently. Wyatt did everything patiently, Shane thought wryly, which was why he usually got his way. "You've been working nonstop for months now, and if you're not careful you're going to burn out. Then you'll be no good to me, and I'll be forced to dump you for someone who's better looking and has a bigger dick."

Shane snorted. "Better looking, maybe. Bigger dick? Keep dreaming."

Eyes gleaming with humor, Wyatt trailed his hand down Shane's chest to wrap it around the dick in question. He let out a happy sigh when he found it firm, thick, and yes, big. He gave it a single, hard stroke, wringing a grunt of pleasure from Shane.

"How are you hard?" Wyatt wondered. "It's only been like, half an hour since we fucked."

Shane glanced at the clock on the wall. "More like forty-five minutes."

"Still." Wyatt gave Shane's cock another long stroke, adding a swipe of his thumb over the trio of piercings at the head. "You're not usually ready to go again so soon."

"It's been a while," Shane reminded him, closing his eyes as Wyatt's thumb dragged against his piercings again. Wyatt's hand was smooth and soft, his grip hard and tight. The contrast always drove him wild. "I've missed you."

"It's been a while because your schedule has been absurd," Wyatt reminded him, and Shane opened his eyes with a sigh.

"You're not letting this go, are you?"

"Nope."

"Babe," Shane began.

"Babe," Wyatt repeated, not giving an inch. "You're not

horning in on my time with Seth. He's going to be doing whatever retreat bullshit the firm has planned most of the time, anyway."

Shane arched an eyebrow. "Some of which will include you."

"Some," Wyatt agreed. "And yes, being with Seth is my priority on this trip. But that's no reason for you not to take advantage of the opportunity. You're not even going to be rooming with us."

Shane frowned. "Yeah, that's another thing. Who is this woman, anyway?"

"A friend of Delia Bell's. You made a sideboard for her."

"Right." Shane flipped through his mental files. "Blonde white woman, kind of a smart ass, stays high all the time?"

"That's Delia."

"The sideboard turned out great," he remembered. Gleaming mahogany, intricate details. Delia had been so thrilled with how it turned out, she'd offered him a joint when he'd delivered it.

"Anyway," Wyatt went on, "according to Delia, her friend —Veronica—was supposed to go on the trip with her boyfriend, but she walked in on him banging the neighbor this morning."

Shane winced. "Ouch."

"Right. So, he's out, but the discount package she bought specifies two people. Which means you're in."

Shane sighed. "Wyatt—"

Wyatt let go of Shane's dick and sat up, his face serious. "Okay, what's your big objection to this?"

"Besides taking a week off of work, you mean?"

Wyatt didn't roll his eyes, but Shane could tell he wanted to. "You told me yourself you're ahead of schedule on your commissions, and you just shipped a bunch of summer stock to the tourist shops. And you don't have any more festivals scheduled until the first week of June. Try again."

"You know how I feel about maintaining healthy boundaries," Shane began.

"Yes," Wyatt said patiently. "Which is why I've been very clear that this is not an 'us' vacation. It's a 'you' vacation. I just happen to be vacationing in the same place, at the same time, with my husband."

"Which is weird," Shane pointed out, eyes narrowed as a sudden thought struck. "Almost like you planned it."

"A happy coincidence, I swear," Wyatt vowed. "And possibly a sign from the universe that you really need this vacation."

"Come on."

"Signs are real, Shane," Wyatt insisted.

"So are boundaries."

"Nobody's crossing boundaries," Wyatt assured him. "I'm going with my husband on a work trip, you're going on vacation. I'm sure I'll have some downtime and we'll be able to hang—"

"Does hang mean bang?" Shane interrupted. He didn't think so, but with Wyatt, it was always best to be clear.

"Any banging on this trip would have to be both discrete and cleared with Seth ahead of time. I won't risk putting him in the position of having to explain our relationship structure to his co-workers."

"Which is another reason why I shouldn't be there," Shane pointed out.

"But even if you can't bang me, that doesn't mean you can't bang someone else," Wyatt went on, ignoring what Shane felt was a very valid point. "Which I think you should do."

"Oh, for God's sake."

"I'm serious. How long has it been since you've been with

a woman? Six months?"

Shane shrugged. "About that. Not since Savanah and I broke up."

"See?" Wyatt gave him a nudge. "Don't you miss girls?"

"Don't you?" Shane countered.

"Hell, yes." Wyatt flopped back onto the bed with a dreamy sigh. "I miss it all. Soft skin and soft hair and soft tits and soft moans."

"So, what you're saying is, women are soft."

"Mostly." Wyatt frowned. "Compared to men. Or at least, compared to my men."

"You're stereotyping," Shane pointed out.

"What I'm saying is, it's been a long time since you've been with a woman."

"I thought you were saying it's been a long time since *you've* been with a woman."

"Well, the last woman you were with was the last woman I was with," Wyatt pointed out logically. "So really, same thing. We haven't had a threesome in forever."

"Six months is hardly forever," Shane pointed out.

"Maybe," Wyatt mused, "if you find someone you like, and she's game, we can both get some vacation strange. I'd have to run it by Seth, and we'd have to be careful..."

"How did this get to be about you?" Shane wondered.

"Just the natural progression of things," Wyatt answered and grinned when Shane snorted. "Where was I?"

"Threesomes."

Wyatt shook his head. "Never mind, I remember. You need to relax, babe. Eat some good food, lie around in the sun, get a good night's sleep for once. And yes, if the opportunity presents itself, get laid."

Shane frowned, considering. The idea of getting away was appealing—he'd been working non-stop for nearly a year now. One of Savanah's big complaints had been that he was always working, and it hadn't helped that he'd been splitting what free time he had between her and Wyatt. Which she had gotten increasingly snarky about. She'd been fine with the occasional three-way romp, but the fact that he needed alone time with his boyfriend had stuck in her craw.

She'd beat him to the breakup punch, but not by much.

Shaking off unpleasant memories, he forced his mind back to the issue at hand. He firmly believed that his relationship with Wyatt worked so well in part because the boundaries were clearly and firmly drawn. Seth was Wyatt's primary partner, and Shane made sure to respect that relationship. He loved Wyatt deeply, and rarely experienced jealousy or envy over his lover's husband, but sometimes the green-eyed monster reared its ugly head. It was simple human nature, and over the years he'd learned to recognize those feelings and deal with them in a healthy way. Honesty was key, he'd discovered, and so were those boundaries. Blurring them in any way, even temporarily, made him uncomfortable.

"I can hear you thinking," Wyatt drawled. "Do you want to call Seth and double-check with him?"

Shane almost smiled. He should've known Wyatt would know where his head was. "No."

"Do you agree that you need a break?"

Shane stifled a sigh. "Yes."

"Do you think we can all be adults and maintain the healthy boundaries we've all agreed work for us?"

"I thought Seth was the lawyer."

"Just answer the question, dickhead."

Shane grinned. If Wyatt was calling him names, he was getting agitated. "Yes."

"Then?"

"We're sure this Veronica woman is cool with it?"

"Completely. She was there while Delia and I were talking.

She doesn't want the ex-boyfriend coming along, and she needs a warm body to fill the spot or she loses the vacation."

"That's it?"

"Well, and half of the resort fees. Which I'm more than happy to cover since this was my idea."

"I can handle the money," Shane told him.

"Is that yes?"

"It's a yes," Shane grumbled, then laughed at Wyatt's loud cheer.

Wyatt dove for his phone. "I'm calling Delia back before you change your mind."

"You do that." Shane sat up. "I'm going to grab a shower."

"Uh-uh." Wyatt slapped a hand on Shane's broad chest, holding him in place. "You stay put."

Shane hid a smile. "For what?"

"For that." Wyatt nodded at Shane's dick. It had softened while they bickered, but was rapidly coming back to life.

"Don't you have to go to work?"

"Nope. I switched my off day with Jane," he said, referring to one of the other nurses on his floor. He raised the phone to his ear. "I want to fuck you this time, but first I want to suck that fat dick."

"Well, then." Shane stretched out on the bed. "Talk fast."

THREE

Veronica shuffled through the Detroit airport a week and a half later, tired and cranky and more than ready to get out of town. Derek hadn't stopped calling every day, though she hadn't listened to any of his messages. Delia had, on the off chance there was anything in them to worry about, and reported with a grin that when he'd found out she'd canceled his plane ticket, he'd called back three times to rant because her voicemail kept cutting him off.

She'd hoped by not engaging, he'd get the hint and go away, but it didn't seem to be working.

She'd packed light for the trip, only toting a carry-on and her messenger bag, so she headed right for the security line and shuffled through with the rest of the bleary-eyed, early-morning passengers. The trip through security went quickly, even with having to be rescanned because she forgot to take her earbuds out of her pocket, and she was sitting on a bench putting her shoes back on when she heard her name.

She looked up and found herself staring at some guy's belt. It was a nice belt, black leather with a plain silver buckle threaded through the loops of faded jeans. The plain black T-shirt tucked neatly into the waistband over a flat stomach was as generic as the belt and jeans, but the gold watch chain made her pause. Curious, because it was such an odd detail, she looked up.

Her fingers went lax on the ankle strap she was trying to fasten, and her mouth fell open. Wow.

The T-shirt didn't look at all generic stretched over a broad chest and broader shoulders, the short sleeves so snug on the bulging muscles in his arms they seemed to cut into his biceps. One arm was fully tattooed, intricate swirls of black ink interspersed here and there with bursts of color, the other bare for the dusting of dark hair across his forearms. Forearms that were, she noted with a little sigh, really sexy. *Forearm porn. Oh my.*

"Oh my, what?" he rumbled, and her gaze darted to his face.

"What?"

"You said, 'oh, my'," he repeated. "Oh my, what?"

"I have no idea," she managed and repressed the urge to laugh. At herself. A lot. Because damn, she was acting like an idiot, and *damn,* he was absolutely the reason.

He was white with olive-toned skin and dark hair tied in a low ponytail, dark brows that were currently scrunched together as he frowned at her, dark brown eyes that held a hint of wariness, and a full beard that looked soft and thick as a mink pelt.

Not that she knew what mink felt like, but Delia had a fake mink coat that Veronica had borrowed once, and it had been soft and smooth and luxurious. She'd loved it so much she'd kept it for six months, always 'forgetting' to return it, and Delia had finally had to threaten her with bodily harm to get it back.

Her palms actually itched to stroke his beard, just to find out if it was as soft as that coat.

"You okay?" he asked, and she realized she was staring at him with her mouth open. Which accounted for the increasing wariness in his teddy bear eyes.

"Sorry." She snapped her mouth shut and tried a smile. "It's early."

"Yeah." His eyebrows relaxed, just a little. "I'm Shane."

"Okay."

"Shane Eklund," he said, his eyebrows getting all scrunchy again.

"Okay," she repeated. It was a good name, she mused. She could easily picture herself screaming it in ecstasy, pinned under that big body.

"My boyfriend is Wyatt Robertson."

"That's great," she said, even as her entire body groaned with disappointment. Of course, he was gay, she thought, and mentally substituted a man's body for hers in her imagination. *Wow. That's pretty hot. Who knew?*

He huffed, and her gaze jolted to his in horror. "I didn't say that out loud, did I?"

His eyes narrowed. "Say what out loud?"

"Never mind," she said and dropped her gaze. Unfortunately, it landed on the little curl of chest hair visible above the collar of his shirt. It was one little curl, slightly lighter than the hair on his head, and she had the completely inappropriate urge to tug on it with her teeth. Realizing that direction of thought wasn't going to do her any favors, she cleared her throat and focused on a spot just over his shoulder. "You were saying?"

"I bought your ex-boyfriend's spot at the resort?" he prompted.

"Oh!" Her eyes snapped back to his. "You're Shane."

"That's what I said."

She winced and pushed to her feet. "Sorry. I'm not usually

so spacey, but I didn't get my coffee this morning. I'm Veronica Black."

He took the hand she offered, gave it one firm shake, and dropped it. "I know."

She frowned. "How do you know?"

He frowned back at her. "I looked you up on Instagram, so I'd recognize you."

"Oh. That was smart." Why hadn't she done that? Then she'd have known she was going to be spending her vacation with a walking, talking wet dream. An unattainable one. *Thanks, Delia.*

"Right." He was staring at her warily, a grumpy, sexy beast of a man who was probably reevaluating the life choices that had brought him to this point. "Well, I just thought I should introduce myself."

She nodded. "Right. Good thought."

"Okay." He shifted the duffle he held, slinging it over his shoulder and making all his muscles move. "I guess I'll see you on the plane."

She blinked her way clear of the hypnotizing effect of his body in motion. "I'm sorry, I'm being so rude."

He grunted, which she assumed meant *yep.*

"I haven't had any coffee," she said again. "Do you, um, want to join me for a cup? My treat."

"Don't drink it."

"Oh."

"But you can buy me a Mountain Dew."

She blinked. "You don't drink coffee, but you drink Mountain Dew?"

He grinned, a sudden flash of bright white teeth in the forest of his beard. "I'm not trying to avoid caffeine, just the taste of burned beans."

She locked her knees—they'd gone weak when he smiled. "I usually disguise it with sugar and steamed milk."

That grin flashed again, further liquifying the bones in her legs that were supposed to hold her up. If he smiled at her one more time, she'd be on the floor. "Mountain Dew's easier."

She grimaced at that. "I'm pretty sure that tastes worse."

He shrugged, making the duffle over his shoulder bounce, and turned. "There's a café in the terminal. We can get something there."

He took a few steps, seemed to realize she wasn't following, and glanced back over his shoulder. "You coming?"

"Yeah. Sure. I just..." She leaned down to fasten her forgotten ankle strap, then straightened and grabbed the handle of her rollaway. "All set."

He grunted again, hitched his duffle bag higher on his shoulder, and headed for the escalator that fed into the terminals.

Her eyes dropped to his butt. The rear view was almost as good as the front, she noted, then gave herself a mental bitch slap. They were going to be sharing a cottage for the week, she reminded herself, and she'd already gotten off on the wrong foot. Thankfully he thought she was a ditzy jerk instead of a horny slut, and for the next week she needed to make a concerted effort to keep her eyes—and her lascivious thoughts —to herself.

Of course, a little harmless fantasy never hurt anything. She trailed after Shane down the escalator, her eyes locked onto his fantasy grade ass, and made a mental note to Google where to buy a vibrator in Bermuda.

***

Shane spent most of the flight staring at the seat in front of him, and the crown of dark hair just visible above it. Veronica Black had plunked herself down in her first-class seat as soon as they boarded, and as far as he could tell she hadn't moved since.

Which suited him fine, because he had no idea what he was supposed to say to her. What he wanted to say was "I like your tits, do you want to fuck?", and that was the wrong move entirely.

Wyatt was right—it had been way too long since he'd been with a woman. Unfortunately, that realization had hit him while standing in front of Veronica, looking down the neck of her shirt at what seemed like an acre of soft white cleavage as she bent to fasten her shoe. Abundant breasts behind a mannish shirt was a visual that never failed to trip his trigger, and if her tailored camp shirt didn't quite fit his fantasies, well, his mind was perfectly capable of substituting one of his own rarely worn dress shirts. And while it was on a roll, his artist's imagination had also stripped away the crisp capri pants, so when she stood, he'd had no trouble envisioning her with her dark hair tousled out of its sleek bob, white skin flushed with desire, and those pin-up curves draped in his dress shirt and nothing else.

The first thought to penetrate the sudden haze of lust was that whoever had cheated on this woman was a grade-A asshole. It was followed closely by the second, which was that springing a boner steps away from TSA was highly uncomfortable.

And the third was the realization that lusting after the woman with whom he was going to be sharing a house for the week was a recipe for blue balls. So, he'd forced himself to pull it together, grunted something at her about not liking coffee, and now he was pretty sure she thought he was a coffee-hating misanthrope.

Which wasn't, despite all indications to the contrary, true. He didn't *hate* people, he just didn't have much use for most of them.

He did hate coffee, though.

He shifted in his seat with a sigh. Thanks to Wyatt booking his flight— "you'll forget, just let me handle it"—he was enjoying the extra legroom and cloth napkins of first class. The napkins he couldn't care less about, but since he was usually chewing on his kneecaps in coach, the legroom was nice—though he wasn't sure the extra money was worth it. Being married to a corporate lawyer who put in a lot of billable hours had given Wyatt a somewhat skewed notion of what constituted a reasonable expense, and even though Shane's business was doing well and he could afford some luxuries, he could never seem to shake the anxiety that came with spending money on something he could easily do without.

He shifted in his seat again, trying to find a position that didn't make his dick feel like it was being pinched. He was still sporting a semi, thanks to Veronica's tailored shirt and bombshell tits, and it wasn't going away. He considered heading to the bathroom to take care of it, but joining the Mile-High Club solo was just too fucking creepy. Besides, the way his morning was going, a flight attendant would probably burst in on him and the whole of first-class see him with his dick in his hand.

For the sake of his dignity, he stayed in his seat. Resigned to spending the rest of the flight to Atlanta—and the connecting flight to Bermuda, and the shuttle ride that would take them to the resort—in discomfort, he sighed again. Maybe a nap would help. He could catch up on some of the sleep he'd lost over the last week of hectic, pre-vacation work, and if he was lucky, he'd have a bad dream that would chase away even the slightest hint of boner.

Except when he closed his eyes, all he could see was big hazel eyes, soft red lips, and the shadowy hint of cleavage tucked behind a crisp white shirt.

Annoyed and aroused, he opened his eyes and glared at the dark hair above the seat in front of him.

By the time they reached the resort, the sun was setting over the ocean and Shane's nerves had been stretched to their breaking point. He'd been seated next to Veronica on the connecting flight, in coach this time. They'd been packed in together like sardines in a can, and no matter how he'd contorted his body, some part of him had been touching some part of her the entire flight. He'd thought it was bad when his thigh had been forced up against hers, but the worst part had been the arms. They were both wearing short sleeves, so when his forearm had briefly pressed against hers it was skin against skin. And hers was warm and soft and smelled somehow of peaches.

Even hours later he could still smell it, and it wasn't until he was walking up the path to their condo behind her and he lifted his duffle bag over his shoulder that he realized it was because she'd somehow transferred the scent onto him. Peaches and cream and something else that teased just underneath the fruity scent and made his dick hard, and he had to stifle what felt like his forty-seventh groan of the day.

Veronica paused and half turned, a look of concern on her face, her pretty lips pursed. "Did you say something?"

He shook his head. "Nope."

"Oh." She bit her lip, her eyes searching his in the dim light of the path. Then she gave a little shrug and began walking again. "I think we're almost there."

He said nothing, concentrating on the back of her head as he walked. Her hair was tangled from the day's travels, reminding him of Wyatt's fuck-hair, which was not helping the boner situation. He'd tried keeping his eyes on his feet, but she'd stopped abruptly to let a lizard scamper across the path, and he'd nearly plowed into her. Since then he'd backed up so there was a good four feet between them and kept his gaze resolutely on her head.

Mostly, anyway. The sway of her hips—round, generous, excellent for grabbing while he buried his face in her cunt—kept trying to draw his attention, and he was only human, after all.

And horny, he thought sardonically. Don't forget horny.

The thick vegetation on either side of the path abruptly gave way to a small clearing, and nestled in the center of it was the tidy cottage that was their destination.

"Oh, thank God," she breathed, and he heard the exhaustion in her throaty voice. "I want a drink and a shower and to fall into bed for eight hours."

"I could use a drink."

He caught the startled look she threw him, and couldn't blame her. It was the most he'd said to her since, "Thanks for the Dew," back in the Detroit airport.

"What's your poison?" she asked, mounting the two shallow steps to the cottage's front door. She had the key card from the front desk in one hand and her messenger bag over her shoulder. He'd offered to take her rollaway by the simple method of picking it up, and after a brief protest she'd let him. They could have had a porter bring their luggage and show them to the cottage, but the staff had been scrambling and neither of them had wanted to wait. So, he'd picked up her bag and his, she'd taken the key and directions to the cottage, and they'd set off on foot.

"I'm not picky," he answered with a shrug as she fit the card into the slot and shoved open the door.

The blast of cool air was a welcome slap in the face. Even though the air held only a hint of humidity, the long day of travel had left him feeling grimy and sweaty, and the fifteen-minute walk hadn't helped. Veronica hit the light switch beside the door, and he stepped past her into the room. "Nice."

It was one large, open space. A small kitchen was to the left, defined by the marble-topped island separating it from the rest of the room, white tiles and shiny appliances gleaming in the light. The living space beyond boasted a huge sectional sofa in white, arranged so part of it faced the gas fireplace and the big-screen television mounted over it, and part faced the wall of glass that made up the entire back of the cottage. There were lights on outside, enough to see the small patio with an outdoor eating area and a hammock, and the beach beyond. On the right side of the room two short steps led to a platform that held a huge bed, mounded high with pillows and scattered with pink rose petals.

"Huh."

He turned to look at her and noticed was chewing on her lower lip. His dick noticed, too. "What?"

She glanced at him, color climbing into her cheeks, then away again. "That," she said and pointed to the bed.

He looked again. Big bed, lots of pillows, flower petals. The whole thing was draped in gauzy curtains that he guessed were meant to act as mosquito netting, or a more romantic, less effective version of it, and more gauzy curtains stretched across the room at the edge of the platform. They were pulled back now, and wouldn't be very effective at creating privacy when they were closed, but he figured it went with the beachy-romance theme.

"What about it?"

She gnawed on her lower lip some more, still staring at the bed. "Do you see another bedroom?"

He looked around. There was a door just inside the entrance that when opened revealed a small closet, and another just off the steps of the platform that held a powder room. He set his duffle down and climbed the steps, ignoring the bed, and found another closet and a full bath done in the same gleaming white tile as the kitchen. It had a walk-in shower that could've comfortably accommodated the defensive line of the Detroit Lions, and a separate soaking tub.

He stepped back out. "Bathroom."

She was sitting on one of the barstools lined up at the kitchen island, the only seating in the room other than the enormous sofa. She looked up when he stepped down from the platform, her eyes wide.

"What?" he asked.

"There's only one bed."

He shrugged. "So? The couch is huge. I'll sleep there."

If he'd thought that answer would bring relief, he'd been mistaken. If anything, she looked even more worried, and started gnawing on her lower lip again.

"I can't let you do that," she protested, her husky voice ragged. "I'm shorter, I'll sleep on the couch."

He shook his head. The manners his mother had spent years drilling into him may have mostly faded away, but a scrap or two still lingered. "Nope. You get the bed."

"Shane," she said, and hearing his name on her lips in that throaty, sexy voice did nothing to stifle the party trying to break out in his pants. "You won't possibly be comfortable on that thing. What if you fall off?"

He rolled his eyes. "Then I hit the floor. I'll survive."

She shook her head, making her dark hair swing. "I insist you take the bed."

"No."

He bent to retrieve his duffle and, ignoring the way her mouth had dropped open, carried it to the sofa and plunked it down on a soft cushion. "There."

She only blinked at him, her mouth still hanging open, so he shrugged and stepped into the powder room. He didn't bother trying to piss through his half hard-on, just splashed cold water on his face until he felt almost human again. He was tempted to take down his pants and run cold water over his dick, but he knew if he took it out, he wouldn't be able to resist giving it a stroke. He'd save it for the shower later, hopefully when Veronica was fast asleep and unlikely to hear him groaning his way toward orgasm.

He wondered if he could convince her to wear earplugs if he told her he snored.

He mopped his face with the pretty pink towel, adjusted the front of his jeans, opened the door, and nearly walked right into her.

"Jesus." He took a quick step back, slamming his shoulder into the doorjamb, and scowled at her. She stood with her arms crossed over her chest and a mutinous expression on her face. "What?"

"You're taking the bed," she announced.

He snorted and stepped around her, careful not to brush against her. If he got any more of that sex-and-peaches smell on him, he was going to jump out of his skin.

"I mean it," she said, trailing behind him as he walked toward his duffle bag.

"Uh-huh." He dug out a fresh T-shirt and whipped the one he was wearing over his head. He'd have liked to get out of the traveling clothes completely, but his pants weren't coming off until she was either gone or asleep. "I'm going to go get some dinner. Want to come?"

"No, thank you." Her voice sounded strangled. "I want to talk about the sleeping arrangements."

He tugged the clean shirt over his head and left it untucked. Maybe it would help cover his dick, which unfortunately had perked up again. Veronica in a snit was pretty fucking sexy.

"Sleeping arrangements are handled," he said, digging out

his phone to turn it on and check the battery. He'd left it off all day, so it was still fully charged. He tucked it back into his pocket and looked at her. Her face was flushed, her eyes wide, and she was biting her lower lip so hard he was surprised it wasn't bleeding. "You, bed. Me, couch. Dinner?"

"I'm not hungry."

He shrugged. That was probably a lie since he hadn't seen her eat all day, but she was a grownup. She could feed herself. "I'm going to take the key card. I'll get another on my way back, once the check -n crowd has died down."

She blinked, clearly thrown off by the change in topic. "Oh. Good idea."

He nodded and scooped it off the kitchen counter. "See you later."

"I'm sleeping on the couch," she called after him.

"No, you're not," he grunted, and let the door slam shut behind him.

He headed up the path, the lights of the hotel gleaming in the distance. He'd check in with Wyatt and Seth, see if they had dinner plans. They'd already been here a full day, so maybe they could tell him where he could get a steak. He wanted red meat, a beer, and to not smell peaches and sex long enough for his dick to go down. If he was lucky, he could stay away long enough for Veronica to go to bed. Then he could get his shower, handle his unruly penis, and catch some sleep.

BY THE TIME he made it back to the cottage, he was all but dead on his feet. Though it was barely midnight, the long day of travel had caught up with him, and he was more than ready to crash. He noticed the room service cart on the side of the small front porch and surmised that Veronica had ordered dinner in. No doubt some invisible staff member would whisk it away before morning.

He shook his head as he shoved the key card into the slot. This place was fancy with a capital F, something that had been made very clear to him at dinner. He'd texted Wyatt, but he and Seth had been at a firm function and unavailable. After making plans to get together the next morning for breakfast, Shane had wandered into the hotel restaurant in search of a steak.

The maître d hadn't exactly sneered at his untucked T-shirt and worn jeans, but Shane could tell he'd wanted to. After scanning his keycard to make sure he hadn't just walked in off the street, he'd suggested a seat at the bar. Shane had been tempted to demand a table in the center of the room just to fuck with the guy, but he'd been too tired and too hungry to care. He'd taken the seat at the bar, ordered a ribeye, and flirted shamelessly with the bartender.

The buxom redhead with the bold pink lipstick had made it more than clear that he was welcome back at her place for dessert when her shift ended at two. He'd been half tempted to take her up on it, except his dick, which had been at half-mast for most of the damn day, had chosen that precise moment to finally clock out.

He'd passed on the redhead and walked the long way back to the cottage. He'd thought about detouring to the beach to watch the moon over the water but knew he'd be shaking sand out of his boots for the next week. So here he was, creeping into the cottage at midnight, hoping Veronica and her luscious tits were already asleep.

He shut the door quietly behind him and toed off his boots, leaving them at the front door, and crept forward on stocking feet. He left the lights off since the open curtains let in plenty of ambient light, and he had no trouble making his way across the room. He glanced toward the bed, saw it was empty, and took two steps forward to peer over the back of the couch.

She'd made herself a little nest with one of the extra pillows from the bed and a spare sheet and was curled up in the corner of the sectional, sound asleep.

"Fuck," he muttered.

She wore some kind of oversized T-shirt as a nightgown, and it was big enough that it had slipped down to bare her shoulder and the upper curve of one breast. Her hair was tousled, as though she'd tossed and turned a bit before falling asleep, and her breathing was slow and deep. Her lips were parted, little puffs of air escaping on every exhale so one wayward lock of dark brown hair fluttered in the light breeze.

She exhaled again, this time with a little rumble of sound that had to be the cutest snore he'd ever heard. And fuck a damn duck, she still smelled like peaches and sex.

He stared down at her, hands on his hips, and considered his options. One: he could leave her there and take the bed. He shook his head, rejecting that notion with barely a consideration. He was not going to take the only bed, and that was that.

Two: he could climb onto the couch with her. Also not an option, he realized. Though it would make his point, climbing into bed with a woman without her express consent violated his ethics. He wouldn't want some stranger climbing into bed with *him* unannounced and uninvited, and he wasn't about to do it to someone else.

Three: he could wake her up and make her move. It was clearly the most ethical option, as he wouldn't need to touch her or engage with her physically, but it would also get him a fight. And he wasn't in the mood.

Four: scoop her up, carry her to the bed, then take the coldest shower possible. Questionable, ethically speaking, as it would require laying hands on her while she was asleep. And if he knew her better, door number four would be his choice. But he didn't like touching a woman when she hadn't asked for it, so he couldn't quite bring himself to do it.

He sighed. Option number three was the clear winner, but man, he didn't like it. Stalling, he looked around for his duffle bag, rolling his eyes when he saw she'd plunked it down on the bed. He picked it up and carried it into the full bath, then went back to stand next to the couch.

He cleared his throat. "Veronica."

She didn't stir.

"Veronica," he repeated, louder this time. She wrinkled her nose, and there was a small pause in her breathing, then her expression smoothed out and she exhaled on a soft snore.

He stifled a snicker and reached down and poked his index finger into her shoulder. "Veronica, wake up."

She frowned and swatted at his hand. "G'way. Sleeping."

He nearly grinned. Fuck, she was cute. But she was in his bed, and he was tired. He poked her again. "Veronica, wake up."

"Grumph," she mumbled and rolled onto her back, her eyes still firmly shut.

He hissed out a breath. The oversized T-shirt was white, with a deep V-neck, and it was painfully obvious she wasn't wearing a bra. He could see the dusky shadows of her nipples through the thin cotton, and the cooler night air was making them pucker.

Goddammit. He ground his teeth together and fixed his eyes on her face. "Veronica, wake up."

She sighed, and her eyes fluttered open. "Why?"

"Because it's time to go to bed," he told her gruffly.

She blinked at him owlishly for a moment, then sat up. "Oh. Okay."

Well, that was easy. He took a step back as she slithered off the couch, the sheet falling away when she stood. He gritted his teeth. The shirt was short, barely covering her crotch, and he'd been right about her thighs—round and firm and smooth, and she had cute, dimpled knees.

Cute knees? Jesus Christ, he was losing it.

She swayed and he reached out to steady her, careful to keep his hands on her shoulders. "Okay?"

She nodded slowly, her eyes hazy and heavy. She smiled at him. "I'm good. How're you?"

"Great," he replied gruffly.

"I have to go to bed now," she informed him and started to sink back down onto the couch.

"No, no, no," he countered and tightened his grip to keep her upright. "The bed is over there."

"Oh." She blinked twice, slowly, then smiled again. "Okay."

He backed up when she started to walk, keeping one hand on her shoulder. She drifted around the sofa, wobbling a little on the stairs, then floated toward the bed. He let his hand fall away from her shoulders and stepped back, then stepped forward again when she stopped.

She pointed. "That's not my bed."

"Yes, it is."

She shook her head. "No. It's Shane's bed. He's supposed to have it. I'm supposed to sleep on the couch."

She started to turn, and he leaped in front of her with a curse. "It's not Shane's bed. They brought an extra one."

Her face wrinkled up in confusion. "Another one?"

"Yep. Different bed. This one's yours."

"Oh." She blinked at him, her eyes hazy, then nodded. "Okay."

His sigh of relief was short-lived because instead of walking to the side of the bed and sliding between the sheets some intrepid hotel staffer had turned down, she dropped onto the mattress on all fours and began to crawl towards the pillows. And Shane, tired and horny and at the end of his already short rope, watched.

It was fucking torture.

Her shirt rode up to reveal pink panties, boy-shorts that cut away to reveal the curves of her ass, round and soft and jiggling as she crawled her way up the mattress. When it came to women Shane was mostly a breast man, but that ass could make a convert out of him.

"Jesus Christ," he ground out and clenched his jaw so hard it throbbed in time with his dick.

"What?" Veronica said and turned to look at him. But of course, she didn't just turn her head. No, she had to turn her entire body so she faced him on her hands and knees, with the deep v of her T-shirt gaping nearly halfway to the bed to give him a clear look at the breasts that had been haunting him all day.

"Jesus Christ," he repeated and closed his eyes, praying for willpower. "Will you just get in the bed?"

"Well, I *was*," she groused, and the blankets rustled as she moved. "Then you said something, and I said "what?", because that's what people *do*, they say "what?" when someone says something they don't understand, and I don't know why you're getting so *snarky*."

His eyes popped open and he frowned at her swaying ass. "Snarky?"

"I gave you the bed and everything," she muttered, finally reaching the pillows. She wiggled and shifted and scooted around, at turns giving him glimpses of tits and ass and sorely testing his willpower and the stitching in the crotch of his jeans.

"This is supposed to be my vacation," she continued and yanked the covers up to her chin. "I'm going to relax, and eat food, and forget about my cheating ex-boyfriend with vacation sex."

"Fucking kill me now," he muttered at the ceiling, then unable to help himself, dropped his gaze to the bed.

She was curled up on her side with her hands tucked under her cheek, sound asleep and snoring. Again.

"Jesus Christ," he muttered again and turned to walk to the bathroom.

He shut the door firmly behind him before flicking on the light. He lifted his bag to the wide marble countertop, dug out his toiletries, and set them in the shower. He yanked the elastic out of his hair to release the low ponytail, then shucked off his clothes. Leaving them in a pile on the floor—surely this fancy-ass resort would have a laundry service—he stepped over to the toilet and emptied his bladder before getting into the shower.

He turned on all the jets, letting out a groan as the criss-crossing sprays hit him. The water was needle-sharp and pounding, the slight sting almost painful. He made himself stand in it until his skin no longer burned, until the bite turned into a caress, reaching beneath the surface of his skin to his muscles, tight and tense from travel and horniness. He stood until the water pounded all the tension out of them, leaving him limp as an overcooked noodle.

Well. Most of him.

He eyed his penis with resignation. He'd gone between half hard and full hard half a dozen times during the day, with brief moments of respite. At the moment he was mostly hard again, thanks to Veronica's pink panty-covered ass and soft, swaying breasts, and he knew he wasn't going to get any sleep tonight unless he took care of business.

He started to grab his bottle of plain, serviceable shampoo to facilitate things, then paused. There was a trio of small bottles set on the recessed shelf, their contents a pale pink, and on impulse he picked up the one labeled 'body wash'. He snapped open the lid and was immediately assailed with the smell of ripe peaches.

"That'll do," he decided and squeezed a small dollop into his hand, inhaling the sweet scent. It didn't have the subtle, musky undertone that it did on her skin, but it was enough. He reached down and stroked his palm over his cock.

Pleasure made him jerk, a groan strangling in his throat. He tightened his grip, dragging his hand from root to tip and back again. He braced a hand on the shower wall, leaning into it as the spray beat down on him and he worked himself in slow, firm strokes with the scent of peaches filling his nostrils and images of Veronica filling his mind.

Soft breasts, round, firm ass. And fuck, those thighs. He wanted to see them spread wide so he could dive face-first into her pussy, then feel them wrapped around his hips as he plunged deep.

He pumped his hips, pushing his dick through his fist, the scent of peaches getting stronger as lather built. His hair hung down to his shoulders, streaming water over his face, down his torso to the fist wrapped around his dick. He closed his eyes as the pleasure spiked, his spine tingling and his muscles tightening, then it burst free in a flood of sensation. A groan ripped from his throat and he opened his eyes, watching his dick jerk in his hand and his come splash against the marble walls while the scent of peaches filled his nose.

He had no idea how long he stood there, letting the water pound at him while he lazily stroked himself, but he was jolted out of his post-orgasmic bliss by a sudden burning in his dick.

"Shit," he muttered and scrambled for the hand-held shower wand. He'd gotten some soap in his urethra, a just payment for liberties taken, and aimed the shower spray at the head of his penis.

After a moment the burning eased, and with a sigh of relief he picked up his own body wash. He scrubbed himself thoroughly, eliminating any trace of peaches, then shampooed his hair. By the time he stepped out of the shower and toweled off, he was practically asleep on his feet. He brushed his teeth, then tugged on a pair of clean boxers. He picked his dirty clothes off the floor and tucked them on top of his duffle, then picked it up and turned off the light.

When he opened the bathroom door, he picked his way across the room on silent feet, deliberately not looking at the bed or the woman softly snoring in it. He dropped his duffle on one end of the couch and lay down on the other, dragging the sheet Veronica had left behind over himself. He sighed and closed his eyes, then opened them with a curse as the scent of peaches hit his nose.

He rolled over with a groan and resigned himself to a long night.

FOUR

When he woke up, Veronica was gone.

Shane lay still, listening to the crash of the ocean coming through the open sliding glass door while the early morning breeze danced over his skin. He strained to hear any sound over the rolling waves, but the cottage was silent. He debated going back to sleep—the couch was surprisingly comfortable—but now that he was awake his bladder was demanding attention. He rolled off the sofa with a grunt, holding the sheet to his stomach while he looked around, just in case she was lurking in a corner somewhere.

The living area was empty save for the pot of coffee sitting on the kitchen counter, and the bed was neatly made. Through the open doors to the patio he spotted a pair of flip-flops by the stairs leading down to the beach, and a plain white coffee mug on the short stone wall that separated the patio from the sand.

Satisfied that he was alone, he dropped the sheet and stretched, then padded in his boxers to the bath. He hit the toilet first, wincing when it burned. He hadn't quite got all the soap out in the shower last night, which just served him right. He finished up and washed his hands, and was walking back into the living area when the doorbell rang.

He frowned. He had no idea what time it was since his pocket watch and phone were still in the jeans he'd shucked off last night—he made a mental note to make sure to pull them out before he sent his clothes to the laundry—and he didn't see a clock anywhere, not even a digital readout on the microwave. He started to turn to the living room to get his watch when the bell rang again.

He glanced down at himself. He was naked but for the boxers, and would normally at least pull on a pair of pants before opening the door. But the bell rang a third time, and this time it sounded as though whoever was out there was holding down the button. With a scowl, he strode toward the door and flung it open. "What?"

Wyatt stood on the front step, his blond hair in casual disarray, his lean body clad in a colorful T-shirt and board shorts, his white, winter-pale skin already showing a hint of a tan. His lips quirked at Shane's greeting. "Good morning to you, too."

"Sorry. Hey." Shane ran a hand through his hair and struggled to wake up. "What are you doing here?"

"You missed breakfast," Wyatt informed him and stepped over the threshold.

Shane automatically closed the door behind him, a frown on his face. "I did? What time is it?"

Wyatt walked past Shane into the living area. "Eleven-thirty."

"Shit." Shane winced. "Sorry. I overslept."

"No big," Wyatt said absently turning slowly in a circle to take in his surroundings. "Nice digs, babe."

Shane scrubbed his palms over his face and tried to wake up. "I guess."

"No, seriously. We're in a room at the hotel, and it's nice, but this is great. Spacious, comfortable." He noticed the pillow and tangled sheet on the sofa and turned to Shane with a raised brow. "Who slept on the couch?"

"I did. Only one bed."

"Really?" A delighted grin lit Wyatt's pretty, tanned face, and he waggled his brows. "Maybe you two should share."

Shane rolled his eyes and went to hunt up a glass of water. "Give me a break, Wy."

"It's a big bed," Wyatt mused, climbing the steps to the platform. "Plenty of room for two."

"You should see the shower," Shane told him, and let out a grunt of satisfaction when he opened the refrigerator and found several bottles of water stocked there.

"Yeah?" Wyatt crossed the room to poke his head in, then popped back out with wide eyes. "Holy crap. You could have an orgy in there."

Shane cracked open a bottle of water. "You want?"

Wyatt walked back toward the kitchen, shaking his head. "I'd love some coffee, though. I assume Veronica made it since you never touch the stuff. Do you think she'd mind?"

"Doubt it. Don't know where the cups are, though."

"I'll find one." Wyatt began opening cupboard doors. "What's she like?"

Shane shrugged. "Seems nice. A little tense. She thinks I'm a jerk."

Wyatt pulled down one of the sturdy white ceramic mugs. "Were you a jerk?"

"Probably."

Wyatt poured himself a cup of coffee and leaned back against the counter. "What were you a jerk about?"

"I wouldn't let her sleep on the couch."

"That's a pretty low threshold for jerk," Wyatt observed.

Shane huffed out a breath. "Yeah, well. I may have been grumpy about it."

Wyatt's eyes widened in exaggerated disbelief. "You? No!"

"Fuck you."

"Maybe later, lover," Wyatt said with an exaggerated leer, and Shane choked back a laugh. "For now, I want to hear about Veronica."

"Why?"

"Because you like her."

Shane snorted. "And you've deduced this how, Sherlock?"

"You're always grumpy to people you like," Wyatt said. "It's your defense mechanism. Remember when we met, and you told me to get the fuck out of your way?"

"You were in my way," Shane reminded him.

"You could've just said 'excuse me'," Wyatt pointed out, "but you wanted me, so you got all flustered and asshole-ish."

"I did not get all flustered," Shane protested, "and asshole-ish is not a word."

"Flustered and asshole-ish," Wyatt went on, ignoring Shane's snort. "It's like all the blood in your brain moves to your dick and you forget how to act like a human being."

Shane opened his mouth to argue, then shut it again.

"Oh yeah, you want her." Wyatt grinned over his coffee. "I bet it's the tits. From what I could see from the pics on her Instagram, she's got nice ones."

"She's a person, you know," Shane pointed out, annoyed that Wyatt was pinning him down so neatly before he'd even had breakfast. "Not a random collection of body parts."

"She's a person with nice tits," Wyatt said, undeterred. "Did you jerk off thinking about her last night?"

Shane sighed. "God, you're annoying."

"I bet you did it in the shower," Wyatt went on, a wicked gleam in his eyes. "A nice, steamy shower with the water beating down, and you took that big, fat dick in hand and stroked one out thinking about Veronica's tits."

Shane gave up. "And her ass. Got a glimpse of that last night."

Wyatt hooted out a laugh. "How'd you manage that?"

Shane thought of Veronica crawling her way up the mattress, her round ass swaying in those pink panties. "Long story."

"Uh-huh. Tell me something about her besides the tits and ass."

"She smells like peaches," Shane said before he could stop himself.

"Peaches?"

"It's her body wash, and maybe her lotion. But yeah, peaches." Shane dragged a hand through his hair and shot his lover a sheepish grin. "I jerked off with her body wash last night."

Wyatt's mouth dropped open, and for a brief moment, Shane had the rare satisfaction of having rendered him speechless.

"You fucking pervert," Wyatt finally said gleefully.

"I know. Paid for it, though."

"Soap in your urethra?" Wyatt guessed and laughed. "Serves you right."

"I know." He scrubbed a hand over his face. "I'm never going to last a week in this cottage with her, Wyatt."

"Yeah, she'll probably notice when she runs out of body wash."

Shane scowled. "Blow me."

Wyatt laughed and set his coffee on the counter. "We can do that later, too. Though since we're inside where none of Seth's stuffy lawyer colleagues might stumble across us..."

He reached out, grabbed the waistband of Shane's boxers, and yanked.

Shane grunted as his body collided with Wyatt's, muscle against muscle. He grunted again when Wyatt's arms wrapped around him, hands clamping onto his ass. "Don't start something you won't be able to finish," he warned.

Wyatt flicked his tongue out, wetting his lips, his pretty blue eyes going dark. "I'm not starting anything. I just want a kiss."

"You want a kiss?" Shane asked roughly and speared his hands through Wyatt's hair. The faint whimper had Shane's lips peeling back in a feral grin. He bent his head slightly to drag his tongue over Wyatt's lower lip. "Ask nicely."

Wyatt's breath shuddered out. "I want a kiss, please."

"Good boy," Shane whispered and slanted his mouth over Wyatt's.

Shane drove his tongue into Wyatt's mouth, taking the kiss deep. They were both breathing hard when he pulled back to nip at his lower lip. "Dammit. You taste like coffee."

Wyatt's laughter vibrated between them. "Sorry."

Shane rested his forehead against Wyatt's, his lips quirked up in a faint grin. "And you got me hard again."

"I know." Wyatt pushed his hips forward, grinding against the erection that wasn't at all contained by Shane's boxers. An impish grin lit his face. "Want to step into the shower and take care of that?"

Shane laughed, then a flash of movement caught his attention. He picked his head up, and Veronica froze in the opening of the sliding glass door.

"Sorry." She cleared her throat. "I'm interrupting."

"Don't worry about it," Shane began, then he noticed what she was wearing and his brain shut down.

Bikini. Red bikini, bright against her white skin. Low on the hips and skimpy on the tits and wet so it clung to her like paint, and *fuck*, he was so screwed.

"Damn," Wyatt muttered under his breath.

See? Shane wanted to say. *See what I'm dealing with here?*

"It's fine," he managed and stepped to the side so his lower half would be hidden by the kitchen island.

Wyatt shot him an exasperated look before turning to face Veronica. "You must be Veronica," he said with a smile, leaning on the counter. "I've heard a lot about you. I'm Wyatt."

"Oh!" She took a step forward, a tentative smile curving her lips. "It's nice to meet you. Delia talks about you a lot."

"All good, I assume," Wyatt said, pouring on the charm.

Veronica laughed, lifting the towel in her hand to her dripping hair. "It's Delia, so no guarantees."

"Fair point," Wyatt agreed. "Listen, I was just about to convince Shane to order some lunch. Want to join us?"

Her hands stilled, and her teeth sunk into her lower lip. "I don't want to intrude."

"No intrusion," Wyatt told her cheerfully. "If you don't mind me invading your space, we can eat on the patio and enjoy the sunshine."

"That sounds great, if you're sure I'm not imposing." Her gaze darted to Shane, who did his best to look like someone who a) genuinely wanted her to join them for lunch, and b) wasn't trying to hide an erection behind the kitchen counter.

"You should eat," he told her.

"Ignore him," Wyatt advised, shooting a *what the fuck, dude?* look over his shoulder at Shane. "He's grumpy when he's hungry."

"Is he hungry all the time?" Veronica wanted to know, and Wyatt laughed.

Shane managed a small smile. "Really. You should join us."

Veronica hesitated a moment, her hazel eyes searching his face for Shane didn't know what, but she finally nodded. "Okay. Do you mind if I take a quick shower first? I want to wash off the saltwater."

"Take your time," Wyatt told her. "I'll wrangle Grumpy here into some clothes, and we can call room service. Do you know what you'd like?"

"A club sandwich would be great." Her smile warmed slightly. "Thanks. I'll be about twenty minutes or so."

"Take your time," Wyatt repeated and waited until she'd disappeared into the bathroom before rolling his eyes at Shane. "Way to go, Romeo."

"Oh, bite me," Shane muttered back, and since the coast was clear, stepped out from behind the counter and headed for his duffle bag.

"Tell me what you want for lunch, Mr. Smooth," Wyatt said, picking up the phone on the kitchen wall.

"A burger," Shane told him and dug clean clothes out of his bag.

Wyatt called in their lunch order, then wandered into the living room to flop onto the sofa. "'You should eat'," he drawled mockingly and shook his head. "I don't know how you ever manage to get laid."

"I'm not trying to get laid," Shane reminded him, fresh jeans in hand. "And I didn't have any trouble getting into your bed."

"Yeah, but grumpy and brooding works for me." Wyatt reached out to toy with the edge of the rumpled sheet. "It means I get to do most of the talking."

"You'd do that anyway," Shane pointed out and hitched his jeans over his hips.

"True." Wyatt wrinkled his nose. "You know, you're at a beach resort. You can wear shorts."

Shane looked down, frowned, and shucked the jeans off. He pulled out a pair of cargo shorts in faded olive green and tugged them on. "Better, Mom?"

"Marginally," Wyatt allowed. He picked up the sheet and began folding it. "She's cute, Shane."

"I know."

"Seriously cute. And built."

"Keep it down, will you?"

"Relax, Grandpa. She's not going to hear anything from the shower."

"I mean it." Shane yanked a white T-shirt over his head. "It's rude."

"You're suddenly concerned with rude?"

Shane scowled at Wyatt. "Making her uncomfortable by talking about her tits would fall under the heading of asshole-ish, don't you think?"

"Okay, fair point. Anyway, I only meant that I like her."

"You don't know her," Shane pointed out.

"That's what lunch is for." Wyatt finished folding the sheet, then with a faint frown, sniffed. "What am I smelling?"

"Peaches." Shane jerked his chin toward the bathroom, where they could hear the shower running. "She was sleeping out here before I made her take the bed."

"It's peaches, yeah, but there's something..." Wyatt put his face to the sheet and inhaled deeply. His eyes drifted closed as he concentrated, then popped wide. "Oh, shit."

"Don't say it," Shane warned.

"But it's peaches and—"

"Don't," Shane repeated, and yanked the sheet out of Wyatt's hands. "Get outside, jackass."

Wyatt waited until they were on the patio and Shane had closed the door behind them. "It's peaches and pussy, Shane."

"I know."

"Peaches. And. Pussy," Wyatt repeated. "Does she smell like that all the time?"

"Yes." Shane dragged his hands through his hair. "Why do you think I'm dealing with a perpetual boner, here?"

"Man." Wyatt dropped into one of the chairs at the small patio table. "What are you going to do?"

"Nothing."

"What?"

"Nothing." Shane sank into the chair next to Wyatt's. "Hitting on her is a dick move under the circumstances."

"She can say no," Wyatt pointed out.

"And then she has to spend the rest of her vacation worrying about whether or not I'm going make things awkward, or worse, ignore the no." Shane shook his head. "Better to just leave it be."

Wyatt looked at Shane with sympathetic eyes. "You're fucking screwed."

Shane laid his head back and closed his eyes. "I know."

When Veronica stepped out onto the patio thirty minutes later, she was feeling slightly more relaxed. Switching out the clinging red bikini she'd let Delia talk her into for a simple tank dress in black cotton helped, as had the stern lecture she'd given herself in the shower. But as soon as she saw them again, sprawled in the patio chairs with lunch waiting on the table, all the dirty, sexy thoughts that had bloomed in her mind when she'd seen them kissing came roaring back.

Surprise had come first—she just hadn't been expecting it—followed swiftly by disappointment. She'd known Shane was gay, of course, but she'd had incredibly vivid sex dreams about him last night that had skewed her sense of reality. She'd forced herself to leave the condo to clear her head, but unfortunately, the image of him lying sprawled on the sofa in nothing but a pair of white boxer shorts had kept popping up. She'd gotten a good look at his back last night when he'd unexpectedly stripped off his shirt, but this morning he'd been lying face up, and the sight of him had nearly brought her to her knees.

The tattoo on his right arm went all the way up, wrapping

around his shoulder and extending halfway across his chest, intricate swirls of black ink interspersed with splashes of color, modern art in flesh and blood. His chest was lightly furred, with curls that began under his collarbone, formed a V to the middle of his chest, then tapered off to a light trail down the center of his abdomen. It circled his belly button and then disappeared beneath the waistband of a pair of white cotton boxer shorts that had no business looking that sexy.

The strength of her desire to see what was behind that plain white cotton had surprised her, and she'd gotten out of there as quickly as she could. She'd hoped the long walk followed by a dip in the ocean would be enough to cool her libido, but she'd still been thinking about licking her way down his belly and diving under those shorts when she'd walked in on him kissing his boyfriend.

It had been, to her honest shock, the hottest thing she'd ever seen in her life. She was clearly missing out by keeping her porn consumption strictly hetero.

It didn't hurt that Wyatt was just as attractive as Shane. He was white, about a head shorter than his boyfriend, with gilded blonde hair and striking blue eyes that danced with charm and mirth. Dimples popped in each cheek when he smiled, and he seemed to smile just about as often as Shane frowned.

So, a lot.

Wyatt spotted her first and stood, smiling. "Perfect timing. The food just got here."

Veronica smiled back automatically and stepped forward. "Great, I'm starving."

She glanced at Shane as he, too, pushed to his feet, then quickly looked away. He was frowning at her—again—and even through the spurt of annoyance she felt a flutter in her belly. His dark hair was unbound, hanging loose nearly to his shoulders, and her fingers practically twitched with the desire to run her fingers through it.

Down, girl, she admonished herself and walked around him to take her seat across from Wyatt.

She eyed the drink on the table in front of her, a froth of pink in a hurricane glass with a pineapple wedge and an umbrella. "What's that?"

"I forgot what the waiter said it was called," Wyatt told her as he sat, and Shane followed suit. "I assume the pink means strawberries, but other than that I have no clue."

She took an experimental sip and nearly choked. "Well, it has rum," she wheezed.

Wyatt laughed. "Is that a good thing?"

She took another sip, the taste of the alcohol fighting with the frozen slush of strawberries, bananas and pineapple. It went down smooth as silk. "Yeah, I think it is."

"Good guess, Shane," Wyatt said and Veronica blinked.

"You ordered this?"

He shrugged and picked up the beer next to his plate. "You looked like a fruity frozen drink kind of person."

"I'm not sure, but I think there's an insult in there somewhere."

Shane grunted, and Wyatt shot her a wink across the table. "How's your vacation so far, Veronica?"

"It's great," she told him and picked up a section of her club sandwich. "Beautiful weather, first class hotel. What's not to like?"

"Getting along with this grumpy bugger okay?" Wyatt jerked his head at Shane, who snorted and sipped his beer.

"Aside from the issue of the sleeping arrangements— which is not yet settled—so far it's been fine."

"It's settled," Shane put in, his tone brooking no argument and automatically putting Veronica's back up.

"Just because you cheated—" she began.

"Cheated?" His scowl was so fierce he looked like he only had one eyebrow.

"Carrying me to bed after I was already asleep on the sofa is cheating," she informed him archly.

"I didn't carry you," he told her.

"Then how did I get from the sofa to the bed?"

He shrugged. "You walked."

"I walked?"

"Yeah, you walked. I poked you, told you it was time to go to bed, and you got up and walked to bed. End of story."

"Hmmm." She took a sip of her drink and wondered what he wasn't telling her. "Still cheating."

He sighed, a long-suffering sound that for some reason made her want to smile, and picked up his burger. "I'm not taking the bed."

"You may as well give in," Wyatt told her as Shane took a bite. He was watching them with his chin propped on his hands and a gleam in his eye. "He's stubborn as hell."

She sighed. "I don't feel right taking the bed and making you sleep on the couch."

"Sorry," he said, looking very not sorry, and took another bite of his burger.

"How about this? I'll take the bed for the first half of the week, you take it for the second."

Shane's eyes were steady on hers as he chewed and swallowed. "Okay."

She paused, eyes narrowed. "You're just saying that to get me to shut up, aren't you?"

"Yes."

Wyatt barked out a laugh. "Welcome to my world."

Deciding to let it lie for now, Veronica picked up her drink and slipped into small talk. "How long have you two been together?"

"Three years," Wyatt said, aiming a warm look at Shane. "He swept me off my feet."

Shane cocked a brow when Veronica choked on her drink. "Don't believe that, huh?"

"No, no, it's not that," Veronica managed. "It's um...it's..."

"Good save," Shane commented.

Wyatt laughed. "It's true. We met when my husband commissioned him to do some built-ins. We were turning the formal dining room we never use into a library, and Seth wanted custom shelves."

"Seth is your husband?"

Wyatt nodded and waggled his ring finger at her, making the shiny silver band wink in the sun. "Just over a year now. Shane was my best man."

Veronica opened her mouth to reply, then closed it again when she realized she had no idea how to respond to that.

Wyatt's smile was knowing. "Hard to wrap your head around it, huh?"

"Honestly, yes," Veronica admitted with a wince. "Sorry."

"Hey, no worries. It bends a lot of brains. But just FYI, we're keeping our relationship quiet this trip," he said gesturing between Shane and himself. "Seth and I are here with his work colleagues, and we're not out as non-monogamous to them."

Veronica blinked. "Oh. Well, I won't say anything."

Wyatt jabbed his fork into his salad. "Appreciate it. And that's enough about our weird love life. I want to hear about yours."

Veronica blinked. "Mine?"

"Yeah. Delia said you just broke up with someone."

She chewed thoughtfully. "You could call it that, I guess," she began as the phone inside the cottage rang.

Shane frowned. "Expecting a call?"

"No. Anyone who knows me would call my cell." She started to rise, then sat again when he waved her down.

"I'll get it."

She waited until he'd stepped inside, then turned to Wyatt. "Is he always this intense?"

Wyatt grinned. "Sexy, isn't it?"

She laughed, her cheeks warming. "I guess it is. I nearly swallowed my tongue when I met him."

Wyatt's grin turned just a little wicked. "I know the feeling. When I walked in on him fitting shelves, he was sweaty and dusty and had his shirt off, and I thought I was going to pass out. Then he told me to get the fuck out of his way."

Veronica polished off one section of sandwich and reached for another. "Now that, I believe."

"The grumpy is only surface," Wyatt said, crunching on a crouton. "Underneath he's a big, cuddly teddy bear."

She couldn't suppress the snort. "Grizzly bear, maybe."

"Trust me. I know he's been a crab ass to you, but that's just because—" He broke off as Shane stepped outside. "What's up?"

Shane spared him a quick glance, then turned to Veronica. "That was the front desk."

Veronica frowned. "Is there a problem?"

"Yeah, you could say that." He dragged a hand through his hair and grimaced, clearly uncomfortable. "Derek's here."

"Derek's here." It took a moment for the words to sink in. "Derek's *here?*"

Shane nodded, his mouth grim. "The desk clerk said he's kicking up a fuss, demanding to be shown to your room, insisting he's on the reservation."

"He's not," she said numbly. "I changed it."

"Which is why they're not giving him any information," he said. "They want to know if you'll come up and talk to him."

"Oh, hell." She sat back with a groan and stared up into the sky. "I don't want to do that."

"Okay, I'll tell them."

"Wait." She took one more moment to look at the sky—blue, cloudless, perfect—then back at Shane. "I'll go."

"You don't have to," he told her.

"Yeah, but maybe I can keep things from escalating." She worked up a smile and pushed to her feet. "If I'm not back in an hour, send out a search party."

Wyatt pushed back from the table and stood. "Oh, we're coming with you."

"You don't have to do that."

"Yes, we do," Shane said and her startled gaze flew to his. He stared back unblinking, his face like a thundercloud.

"Really, it's ok. Stay and finish your lunch."

"We're going," he told her and turned back to the cottage. "I'm getting my shoes."

Veronica stared after him, completely nonplussed, then looked at Wyatt.

He shrugged. "He's getting his shoes."

FIVE

The walk from the cottage to the main hotel seemed to take forever, but in reality, it only took ten minutes. Veronica chatted amiably with Wyatt along the way about nothing in particular—her job, his job, the fact that Delia was a loose cannon and would surely, at some point, cause a great big scandal somewhere, likely involving huge quantities of marijuana and a rescue squad. Shane was silent, apparently content to let Wyatt carry the conversation.

By the time they approached the wide front doors of the hotel lobby, Veronica was feeling almost relaxed. Then they pulled open the doors and heard the shouting.

"I *demand* to be taken to my room immediately. This delay is unacceptable. I want to speak to a manager."

"Oh, for God's sake," Veronica muttered. The check-in desk was around the corner, so she couldn't see Derek, but she could hear him, along with everyone else within a hundred feet.

"He sounds like a prize," Wyatt commented, and Shane grunted in agreement.

"I told you, I've called my fiancé, but she isn't answering her cell phone. The reception here is terrible."

"Fiancé?" Shane asked.

Veronica glanced up at him. "No," she said firmly and saw a hint of amusement creep into his dark eyes.

"How do you want to do this?" Wyatt asked.

Veronica wrinkled her nose. "He's not going to go away unless I make it clear that I don't want him here."

"Honey, if uninviting him from this trip didn't convince him, I'm not sure what will."

She looked at Wyatt. "I have an idea, but it's kind of underhanded."

"I love underhanded," Wyatt proclaimed.

"How do you feel being party to a big, fat lie?"

He grinned, blue eyes dancing. "Oh, I'm in. Shane?"

Shane grunted, and Wyatt shot Veronica a wink. "That's his "game on" grunt. Let's do this, beautiful."

She squared her shoulders. "Okay, follow my lead."

She strode forward, Shane and Wyatt close behind, and rounded the corner. Derek was at the check-in desk, leaning so far over the counter that the poor girl behind it had taken a couple of steps back to avoid the finger he was trying to jab into her face.

"That's him?" Shane rumbled, his voice just loud enough to carry. The sneer on his face had Veronica holding back a laugh. "Think you can do better, babe."

The 'babe' made her blink, but she recovered quickly enough. "I agree," she said and Derek spun around at the sound of her voice.

"Veronica, *there* you are," he exclaimed and strode forward, arms outstretched.

Shane stepped neatly in front of her, and Derek skidded to a halt.

"Excuse me," he said icily.

"No," Shane said and Wyatt snorted out a laugh.

Veronica leaned to the side to peer around Shane. Derek was attempting to look down his nose at Shane, which, considering their height difference, was pretty funny.

"What do you mean, no?"

Shane shrugged. "No, I don't excuse you."

Derek's eyes narrowed. "Please move. I would like to speak to my fiancé."

Shane didn't budge. "No."

Veronica rolled her eyes at Wyatt, who winked back, a wicked grin on his face. "Derek, why are you here?"

Derek's gaze darted from Shane to Veronica, a wide smile pasted on his face. "I'm here for our vacation, of course."

"It's my vacation," she corrected. "You were uninvited."

Wyatt spoke up. "Yeah, uninvited. Scram, pal."

Derek barely spared him a glance. "Veronica, I know we argued—"

She laughed in his face.

"That's what he's calling it?" Wyatt wondered out loud, and before Derek could open his mouth, Veronica stepped to Shane's side and smiled at the girl behind the counter.

"I'm so sorry about all of this...Lacy," she said, reading the clerk's name tag. "I wonder if there's someplace we could go to hash this out, so we don't have to continue disrupting your guests."

Lacy's smile was pure relief. "Of course. There's a small conference room just down this hall." She tapped at her keyboard. "It's free all day."

"I'm sure this won't take long." She accepted the keycard with a smile, then raised a brow at Derek. "You coming?"

"Veronica, I don't think this is necessary," Derek began.

"Oh, I think it is." She began walking down the hall, Shane and Wyatt on either side of her. "This is the only chance you're getting, Derek. Take it or leave it, it's up to you."

She smiled when she heard him scramble behind her, and Wyatt leaned down to whisper in her ear. "I take it we're going to make it clear he's been replaced?"

She flashed the key card at the reader on the conference room door. "Okay by you?"

"Oh, yeah," he chuckled and held the door for her.

The room was small, with a round table and eight chairs in front of a wall of windows that showcased lush green foliage and vibrant blooms. In the distance she could just make out the blue of the ocean rolling in, white foam capping the waves as they crashed toward the golden stretch of sandy beach.

"We should go to the beach after this," Wyatt commented, coming up behind her. "You know how to surf?"

She shook her head and smiled up at him. "No, I never learned."

He draped an arm over her shoulder and pressed a kiss to her temple. She nearly jumped, catching herself just in time. "I'll teach you."

Shane stepped up to her other side, his big hand sliding to the small of her back. "You'll teach her how to fall, you mean."

"Sure." Wyatt's lips curled in a sexy smirk. "Then I can catch her."

Veronica laughed, enjoying both of them. Then the door slammed, and their hands fell away, and she turned her back on the view.

She regarded her ex dispassionately. "What do you want, Derek?"

"I want to talk," he told her stiffly and glared pointedly at Shane and Wyatt. "Alone."

She shook her head. "I thought I made it clear I was done talking."

"You canceled my plane ticket," he accused.

She raised a brow. "I did. And as I'd bought it with my airline miles, I was well within my rights to do so."

"Dammit, Veronica," he began and took a step forward.

Shane's low growl had him halting in his tracks.

"Watch it, Derek," Wyatt said quietly. "You're here because the lady allowed it, but there are lines. You don't want to cross them."

"You can't threaten me," Derek blustered.

"Can, and did." Wyatt grinned, feral and sharp, all his boyish charm gone. "Want to test me?"

Derek's eyes were furious, but his voice was cajoling. "I made a mistake, but I can make it up to you."

"No, thank you," Veronica countered coolly. "If that's all you came to say, you can go ahead and leave."

His expression darkened, his cheeks flushing with temper. "I paid for half of this vacation. I have every right to be here."

Veronica merely raised a brow. "Your name has been removed from the reservation. I'm sure Lacy told you that."

"I paid for it!" he repeated and actually slammed a fist on the table. "I'll sue them."

She shrugged. "You never made any payment to the resort, so I doubt you have any legal standing. But of course, you're welcome to try."

"I'll sue you," he returned, a combative glint in his eye.

"Okay."

He paused at that, blinking in confusion. "Okay, what?"

"Okay, sue me." She glanced at Wyatt. "Would that be small claims court, do you think?"

Wyatt pursed his lips as though he was considering the matter. "If we're talking about less than five grand, yeah."

"So, I'll see you in small claims court," Veronica went on calmly. "I'm sure you'll win. I might even have to pay court costs, once we explain to the judge exactly why you didn't get to go on this vacation. In open court. Where it's a matter of public record available to anyone with an internet connection.

Like say, the HR departments of large marketing firms running background checks."

Out of the corner of her eye, she saw Shane's beard twitch as he cracked a smile.

Derek went red as realization dawned. "You bitch."

"Are we done here, babe?" Shane asked, sounding like he was about to yawn, and she turned to look at him. He was leaning back against the window frame, his hands shoved into his pockets and his sandaled feet crossed at the ankles. The curtain of dark hair shadowed his face, and his eyes were glittering with unmistakable heat as his mouth curved into the faintest of smiles. He looked relaxed and a little bored and so ridiculously hot it nearly stole her breath. "I thought we were going to have some fun today, and this isn't it."

"Yeah," she said when she found her voice—though it didn't sound like her voice. It was husky and soft with a subtle vibration that he absolutely heard because he suddenly looked a lot less bored. "Yeah, we're done."

"Thank God," Wyatt muttered, and Veronica jolted when he slid a hard arm around her waist. She dragged her gaze away from the magnetic pull of Shane's eyes only to be snared in Wyatt's clear blue ones, so full of heat and humor, the *I want to fuck you* vibes pumping off him in waves, and she forgot all about Derek as her knees went liquid along with the rest of her.

"Just a damn minute," Derek thundered, breaking through the haze of lust that had somehow filled the room when she wasn't paying attention, and Veronica turned to him with a scowl.

"What?" she said, her exasperation clear.

"I'm your boyfriend," he began, and she sighed as both Shane and Wyatt began to laugh.

"You stopped being my boyfriend the minute I saw your dick in Cami," she informed him. "Do you remember me throwing you out of my apartment, taking my key back, and threatening to kneecap you?"

"Wait, he did this in *your* apartment?" Wyatt asked, astonished. At her nod, he looked at Derek with a combination of pity and disgust. "What an asshole."

"And then some," Shane agreed in his rumbling voice. He pushed away from the wall. "She's done with you, Derek. Fuck off."

"Who the hell do you think you are?" Derek blustered, his hands curling into fists at his sides.

Shane and Wyatt both looked at him with amused pity.

"Oh, right, you haven't been introduced." Veronica beamed a smile and hooked one arm through Wyatt's, then the other through Shane's, so the three of them were linked. "This is Wyatt, and this is Shane."

"I'd say nice to meet you, but it's not," Wyatt said baldly, and Shane snorted.

"We should probably say thank you, though," Wyatt went on, his tone thoughtful. "After all, if he hadn't been such a douche, we wouldn't be here."

"True," Shane rumbled, then frowned. "But I don't want to."

"Me neither," Wyatt said with a shrug.

"Well, then."

"But who *are* they?" Derek demanded, ignoring both men to glare at Veronica.

"They're my friends," Veronica purred in a tone that clearly said *naked friends*.

"And also, your replacements," Wyatt put in, apparently not willing to leave it up to innuendo.

"My what?"

"Well, technically I guess Shane is your replacement," Wyatt mused, "since he took your place on the reservation. But I'd like to think I get at least an honorable mention."

"Oh, don't worry," Veronica drawled, her low voice practically dripping with lust, "you do."

Derek's eyes bugged out. "He's staying with you?"

"He is," Wyatt said, pointing helpfully at Shane. "Technically, I have my own room. Which reminds me, I should pop in there for a change of clothes."

Shane looked at him over Veronica's head. "Get more condoms while you're at it."

"I don't believe this," Derek sputtered.

"Why don't we all go to Wyatt's room?" Veronica suggested silkily, ignoring Derek's look of jaw-dropping disbelief. She shifted to wrap her arms around their waists, tugging them both closer. She looked up at Shane. "I could use a nap."

"A nap?" Shane rumbled, his lips twitching as he turned to face her. He laid his hands on her hips and turned her, nudging her backward until her back bumped up against Wyatt's chest. Wyatt's hands came up to hold her by the shoulders, and the gleam in Shane's dark eyes made her shiver. "You think you're going to get to sleep?"

The sound that slipped from her lips had nothing to do with the show they were putting on, and everything to do with the heat flooding her body. He was standing so close that the skirt of her dress snagged on his shorts, and Wyatt was a solid wall of muscle behind her. She licked her lips, shivering when his eyes tracked the movement. "You have to let me sleep sometime," she managed.

"Yeah, Shane. Have a heart," Wyatt put in. He slid an arm around her, his palm flat on her belly, and tugged her back so her back pressed to his chest, her ass to his groin. His breath skimmed her ear and made her skin break out in goosebumps. "Can't you see she's tired?"

"Fine." Shane took another step forward, so close now his hard thighs brushed hers. His hips rolled, a subtle flex that wasn't quite a thrust but close enough for her to tell that his thighs weren't the only thing that was hard. Heat flooded her face, and she knew her cheeks were probably glowing. The sexiest smile she'd ever seen curled his lips and he raised a hand to cup her cheek. He stroked his thumb over her mouth and almost sent her into cardiac arrest. "We'll do all the work."

Dimly, she realized it was her turn to say something. Shane was looking at her expectantly, Wyatt had tensed behind her, and Derek stood mere feet away, his mouth still open as he made noises like a constipated goat. But her mind had gone blank, all thoughts burned away by the look in Shane's eyes.

If he was acting, the man was absolutely *wasted* making furniture.

Then there was Wyatt, looming behind her, his big hand still splayed on her belly only inches above her pussy, where all hell was currently breaking loose. She was trying to ignore the fact that her butt was pressed right against his pants, and she was *really* trying not to notice that his pants were pressing back. Here she was sandwiched between two gay men who, if her senses weren't playing tricks on her, both had serious wood happening.

Was it for her? Each other? Did they both have some kind of odd improv fetish? *What the hell is going on here?*

"Veronica," Wyatt said, his breath skimming over her ear, his tone just questioning enough that she knew he was checking in, but it was also so drenched in lust she went a little dizzy, swaying in his hold. His hand tightened on her belly, the heat of it almost searing through the thin cotton of her dress, and she let out a whimpering moan that if she'd been in her right mind would've embarrassed the hell out of her.

In her current state, she couldn't have cared less.

The sound had a galvanizing effect on all three men in the room. Wyatt's hand tightened even further on her abdomen, tugging her more firmly against him. Shane's eyes narrowed, his fingers shifting to cup her jaw as he began to lower his head.

And Derek shouted, "What the fuck is going on?", jerking her back to reality and killing the mood.

Mostly.

Shane turned his head slowly, the look on his face not boding well for Derek's continued good health. Veronica was half tempted to step back and see how this played out, but she realized she just wanted him gone.

"Go away, Derek."

"Yeah, go away," Wyatt echoed, still holding her firmly, and turned to glare at her ex-boyfriend. "You're not invited to my room."

Veronica bit down on her lip to kill the laugh as Derek's face went fire-engine red. Shane's expression didn't change, his hand still cupping her face. "I think that makes it unanimous." He jerked his head toward the door. "Bye."

"I don't believe you," Derek said, ignoring Shane to focus on Veronica. His breath was puffing out in outraged huffs, his eyes filled with outraged disbelief. "I don't believe you're...you're..." He waved his hand in the air as if he could magically conjure the words. "Doing that with them."

"Doing that?" Wyatt's low chuckle made her hair flutter. "What is he, twelve years old?"

Veronica shrugged. "I don't care if you believe me. Go home, Derek."

"I can't believe I flew down here to try to get back together with you."

"I can't either," Veronica snapped, sick of him. "I kicked you out of my apartment, changed the locks, and gave away all your shit. What the *hell* made you think there was ever a chance we were getting back together?"

His eyes bugged out. "You gave away my stuff?"

"Everything but the unopened face creams." She sent him

a sunny smile. "I returned those to Nordstrom's and bought this dress."

"Nice," Shane rumbled, and she smiled up at him.

"Thanks. You don't think it's too plain?" She glanced down at the simple, unadorned black. "Delia thought it needed sparkle."

He shook his head. "You're the sparkle."

She blinked, and even though she knew he was just playing his part, melted a little. "Wow."

"Shane, you're such a romantic," Wyatt said and gave her a light squeeze. "Did you buy that red bikini with face cream money?"

She turned slightly to smile over her shoulder at him. "You liked that?"

"I loved that," he told her with unabashed relish and an exaggerated leer. "I wanted to peel it off you with my teeth."

"Oh. Well."

"Excuse me!"

Veronica turned back to Derek with a sigh. "You're still here?"

"You gave away my stuff?"

"Shirts, pants, ties, shoes. Oh, and the suit."

"The suit? The suit?" He flapped his arms in the air as though he was trying to take flight. "It was nearly brand new. I'd only worn it once!"

"Well, now someone else is going to be wearing it."

"I can't believe—wait. You said shoes. Not the loafers."

"The lady at the agency was thrilled to get them," she said and watched him close his eyes in pain. "I'm sure whoever got them will put them to good use."

"Agency?" Wyatt asked.

"Fresh Start," she told him. "They specialize in helping recently incarcerated people find jobs. They help with resume writing, provide clothes for interviewing, stuff like that."

"Nice," Shane told her.

"I thought so."

Derek's face filled with rage, his mouth twisting with it. "You bitch."

"Well, ouch," she said mildly.

"You owe me what I paid for my half of this vacation, the two thousand dollars I had to shell out for the last-minute plane ticket down here—"

"Is he high?" Wyatt wondered.

Shane grunted and tried to take a step towards Derek, but Veronica curled her hands into his shirt, shaking her head.

"Not worth it," she said when he looked at her.

"—plus the cost of the suit, *and* the shoes, and all my skin-care products," Derek finished.

She rolled her eyes. "Go away, Derek."

"I will not," he declared haughtily, his cheeks still flushed with temper. "Not until you write me a check."

"Is he really this clueless?" Wyatt wanted to know.

"I guess," Veronica said and sighed when Shane broke free from her grip to stomp across the small room.

"Stay away from me," Derek warned in a quavering voice, then squeaked when Shane fisted a hand in his shirt and started towing him toward the door. "You can't do this! This is assault!"

Veronica glanced up at Wyatt. "Is he going to hurt him?"

Wyatt shook his head. "Nah," he said, then pursed his lips when Shane slammed Derek against the wall and lifted him off his feet. "Well, maybe."

"Here's how this is going to go, Derek." Shane's voice sounded like a dog chewing gravel. Veronica couldn't see his face, but since Derek's eyes bugged out and the angry flush drained away, she assumed a smile was not present. "You're going to get the fuck out of here. You're going to leave

Veronica alone. Failure to do these things will make me angry. You won't like me when I'm angry."

Wyatt snorted out a soft laugh. "Go, Hulk."

"You can't make me do anything," Derek protested in a show of bravado that would've had more impact if his feet weren't four inches off the ground. He looked like a worm on a hook, squirming and twisting despite being thoroughly skewered.

"You don't think so?"

Whatever Derek saw on Shane's face made him go even paler. "But I can't go," he whined. "My return flight isn't for a week."

"Change it."

"That costs money."

"I don't give a fuck," Shane said and dropped him to his feet.

Derek lost his balance and crumpled to the ground, then yelped again when Shane reached down and hauled him back up. "Time for you to go, Derek."

"Veronica," Derek began, his eyes pleading with her as Shane dragged him toward the door. "You can't just—"

"No talking," Shane ordered, and with Derek babbling behind him, dragged him out the door.

Veronica's breath left her in a whoosh, and she sagged against Wyatt's restraining hold.

"Hey, hey," He turned her carefully around, ducking down to peer into her face. "You okay?"

"Yeah." She inhaled deeply, smelling the faintly citrus scent of the hotel soap on his skin. "Yeah, I'm okay. Just relieved."

His blue eyes searched her face, concern stamped on his features. "That he's gone?"

"And that he's no longer my problem."

"I'll bet." He pulled out a chair and eased her into it with gentle hands. "That was pretty slick, playing the two of us against him."

"It was, wasn't it?" Her lips twitched. "I've never actually seen anyone's face turn purple before."

He grinned. "He's going to be torturing himself with mental pictures of the three of us "doing that" for weeks."

She snorted. "Oh God, he's such a tool. I can't believe I ever thought I was in love with him."

"Were you?"

She sighed. "No. I think I had myself convinced I was, otherwise I wouldn't have stayed with him. But I wasn't hurt that he cheated, just pissed. I think my ego took more of a whack than my heart."

He settled himself into the chair next to her, and she sent him a grateful smile. "You guys are sweet for playing along."

He raised a brow, his mouth curled in amusement. "Is that what you thought we were doing?"

"Well, yeah."

"Oh. You think we're gay." The amusement deepened. "A reasonable assumption to make, but inaccurate. Which you probably guessed, since I know you felt my dick trying to force its way out of these shorts a few minutes ago."

The shocked little gasp caught in her throat. "I thought maybe you'd shoved a banana in your pocket."

"I'm bi-sexual," he said baldly, still amused but now watching her with a focused intensity that seemed at odds with his usual cheer. "Surprised you didn't clue into that."

Unsure what to do with this information—or the effect it had on her still present lust—she felt back on wit. "I wasn't thinking very clearly. My brain kind of fogged over."

He barked out a laugh, though the heat in his eyes remained. "I know the feeling. Shane is too, you know."

"Shane is what?" Shane asked, coming through the open door, and Veronica jumped up.

"Glad we could help out," Wyatt said easily and pushed to his feet. "You take out the trash?"

"Hotel security is on it." Shane's eyes searched her face, his big body tense. "You okay?"

"Yeah." She rubbed damp palms on her thighs. "I'm okay."

"If he gives you any trouble when you get back home, I want to hear about it."

"It's not going to be an issue, Shane."

"I want to hear about it," he repeated.

"He's cute when he's in protector mode, isn't he?" Wyatt asked Veronica.

"Adorable," Veronica agreed through the haze of confusion and hormones, and Shane gave a low, bad-tempered grunt.

"And so eloquent," Wyatt continued, grinning when Shane glared at him. "Now, since none of us got to finish lunch. I think we should go out for a bite. The concierge told me there's a great seafood place not too far from here."

"Thanks," Veronica managed and took a step backward. "But I think I want that nap."

Shane frowned. "You should get some food."

"I ate almost half of my sandwich," she told him and took another step back. It was suddenly imperative that she be alone. "You guys should go, though. Let me know if the shrimp's any good."

"You okay?" Wyatt asked, concern in his pretty eyes.

"I'm fine," she assured him, edging toward the door. "Thanks for the help."

"Anytime," Wyatt said, watching her with a mix of concern and confusion. Shane just stared.

"I'll see you later," she said and ducked out before they could respond.

She made her way quickly down the hall, surprised when

she didn't hear any footsteps behind her. She stopped at the front desk to leave the keycard with Lacy, thanked the young woman for her help, then headed out into the midday sunshine.

She finally managed to exhale when she hit the path to the cottage, but there was no calming her racing heart. Jesus, she'd had actual sex that hadn't turned her on this much. She wasn't sure what had just happened, or what it meant, but she knew she needed to be alone to figure it out.

And to maybe take advantage of the handheld shower massager.

Six

"Well." Wyatt turned to Shane. "That was interesting."

Shane grunted. "Asshole deserved it."

"No argument, but that's not what I was talking about."

Shane was staring at the empty doorway, a concerned frown on his face. "You think she's okay?"

"She's fine," Wyatt said, and his tone had Shane turning to him. One tawny brow rose, and there was a smirk on his pretty face. "How're you?"

"I'm fine. Guy was a lightweight."

"Again, not what I'm talking about."

"What?"

"I'm talking about this," Wyatt said, laying his hand on the hard ridge of flesh behind Shane's zipper.

"That's nothing," Shane began.

"You sure?" Wyatt gave an experimental squeeze, grinning at the responding surge of Shane's hips. "Doesn't feel like nothing. Feels like pretending to be Veronica's lover turned your crank."

"Just going with the program."

"That's all that was, huh?"

"Are you seriously giving me shit over this?" Shane wanted to know.

"Only if you don't do anything about it."

Shane shoved Wyatt's hand away from his dick. His dick protested the loss, and Shane ignored it. He was getting pretty good at it. "Don't start this again."

Wyatt held out his hands in surrender. "I know, I know, you don't want to make her uncomfortable. But you're so busy convincing yourself that you were just 'going with the program' that I think you missed something."

Shane started for the door. "Come on, I'm hungry."

"She wants you," Wyatt said and Shane stopped in his tracks.

"What are you talking about?" he said carefully, his body tight with tension. He hadn't quite burned off the adrenaline surge of dealing with Derek—he'd barely gotten to toss him around at all, and no punches had been thrown—so he still had a lot of energy and nowhere to go with it.

"She wants you," Wyatt repeated. "I can't believe you didn't notice."

He crossed his arms over his chest and glared at his lover. "Notice what?"

"Oh, I don't know. How about the way she almost melted into a puddle when you touched her mouth? Or the little whimpering sound she made when you nearly kissed her? And don't tell me you couldn't smell her."

Shane bit back a curse. He had been able to smell her, that intoxicating mix of peaches and the richer, spicier scent of arousal. He'd nearly forgotten all about their audience, thinking only of the soft, supple mouth under his thumb and the surprised heat in her wide hazel eyes, and he'd been about to get a taste of all that spicy sweetness when Derek the

Asshole had interrupted and poured a metaphorical bucket of cold water over his head.

He could almost be grateful for it. Once he crossed over that line, he couldn't uncross it, and no matter what his dick wanted, he had been serious when he'd told Wyatt he wasn't going there.

"Not going there, Wyatt," he said out loud, as much to convince himself as his lover.

"Why?" Wyatt asked, genuinely baffled.

Shane scrubbed a hand over his face, unsure how to explain. While Wyatt loved women just as much as Shane did, the bulk of Wyatt's romantic relationships had been with men, and he didn't always recognize the power imbalance inherent in most opposite-sex relationships. Shane, however, was hyper-aware of the fact he held a distinct physical advantage over most women. Since there was nothing he could do about that, he went out of his way to be as non-threatening as possible. He didn't reach for or touch women who weren't expecting and receptive to it, and he always tried to maintain a respectable physical distance. Their temporary living arrangement made Veronica even more vulnerable, and no matter how much he wanted her, he just couldn't take the chance.

"I told you," he said to Wyatt, "I'm not doing anything that would make her uncomfortable."

Wyatt arched a brow. "I'd bet you a thousand dollars that she just went back to the cottage to rub one out."

"Jesus, Wyatt."

"I know it's been a while for both of us," Wyatt went on, "but that was a seriously turned-on woman. Her knees were shaking."

"Her ex-boyfriend was screaming at her," Shane protested, but it sounded weak. "She was scared."

"Please," Wyatt scoffed. "She barely even twitched when

that jackass started braying. Hell, she barely *looked* at him. She was focused on us. On *you*."

"She was just pretending to be into us so he'd get the message and leave," Shane began.

Wyatt shook his head. "Yeah, that's how it started. But that's not how it ended."

Shane scowled at him. "Shut up."

"Shane—"

"Shut. Up. I've had a hard-on for almost twenty-four hours now, and you're not fucking helping."

"I'm *trying* to help," Wyatt muttered.

"Give it up, Wyatt."

"You're wasting an opportunity," Wyatt protested.

"Then it's wasted," Shane said, exasperated. "Can we go eat now?"

Wyatt eyed him thoughtfully. "Maybe you want to go find a truck to push up a hill first. You seem like you have some energy to burn off."

"Fuck you," Shane said mildly and turned for the door. "You're buying lunch."

"I still say she's down there taking care of business," Wyatt muttered as he trailed after Shane.

Shane merely reached back and slapped the side of Wyatt's head.

"Okay, okay, I won't bring it up again. Say, I wonder if the restaurant has warm peach pie on the menu?"

Shane just kept walking, Wyatt's laughter ringing in his ears.

***

Veronica sat on the warm sand and watched the sunset, the vibrant pinks and oranges slashing across the sky as the glowing ball of the sun sank slowly into the ocean. It was gorgeous, the most breathtaking sunset she'd ever seen. And a damn shame, because she barely noticed any of it. Her thoughts were where they'd been all day—on Shane, Wyatt, and the hottest moment of her life that had been interrupted by her dumbass ex-boyfriend.

She sighed and rested her chin on her updrawn knees. After she'd fled the conference room, she'd run back down to the cottage and immediately pulled out the little battery-operated accessory Delia had so thoughtfully packed for her. When she'd unpacked and found it, along with a note from Delia, she'd been annoyed at her friend for tucking it into her suitcase without telling her. How she'd gotten through TSA without it being flagged was beyond her, but after her brilliant little brainstorm—*hey, how about I make my ex think I'm banging these two ridiculously hot guys, that'll make him go away without a fuss and won't blow up in my face at ALL because they're gay, cool!*—she'd made good use of Delia's gift.

Twice. Then she'd taken a shower and made good use of the adjustable, handheld shower wand.

Even now, with her vagina pleasantly sore and her lust sated, she couldn't stop thinking about those moments in the conference room. The heat of Wyatt's hard, muscled body behind her, Shane looming in front. His hand on her face, the scrape of his calloused thumb over her mouth. If Derek hadn't chosen that exact moment to start squawking, he would've kissed her. And she would've let him.

She closed her eyes with a groan and resisted the urge to beat her head on the beach. It was too soft to knock some sense into her, and she'd just have to wash her hair again.

She'd thought he was gay. She'd thought they were *both* gay. When the idea came to her to pretend that she was sleeping with them, it had seemed harmless enough. Nobody wanted to hang around and watch their very recent ex canoodle with a new lover—much less two of them—so what better way to convince Derek to leave? Both men had fallen in instantly with the plan, and it had been working beautifully until her hormones had gotten in on the action.

"Asshole hormones," she muttered. This was all their fault. By the time Shane had lost his patience and escorted a squawking Derek out of the room, she'd been a tangled mess of arousal and confusion. She'd hoped to play it off as exceptional acting—*I was just playing the part really, really well, it's not like I'm wildly and inappropriately attracted to you and your lover, two gay men who are being nice enough to help me out. That would just be silly!*

But she hadn't fooled Wyatt. If she had, she doubted he'd have felt the need to correct her assumptions about their sexuality.

"Bi," she muttered to her knees. They're both bi, and their relationship wasn't monogamous, and if the erect penises were any indication, they both seemed to be attracted to her and what the fuck was she supposed to do with all of this information?

Her hormones had cast their vote—she didn't think she'd ever masturbated three times in a single day in her life, much less three times in as many hours—but her brain was still struggling to wrap her mind around Wyatt's little truth bomb.

She shifted to stare out over the water, glowing now with the reflection of the setting sun. So, okay, if jumping Shane's bones turned out to be an option, she wasn't going to be mad, exactly. Confused, but not mad. And, despite her vagina's very clear opinion on the matter, she was also going to be cautious.

She had no idea what the parameters of Shane's relationship with Wyatt allowed, and she wasn't going anywhere near either of them until she knew more. Having just been cheated on, she had no desire to switch roles and suddenly become the other woman.

"This is complicated," she told the ocean.

"Then you should probably have a drink," the ocean said back, and her mouth dropped open in shock. Then she realized Wyatt was standing four feet away with a couple of frothy pink drinks in his hands.

He sent her a dimpled smile, the breeze ruffling his hair. "How's it going?"

Well, I thought the ocean was talking to me, so there's that. "What are you doing here?"

He stepped forward. "Brought you a drink."

She automatically took the glass and he dropped down beside her. He was wearing nothing but a pair of board shorts and sunglasses, the wide expanse of his sleekly muscled chest on display. Her pussy gave a little twitch in response, and Veronica sighed.

"You okay?" he asked.

"Yes," she told him, and mentally admonished her vagina. *You've gotten all you're getting tonight, my girl, so settle down.* "Why are you bringing me drinks?"

"You didn't get to finish the one from lunch."

"Oh." She took a sip, grateful that the bartender hadn't stinted on the rum. "Thanks."

"You're welcome. So." He shoved his sunglasses up onto his head and smiled at her. "What'd you do today?"

She studied his face while she sipped, for some reason wary of that open, seemingly guileless expression. "Not much," she said vaguely.

"Seen Shane?"

She shook her head. "Not since lunch. Why, is he missing?"

He shrugged, shifting his attention to the ocean. "No. I had dinner with him earlier."

"Okay," she said, and not knowing what else to say, sipped her drink again.

They sat for a moment in silence, staring at the ocean and sipping their drinks, before Wyatt spoke again.

"Sorry if I freaked you out earlier."

She turned to him with a frown. "When?"

"Earlier," he repeated and gestured with his drink. "In the conference room, when Shane was throwing the idiot out."

She shook her head in confusion. "You didn't freak me out. Why would you think you did?"

He shrugged again, his blue eyes surprisingly sober as he turned away from the sea to look at her. "The information that Shane and I are bi-sexual seemed to catch you off guard."

"Oh. That." Because it was there, and she didn't know what to say, she took another sip of her drink. A long one.

"So, if it freaked you out, I'm sorry."

She let the straw fall from her lips. "'Freaked out' is the wrong term."

"Yeah?" A glint of humor lit his gaze now. "What's the right one?"

"Um. Nonplused?" she ventured, and smiled at him. "Taken aback? Gobsmacked?"

"Gobsmacked, huh?" He smiled back. "Sounds kinky."

"It does, doesn't it?" She laughed, oddly comfortable with him despite the little tingles of desire bubbling through her. "Anyway, no offense taken."

"Good." He was silent for a moment, sipping his drink, then set it down, twisting it to wedge it into the sand. "Can I ask you a personal question?"

"Sure," she said absently. She was watching his arm flex as he worked the glass into the sand, fascinated by the play of muscle under his skin. He had fabulous arms, rippling with lean muscle and dusted with fine golden hair. Her fingertips itched to stroke, just a little, to see if that hair was as soft as it looked.

She took another drink instead.

"Did you come back to the cottage and take a nap today, or did you rub one out?"

She choked in surprise, spewing her drink onto the sand, and Wyatt pounded her helpfully on the back. She stared at him, eyes watering as she coughed. When she had her breath back, she wheezed out, "Boy, when you said personal, you weren't kidding."

"Sorry." He gave her a last pat on the back. "You okay?"

"Yeah." She sucked in a deep breath and spent a few seconds digging her glass into the sand next to his to buy herself some time. "Why do you ask?"

He shrugged. "Because I know you were turned on when you left, and it's what I would have done."

"Would have done, or did?"

A dimple winked in his cheek when he grinned at her. "I asked you first."

"Three times," she admitted with a sheepish grin, and he hooted with laughter.

"Go, V," he said with a chuckle. "I only managed one, but I did jump Seth when he got back from his team-building workshop this afternoon. He says thanks, by the way."

Veronica stared at him. "I think this is the weirdest conversation I've ever had."

"Yeah, I can see how it might be." He tiled his head, regarding her thoughtfully. "You don't have any experience with non-monogamy, do you?"

"No."

"Want me to tell you how it works for us?"

She shifted on the sand, intrigue outweighing discomfort. "I'm dying of curiosity, but you don't have to tell me. It's none of my business."

"You don't think so?" He shot her a considering look, then shrugged and looked back out to sea. "I don't mind talking about it. I've always known I was poly."

"Poly?" she asked.

"Polyamorous," he explained. "It basically means I can, and do, have more than one romantic relationship at a time."

"How is that different from non-monogamous?"

"It's mostly semantics. I go with poly because my relationship with Shane isn't just about sex. I love him, he loves me, we're committed to each other as partners even though our relationship isn't primary for either of us. But Seth doesn't conduct his outside relationships the same way, and he feels like non-monogamous fits him better."

"Delia said she didn't think he was seeing anyone else right now."

"He's not. He usually doesn't, actually." He shifted around on the sand so they faced each other. "Seth likes to have sex with other men—he is gay, by the way—but he doesn't want another relationship."

"Oh."

"He says he doesn't have time for one, which is true," Wyatt went on. "But even if he did, he'd still prefer to keep his other partners casual."

"And that's okay with you?" Veronica asked. "You don't get jealous?"

"Sure, I do." He said it so easily, so casually, Veronica blinked in surprise. "He used to come home from a date and tell me all about it, and let me tell you, there's nothing worse than hearing my man gush about the firm young thing that just blew his mind."

Veronica winced. "Oh, ouch."

"It wasn't pretty," Wyatt agreed. "Some poly couples like to share details about their dates and other partners, but it just makes me anxious. I start comparing myself, and that way lies madness, you know?"

She nodded. "That would make me nuts. How'd you work it out?"

"He stopped gushing about the firm young things, which helped me stop comparing myself to them. That's our first rule. And if he has plans with someone, I try to make sure I'm not just waiting around the house with nothing to do. Even if I just take myself to the movies, it helps to be busy, or have something else to focus on."

Veronica nodded slowly. "That makes sense."

"We make sure to carve out time for each other, and we make sure to communicate."

"What do you mean?"

"I mean, if anything is bothering me—about the scheduling, someone he's seeing, how he's acting about it—I make sure to tell him, and he does the same. Expecting your partner to read your mind is a disaster when you're not seeing other people. With non-monogamy, it's an atom bomb."

"Do you get jealous of Shane, too?"

"With Shane, it's a little different," he began.

She shook her head when he hesitated. "You don't have to tell me."

"It's okay. I was just trying to figure out how to say it. Shane doesn't date other men. He says I'm enough," he explained with a wink. "So when he does date, it's usually women. Somehow that makes it easier. It also helps that he's willing to share."

"You mean..." She had to clear her throat. "You mean you date them too?"

He shook his head. "As much as I love women, I'm not interested in having a girlfriend. I'm at my poly limit with my two guys. But I like having sex with women, and some of Shane's girlfriends have been into threesomes. So..."

"Oh." She swallowed. Hard. "Wow."

"Am I freaking you out yet?"

"Getting closer," she managed.

"Sorry."

"It's okay." She blinked away the haze of lusty thoughts and refocused on him. "Any other bombs you want to drop on me?"

"I think that's about it," he said. "Any thoughts?"

"It sounds hard," Veronica said honestly.

"It is, sometimes."

"Is it worth it?"

"Yeah, it's worth it." He smiled at her. "I've got two wonderful men in my life who love me and want me to be happy. Doesn't get better than that."

"Well, that's romantic."

"You sound surprised."

"I am," she admitted and grimaced. "Sorry."

"No need to be. Most people think of non-monogamy, they think of cheating, which is pretty much the opposite of romance."

"I can attest."

"You're thinking pretty hard there, beautiful," he observed. "Care to share with the class?"

"It sounds complicated and fraught and the possibility for heartbreak seems huge, but it also sounds kind of..."

"Insane?" he guessed when she trailed off.

"Wonderful," she finished. "It sounds kind of wonderful."

"It is." His smile was contented. "It's not for everyone, but it works for us. Which brings me to the reason for my visit."

Her eyebrows shot up. "It wasn't to bring me a drink and enjoy the lovely sunset?"

"That was my secondary purpose. My primary purpose was to find out if you're as into Shane as he's into you."

Her mind went blank. "What?"

"Seems to me like you are," he went on, ignoring her slack-faced shock. "But since I just got done explaining how poly requires clear communication, I figured I'd ask."

It took her a while to find her voice. "Ask what, exactly?"

His dimple winked again. "Do you want to fuck my boyfriend, Veronica?"

"Well, that's clear," she muttered, and he laughed.

"It's not a hard question," he chided, his tone surprisingly gentle. "And it's not going to hurt my feelings if the answer is no."

"Hang on a second." She picked up her drink, now mostly melted, and slugged it back in one gulp before reaching for the glass beside it. "Are you going to finish that?"

"Go ahead," he said, amused, and she drained his glass.

"Okay." She set the empty glass next to the first, her head swimming a little from the rum. "What was the question again?"

"Do you want to fuck my boyfriend?"

Not sure if her head was spinning from the rum, or from the idea of fucking Shane, she huffed out a breath. "Well, yeah."

His dimples winked at her. "I had a feeling. So, what are you going to do about it?"

Veronica just stared at him, her mind a complete blank. Well, not a *complete* blank. There were images dancing through her brain, most of them featuring a very naked, very aroused Shane. Over her, under her, his mouth on her body, his cock in her—

She shook them away. "Are you asking for him, or for both of you?"

"Him." Wyatt's smile was devilish. "For now."

"Right. Well. Anyway." She cleared her throat. "I don't think it would be a very good idea."

"Why not?"

"Because."

He arched one tawny eyebrow. "Flawless reasoning."

Giving into frustration, she flopped backward onto the

sand with a groan. "I don't need these kinds of complications, Wyatt."

"What complications?" Wyatt asked with disgusting reasonableness. "You like him, he likes you—"

"I highly doubt that," Veronica said, sitting up. She ignored the cascade of sand down the back of her dress to frown at Wyatt. "He barely talks to me, and when he does it's mostly grunts."

"Well, he's a grunter. Trust me, he likes you. He threw your ex-boyfriend out of a hotel for you, remember?"

That gave her pause, then she shrugged. "I'm pretty sure he'd do that for just about anyone."

"True enough," Wyatt conceded. "Look, we've talked about this."

She was thoroughly confused now. "We're talking about it now."

"I mean Shane and I have talked about this—"

Her jaw dropped open in shock. "Excuse me?"

"—and trust me, he wants you. So do I, actually, but one thing at a time."

She lifted her hands to her head. "I don't know what to do with all of this information. He doesn't act like he's into me at all, Wyatt."

"Which is where the trusting me comes in," Wyatt said patiently.

"Look, it's sweet that you're trying to hook me up with your boyfriend," Veronica began, then let out a laugh. "Boy, that's a sentence I never thought I'd say."

"Welcome to the dark side," he quipped.

"But I just got out of a shitty relationship."

"Which makes it the perfect time to have a little vacation fling," Wyatt pointed out. "I'm not saying you have to marry the guy—"

"Thank you so much," she said wryly.

"—or even fuck him. I'm just saying, if you make a move, he's not going to say no."

She frowned. "Why do I have to make the move?"

"Shane has it in his head that hitting on you would be ethically inadvisable, considering the circumstances."

"Which circumstances?"

"The ones where you're sharing a house for the next week." Wyatt shrugged. "He thinks if he hits on you and you don't hit back, it could make things uncomfortable for you."

"Oh." Veronica blinked. "That's...really thoughtful."

"He's a thoughtful guy." Wyatt winked. "And a helluva lay."

Veronica snorted. "Why are you trying to sell me so hard on this?"

Wyatt shrugged. "I'm not. I just wanted to make my feelings clear, in case that's what's standing in your way."

"It was a consideration," she said carefully. "I just got out of a relationship where someone cheated on me, and I didn't want to do that to someone else."

"An admirable sentiment, but in this case, misplaced. You have my blessing to fuck his brains out."

"Um. Thanks?" she ventured.

He laughed and before she could blink, leaned over to kiss her. It was quick, a brush of his lips that lasted only a few seconds, but the barest hint of tongue dancing along the seam of her lips made it anything but innocent. Then he was pushing to his feet. "You're welcome. Now, I better get back to the hotel before Seth sends out a search party. We're supposed to be meeting his partners for drinks."

She managed a smile for him, even with her lips still tingling from the kiss. "Not looking forward to it, huh?"

"Lawyers are boring." He bent to pick up the empty glasses. "They'll talk case law and tort reform until last call, and Seth will have to kick me under the table to keep me from falling asleep."

"The things we do for love," she quipped.

"Tell me about it." He paused, eyes glinting down at her in the deepening twilight. "You okay out here by yourself?"

"Sure." Her smile came easier this time. "Thanks for the drink."

"Anytime, beautiful. I'll see you later?"

"Sure. Maybe we can all go snorkeling or something," she suggested.

"Ah, if only that were sexual innuendo," he sighed.

She sputtered with laughter. "You're terrible."

He grinned. "I know. Night."

"Night," she echoed and watched him walk away down the sand. He was so pretty, she mused, all surfer-boy good looks and charm, with those dimples that winked every time he even thought about smiling. He was easy to talk to, easy to laugh with, and easy to lust over in a benign, uncomplicated sort of way. Easy.

Unlike Shane, who had her tongue in knots and her libido showing fangs every time she even thought of him. And there was nothing benign about the way she wanted him.

She sighed and pushed to her feet, heading for the cottage. If she was lucky, he wouldn't be back yet, and she could take a quick shower to wash off the sand. Then she thought she might come back outside and lie in the hammock for a while. It was a warm night, the air still but for a wisp of a breeze coming from the sea, and the stars were starting to pop out. She'd stay in the hammock until she got sleepy, then go to bed. And if Shane was back by then, well, she'd just have to deal.

SEVEN

Shane woke the next morning and turned to frown at the empty bed across the room.

Veronica hadn't come back last night.

It had been late when he'd gotten in, after two. He'd found a local bar that had decent live music, and had stayed through last call. He'd ignored his phone most of the night, and the dozens of texts from Wyatt. They'd started out subtle, then gradually increased in boldness until "fuck the girl" followed by eggplant and peach emojis was popping up on the screen over and over again.

He'd responded once, with a gif a cartoon monster swallowing a man whole, then turned off his phone.

When he'd gotten back to the cottage, Veronica wasn't there. She hadn't shown up while he showered, still wasn't there by the time he turned off the lights and settled onto the sofa. And now it looked like she hadn't come back at all.

Biting back a curse, he fought his way out of the tangle of sheets and stumbled to the bathroom. He took care of business, then stumbled back out again and dragged on shorts and a T-shirt. He grabbed his phone off the kitchen counter and thumbed it on.

He snagged a Mountain Dew from the fridge—he'd taken advantage of the all-inclusiveness of the resort and had them deliver a twelve-pack—then picked up his phone and called Wyatt.

It rang five times before Wyatt's sleepy, "H'lo?" sounded in his ear.

"Did you see Veronica last night?"

There was a muffled rustling of sheets, a low murmur, then, "Shane?"

"Yeah. Did you see her?"

"About sunset," Wyatt mumbled. "We had a drink on the beach and talked for a few minutes. Why?"

Shane popped the tab on the can of pop. "She didn't come back last night."

"Hang on a second." There was a soft grunt and a rustle of sheets. Shane raised the can to his lips for a drink, relishing the ice-cold sweetness as he listened to Seth's sleepy voice murmuring in the background. Then he heard footsteps, followed by the click of a door shutting.

"Okay, I can talk now."

Shane winced. "Sorry. I didn't think you guys would still be in bed."

"We had a late night, and there's nothing on the schedule till after lunch today. Don't worry about it. What about Veronica?"

"She didn't come back last night." He set the can on the counter. "She didn't say anything to you about going out?"

"No, but why would she?" The shrug in Wyatt's voice was clear.

"What time did you see her? Where was she?"

"I don't know, it was after dinner. She was sitting on the beach in front of the cottage, watching the sunset."

Shane narrowed his eyes on the glass doors that led to the patio, and the empty beach beyond.

"If you're worried, try calling her."

Shane frowned. "I don't have her cell number."

"Want me to get it?" Wyatt said with a yawn. "I can call Delia."

Shane opened his mouth to reply, then his eyes narrowed as a flash of something moving at the edge of the patio caught his eye. Something that looked like...a hand? "I'll call you back," he said and hung up on Wyatt's confused reply.

Leaving his pop on the counter, Shane strode toward the glass doors, his attention focused on the small shape just off the edge of the patio. By the time he got to the door, he knew what it was. Muttering under his breath, he slid open the door and marched across the patio to the hammock strung there, and the woman asleep in it.

She was snoring, lying on her back under one of the knitted throws from the couch. One hand was curled up by her face, the other hanging over the edge of the hammock so it nearly touched the ground. If it hadn't been for that hand, he might not have spotted her.

Relieved—and irritated that he'd been worried while she'd been twenty damn feet away the whole time—he scowled at her sleeping form.

She was so damn cute, with her hair all tangled and frizzy from the sea air, her cheeks flushed with sleep. Her mouth was parted slightly, soft and pink. It was sexy as hell, even with the snoring. Though all he could see were the straps over her shoulders, he'd wager she was wearing the same simple black cotton dress she'd had on the day before.

When his fingertips started itching to tug the blanket away so he could see the rest of her, he gave the hammock a nudge with his knee. "Veronica."

She frowned as the hammock swayed, then continued snoring.

He put a little more boom in his voice and hit the hammock harder. "Veronica."

Her eyes shot open so fast he nearly took a step back. Immediately, she slapped a hand to her head, the other reaching out to grab the side of the hammock. "Oh God, make it stop moving."

Taking her literally, he reached out and wrapped a hand around the webbing, pulling the swaying hammock to a halt.

"Thank you," she whispered, and the heartfelt relief in it almost made him smile.

Then he remembered he was irritated with her, so he grunted instead. "Hungover?"

"No," she mumbled and gave a jaw-cracking yawn. "I just get motion sick easily."

"What are you doing out here?"

She blinked up at him, looking befuddled. The hammock pattern was pressed into her right cheek. "Huh?"

"What are you doing out here?" he repeated gruffly.

"Um. Sleeping."

He scowled. "You slept out here? All night?"

"I guess so." She shoved her hair out of her face and looked around. "What time is it?"

"Nine-thirty," he said. "What do you mean, you guess so?"

"Wow, I was out." She looked up at him. "Can you help me out of this thing?"

He didn't want to touch her—it was hard enough to resist her sleepy sexiness without adding *touching* to the mix. But she looked like she'd fall on her ass if he left her to her own devices, and while he was willing to be an asshole if he had to, he couldn't bring himself to be that much of an asshole. So he held out a hand, waited for her to grab on, and hauled her up.

She came flying out of the hammock and crashed into him.

He staggered back a step but kept his feet, and mostly because he didn't know what else to do, scowled at the woman he now held in his arms. "You okay?"

Her eyes were wide as saucers, her lips parted in surprise. He could see the flecks of green and gold in her eyes, the thickness of her lashes. Her cheeks were pink and getting pinker, her mouth a lush temptation a saint would struggle to resist. The rat's nest hair and the traces of makeup crusted in the corners of her eyes should've made her less appealing, but to his annoyance, they didn't. Not even the distinct whiff of morning breath coming from that fuck-me mouth was enough to put him off.

"I'm fine," she said in a husky rasp. Her lashes fluttered down to shield her eyes, and she stepped away.

He resisted the urge to haul her back. "Come inside. I'll make coffee."

He turned to stomp across the patio without waiting to see if she followed, and was pouring water into the coffee maker when she came in.

She stepped through the door, the knitted throw draped over her shoulders like a cape. She still looked befuddled, like she hadn't quite woken up yet. She tossed the throw onto the sofa, the strap of her dress sliding down her arm to reveal the curve of one generous breast. Cursing under his breath, he focused on the coffee maker.

"You don't have to do that," she told him, her voice hesitant, and he made an effort to relax his shoulders and take the grumpy motherfucker out of his tone.

"Not a problem," he said with a glance over his shoulder. She'd pulled the strap of her dress back in place, and he felt a purely selfish pang of disappointment. But at least he could look at her without wanting to fall on her like a rabid dog. Much.

"This'll take a minute," he told her. "You want food?"

Her brow furrowed. "We have food?"

"Fruit," he said, jerking his head toward the bowl on the counter. "Or room service."

"I'm good with fruit." She cleared her throat. "I'm going to shower and try to wake up."

He shrugged and tried to act like he had no intention of imagining her naked. "Coffee will be here when you get out."

He busied himself slicing fruit while the shower ran, hacking into the apples and pears with more enthusiasm than finesse. By the time he got to the bananas and mango, the water had shut off, and a few minutes later she emerged from the bathroom.

He looked up from his slicing and nearly took off a finger.

Her dark hair was still wet and sleeked back from her face, leaving it unframed. Her skin glowed pink from the heat of her shower, her mouth soft and full. She'd put on some kind of oversized tunic that fell to the floor in swirling shades of blue, with long, wide sleeves and a narrow V-neck. It shimmered and slithered as she walked, her bare toes playing peek-aboo with the trailing hem. It was big as a tent and should've been the least sexy garment on the planet, but the silky material clung to her skin and made it obvious that she wore nothing underneath, and he was happy to once again be standing behind the counter.

At this rate, by the time his 'relaxing vacation' was over, he was going to have a permanent case of blue balls.

To keep himself from drooling, he shoved a piece of mango in his mouth.

She sent him a tentative smile. "The coffee smells great. Thanks for making it."

He grunted around the chunk of mango and slid the mug he'd already filled across the counter.

Her eyes widened in surprise. "Thanks. Um. Do we have any milk?"

He swallowed the fruit and shook his head. "There's some of that non-dairy creamer crap."

"That's okay." She took a sip, those gold-flecked eyes watching him over the rim.

He shoved the bowl across the counter. "Fruit."

"Thanks." She plucked out a slice of mango and popped it into her mouth. "You didn't have to cut it up, I could've just eaten a banana."

Yeah, and made my head explode, he thought. Out loud, he said, "No problem," and turned to set the knife in the sink and wash his hands.

"I'm going to move my stuff out today," he told her.

"What? Why?"

He kept his eyes on his hands. "Because you're sleeping in the hammock."

"I didn't sleep in the hammock on purpose," she said, and he could hear the eye roll in her tone. "I was watching the stars and I fell asleep."

He concentrated on the suds swirling down the drain. "You're uncomfortable."

"I'm not," she protested, and he shut off the water and turned to look at her with blatant disbelief.

"Okay," she conceded, the pink on her cheeks deepening. "I'm a little uncomfortable. But that's not because of anything you've done, and I really did just fall asleep in the hammock last night."

He dried his hands on the dishtowel and laid it carefully over the handle of the dishwasher to dry. "Still."

"You know, if you want to make me more comfortable, you can take the bed."

That surprised him into smiling. "Funny. No."

"Then it's ridiculous for you to move out," she began, then frowned. "Unless...wait. Am I making *you* uncomfortable?"

"No," he said with conviction while his penis scoffed and his balls turned a deeper shade of blue. "You're not."

"Great. Then neither one of us is uncomfortable and you're staying."

He frowned. "Are you sure? I can call the hotel, get a room up there."

She shook her head. "They're fully booked. That's why we got upgraded to the cottage. And yes, I'm sure."

Her voice was rock solid, but she was nibbling on her lower lip. "You don't seem sure."

"No, I am. I just had a question, but it's not important."

"What is it?"

She shook her head and picked up her coffee. "Nothing, never mind."

"Veronica," he said, trying not to sound pissy. "What?"

"I don't want to ask now," she said, her mouth going mulish. "It might make you uncomfortable, and it's not important."

He reached for his forgotten can of Mountain Dew. "It was important enough for you to think of it, so spill it."

Her teeth dug harder into her lower lip, indecision in her eyes, and he gestured with the can. "If you don't ask, I'm calling the hotel."

"That's a pitiful threat that shouldn't work."

He sipped his soda and grimaced. It had gone lukewarm. But he needed something to do, so he kept sipping while she tried to stare him down.

She finally gave up with a sigh. "Fine. I talked to Wyatt last night."

He nodded. "He told me. Go on."

That made her pause. "Oh. Did he tell you what we talked about?"

"No. He just said he'd seen you on the beach."

"Oh." She nibbled her lip again. "Well, he ended up explaining a lot more about your relationship. The whole non-monogamy thing, and how it works for you guys."

"Okay.

"And, well, something he said got me to thinking. I was going to ask you about it, but…"

"Just ask, already," he said, exasperated, and took another drink of lukewarm pop.

"Do you want to fuck me?" she asked, and he spewed Mountain Dew all over the counter.

Eight

Veronica eyed the wet counter, then lifted her gaze to Shane's. "Is that a yes or a no?"

He glared at her, still coughing, and grabbed a dishtowel. "What the hell kind of a question is that?"

"An honest one?" she ventured.

"Did Wyatt put you up to this?" he demanded, mopping the Mountain Dew out of his beard and swiping at the countertop.

"Of course not," she said, offended, then wrinkled her nose. "Well, kind of? He said he told me how your relationship works because he wanted me to know that if we slept together, it wouldn't be cheating. Which, honestly, I appreciate. And he said you probably wouldn't ask me, because you were worried I'd feel pressured since we're sharing the cottage. So, I guess, in a way, he sort of put me up to it, but he didn't tell me to ask you, if that's what you're asking."

He was staring at her, the dishtowel hanging limp in his hand. "I'm not sure I followed all that."

"Oh. Do you want me to say it again?"

"No." He set the towel down. "But I do have a question."

"Okay."

"Do you want to fuck me?"

"Um. Well. Yes." She chewed her lower lip and tried to project both sexual confidence and indifference. "But not if you don't want to."

He stared at her for so long that she lost her nerve. "Okay! Well, good talk," she babbled and slid off her stool. "I think I'm going to head into town, maybe do some shopping. Is there anything you want me to pick up for you? More Mountain Dew, maybe?"

She took a step toward the closet where she'd stashed her bag, keeping her eyes resolutely ahead, and didn't see him move until he was right in front of her.

She drew to a halt with a little squeak, barely stopping herself from crashing into him for the second time that morning. It was tempting to pretend she couldn't catch her balance, just to see if that broad chest was as hard and warm as she remembered. She'd gotten so little time to savor it when she'd come flying out of the hammock earlier, just a fleeting moment of bliss when his hard muscles had pressed into her aching breasts, and she was sorely tempted to fake a stumble now. But she reminded herself firmly that pretending to fall just to cop a feel was awful no matter who did it, and kept a respectable distance between his chest and her disappointed boobs.

He crossed his arms over his chest, making his muscles bulge and his tattoos ripple so she had to stifle a sigh. "Tell me something."

She looked up, annoyed to see the familiar stony look on his face. He could at least have *some* reaction to her declaration of lust, the grumpy bastard. "What?"

His eyes widened at her sharp tone, then narrowed again. "Was that question supposed to help make things more comfortable around here?"

She let out a huff of breath. "That's why I said never mind."

"Uh-huh. Why do you want to fuck me?"

She blinked. "I don't understand the question."

"I mean, why do you want to fuck me?" He tilted his head, considering her. "Revenge?"

"On who?" she asked, so completely confused she forgot to be embarrassed.

"Your ex."

"I got my revenge on him by giving away all his clothes," she said, still baffled. "Besides, he already thinks I'm fucking both you and Wyatt, I don't have to actually do it."

"Right. Is it because I'm bisexual?"

"Why would that make me want to fuck you?"

He shrugged. "Some women do."

Now her eyes bugged out. "Women try to fuck you just because you're bisexual?"

"It's a common fantasy," he pointed out. "A sexual bucket list item, if you will."

"I don't have a sexual bucket list, and I wanted to fuck you before I knew you were bi."

That got her a raised eyebrow. "You did?"

She could feel her cheeks burning with embarrassment now, but there wasn't much she could do about it. "Yes. Can I go now?"

He took a step back, giving her room to go around him, but he didn't take his eyes off her face. "When did you first want to fuck me?"

In for a penny. "When I saw you in the airport."

Now he frowned. "You thought I was a jerk at the airport."

She threw up her hands. "You were a jerk. I still wanted to bite your neck. Happy now?"

"Bite my neck?" he echoed.

"Yes." Exasperated, and resigned to never being able to look at him without blushing again, she pointed. "Right there above your collarbone, where the tattoo ends in that little curlicue."

Out came the scowl. "My tattoo does not have a curlicue."

"Well, whatever word dudes use for curlicue, then." She stepped around him to the closet and dug out her bag.

"Yes."

Slinging the bag over her shoulder, she spun around to frown at him. "Yes, what?"

"Yes, I want to fuck you."

Her purse slid to the floor. "You do?"

"I do."

"Oh." She stared at him, at the heat she could see now in those dark, piercing eyes. "Then what am I yelling about?"

"Beats the hell out of me," he said and reached for her.

She squeaked again as she went suddenly airborne, then she was crushed against his chest.

"Oh," she breathed, staring up into his face. His chest was hard and unyielding, delighting her no longer disappointed boobs, and his skin warm where she clutched his arms.

He stared down at her, a little smile curling his mouth under his beard. "You want to do this now?"

"Yes, please."

"We use condoms, agreed?"

She nodded, nearly dizzy with lust. "Yes."

"Anything I do that you don't like, you tell me."

She had to lick her lips. "Okay."

"Anything you want me to do, just ask."

"Uh-huh."

"If you want me to stop, I'll stop." He sobered when he said it, his eyes dark and serious, and she remembered what Wyatt had said about Shane's determination not to make her feel pressured or uncomfortable. "Just say the word."

She nodded. "Thank you."

"You're welcome. Anything else?"

"No. Can you kiss me now?"

"Sure." He slid his hands from her waist to her ass, yanked her higher, and covered her mouth with his.

Sweet Jesus, the man could kiss. He didn't bother teasing, didn't bother to cajole. He just slanted his lips over hers, opened his mouth, and plunged his tongue inside, and it was the most awesome thing she could imagine.

His beard was soft against her skin and he tasted amazing, like mangos and cinnamon toothpaste and not at all like Mountain Dew, thank God. She opened her mouth wider in a silent plea for more and whimpered when he gave it to her. His low growl vibrated against her breasts, and her nipples drew into tight little buds as he moved one hand from her ass, grabbed a fistful of hair, and tugged her head further back.

He lifted his head at her startled moan. "Good noise or bad?"

"Good," she panted, and arched her neck back even further, pressing into his hand. "Very good. Don't stop."

He hummed appreciatively and skimmed his lips down her neck. "Where was it you said you wanted to bite me? Here?"

Her eyes nearly rolled back in her head when he lapped at the hollow of her throat. "Not...not there."

"Maybe it was here, then."

"Uh-uh," she managed, shivering as his teeth nibbled along her jaw.

"No?" He lifted his head and raised a brow. "Maybe you should show me."

Delighted, she shifted her grip from his biceps to his shoulders and hitched herself higher. She held his gaze for a long moment, the heated glitter making her belly clutch and her pulse race, before lowering her mouth to his neck. "It was here," she said and dragged her tongue along the edge of his T-shirt.

He rumbled in approval and shifted his grip, one thick forearm wrapping around her hips to hold her snug against him. Her feet dangled off the ground and she wriggled, trying to get closer as she followed the line of his collarbone with her tongue.

"You're not biting," he said, his gravelly voice thick with amused lust.

"I'm savoring the moment," she panted. "Deal with it."

He grunted out a laugh and his hand tightened in her hair, her scalp coming alive with tiny prickles of sensation. He stopped just shy of pain and gave a little tug. "Get to it."

She laughed, breathless with giddy lust, and sank her teeth into him.

"Fuck!"

His hand tightened painfully in her hair, his big body jerking when she licked the marks she'd just made, then dragged her tongue up the side of his neck. She nibbled daintily on his ear before dipping her tongue in briefly, shivering with delight when he groaned.

"You taste good," she said, making her way across his bearded jaw to his mouth. She hovered there for a moment, her breath mingling with his while his heart hammered against her breast. "Kiss me again?"

His hand immediately tightened in her hair, tilting her head and angling his own. His tongue filled her mouth, flavor and texture seducing her until she writhed in his hold, seeking deeper contact. Her legs tried to rise to wrap around his hips, but the flowing caftan she'd put on for comfort was caught between them, effectively pinning her legs.

"We need the bed," she mumbled into his mouth, and he lifted his head.

His breath was coming in harsh pants, and a red flush stained his cheekbones. Still, he hesitated. "You're sure?"

"No, this is just my sneaky way of getting you to take the bed," she drawled, and he snorted out a laugh. "I want you to fuck me, Shane. Now."

"Yes ma'am," he rumbled and tossed her over his shoulder.

She squealed, laughter bubbling up as she found herself upside down, holding onto the waistband of his shorts for balance as he climbed the two short steps to the bedroom. She was still laughing when he tossed her onto the bed and followed her down.

She gasped, the laughter strangling in her throat when his big body pressed her into the mattress. Her legs parted to cradle his hips, rolling against him as the thick ridge of his dick settled against her. It felt so good she did it again, and his hips surged in response.

He stared down at her, braced on his hands, his hair falling forward to curtain his face. "This what you had in mind?"

She shook her head, her hands fumbling for the hem of his T-shirt. "Naked."

He helped her get his shirt off, reaching behind his neck to drag it off over his head, and she sighed with pleasure as his torso came into view.

She ran her hands up his arms, over the swirls and splashes of ink. "This is pretty."

"Thanks."

"Does it mean anything?" she asked, tracing the curlicue at the edge of his collarbone.

He shook his head. "No. I just like it."

"So do I." She splayed her hands over his pecs, bumping into his tight, flat nipples. She danced her fingertips over them, teasing, testing. He leaned into her touch with obvious delight.

"You like that," she said and dragged her thumbs over them.

"Yeah," he muttered, his eyelashes fluttering a bit. "Do it again."

She did, her breath catching as the roll of his hips pressed hers hard into the mattress. "God, you're sexy," she breathed, and going with instinct, pinched his nipples lightly.

He groaned, his hips rolling. His penis bumped her clit, and the little whimper escaped her throat before she could stop it.

His eyes opened, gleaming in a way that made her breath catch again. He rolled his hips again, deliberately this time, and his lips curled up in a faint smile when she moaned.

"I can feel your pussy," he told her. "Hot and wet, even through all this cloth. What is this you're wearing, anyway?"

She struggled to find her voice. His hips were grinding against hers, slowly, purposefully, pressing right against her clit, and her ability to speak was rapidly fading. "A caftan."

"It looks comfortable," he said.

"Not right now, it's not."

He grinned. "Is it silk? Feels like silk."

She nodded, trying in vain to spread her legs wider. "Yes."

"Silk's expensive," he noted casually like he was just making conversation, except Shane never just made conversation. "Was it expensive?"

"Hideously," she panted. "Rip it off."

"Okay," he said agreeably, and rearing back on his heels, grabbed two fistfuls of fabric and yanked.

Her eyes popped wide as the silk rent right down the middle, from the neckline to her belly button, falling away from her bare breasts to hang off her shoulders. Her mouth dropped open in shock. "I meant over my head," she protested feebly.

He hesitated a second, then shrugged. "Oops," he said and

she opened her mouth to yell at him just for form when he leaned forward and placed both big hands over her breasts.

"Oh," she said, her voice strangled, and arched up into his firm, heavy hands. He squeezed, his calloused palms rubbing her nipples as his long, strong fingers compressed her flesh. It felt glorious. "Oh, more."

"More of this?" he asked, grinding his palms in tiny circles that abraded her nipples and made them sing. "Or more of this?" he asked and squeezed harder.

"The squeezing." She reached up and covered his hands with her, pushing down so the pressure on her breasts increased. It wasn't enough. "Harder."

"Like this?" he rumbled and squeezed so hard her eyes rolled back in her head.

When she had her breath back, she said, "Yes," and he did it again.

"Tell me how this feels," he said and let go of her breasts.

She blinked her eyes open to frown at him. He wanted to know how it felt to *not* do something? *It feels like nothing, you dork*, she thought and opened her mouth to tell him just that when he wrapped both big hands around her right breast, squeezed firmly, and sucked her nipple into his mouth.

She let out a high, keening wail and plunged her hands into his hair, fingertips digging into his scalp. Her back arched, shoving her breast harder into his hands, his mouth. He pushed her back down, his low growl vibrating against her flesh.

When she thought she couldn't stand it anymore he lifted his head, his mouth red and wet, and switched his attention to her other breast.

By the time he lifted his head again her hips were rolling, pumping helplessly into the air. She stared at him through blurry eyes, frantic need pumping through her as she fought with the button on his shorts. "Naked," she managed, her voice guttural and breathless. "Now."

He shoved her hands away and stood, shucking his shorts down in one quick motion, then reached down and ripped the caftan the rest of the way down the middle. She barely noticed —all her attention was on his hard, gloriously thick cock.

She sat up abruptly, blinking in shock. His hard, gloriously thick, *pierced* cock.

"Oh, my god," she breathed. "You have a piercing."

"Technically, it's three piercings. Is that a problem?"

"No, no. No." She swallowed, unable to take her eyes off the trio of metal studs penetrating the ridged head of his dick, one in the center and the other two on each side. "No. Does it hurt?"

"No. Never been with someone who's pierced?"

She could hear the amusement in his voice, but couldn't take her eyes off his dick. "No."

"Want to touch it?"

So much yes. She forced herself to look up. "Can I?"

He wore a half-smile, a sort of gentle amusement that somehow managed to shine through the crazed lust. "Yeah. Here."

He reached for her hand, taking her fingers and placing them on his shaft just behind the trio of metal studs. "You can play with them, you won't hurt me."

"Okay," she breathed and stroked her fingertips over the metal.

They were warm, heated by his body, the hard metal a sharp contrast to the soft skin around them. She dragged her fingertip across the ball of the centermost stud, watching with fascination as the barbell rotated slightly. He hissed out a breath, and her gaze shot to his face.

The amusement was gone, buried in lust, and she felt an answering tug low in her belly. "You like that."

"Yeah," he said. "Do it harder."

She did it harder, keeping her eyes on his face this time. An expression of pure, sensual bliss crossed his face, his eyes drifting shut as a moan slipped from his lips. "Again. Tug on it."

She reached up with her other hand to grasp his shaft to hold it steady. It was both hard and soft, velvet over steel, and she couldn't resist giving him a stroke as she pinched the tiny barbell between her fingertips and gave it a short, firm tug.

"Fuck." His hips surged forward, shoving his dick through her fist, and she tightened her grip.

Veronica rose to her knees, wanting the leverage, and settled on her haunches at the edge of the mattress. She continued to work her hands, stroking and squeezing with her left and playing with the piercings with her right, watching with fascination as his dick got harder and the tip got redder. It was starting to drip, fluid bubbling up and running down the underside so her stroking hand grew slick and sticky.

She glanced up at his face, a rush of purely sexual power hitting her when she saw his expression of pleasure-filled agony. She continued to stroke, her left hand gliding up and down his shaft, aided by the pre-come that was now flowing freely down his shaft, while her right tugged and rolled and rubbed at the piercings.

The difference in textures was delightful, from the soft, spongy head to the hard, slick metal of the piercings. She slid her hand over them hard, loving his harsh moan, then oh so slowly, hooked her fingernail behind the ball of the center piercing and gently, steadily, pulled.

Then she squealed as the world turned upside down, righting again when she hit the bed with a thump. He came down on top of her, strong hands spreading her thighs apart as he settled on his belly between them. "Did I hurt you?"

He stared up at her from between her thighs with blazing eyes. "No, you almost made me come."

"Oh." She was panting so hard she could barely hear him, so turned on she could barely think. Seeing his face framed between her thighs was so hot. "Isn't that a good thing?"

"No," he replied, his voice so deep and rough she'd swear the bed vibrated. "I don't want to come until I'm inside you."

"Then get inside me," she ordered and reached down to drag him up.

"Uh-uh." He shook his head, his hair tickling the sensitive skin of her inner thighs. "You're not ready."

Not ready? She nearly rolled her eyes. If she got any more ready, she'd be done. "Trust me, I am."

"Trust me, you're not," he replied.

"Hey," she said with a scowl. "I think I know when I'm ready or not—oh, *shit!*"

He chuckled against her pussy, and his teeth scraped gently against her clit again. "Want me to stop?"

"I'll kill you if you do," she told him and dug her fingers into his hair.

He laughed again, the vibrations making her squirm, then he stuck out his tongue and dragged it from her taint to her clit in one long, thick lick that stole her breath.

Then he went to work.

Nibbles and licks, sucks and flicks, he destroyed her with tongue and teeth and lips until she was hanging on the edge of madness. Her hips ground up into his face as she tried to push herself over, but he kept her hovering there, a panting, desperate, whimpering mess of a woman until she wanted to flip him over and ride his face into oblivion.

She would have if she'd had the strength. But all she could do was yank his hair harder and hitch her hips higher and choke out, "Harder, more. *More,* I'm close I'm close, fuck fuck fuck."

Apparently this display of sexual desperation was the signal he was waiting for because he suddenly shoved two fingers deep in her clutching pussy and rubbed the flat of his tongue hard just above her clit and she went off like a rocket.

When she could see and hear again, she opened her mouth to speak—to say what, she wasn't sure, probably something along the lines of "thank you for the amazing orgasm, now put your dick in me already"—and then he put his dick in her already.

Nine

"Oh my God," Veronica choked out, her hands coming up to dig into his chest. He was thick and hard inside her, and even though he was moving slow the pressure was intense. "Shit, shit, shit."

Shane froze, his jaw clenched and his eyes worried. "Do I need to stop?"

She shook her head wildly, hair tangling on the pillow as she struggled to catch her breath. "No, no. Just give me a minute, okay?"

"Take all the time you need," he told her. His hands were on her hips, his grip going from bruising to caressing while he waited, patient and still until her body adjusted and she gave him a slight nod.

"Go slow," she told him, and he eased forward another inch.

She winced, the burn and the pinch getting the better of her, and he stopped again.

"I'm going to pull out," he told her, and she dug her hands harder into his chest.

"Stay," she protested, and he frowned.

"I'm hurting you."

"Only a little," she assured him, but his frown only deepened. "I'll be fine in a minute."

"I don't want you to be fine," he said with a scowl. "I want you to enjoy this."

"I will," she promised, digging her fingers into his chest harder when he didn't look like he believed her. "It's just going to take a minute, that's all. It would be better with lube, but I don't have any."

"I have lube."

"You do?" she asked, wincing when he pulled free.

"Yeah." He got off the bed and jogged over to the couch, rummaged around in his duffle bag, and came back with a small bottle of clear liquid.

"Why do you have lube?" she asked.

He flipped the cap open and poured a generous amount into his palm. "I fuck men. Men usually need lube."

"Right," she said faintly, her level of interest in why he carried lube fading as she watched him stroke it over his condom-covered cock.

He glanced at her. "Think that'll do it?"

The latex gleamed, shiny and wet, but she held out her hand. "Give me a little"

He poured a small amount into her outstretched palm. "How's that?"

"Good." She brought her hand to her pussy, flinching when the cold liquid hit her heated flesh. She rubbed it into her labia to warm it up, then slid two fingers deep.

"Shit, that's hot," he muttered, his eyes locked on the hand tucked between her thighs.

"What's hot? This?" she asked, her voice husky with renewed desire. She pulled her fingers out, spreading them apart so the opening of her cunt was clearly visible. A growl rumbled in his throat, thrilling her, and she swirled her fingers up to her clit. "Or this?"

"All of it," he said, squeezing his dick. "Fuck yourself again."

The graphic command made her blush but she obeyed, pushing her index and middle fingers deep and grinding the heel of her hand against her clit. "Like that?"

"Yeah." He climbed onto the bed between her spread thighs, dick in hand, his eyes trained between her legs. "Spread yourself open."

She pulled her fingers free, shuddering when her cunt clamped down like it didn't want to let go, and using both hands, laid her fingertips on her lube-slick labia and pulled them apart. "Like this?"

"Yeah." He was panting, his eyes glued to her pussy, open and shiny with lube. "Look at that pretty pink pussy."

She had to swallow before she could speak. "Are you just going to look?"

His eyes darted to her face, dark and hot and just a little feral. "You ready?"

She nodded and licked her lips. "Yes."

He inched up the mattress until his knees nudged her butt. "Lift up a bit," he told her, and she planted her feet and raised her hips off the bed. When she lowered back down, her buttocks rested on his muscled thighs and his cock was so close to her pussy that his knuckles bumped against her as he stroked himself.

"Don't let go," he told her, and leaning forward just enough to lodge the head of his dick against her spread opening, pushed.

The thick length of him slid deep, the lube cutting the friction so he glided forward unimpeded until his balls pressed against her ass and his pubic hair tickled the backs of her fingers. She let out a strangled groan, because *God,* he felt good.

"Jesus," he groaned, his eyes locked on the spot where they joined, and pulled back to do it again.

"Lube is so awesome," she panted, loving the slick slide of him going in and out, reveling in the press and stretch without the pinch of pain.

"Yeah," he replied and shoved into her just a little harder.

"Oh," she cried, and her hands, slick with lube and her own arousal, flew to his arms.

"Too much?" he asked, holding himself deep.

She shook her head. "No. You just surprised me. Keep going."

He pulled back slowly. "I want to go hard," he warned. "You okay with that?"

"Yes, that. Hard."

He took her at her word, his hips hitting her with a jolt that she felt all the way to her toes. Then he lowered himself down so his arms were braced by her head and his chest rubbed against her breasts and kept doing it.

She lost track of time. Skin grew slick with sweat, his and hers, making her breasts rub and glide against his chest. Her hands slipped off his arms to clasp his ribs, to run them over his back and feel his muscles bunch and clench as he drove into her over and over again. He paused once to add more lube, then dove back in at the same steady, driving pace.

And the whole time, he talked.

He talked about how good she felt, how hot and slick her pussy was, how good it had tasted. He told her how sexy she looked, flushed and dazed from one orgasm, and how much he wanted her to have another. He talked about the softness of her skin, the hardness of her nipples, how she smelled like ripe peaches and sex and how hard it made him and how much he wanted to come inside her. He talked so much he started to go hoarse, and every word pushed her harder toward a second orgasm that suddenly, didn't seem so impossible.

Her fingertips dug into his ribs as she felt the slow, steady build between her legs, deep in her belly. "I think I might come again," she moaned and triumph flashed in his eyes.

"What do you need?" he asked, his pace never slowing.

"I don't know." She knew if he touched her clit directly right now it would be too much, but she needed *something* to push her over. "I don't know."

"How about this?" he asked, and sat up, shoving his knees under her butt again. He grabbed her hips and dragged her even further forward, then began moving again in sharp, short thrusts.

"Oh, my God!" Her eyes popped wide as the angle forced his dick against the front wall of her cunt. "What is that?"

"Piercings," he grunted. "Good?"

She nodded frantically and her hands locked onto his wrists, digging in as the pleasure built. "Don't stop, ohmigod, don't stop don't stop don't—oh!"

Her head went back on a choked scream as the orgasm burst free, her body jolting and jerking as her cunt clamped down on him. He kept thrusting, forcing himself through the spasming tissues, and it was so fucking good she just kept coming.

She was still coming when he abruptly shoved her legs wide and came down on top of her again, his forehead pressing hard into her breastbone as he ground into her once, twice, then stiffened and came.

He throbbed inside her, filling the condom with pulsing jets. His head was grinding into her sternum hard enough to bruise, but she was still coming and didn't care.

Then they both collapsed, sweaty and spent and quivering with aftershocks, and Veronica marshaled what brain function she had left to concentrate on getting her breath back.

Just when she was starting to think she might regain the power of speech, he picked up his head and pressed his mouth to hers. The motion shoved him deeper and she jolted, moaning into his mouth. He kissed her slowly, leisurely, stroking his tongue over hers as though he had all the time in the world, and by the time he raised his head she was breathless again.

"Sorry," he murmured, and he was still so close that his lips brushed against hers when he spoke, every word a whispering kiss. "I just realized I forgot to do that."

God, he was sweet. "You didn't forget to kiss me."

"I forgot to do it enough." He shifted to wrap a hand around the base of his penis to keep the condom in place and lifted himself off her.

She winced when he pulled free, her pussy sensitive and sore, and he noticed. "You okay?"

"Just a little sore. In a good way," she assured him when he frowned.

He glanced down at her pussy, on display between her spread legs, and his face tightened. "Damn," he muttered hoarsely, and when he lifted his gaze to hers, she caught her breath at the blazing heat in his eyes.

"You have any idea how sexy you look right now?"

"Um." She licked her lips, her eyes widening as his penis began to show definite signs of new life. "I don't know how to answer that."

He huffed out a laugh and rolled off the bed. "Stay put, I'll bring you a washcloth."

"Okay," she said weakly and curled up on her side to watch him walk away.

The view was spectacular, from muscled calves to broad shoulders. Her gaze lingered on his butt, round and firm with cute little dimples just above it on either side of his spine, and despite her soreness felt a little glimmer of interest.

Then she moved and her pussy gave a distinct *not happening, sister* twinge that was echoed in the sore muscles of her thighs, and she sighed. The spirit was willing, but her body was down for the count, so she moved off the bed. She shucked what was left of the caftan off her shoulders, peeled back the duvet, and was just sliding between the cool, crisp sheets when he emerged from the bathroom.

He approached the bed, gloriously naked with a washcloth in his hand. "You settling in?"

"I got chilly," she said, thrilled when he pulled back the covers and slid in beside her.

He sat next to her hip. "Spread your legs," he said and she obeyed without thinking. She flinched when he placed the wet washcloth between her legs, then sighed with pleasure as the heat soaked in.

"Good?"

"Great," she said, her eyes on his face. "Thanks."

He grunted, and she laughed.

His gaze, which had been focused on her bare breasts, darted to her face. "What?"

"Nothing," she said, lips twitching. "It's just...you're grunting again."

"So?" he grunted, and she laughed again.

"What happened to the chatty guy who just fucked me?" she teased and was rewarded when his beard twitched in a smile.

"Sex makes me less grumpy," he said and drew the washcloth away. He tossed it onto the floor beside the bed and sliding down under the covers, rolled onto his side to face her.

She winced. "Ew. Don't leave that on the floor."

"I'll get it in a minute. I want to talk first."

"More talking?" she teased, then sighed. "Do we have to? I want to take a nap."

"It's barely mid-morning," he pointed out.

"So?" She snuggled into the pillow and closed her eyes. "I have the post-sex sleepies."

"Post-sex sleepies?" he repeated, amusement clear in his tone. "That's a thing?"

She opened one eye to frown at him. "It's quiet time. Shush."

He snorted. "You're seriously going to go to sleep"?

"I will if you shut up," she said and he laughed.

"Okay, take your nap. We'll talk after."

"Fine," she muttered and closed her eye. "Pick the washcloth off the floor."

The bed shifted as he got up. "We get housekeeping service here, right?"

"We do not leave come rags lying around for the maid service, Shane," she told him without opening her eyes and smiled when he laughed.

She opened her eyes a slit to watch him walk away, enjoying the view of his muscled butt once again, then she closed her eyes and gave in to the post-sex sleepies.

Ten

When she woke, the cottage was empty. She lay quietly for a moment, listening to the sound of the waves crashing on the beach through the open doors. She was so relaxed she thought about just going back to sleep, but the room had grown warm, even with the ocean breeze coming through, making her just sweaty enough to be uncomfortable. Plus, her bladder was demanding her attention, so after a few peaceful moments of watching the curtains flutter in the breeze, she fought her way out of the covers and headed for the bathroom.

After taking care of her most pressing need, she considered her options for cleanup. She was sticky from the sex despite Shane's attempt at a sponge bath, and a little sweaty. But she didn't need to wash her hair again, and while she'd already experienced—and thoroughly enjoyed—the adjustable showerheads, she hadn't tried out the deep soaking tub yet. And it was calling her name.

She turned on the taps and went hunting for some bubble bath as steam filled the room. She found a couple of bottles in the basket of resort-supplied toiletries on the counter, but they smelled too much like flowers, so she grabbed her peach-scented body wash out of the shower and squeezed some into the tub. It foamed up nicely, so by the time she turned off the taps, the tub was piled high with peach-scented bubbles.

She left the bathroom door open so some of the heat could escape and slid into the tub. The hot water eased the slight soreness in her thighs, relaxing muscles she hadn't even realized were tense, and with a happy sigh she laid her head back against the curved rim of the tub.

She wasn't sure how long she lay there, drifting peacefully, when the closing of the front door made her jolt.

She sat up, bubbles sloshing to the edge of the tub. "Hello?" she called out.

"Just me," Shane called back. "Where are you?"

"In the bathroom," she replied and laid back again.

She heard him walk across the floor and turned her head so she could see the bathroom door. She frowned when the footsteps stopped and he didn't appear, then rolled her eyes when he said, "You on the toilet?"

"No, I'm in the tub. You can come in."

He stepped into the doorway, dressed in cargo shorts and a black T-shirt with a familiar grumpy look on his face and an insulated cooler in his hand. "Why are you giving me that face?" she asked.

"What face?"

"Like I just called your sister ugly."

"I don't have a sister," he told her, still frowning. "Where'd you find peach bubble bath?"

"I didn't, I used my body wash." She cocked her head. "There's that face again."

"There's no face," the face told her. "You going to be a while in here?"

She lifted a hand to judge how wrinkled her fingertips were. "I'm about done. Why?"

He lifted the cooler. "I brought food. Come out to the patio when you're ready."

He disappeared before she could respond. Suddenly starving, she pulled the drain and climbed out of the tub. She rubbed the bubbles clinging to her skin off with one of the huge, fluffy towels before wrapping it around her torso and padding into the bedroom. She pulled the red bikini out of the drawer and slipped it on, intending on finding a patch of sand for some sunbathing later, and covered it up with a loose cotton tunic in gauzy white.

Then she walked out to the patio and stopped dead. "Wow. How hungry are you?"

Shane, already seated, just shrugged. "You said you liked shrimp."

She was surprised the little patio table wasn't buckling under the weight of the pile of fried shrimp in the center. There was a plate of lemon and lime wedges, little dishes of cocktail sauce, what looked like melted butter, and— "Is that ranch dressing?"

"Yeah." He dipped a shrimp in the little container and bit into it with obvious relish.

She took the chair next to his with a grimace. "I don't want to judge, but after seeing that, I don't think I can kiss you again."

He just raised one eyebrow and popped another dressing-coated crustacean into his mouth. "Want a beer?"

She took a shrimp and reached for the dish of melted butter. "Sure."

He dipped into the cooler at his feet and came up with two bottles of Corona. He popped the caps, shoved a wedge of lime into each, and handed her one.

"Thanks."

They ate in silence for a moment, hunger taking precedence over conversation, until he sat back, hands crossed over his belly, and raised an eyebrow. "We should have that talk."

"Okay." She popped a shrimp, dripping with butter, into her mouth. "Go ahead."

"Sorry about the whatdayacallit."

"The what?"

"The thing," he said, swirling his hand in the air in a gesture that she assumed he thought was helpful. "The dress thing you had on."

"The caftan?"

"Yeah, that. Sorry I ripped it."

"It's okay." She shrugged. "It wasn't mine, anyway, and Delia can always buy more."

"I'll replace it."

She wasn't going to let him do that, but she didn't see the point in fighting about it now. "Okay."

"Anything we do giving you a hard time?"

"The ranch dressing thing is pretty gross, but you do you."

His beard twitched. "I meant the sex."

She reached for another shrimp. "No. Why would it?"

"Just making sure all parties were satisfied."

She cocked her head. "Do you do a morning after debriefing for all your sexual partners, or is this a special case?"

His grin flashed, quick and bright. "The first rule of poly is communication."

"I'm not poly," she reminded him and bit into another shrimp.

"Habit, I guess."

"Fair enough." She licked the butter from her fingertips, smiling when his eyes tracked the movement. "Except for not getting to put your dick in my mouth, I'm very satisfied, thanks very much."

He chuckled, low and rough, the sound doing interesting

things to her heart rate. "I assume we're sharing the bed from now on?"

"Well, I want to," she said. "But you get a vote, too."

He shifted in the chair, stretching his long legs under the table. "I vote yes, but we should probably clarify what we want this arrangement to entail."

"More orgasms."

He saluted her with his beer bottle. "Same. Other than that?"

"I don't know." She grimaced and picked up her beer. "It's been a while since I've done this."

"Had sex?"

She swallowed her beer. "Had sex with someone new. I was with Derek for almost two years."

He shrugged. "Me neither."

"Really?"

"Other than Wyatt, I haven't been with anyone else since I broke up with my last girlfriend six months ago."

"Oh." She thought back to her conversation with Wyatt. "Was this one of the girlfriends you shared with Wyatt?"

He froze, the beer bottle halfway to his mouth. "Wyatt tell you that?"

"Yes. Is that okay with you?"

"It's not *not* okay," he replied, but he didn't look happy.

"You sure about that?" she asked, keeping her voice light.

He stared at her for a long moment, sipping his beer. Finally, he said, "I have a hard time finding women to date."

She looked at him, six feet plus of muscle and tattoos and dark brooding sexiness with a larger-than-average penis. "I find that hard to believe."

"I didn't say I had a hard time finding women to fuck," he said, his beard twitching again, and she was relieved to see the light come back into his eyes. "Dating's another issue."

"Why?"

"Once I make it clear I have no intention of leaving Wyatt, things can get...tense. Women tend to think I'm using Wyatt as some kind of a placeholder until they come along, then expect me to drop him. Or they think we're a package deal."

"A package deal?" She frowned. "Is this the sexual bucket list thing again?"

"Hot bi-sexual threesome is a pretty common fantasy. But Wyatt makes his own choices about who to fuck, and sometimes he's not into it."

"Okay. Well, I already know you're not going to leave Wyatt, and I don't have a sexual bucket list. Although if I did, a hot bisexual threesome would be on it." She closed her eyes and allowed herself to picture it, just for a moment. "Oh yeah, it'd definitely be on it."

"And here I was worried this would be weird for you."

She opened her eyes to find him watching her with amusement. "Sure, it is. There's a part of me cringing because it looks so much like cheating. If Wyatt hadn't explicitly told me he was okay with it, I never would have said anything to you."

"He's a romantic," Shane said, "and likes to play matchmaker."

"It's sweet," she decided, a little surprised to find that it was true.

"Back to the question..." Shane began.

"What was it again?"

"What do we want this arrangement to entail?"

"Oh, right." She picked up her beer, saw the bottle was empty, and set it down again. "What are my options?"

"Are we having a fling? Dating? Just fucking whenever we happen to be in the same room?"

"I appreciate your dedication to communication," she told him after a beat, "but this conversation is not sexy."

"Welcome to polyamory," he said drily and made her laugh.

"Okay, okay." She pushed back from the table. "Other than seeing you and Wyatt kiss again..."

That got her a smile. "Liked that, did you?"

"Yeah," she sighed, shivering at the memory. Only this time they were naked. And instead of standing in the kitchen, they were lying on a bed. Naked. And there was lube. And maybe she was there, too.

"Focus," he chided her with knowing amusement.

"Right." She shook off the fantasy. "How do you define 'fling'?"

"Hang out and do stuff besides fucking, but also fuck."

"That sounds good. Let's do that."

"Works for me," he said genially and pushed to his feet. "What do you want to do today?"

"I was going to hang out on the beach," she said and watched him begin clearing away their lunch debris. "Read a book, take a nap. Maybe go for a swim."

"Want some company?"

"Sure. Hey, I just realized something."

He paused in the act of fitting the lid on the container of ranch. "What?"

"You haven't grunted at me once since I sat down, and you talked. A *lot*."

"Again, welcome to poly." He finished packing up the cooler. "I'm at my word quota for the day, though."

"Oh, good. Because I don't know if you know this, but the grunting is hella sexy."

He picked up the cooler and let out a deliberate grunt. She sagged back in her chair and let out a sigh, fanning herself with her hand. "Oh, baby."

He snorted out a laugh and walked back inside, and she grinned at the cloudless blue sky. "This vacation rocks," she decided, and making a mental note to send Delia some of her favorite THC-infused chocolates, followed Shane into the cottage.

SEVERAL HOURS LATER, Veronica woke from another post-sex nap, feeling loose and relaxed. She stretched, loving the slight soreness in her muscles, then rolled over and opened her eyes with a happy sigh. And immediately let out a shriek when she saw the man standing beside the bed. "Jesus! You scared the crap out of me!"

"Sorry," Wyatt said, his blue eyes twinkling even as his mouth twisted with remorse. "I didn't mean to wake you."

She clutched the sheet to her breasts and tried to catch her breath. "So, what? You were just watching me sleep? That's not creepy at all."

He held up a piece of paper. "I was leaving you a note. Do you know you snore?"

"I do not snore." She sat up, making sure to keep the sheet tight against her chest, and shoved her hair out of her face. "I breathe with emphasis."

"I stand corrected."

She ignored the laugh in his eyes. "Why are you leaving me a note? How'd you get in here? What time is it?"

"It's almost seven," he explained, taking the questions in reverse order. "Shane let me in. And I was leaving you a note to tell you to come up to the hotel to join us for dinner."

Her brain didn't seem to want to engage. She looked around but didn't see any sign of Shane. "Where is Shane?"

"In the shower," Wyatt said, jerking his head toward the bathroom door, and the faint sound of running water coming from behind it. "You hungry?"

"Um." She pressed a hand to her stomach. "Yeah."

"Want to get dinner? Seth has the night off from forced socialization, so we're going to get a steak."

"Forced socialization?"

Wyatt flashed a grin. "Yeah, all the team-building rah, rah, rah stuff the firm has planned. Tonight's their 'free night', so we're going to take advantage. You should come."

"A steak sounds good," she said, and it really did. But... "I don't want to intrude."

"You won't," Wyatt assured her. "Besides, Seth is dying to meet you."

"He is?" She fought back a yawn. "Why?"

"Because I told him you were making Shane drool, and he thinks it's hilarious."

She was not awake enough to have this conversation. "Um. Okay."

Wyatt opened his mouth, then turned when the bathroom door opened and Shane emerged.

He walked past the bed, shooting Wyatt a disgruntled look. "I told you not to wake her up."

Wyatt held out his hands. "I didn't, I swear."

"He didn't," Veronica said around another giant yawn.

"Uh-huh." Shane picked his duffle off the floor and set it on the end of the bed.

Veronica made an effort to focus her bleary eyes on Shane, naked but for the towel around his waist. "Wow. You got a lot of sun today."

"You, too," he said and she looked down at her chest above the sheet, much pinker than usual. "You coming to dinner?"

"If it's okay with you."

"Sure." He pulled pants and a T-shirt out of his bag, then tossed it back on the floor. He did not, she noted, pull out underwear.

"You know, you can put your stuff in one of the drawers,"

she pointed out, mainly to distract herself from the fact that he apparently planned to go to dinner commando.

He grunted and gathered up his clothes. "We'll give you some privacy to get dressed."

"Okay," she said faintly, still focused on the lack of underwear, and watched him walk back to the bathroom.

He paused in the doorway, a scowl on his face. "Wyatt."

"What? Oh, right." Wyatt hurried to catch up to Shane, throwing a smile over his shoulder. "Privacy. Sorry."

"No problem," she managed, but the door had already shut behind them, leaving her alone in the bedroom with her lascivious thoughts.

"Dinner," she reminded herself and climbed out of bed to find something to wear.

Wyatt leaned against the sink and waggled his eyebrows at Shane. "Well, that didn't take long."

Shane dropped his towel and reached for the underwear he'd left on the counter. "What didn't?"

"Don't play the grunting fool with me, my love," Wyatt admonished playfully. "You know what I mean. You and Veronica."

Shane tugged his boxers on. They stuck to his damp skin, forcing him to wiggle. "Me and Veronica what?"

"Fucked," Wyatt said with a gleam of triumph. "She made a move, didn't she?"

Shane grabbed his T-shirt. "Thanks to you, matchmaker."

"You're welcome," Wyatt said and was wearing a satisfied grin when Shane's head emerged from the shirt. "I can't wait to tell Seth. How was it?"

Shane grabbed his pants and yanked them on. "Really?"

"Okay, okay, that's a little crass." Wyatt pursed his lips. "Fuck it, I still want to know."

"Ask her," Shane said, then frowned. "On second thought, don't ask her. You'll just make it weird."

"I'm going to take that as a sign that it was good, and you'll be doing it again," Wyatt said. "She's gorgeous."

Shane grunted and finished putting on his pants, then reached for his hairbrush.

"And built," Wyatt went on, well used to Shane's silence and undeterred by it. "And she smells amazing. Hell, even the snoring thing is cute."

Shane reached for the elastic on the counter and tied his hair back in a low tail. "She has a personality, you know."

"Say it ain't so," Wyatt said with mock shock and rolled his eyes at Shane's dark look. "I know she has a personality, Shane. I like her personality. I'm also jealous that you get to fuck her and I don't. You think she'd be up for a threesome?"

Shane picked his towel up off the floor and hung it over the shower door. "I have no idea. And no, you can't ask her."

"You like her," Wyatt said, and his quiet voice made Shane turn.

"I don't fuck people I don't like."

"You know what I mean."

Shane shrugged, a trickle of unease curling through him at Wyatt's knowing look. "I've known her for less than forty-eight hours, Wy. How about you just let it go for once?"

"Fine. But can I ask her how you were in bed?" Wyatt wanted to know, then choked out a laugh when Shane whacked him on the side of the head.

"No," Shane said. He opened the door a crack and called out, "You dressed?"

"Yeah, come on out," Veronica replied.

He opened the door to find her standing beside the bed, draped in a flowing green dress that skimmed the floor and left her shoulders bare. "You look good."

"Yeah?" She frowned down at the dress. "It's not too casual?"

"Honey, look at what this one is wearing," Wyatt said drily, pointing to Shane's cargo pants and black cotton T-shirt. "Trust me, you look great."

"Really great," Shane managed when her soft gaze flicked back to him, and she smiled.

"Okay. Give me a second in the bathroom and I'll be ready to go."

Wyatt waited until the bathroom door was shut and they could hear water running on the other side before he spoke. "She's really hot."

"I know."

"Amazing tits."

"I know."

"And that ass."

"I know, Wyatt."

"Maybe I should—"

"Maybe you should shut up," Shane suggested, and Wyatt closed his mouth just as the bathroom door opened.

"Ready," Veronica said, then frowned, her gaze darting between him and Wyatt. "Is something wrong?"

"Not a thing, gorgeous," Wyatt said easily. "Let's go to dinner."

ELEVEN

Veronica glanced at Shane as she slid her key card into the slot. "You were awfully quiet at dinner."

He raised a brow. "Between you and Wyatt, I couldn't have gotten a word in if I tried."

She pushed the door open. "We weren't that bad."

He stepped in behind her and closed the door. "Uh-huh."

"We weren't," she insisted. "Seth didn't mind."

"He's used to Wyatt running the conversation."

"He seemed nice."

"He is." Shane eyed her curiously as she walked into the living area and set down her purse. "Did you think he wouldn't be?"

"No." She frowned slightly, slipping off her sandals. "I guess I expected him to act weird around you."

"Why?"

"Because you're dating his husband?" She wrinkled her nose. "I'm still having trouble wrapping my head around it all."

"Understandable." He tossed his key card on the kitchen counter and went to the fridge. "Were you uncomfortable?"

"Not really. Seth seemed amused, but I figure that's just because I was acting like a wide-eyed rube."

"No, that's because of Wyatt." He held up a bottle of water. "Want?"

"No, thanks. What do you mean, it's because of Wyatt?"

He closed the fridge and twisted the cap off his water. "He can't stop talking about you, which amuses Seth."

Her mouth formed a silent 'O' of surprise. "He can't stop talking about me?"

"It's your tits." Shane gestured with the water bottle. "He's obsessed."

Veronica looked down at her breasts with a smile. "Well, they are excellent."

"He likes all of you, actually," Shane amended, not wanting to give her the wrong idea. "He has a little crush on you."

The smile morphed into a grin. "Aw, really?"

"Completely un-romantic," he clarified. "But he'd definitely like to fuck you."

She hitched a hip on the arm of the sofa. "He mentioned that the other night on the beach."

"Did he?"

"He's shameless. And cute."

"Adorable," Shane agreed drily. "Can I ask you a couple of questions?"

"Sure."

He gestured with the water bottle. "We're sleeping together tonight, right?"

"I thought we were." She tilted her head, curiosity and a tinge of disappointment in her gaze. "Have you changed your mind?"

"No, I was just making sure you hadn't."

"Oh." Her smile bloomed. "No, I haven't changed my mind."

"Good. Second question. What do you have on under that dress?"

"My dress?" She glanced down, and when she looked up again, her cheeks were tinged the softest pink under her tan. "The usual."

"Panties?" he asked.

Her tongue came out to wet her lips. "Yes."

He set the empty bottle down on the counter, his eyes trained on her face as he took a step forward. "A bra?"

"It's built into the dress," she explained.

Another step. "So, no bra."

"It's more than you're wearing," she said archly.

Confusion clouded his eyes. "What does that mean?"

"It means you, going to dinner with your boyfriend, his husband, and whatever I am with no underwear on." She tsked. "Naughty."

"Whatever you are?" he asked, a rare grin splitting his face.

"Lover? Friend with benefits? Vacation strange?"

He snorted out a laugh. "Lover works. And I'm not commando."

"I saw you take your clothes into the bathroom to get dressed," she countered, eyes narrowing when he resumed his slow approach. "No underwear."

"I already had it with me in the bathroom."

"Oh. Well, now I'm disappointed."

He came to a stop in front of her. "Seriously?"

"I was picturing you freeballing all night," she complained and made him laugh again. "I guess fantasy just never lives up to reality."

He leaned down slowly, his eyes on the pulse that fluttered in the base of her neck. "Is that right?"

"That's been my experience."

"Hmmm." He braced his hands on the arm of the sofa on either side of her hips. "I'm sorry to hear that."

"Life is full of disappointments," she said with a dramatic sigh, and he would've laughed again if he hadn't taken a deep breath, filling his nostrils with the scent of warm, ripe peaches and Veronica.

He loved the way she smelled.

"It's still early," he murmured. He nudged her hair aside with his nose and rubbed his lips against her neck. "Want to watch a movie?"

"Not really."

"Play cards?"

"I'm terrible at games."

"Walk on the beach?"

"Too much sand."

"Hmm." He flicked out his tongue to taste her, his lips curving when she shivered. "What else could we do?"

"Um." With his lips against her throat, he felt her swallow. "We could look up instructional videos on YouTube. I've always wanted to learn how to rebuild a carburetor."

He nibbled his way along her jawline, appreciating her humor almost as much as he appreciated how soft her skin was. "I didn't bring my tools."

"I don't think that's true at all," she said with a breathless laugh. "Shane?"

"Hmm?"

"Are you trying to seduce me?"

He teased the delicate lobe of her ear with the tip of his tongue. "That okay with you?"

"Yeah." Her breathing hitched when he dipped his tongue into her ear. "But, you know, you don't have to. I'm kind of a sure thing."

He nipped at her ear once more before pulling back to look at her face. The flecks of green and gold in her eyes were all but glowing, her cheeks a dark pink. His gaze dropped to her mouth and found it red and wet, her teeth sunk into the lush lower lip.

He leaned forward and, keeping his eyes on hers, traced it with his tongue. He watched, fascinated, as her pupils dilated and her flush deepened. The soft sound that slipped from her lips—part sigh, part whimper—had him going rock hard.

"Does that mean you don't want me to seduce you?" he asked and licked her mouth again.

Her lips parted and she swayed, leaning into him. "I didn't say that."

"Then shut up."

Her hands came up to cling to his ribs, her fingers curling into his skin. He skimmed his tongue over her mouth again, then slipped inside. Soft and warm and tasting of the Crème Brule she'd had for dessert, he took his time exploring, enjoying the flavor and texture of her, savoring the small sighs and moans that vibrated against his lips.

He angled his head to take the kiss deeper, wrapping one arm around her waist. She slipped off the arm of the couch and arched into him, pressing her breasts against his chest and returning the kiss with equal fervor. Her tongue tangling with his sent tingles down his spine, and a low growl vibrated in his chest.

He lifted his mouth slightly. "Who's doing the seducing here?"

She pursed her lips, shiny and swollen from his, a languid sort of heat shining in her eyes. "I can't participate?" she purred and rolled her hips.

"No, you can," he muttered against her mouth and swallowed her laugh with another kiss.

He returned to her mouth over and over again, getting drunk on the taste and the feel of her. She kissed him back with voracious enthusiasm, the desperate little sounds she made making his head spin and his dick throb.

Her hands moved from his rib cage to his shoulders, digging in as she strained to get closer, and he broke free from her mouth with a laugh. "Are you trying to climb me?"

"Yes. Your penis is too high."

He wanted to laugh but managed to coolly arch an eyebrow. "Too high?"

"It's poking me in the stomach," she pointed out and wriggled against him to demonstrate. "I need it lower."

The laugh escaped. "Are you always this blunt?"

She wriggled again and bit her lip. "Yes. Are you going to help me out here, or what?"

"I kind of want to see if you can get up here without help," he mused and had to bite back a grin when she scowled.

"Fine," She muttered, her hands tensing on his shoulders. He shifted his grip to her waist and looked on, fascinated, as she flexed her knees once, twice, then rolled to the balls of her feet and jumped.

"Shit!" he exclaimed, staggering back a step. He grabbed her ass and tried not to fall while she laughed in his ear.

"Nice catch," she told him and wiggled herself into place with a happy sigh.

He grunted as the heat of her pussy settled against his cock. His hands shifted to wrap around her upper thighs, digging into the round, firm flesh. "Fuck, you feel good."

"You too." She lowered her head to nibble at his mouth. "God, I want to ride you like a...like a..."

"Like what?" he prompted.

"I can't think of anything," she admitted. "Something you ride really hard until you come."

Laughter and lust were a tangled mess inside him. "Like this?" he asked and flexed his hips.

She shuddered against him, breathless and flushed. "Oh God, do that again."

He did, shuddering along with her. "We need to get horizontal. Bed or couch?"

"Where are the condoms?" she asked, panting in his ear.

"My bag. By the bed."

She dragged her teeth along the sensitive curve of his neck. "Can you get us there without dropping me?"

"Not if you do that," he warned, and she laughed.

"Hurry," she urged, and he dug his fingers into her thighs and shuffled his feet forward until his toes knocked into the platform. He stepped up carefully, taking more of her weight onto his hands and bouncing her a little, then he was on flat ground again and striding toward the bed.

"Hold on," he warned and fell across the bed with her.

She sprawled on top of him, temporarily knocking the wind out of him, and by the time he got it back she was sitting up, straddling him and working the dress over her head. He reached out to help, yanking it off and tossing it aside, then pulled off his shirt before sitting back to enjoy the view.

"Goddamn, you're pretty," he muttered and reached up to take her bare breasts in both hands.

They were heavy and round, spilling over his hands, tight little nipples stabbing into his palms and making his mouth water. He squeezed gently, then harder when she arched into his hands, remembering how much she'd loved it the night before.

Her hands came up to wrap around his wrists, her eyes closing on a moan. "You really like that," he muttered and squeezed harder.

She leaned into his grip, her hair falling forward to curtain her face. Her eyes fluttered open, glowing gold and green.

"Too many clothes," she groused and dropped his wrists to fumble with his fly. She wrenched the button free and dragged the zipper down, and he lifted his hips to help. She rose to her knees to give herself more room to work, and he got distracted by the tiny swatch of green lace across her hips.

"This is nice." He trailed a finger at the band of lace under her belly button, fascinated when the muscles rippled under his touch.

She gripped the waistband of his pants and boxers and yanked, dragging them below his ass and working them down. She got them to his knees and then he took over, kicking them free and onto the floor.

She gave a hum of delight, her gaze focused on his freed cock. It bobbed in the air, the light glinting off the trio of piercings. She reached out, wrapped a hand around him, and squeezed.

He grunted, pumping up into her grip. "Let me get a condom."

"In a minute," she said absently, all of her focus on the plump head. She slid her hand up, her fingertips swirling through the fluid already bubbling up. He hissed out a breath when she bumped over the piercings, pleasure spiking through him at the soft touch. Her gaze flicked to his face as she repeated the caress. "Shane?"

"Yeah?"

"Will these—", she tapped her fingernail against the centermost piercing, the dull clack loud in the quiet room, "— get in my way if I go down on you?"

"Shouldn't," he managed, trying not to overheat at the idea. "You want a condom?"

She blinked in surprise. "Do I need one?"

He struggled to concentrate. "My last STI panel was clear, less than a month ago. But it's up to you."

"I'm okay not using one for oral," she said and smiled. "But thanks for thinking of it."

She wriggled her butt down his thighs and leaned over. He held his breath, his eyes locked on her mouth as she lowered her head. Her tongue came out to lap at him, and he ground his teeth to keep from shoving his dick into her face.

"Yum," she whispered, and he didn't think she was saying it for his benefit. She shifted, sliding further down his thighs and tightening her grip at the base. She pointed the head at her mouth, lifted her lashes so she was staring directly into his eyes, and sucked him in.

"Jesus fuck." His hands fisted on the sheet under him, his hips arching up as the wet heat of her mouth engulfed him. She slid down, her tongue swirling along the underside of his shaft, then back up again, and her teeth bumped into the piercings.

He jerked and she lifted her head, her eyes dark with concern. "Too much?"

He shook his head. "Tugging on them feels good," he rasped. "Just be careful."

"I will," she promised and lowered her head again.

Her tongue danced around the sensitive head, flicking over the piercings with the softness of butterfly wings. Then her teeth caught the small steel balls, tugging just enough to make his eyes roll back in his head. Soft and hard, sweet and sharp, the pattern repeating over and over again until he was breathing in growls and his hips were pumping, trying to drive deeper into her mouth.

"Stop, stop," he finally gasped, so close to the edge that he could feel his balls drawing up tight.

She pulled off him with a soft pop, a pout on her pretty, puffy mouth. "Why?"

"Because if you don't, I'm going to come in your mouth." He peeled his fingers off the bedsheet and slipped a hand around the back of her head. "Come up here."

She obeyed, though the pout stayed as she crawled up his body to perch on his abs. "I wouldn't mind you coming in my mouth."

"Later," he promised and dragged her down to lie on his chest so he could capture her mouth. He sank into the kiss, fisting both hands in her hair to move her where he wanted her. She moaned into his mouth, digging her fingernails into his chest as a full-body shiver shook her.

He pulled back slightly. "Yeah?"

Her eyes were heavy, her cheeks flushed. "I like having my hair pulled."

"I guess you do." He tightened his hands in her hair again, tugging slowly and steadily to give her plenty of time to stop him, and she shuddered again.

"A little harder," she panted, letting out a whimper when he obliged, and her hips rotated, rubbing her pussy against the hard muscles of his abdomen.

"You're really wet."

She licked her lips. "I liked sucking your cock."

"Yeah?" He would've smiled, but he was too busy trying not to come.

"Yeah. I want to come back to that later."

"Twist my arm," he muttered, and she laughed. "Still want to go for a ride?"

Her cheeks flushed a deeper pink. "Yes."

"Condoms are in my bag," he told her, and she scrambled off him to reach over the side of the bed, giving him an excellent view of her round ass and round thighs and the sweet, slick pussy between them.

He pushed himself up on one elbow, and unable to resist, stroked a hand down one smooth cheek. "Look at that ass," he marveled, chuckling when she wiggled in response.

"I'm trying to accomplish something here," she reminded him, fabric rustling as she dug into his duffle. "Why don't you put your stuff in the dresser?"

"Too much bother," he said absently, his attention on the curve of her butt. He shifted to cup both cheeks and squeezed, fingers digging into the supple flesh. He squeezed again, harder this time, and was rewarded with a squeal.

"Feel good?" he asked, watching her hips wiggle and press back more firmly into his hands.

"Yeah," she panted. One hand still rummaged around in his duffle, but she was watching him over her shoulder. "Do it again?"

He obliged, squeezing hard. Her eyelids fluttered closed for a second, and when they opened, he felt the punch of that gold-flecked gaze right down to his balls. "You like being handled rough."

"I guess so," she managed. Her hand had stilled in its search, her arm half-buried in the bag while she watched him with those sexy, smoky eyes.

"You guess so?" He eased his grip, stroking his hands in a circular pattern over the rounded cheeks. "You don't know?"

She shook her head, her tangled mass of dark hair swishing over her shoulders. "It's never come up."

"That's a shame," he said mildly, hands still stroking. "Want to try something?"

Her tongue flicked out to lick her lips, making his dick jump. "What kind of something?"

"A spanking something," he said and watched with fascination as her whole face went bright red.

"I'm not really into BDSM," she told him breathlessly, her face flaming.

He shrugged. "Me neither. I'm not talking about an over-the-knee paddling. I'm talking about one swat, right here." He tapped her right butt cheek.

"One?"

"One," he assured her.

She licked her lips again. "Okay. One."

He raised his hand slightly, no more than six inches above her butt, and lowered it again in a short slap. Her ass jiggled under the impact and the sound cracked through the room, and a faint red mark bloomed on her smooth skin. But it was the look on her face that held him captive.

It was a look of pure, carnal delight. Her eyes were unfocused, her lips parted on a startled moan. Then they curled faintly at the edges and her eyes refocused on his, shining with giddy delight.

"Wow," she breathed.

"Good?" he asked,

She nodded. "Can you do the other side? You know, for balance."

"Balance is important," he agreed and repeated the short smack on the other side, She wiggled and blushed, her reaction feeding his lust, and he was suddenly desperate to be inside her.

He gave her cheeks another squeeze. "Condom," he reminded her.

"Right. Condom." She began digging in the bag again, her movements jerky. "It's your fault for distracting me."

"It's your fault," he corrected.

She sat up, a strip of condoms in one hand, the bottle of lube in the other, and outrage on her face. "How?"

"You put this delicious ass in my face," he reminded her and squeezed the ass in question one more time before she spun around to crawl back on top of him.

"Compliments will get you fucked," she said breathlessly, straddling his thighs, and tore a condom off the strip. "Here."

He took it from her and ripped off the wrapper. "Hand me the lube?"

She handed it over, watching with curious eyes as he squeezed a drop onto the ruddy head of his penis.

"What's that for?" she asked, taking the bottle back.

"Makes it feel good," he replied, rolling the latex down his shaft. "Want some on the outside?"

She nodded and poured a small puddle into her hand before clicking the lid back on the bottle and tossing it aside. She wrapped her palm around the base of his dick and stroked upward, her fingers slippery and sure.

He gritted his teeth because the feel and the look of her hand on him were ridiculously hot, and he was close enough to the edge as it was. When he was shiny and slick, he pulled her hand away. "Enough."

"You are all about killing my fun tonight," she scolded, and he opened his mouth to retort when she lifted up and impaled herself on him in one smooth motion. The words fell away, and all that came out of his mouth was a strangled groan when her wet heat swallowed him whole.

"Oh," she breathed and wiggled. "You feel so thick."

He clamped his hands onto her hips, desperate to keep her still. He was right on the edge, that feathery sensation crawling up his spine and down his balls, but he didn't want to come yet. "How close are you?"

"I'm not," she told him, a faint, knowing smile curling her lips. "How close are you?"

"Right on the edge," he managed, panting with the effort of holding back. "Shit, sorry."

Her smile only deepened, and she rocked her hips forward. "Don't be," she said when he groaned. His hands tightened on her hips, and she reached down and peeled them off. She placed them on her breasts and leaned into his grip, a happy little sigh spilling from her throat as his hands tightened.

"Yeah, do that," she instructed in a husky voice as her hips began to move.

"You like my hands on your tits?" he managed to gasp, the hot clasp of her pussy all but stealing his breath.

"Yes." Her eyes drifted closed. "God, your hands are big."

"Your tits are bigger," he pointed out, and she let out a breathless laugh.

"I know." She picked up her pace, rising and falling on him faster. The faster she moved, the harder he gripped her breasts until her hips were slapping into his with a wet smack, he was gripping her tits so hard he was afraid she might bruise, and they were both moaning.

"You have to stop, or I'm going to come," he choked out.

"Good." Her hips rose and fell faster, her hands coming up to press his into her breasts as she panted. "I want you to come. I want to watch you do it."

"What about you?" he asked through gritted teeth.

"I'll get mine," she assured him. "Come on, I want to feel it. I want to see it. Come in me, Shane. Come in my hot, wet pussy."

The dirty talk did it. He ground his teeth together, his hands spasming on her breasts as pleasure blasted through him. He shoved himself up, lifting her knees off the bed. She gasped, her pussy tightening on his throbbing dick, then he was coming in long, heavy spurts that seemed to come from the soles of his feet.

When he sagged back onto the mattress, quivering and shivering in the aftermath, he heard her whispered "Wow", through the roaring in his ears.

He fought his eyes open to look at her. She was leaning over him, her hands holding his in place against her breasts, a look of fascinated wonder mixed with the heat in her eyes.

"That was hot," she said, her cunt tightening on his twitching dick.

"Did you come?" he asked, though he already knew the answer, confirmed when she shook her head.

"No, but watching you..." She leaned down and kissed him, lingering over it. "It was almost as good."

"Glad you liked the show," he managed. "Okay, your turn."

Her eyes widened in surprise. "I can take care of that myself."

"Yeah?" He was leveling out, the blood flow to his brain restored, and he had the wit to arch a brow at her. "I'm going to want to see that later, but right now, get up here."

"Get up where—hey!" She squealed as he grabbed her waist and lifted her off him. "What're you doing?"

"Putting your pussy on my face," he replied, and dragged her up his body, scooting down at the same time, until her knees were planted on either side of his head and her pussy was hovering above his mouth.

She grabbed the headboard in a white-knuckled grip. "I'm going to taste like latex and lube," she protested feebly.

Shane grabbed the pillow next to him, shook it free of the case, and used the linen to swipe at her pussy. "There," he said, throwing it aside. "Any other objections?"

She peered down at him, curling forward to see past her tits. Her teeth were sunk into her bottom lip, her eyes wide. "No, but you really don't have to—ohhhhhkay, you're just going to go for it," she panted.

In answer, he wrapped his hands around her thighs and yanked her down onto his mouth.

He grunted against her pussy and speared his tongue up, delving through the slick folds of flesh to find the soft opening. He grunted again when he found it, burying his tongue as deep as it could go, tasting yes, latex and lube but also Veronica, sweet and spicy and delicious.

"Shit, shit, shit," she breathed, rocking her hips and rubbing her pussy against his face while he struggled to keep his tongue inside her. "Fuck, you're so good at this, don't stop."

He wanted to assure her that he had no intention of stopping, but that would've required stopping, so he just tightened his grip and kept fucking her with his tongue and rubbing his beard against her labia and nudging her clit with his nose while she squirmed and gasped and squealed into the wallpaper.

"Wider," she gasped, and he loosened his grip so she could spread her thighs, bringing her even closer to his mouth and giving his neck a break. Then she reached down, bumping into his lips and nose as she tried to get her fingers in there, and he suddenly understood.

He pulled away long enough to mutter, "Like this?", and shifted his grip on her thighs so he could dip his fingertips between her legs. Using his long middle fingers, he pulled her labia apart.

"Harder," she rasped, and he obliged, pulling her wide until his entire view was her inner labia, pink and gleaming wet, and the darker, wetter red of her pretty hole.

"Just like that, oh shit, oh fuck," she whispered, and her hips started to roll.

He gave up on directing her and just kept his head still and his tongue out, letting her fuck his face. She ground against him, hips moving in quick jerks now as she'd found the right spot. He heard the thump of her head hitting the wall and nearly lifted her off him to make sure she was okay. But then the words started, *fuck* and *oh, god* and *shit, shit, shit,* whispered so low he could barely hear it with her thighs clamped around his head.

Her body shifted and her fingers bumped into his, and he realized she'd reached down and back and had grabbed onto her ass, pulling the cheeks apart hard while he held her labia spread wide. Her breath began to stutter, her words getting more and more garbled as she bore down.

Then she froze above him, her cunt planted firmly on his face, his tongue buried so deep inside her that he felt the contractions of her orgasm start. Then she was wailing and shaking and he concentrated on not moving, letting her grind it out on his face until she collapsed in a sweaty, satisfied heap, held up only by his face under her and the wall in front.

He moved his hands to her waist, shifting her carefully to lie on top of him, shaking and shivering, little sighs breaking from her throat. He stroked her back, her hair until she'd quieted and stopped shaking, and she lifted her head to stare at him from slumberous eyes.

"Shit," she said, a tinge of awe in her tone. "I don't think I've ever come that hard in my life. I can't move."

"Eventually, you have to," he told her. "I'm still wearing the condom."

"Oh." She wriggled, grimacing. "Is that the clammy thing poking me in the hip?"

"Yes," he said, "and stop wiggling or it's going to come off, then we'll have to ask housekeeping for a new duvet cover."

Her opinion of that was a succinct "Ew", and she carefully lifted herself up and off, collapsing on the mattress beside him on her belly, a limp tangle of sweaty limbs.

She waved a hand limply in the air. "Condom. Garbage. Go."

He snorted and heaved himself off the bed, one hand clamped around the now dangling condom to keep it—and its contents—from falling to the floor, and padded to the bathroom. He disposed of the condom, then did a quick clean-up before dampening a washcloth and carrying it back to the bed.

She hadn't moved except to close her eyes, and those didn't even flutter when he tapped her shoulder. "Roll over," he instructed, lips twitching when she obeyed by shifting to her back in an inelegant sprawl. "You okay, there?"

He stroked the washcloth over her torso. "That feels nice," she sighed and opened her eyes to slits. "You perform this service for all the women you hook up with on vacation?"

"Part of the package," he grunted and she giggled, making

her breasts jiggle. Her belly rippled as he dragged the cloth down, and he raised a brow at her. "What's so funny?"

"I just love how as soon as the sex is over, you go back to communicating in grunts."

"Glad I could amuse you," he replied. He reached her thighs with the cloth, and his lips twitched when they fell open with barely a nudge. He wiped her down slowly and carefully before flipping the washcloth over and moving on to her thighs and calves. When he was done, he took the cloth back to the bathroom, rinsed it out, and laid it over the edge of the tub to dry.

He was back in the bedroom and pulling on a pair of clean shorts when he noticed she hadn't moved. "You going to sleep?"

"I could." The gold and green flecks in her eyes were muted, hazy and soft with contentment. "I'm so relaxed, it'd be a short trip to sleepy town."

"Still pretty early," he pointed out. "Want to watch a movie?"

Surprise chased some of the softness from her eyes. "Okay. Can I wear your T-shirt?"

"Sure." He started to dig out a clean one, but she picked up the one he'd stripped off earlier and slipped it over her head. It settled halfway down her thighs, clinging to her hips and ass in a way that made his gut clench.

She dragged her hands through her hair and gave him a sleepy smile as she padded past him to the couch. By the time he'd pulled on a shirt and joined her, she was curled up in the corner of the huge sectional, remote in hand.

"Ooh, there's a horror movie channel," she enthused, then scowled when he reached out and stole the remote. "Hey!"

"No horror movies," he told her firmly, settling in beside her.

"Why not?"

"I don't like them," he muttered, pointing the remote at the flat screen.

"Do you get scared?" she asked teasingly.

"Yes," he said baldly. "The last time I saw a horror movie I didn't sleep for almost a week."

"Aw," she said, and he could tell she was trying hard not to laugh. "When was that?"

"When I was twelve."

Now she did laugh. "So, what, twenty years ago? Do you think you might have a different view of things now?"

"No," he said emphatically. "No horror movies."

"Fine," she said with a roll of her eyes, and she scooted closer. "I'll watch whatever you want."

He lifted his arm so she could snuggle against his side, then draped it over her as he flipped through the channels. She let out a contented sigh, her breath dancing over his skin, and just for a moment, he let himself dream.

Twelve

Wyatt frowned at him, the golf club in his hand lined up for a swing. "What did she want to watch?"

"Night of the Living Dead."

Wyatt nodded. "Which you, of course, vetoed."

"Yep."

"What'd you want to watch?"

Shane shrugged and leaned on his five-iron. Or his nine-iron, he could never tell the difference. "Whatever, just not horror."

Wyatt straightened, a grin creasing his face. "You wanted to watch Dirty Dancing, didn't you?"

Shane scowled. "It's a good movie. A classic."

"Dirty Dancing is not a classic, love."

"It was on a list of top twenty classic romantic movies," Shane shot back.

Wyatt merely lifted a brow. "And who published this list?"

"Teen Vogue," Shane muttered and sighed when Wyatt laughed. "Are you going to hit that thing or not?"

"In a minute." Ignoring the ball, Wyatt continued to grin at Shane. "Did she go along with Dirty Dancing?"

"Yes."

"Did you cry when Johnny said 'Nobody puts Baby in a corner'?"

"Just hit the ball," Shane said with a scowl.

Wyatt hit the ball, but he was laughing so hard he sent it skipping off into the trees.

"Shanked it," Shane said smugly.

"Who cares? God, I hate golf."

Shane stepped up to the tee and placed his ball. "Then why are we here?"

"Because all the lawyers are going deep sea fishing and I get seasick."

"We could've just hung out on the beach," Shane pointed out.

"Yeah, but this way I have something to talk about at dinner tonight. If I stare at you in swim trunks all afternoon, all I'll have to talk about is your ass."

Shane eyed his club. "Is this a five-iron or a nine?"

"Like I would know. Where's Veronica?"

Shane rolled his shoulders and set his club into place. "She had a spa thing first thing this morning, then she said she had a book she wanted to read."

"You should've asked her to come along," Wyatt said. "This would be more fun with her around."

"I did ask. She hates golf." He drew back his club and swung.

"Join the club," Wyatt muttered, squinting as he watched Shane's ball land on the green a couple hundred yards away. "Show off."

Shane slipped the five/nine iron back into the rented golf bag and hoisted it onto his shoulder. "This was your idea," he reminded Wyatt.

"I know, I know." Wyatt shouldered his bag and they started down the fairway. "So, aside from your very different tastes in movies, how's it going with her?"

Shane thought back to that morning, when he'd woken to find her warm, wet mouth wrapped around his dick. And this time, she hadn't let up when he'd warned her he was about to come. "It's fine."

Wyatt rolled his eyes. "Fine, he says. I see that smirk, Shane Eklund, and I know what it means."

"If you know, why'd you ask?"

"Because I'm a nosy pervert, and I want all the dirty, dirty details." He raised a brow as Shane snorted. "So, come on. You've had a few days to gather intel, it's time to debrief."

Shane didn't bother to roll his eyes. "You have to stop watching bad spy movies."

"Bad spy movies are my catnip," Wyatt said and nudged Shane with his elbow. "Come on, spill it. What's she like in bed?"

"I'm not telling you that."

"Why not? You always tell me what your girlfriends are like in bed."

"I do not."

"Yes, you do." Wyatt held up a hand and started naming names, ticking them off on his fingers. "Julia, Savanah. Beth, unfortunately."

Shane ignored the jibe. "Those were all women you were fucking, too."

"So?"

"So, the only reason I talked was so we could make sure they had a good time, not to swap sex stories."

"You're in half my sex stories," Wyatt told him.

"And the ones I'm not in are none of my business," Shane finished.

"Jeez, you're such a grown-up," Wyatt complained.

"Look, if she's ever interested in having you be a third, I promise I'll tell you everything you need to know."

Wyatt perked up. "Is she interested in that?"

"Not so far," Shane told him, and watched, amused, as Wyatt's face fell. "She said she doesn't have a sexual bucket list, but if she did, a hot bisexual threesome would be on it."

"So you're saying there's hope," Wyatt mused.

Shane climbed the last little rise to get to the green and set his bag down with a thud. "You're such a pervert."

Wyatt set his bag next to Shane's and aimed a knowing look. "Like you haven't thought of it."

"Of course, I've thought of it," Shane replied and ignored Wyatt's triumphant "Ah-ha!". "But I'm not going to pressure a woman I've known for less than a week into group sex."

"Well, of course not. But if it does come up, I got the green light from Seth."

Shane rolled his eyes. "I should've known you'd ask."

"Normally he wouldn't care, you know that," Wyatt went on. "But considering the circumstances..."

"I get it." Shane paused, his hand on his three wood—or was it his driver? "No pressuring her, all right?"

"I won't, I promise."

Satisfied, Shane pulled out whatever club was closest at hand and eyed his ball.

"But if it happens to come up..."

"Jesus Christ. Go get your ball, asshole. It's that way," Shane reminded him, pointing at the tree line fifty yards away.

Wyatt sighed. "Can I pretend I already went in there, found it, and took seven strokes to get it into the hole?"

Shane's lips twitched. "No."

"Shit." Wyatt pulled a wedge out of his bag. "You're buying the beer," he said and stomped off toward the tree line.

Veronica was cozied up in the hammock in another borrowed caftan with a book and a bottle of water when Shane and Wyatt came walking through the sliding doors. "Hey, there. How'd the golf game go?"

"Don't ask," Wyatt muttered, an uncharacteristically grumpy look on his handsome face.

Shane shook his head. "Don't mind him. He's always been a sore loser."

"Aw." Veronica bit her lip to keep from laughing. "Sorry, sweetie."

"I'm not a sore loser, I just hate golf," Wyatt declared, still grumpy.

"He's a sore loser who hates golf," Shane amended and bent down to kiss her. "How was your spa thing?"

"Awesome," she replied. "I've been buffed and plucked and polished and painted."

"Yeah?" He raised a brow, a flirty look in his eye. "What got plucked, exactly?"

"Not that," she told him with a laugh. "Sorry. I like having pubic hair."

He shrugged, unconcerned. "I'm interested in what's under it, anyway."

"I noticed."

He straightened and turned to Wyatt. "Beer?"

"God, yes." Wyatt collapsed in the lounger closest to the hammock with an exaggerated sigh, and Shane rolled his eyes.

"You?" he asked Veronica.

"I'm good, thanks." She watched him walk into the cottage, then turned to Wyatt. "Was it really that bad?"

"Nah." He crossed his feet at the ankles and hooked his hands behind his head. "It was nice, except for the golfing part."

"So, the walking, then?"

"And catching up with Shane. I haven't seen him much this trip."

She winced. "My fault?"

"Nah," he said again. "We knew it would be like this."

"Still," Veronica said. "I feel a little guilty for monopolizing..."

"My boyfriend's dick?" Wyatt offered and laughed when her mouth fell open. "Sorry, I couldn't resist."

"Neither can I, that's why I've been monopolizing it."

"Nice," he said, eyes gleaming with good humor. "He likes you, you know."

"I like him, too," she said.

"And he's more relaxed than I've seen him in months, so thanks for that."

"I don't think that's my doing," she protested, then snorted at his exaggerated leer. "You're such a pervert."

"So Shane informed me only hours ago," he replied and sighed dramatically. "I'm so misunderstood."

"Oh, I think we understand just fine."

He grinned, unrepentant. "I asked him to share all the dirty, dirty details with me, and he wouldn't."

Her brows shot up. "Good for him."

"So I thought I'd ask you."

She cocked her head, enjoying herself. "Don't you already know what sex is like with Shane?"

"Delightfully, yes," he replied with a look of such reverent lust that she felt a little twinge herself.

"And don't you already know what Shane is like having sex with women?" she continued.

He gave a wistful sigh. "Good times."

"I'll bet," she said with a grin.

"Which Shane says isn't your thing. The sexual bucket list thing," he elaborated when she frowned.

She shrugged. "No."

"There's nothing you've always wanted to try? Sexually, I mean."

"Believe me, I know what you mean." She leaned over the side of the hammock to snag the bottle of water she'd set there. "And no, not really. I already have good sex. I have great sex, actually."

"Thanks," Shane said and she looked up to see him crossing the patio, a pair of Corona's in one hand and a scowl his face he directed at Wyatt. "What'd I say about being a pervert?"

Wyatt rolled his eyes. "Calm down, Sister Mary Tight-Ass. We're just having a conversation."

"It's fine," Veronica assured him with a laugh. "I was just explaining why I don't have a sexual bucket list."

"There's got to be something," Wyatt said, taking his beer from Shane without looking away from Veronica. "Something wild and crazy that you want to do just once, just to say you did."

She shrugged. "I had my share of wild times. They were fun."

"What's the wildest thing you've ever done?" Wyatt asked avidly, then said, "Ow!" when the flat of Shane's hand connected with his head.

"Grow up," Shane growled as Veronica laughed.

"Buzzkill," Wyatt said, sulking into his beer.

Shane looked at Veronica and winked, humor dancing in his eyes. "Did you eat lunch?"

"Just a smoothie at the spa."

"Let's order in and watch a movie." He looked down at the sulking Wyatt. "You can stay if you promise to act your age."

"Where's the fun in that?" Wyatt muttered.

"I'm not watching Dirty Dancing again," she warned.

Shane sighed. "Fine. But no horror."

"Comedy?"

He nodded. "Acceptable."

"Cool." She swung her legs out of the hammock. "I know just the thing."

"Is it going to make Shane cry?" Wyatt rose from the chaise. "I'd like to watch a movie that makes Shane cry."

"Um, I don't think it's a crying kind of movie," she began, stifling her laughter as Shane swiped at Wyatt's head again. Wyatt saw it coming and dodged, sticking his tongue out. "But then again, he cried at Dirty Dancing, so what do I know?"

Wyatt grinned. "When Johnny says, 'Nobody puts Baby in a corner'?"

"It was sweet." She pushed out of the hammock and patted Shane's arm. "Don't worry. It's not a crying kind of movie."

"Five bucks says he'll do it anyway," Wyatt said.

Shane just grunted. "Come on. I'm hungry."

Three hours later Veronica set down the remote and shot an apologetic look at Shane. "I'm sorry. I really didn't think Defending Your Life would make you cry."

"Are you kidding?" His eyes, still damp, glared at her in disbelief. "He's risking everything to be with her."

"Told you he'd cry." Wyatt leaned over to kiss Shane's cheek, then snagged the box of tissues off the coffee table and passed them over. "He may be all gruff and grim on the outside, but on the inside? Marshmallow."

"I'm sorry you didn't like it," she began.

"Of course, I liked it," Shane said and pulled a tissue from the box. "It was great."

"Oh. Okay. Good."

"I'll tell you a little secret about our boy, here," Wyatt said, leaning over Shane to see her better. "He likes it when movies make him cry."

"Well, then." She patted Shane's shoulder as he mopped his eyes. "Want to watch another one?"

"I'm out," Wyatt said, levering himself off the sofa. "I have to get back and get changed for dinner. Veronica, it's been a pleasure."

He bent to kiss her cheek, and she smiled up at him. "Wyatt, you could charm the panties off a nun."

"Nuns don't wear panties," he said with a waggle of his brows. "Don't ask me how I know that."

"Don't encourage him," Shane said to Veronica and started to stand. "I'll walk you out, Wy."

"I can find my way," Wyatt said, laying a hand on Shane's shoulder to keep him in place. He glanced at Veronica. "Do you mind if I kiss my guy here goodbye?"

"Not at all. Do you mind if I watch?"

A devilish grin curled his lips. "Not at all."

He turned to Shane, humor and heat dancing in his blue eyes. "She wants to watch, Shane. Should we give her a show?"

Shane opened his mouth to warn Wyatt about being a pervert again, but he didn't have the chance. Wyatt's mouth was on his, soft at first because Wyatt was always patient, then firmer, with a hint of tongue. After five years Shane could map out Wyatt's kisses moment by moment, but they never failed to stir him.

The rumble started in his chest, working its way up his throat to spill out against Wyatt's lips, and they curved in what Shane knew would be a smug, self-satisfied smile.

Impatient, and suddenly ravenous for his lover's taste, Shane opened his mouth. He nearly groaned again as Wyatt slid his tongue inside, slow and teasing at first, then more aggressive. It was rare for Wyatt to be the aggressor, though he'd been known to if he was feeling particularly randy. Shane figured their hands-off policy this week, combined with the fact that Shane was sleeping with Veronica, had lit a fire in his lover.

Then Wyatt shoved both hands into Shane's hair and took the kiss deep, fast and hard, and Shane was half a step away from dragging him down and ripping into him when Wyatt broke free.

Panting, his mouth wet from the kiss, Wyatt stared into Shane's eyes for a long moment. All the playfulness was gone, replaced with raw, unfettered lust. Then he smiled, laughter dancing back into his eyes, and licked his lips.

"That ought to hold me," he said breezily and straightened with a wink. "See you later, babe. Bye, Veronica."

"Bye," Veronica said faintly, and Shane turned to look at her as the door clicked closed behind Wyatt.

"Wow," she breathed. "That was hotter than I remembered."

Shane was still trying to catch his breath. "Yeah?"

"Uh-huh. Can I ask you a question?"

"Sure."

"You're turned on right now."

"Yes."

"By Wyatt."

"Yes."

Her eyes were locked on his, her pupils dilated and the green and gold flecks in her irises glowing. "Would it be incredibly tacky for me to take advantage of that?"

"Tacky?" he echoed.

"Yeah. Rude, uncouth, vulgar, ill-mannered." She waved a hand in the air. "Tacky."

"To...?"

"To want to fuck you right now."

He blinked, his brain struggling to shift gears. "You want to fuck?"

"I want to fuck."

"Now?"

"Oh yeah." She slid to her feet and whipped the caftan off to reveal what she had on underneath—nothing. "Right now."

"Damn." He would've smiled if there had been enough blood left in his brain to send the signal. As it was, he barely had the wit to shift over on the sofa to give her enough room to straddle him. "You mean *right now*."

She flipped the button on his shorts open and slid her hand inside to wrap her fingers around him. "That okay with you?"

He had to swallow before he could answer. "There's a condom in my pocket."

Her smile was sharp as a blade. "Get it ready. I'm going to need it in a minute."

His last coherent thought as she lowered her mouth to his dick was that he should've made out with Wyatt days ago.

Fifteen minutes later Veronica rolled off Shane to lie on the couch, sweaty and panting and a little hoarse from all the screaming. "Damn."

He let out a rough grunt. "That's what I was going to say."

"Okay," she managed between breaths. "Go ahead."

"Damn," he said.

She laughed breathlessly, then sighed. "I'm going to need another shower, but all my bones melted during that second orgasm, so you might have to carry me."

He grunted again, and she laughed. "God, you're cute."

"Cute?" Out of the corner of her eye she saw him roll toward her. "I'm cute?"

She mustered up the energy to move, curling into his side. "Fucking adorable."

"Well." He seemed genuinely nonplused by that observation. "That's a new one."

She laid a hand on his chest. He was sweaty, and she could feel his heart pounding under her palm. "You must have heard that before."

"Not really. Wyatt gets cute a lot, though."

"And he is," she said with a sleepy sigh, and her eyes drifted closed. "But so are you."

He shifted his body, turning on his side to face her. "You got all cranked up watching Wyatt kiss me, Miss I Don't Have A Sexual Bucket List."

She forced her eyes open, a little surprised to find his face so close to hers. His eyes were so dark, still cloudy from passion. "Just because I don't have a list of sexual 'must do before death' items doesn't mean I don't find the idea of you, me, and Wyatt all naked together hot."

His lips quirked. "Yeah?"

"Ridiculously hot." The sweat was drying on her skin, making her shiver, so she snuggled closer. He wrapped his arm around her, stroking her arm with an absent sort of intimacy that made her heart sigh. "Smoking hot. Incendiary. Lava."

He chuckled. "Okay, you think it's hot."

"In theory," she said, her eyes drifting shut. "Never having had a threesome with two guys, I don't know if it would be hot in practice or just annoying."

"Why would it be annoying?"

"Logistics," she said around a yawn. "Are all three people equally involved, or is one waiting to tag in?"

"What, like wrestling?"

She shrugged. "If penis number one is in my vagina, where is penis number two? Is it patiently waiting its turn, or am I going to have to suck one and fuck the other at the same time? Because I gotta be honest, I don't think I'm that coordinated."

His chest rumbled with laughter under her cheek as she

went on. "How do we decide which penis goes first? Do we flip a coin? Will there be butt stuff? Because okay, that can be fun, but I've seen double penetration in porn, and that doesn't look like a good time. Also, am I solely responsible for the penises, or will there be crossing of the swords?"

"Crossing of the swords?" he echoed, sounding confused, and she opened her eyes.

"That's probably not an issue for you two, but I understand in a hetero group sex situation, it can be very awkward if there is errant and unexpected penis touching."

He was shaking with laughter. "No, that's not a problem for us."

"One less thing to worry about." She snuggled back up against his chest. His hand was still stroking her arm, the rhythmic motion lulling her to sleep. "But still. These things need to be considered."

"I have to say, I never gave my threesomes this much thought," he said, laughter brightening his usual gravely, post-sex voice.

"That's because you're a guy." She yawned hugely. "Guys just go 'ooh, dick getting wet, threesome good'."

"Is that what we do?"

"I'm speculating," she admitted. "Probably there's more to it than that."

"Probably."

"But I bet it's easier when you love somebody, the way you and Wyatt love each other."

"Maybe it is," he conceded as she drifted off to sleep. "Maybe it is."

THE REST of the week passed by in a blur of sun, food, and sex, and Veronica couldn't remember ever being so relaxed. She lost track of the days, so when Shane asked her about her flight the day before they were due to leave, it came as a complete shock that their vacation was almost over.

She didn't handle it well.

"Are you going to pout all day?" Shane demanded after her third heavy sigh.

"No." She stopped poking at her breakfast of fresh fruit and yogurt to send him a grumpy look across the patio table. "Maybe just for the next hour."

"Well, let me know when you're done," he commented, and bit into a slice of bacon.

She frowned at her fruit plate. "Why didn't I get bacon?"

"You didn't order it. You said you'd been eating like crap and you wanted something healthy."

"Dammit," she muttered.

"What do you want to do today?" he asked, biting into his bacon again. Smugly, she thought.

"I don't know." She pushed her plate aside and dropped her chin into her hands. "We could fuck, I guess."

"We could fuck, you guess? Nice enthusiasm," he said and polished off the bacon as she laid her head back on the table hard enough to rattle the flatware. "You're going to get yogurt in your hair."

"Oh, shut up. You didn't even share your bacon."

He snorted, then glanced over as Wyatt stepped onto the patio from the beach path. "Hey."

"Hey, baby." Wyatt raised a brow at Veronica. "What's with her?"

"She's pouting," Shane said, reaching over to move her plate away from her head.

She aimed her most pitiful look at Wyatt. "Shane didn't share his bacon."

"What a bastard."

The bastard in question just rolled his eyes. "She's blue because it's our last day."

"Man, me too." Wyatt walked over to sink into the hammock with a sigh. "Leaving this place is going to suck."

"See? He gets it." Veronica sniffed without raising her head. "He also would've shared his bacon with me."

"Of course, I would, darling," Wyatt soothed.

"Are you both going to waste our last day here pouting?"

"Not the whole day," Wyatt said. "Maybe like an hour."

Veronica picked her head off the table. "That's what I said!"

He set the hammock to swinging and grinned at her. "Synchronicity, baby."

Shane tossed his napkin on the table. "I'm going to go for a run," he declared. "When I get back, if the two of you are done with your pity party, we can figure out something fun to do on our last day."

"Fine," Veronica sighed and laid her head on the table again with a pitiful moan.

Wyatt laughed. "Go. I'll cheer her up."

"Don't be a pervert," Shane warned.

"Yeah, yeah, blah, blah." Wyatt waved him off. "Go."

Veronica lifted her head to look at Wyatt as Shane's footsteps faded away. "You can be a pervert if you want. That might cheer me up."

"Yeah?" He grinned. "How depressed are you?"

"A little bummed," she admitted. "But sometimes I like to wallow."

"Me, too. Shane's too practical to wallow."

She laughed at that. "Oh God, he is."

"This is pretty comfortable." Wyatt lowered a foot to the ground to push off, setting the hammock swinging again. "I should get one of these at home."

"I've napped in that thing every day," Veronica told him. "I'm going to miss it."

"I can see why." He nestled back into the pillows, then lifted his head to eye her curiously. "You guys haven't done it in this, have you?"

"God, no," she said with a snort. "We'd probably kill ourselves."

"Yeah. Not a lot of...stability," Wyatt mused.

Veronica raised a brow. "Is that it?"

"Is what it?"

"You being a pervert," she explained. "I mean, based on past conversations, I was expecting something more than just speculation about hammock sex."

"Okay," he said agreeably. "When Shane gets back, wanna have a threesome?"

"Um....maybe?"

He started, making the hammock jerk. "Seriously?"

"No," she said, half wishing she wasn't. "And neither are you, you're just trying to spook me again."

He eased back onto the hammock, his gaze amused. "Would I do that?"

"Absolutely," she said and tried to ignore the butterflies in her belly. "

"Okay, I would." He sent her a wink. "But I'm serious about the threesome."

"Oh."

"If you're not into it, that's fine," he went on, a watchful glint in his playful gaze. "I promised Shane I wouldn't push. He'd kill me if he thought I was making you uncomfortable."

She wasn't uncomfortable, exactly. The little wiggle in her belly was something far warmer, and far more interesting, than discomfort. "I'm not *not* into it," she hedged.

"But you're not sure turning fantasy into reality would be a good idea," he replied. "Okay. I won't perv you into it."

She had to laugh. "Perve me into it?"

"I have this power," he said with an exaggerated smolder.

"Oh, I can tell." She propped her chin on her hand. "Just out of curiosity, what does a threesome include?"

"It includes whatever you want, and nothing you don't. I don't even have to fuck you."

She snorted. "You want to have a threesome with me, but you don't want to fuck me?"

"I want to fuck you almost as much as I want to fuck Shane."

"Wow." She blinked. "That's a lot."

"But the question isn't do I want to fuck you, it's do you want to fuck me."

She chewed her lip, considering. "Honestly?"

He spread his hands. "That's the only way this works, sunshine."

"It depends."

He tilted his head. "On?"

"On whether or not Shane is okay with it."

"Aw." The small smile curling his lips spread. "You like my boyfriend."

"Shut up," she said, her face heating, and cleared her throat. "Anyway. He'd have to be okay with it."

"That's actually my rule, too."

"Well. That makes things…"

"Easier and more complicated at the same time?" he finished when she trailed off.

"Polyamory is some tricky shit," she sighed, and he laughed.

"Baby, you don't know the half of it."

She was beginning to see that. "Anyway, I appreciate the offer, but we'll have to come up with something else to keep us busy today."

"Fair enough. How do you feel about snorkeling?"

"I'm good with that," she decided, relieved the conversation had moved to safer territory. She pushed her chair back and stood. "Can you reserve the equipment?"

"Sure. One thing, though."

She paused as Wyatt stood and walked toward her, his blue eyes strangely dark. "What is it?"

"Just this," he said and kissed her.

She squeaked in surprise, then squeaked again when he took advantage of her parted lips to slip his tongue inside. He was bold, sliding his tongue over hers with sure strokes, flicking over the roof of her mouth before pulling back to nibble on her lips. Heat curled in her belly, and just as she leaned into him, wanting more, he was gone.

She blinked her eyes open to find him watching her with a kind of heated satisfaction. "Just wanted to make it clear where I stand."

"Yeah," she managed. Her lips tingled, and she could still taste the coffee he'd had with breakfast. And something else. "Did you have cinnamon rolls for breakfast?"

He grinned at her. "With extra icing."

"Fucking fruit plate."

"Go get changed," he told her, laughing. "I'll go get the equipment and meet you back here."

"Take your time," she told him, heading for the sliding door. "I suddenly feel the need for a shower."

"Before snorkeling?" he asked.

"It's not to get clean," she informed him tartly and closed the sliding door on his delighted laughter.

Thirteen

On Monday morning she woke back in the real world, in her own bed, with the sheets cold and empty beside her.

"Nuts," she muttered and shoved her way clear of the blankets.

The floor was freezing on her bare feet, even though the temperature was supposed to be in the high sixties for the day. Spring in Michigan was nothing like spring in Bermuda, and her toes could tell the difference.

She stopped at her dresser for a pair of thick socks, then made her way to the bathroom. After taking care of business and covering her feet, she headed for the kitchen.

She had thankfully had the presence of mind to set the coffee to brew automatically the night before, so it was already hissing and spitting out life-giving caffeine. She pulled a mug from the dishwasher she hadn't bothered to empty before she'd gone on vacation and leaned against the counter, yawning, while she waited for the pot to fill.

The knock on her door made her frown, and she glanced

at the clock on the microwave. Who would be at her apartment at six-forty-five in the morning?

She glanced down at herself. In addition to the socks, she wore the plain black cotton T-shirt she'd slept in—one of Shane's. It had somehow wound up in her luggage by mistake, and she'd found it last night when she'd unpacked. She'd started to throw it into the basket with the rest of the laundry, then had given in to impulse and pulled it over her head instead.

It fell nearly to her knees, covering all the vital bits, so she walked to the door. "Who is it?"

"It's me," Delia called back. "Open the door."

Veronica flipped open the locks. "Why didn't you just use your key?"

"Because my hands are full," Delia replied and held out a to-go cup of coffee. "Here. I thought you might need this."

"You're a lifesaver," Veronica said reverently, forgetting all about the pot brewing in the kitchen.

"I know. I also brought muffins." Delia walked to the sofa, rattling the paper bag in her hand.

"Coffee and muffins, before seven a.m.?" Veronica wrapped both hands around her cup and perched on the sofa. "And you got dressed to bring them to me?"

Delia snorted, her messy knot of blonde hair bobbing as she dug into the bag. "Please. These are my pajamas."

Veronica's eyes narrowed on Delia's clothes, which, yes, seemed to be pajama pants with... "Is that Strawberry Shortcake?"

"Yep."

"I didn't know they made them for grownups."

"They don't. I found the fabric and had them made."

"Of course, you did." Veronica sipped her coffee. "To what do I owe the honor?"

Delia dug into the bag and came up with a muffin, fat with blueberries and glistening with sugar. "I'm bribing you."

Veronica eyed the muffin with interest, suddenly very aware that she hadn't eaten since four o'clock the previous afternoon. "Why are you bribing me?"

"Because I want to hear all about your vacation."

Veronica reached for the muffin. "You don't have to bribe me for that."

Delia jerked it out of reach. "Ah, but I want the good stuff. The dirty, nitty gritty. No dirt, no muffin."

"What dirt? There's no dirt."

"Oh really?" Delia gave her an arch look, still holding the muffin aloft. "Then why did Derek come to my house, ranting and raving about you joining a sex cult?"

Veronica's eyes bugged out. "He did *what?*"

Delia nodded smugly. "Came right up to my front door, pounded on it until I let him in, then demanded I help him rescue you."

"Oh, for God's sake." Veronica fell back against the back of the couch with a groan. "What an ass."

"After he did some weed, he calmed down and told me the whole story." Delia's mouth curved into a small smirk. "Not that he knew he was doing weed."

Veronica's eyes popped wide again. "Delia!"

"What?"

"Tell me you did not drug Derek without his knowledge."

"It was just one little brownie. What harm could it do?"

"Delia!"

"Oh, calm down, I'm kidding." Delia waved a hand. "I offered, he declined. He had two fingers of Scotch and spilled his guts."

Veronica glared at her best friend and snatched the muffin out of her hand. "Don't do things that make me feel sorry for Derek."

"You wouldn't feel sorry if you could've heard the way he was ranting and raving about what a slut you are."

"He did not say slut."

"Oh, but he did." Delia's face was grim. "That's about when Julian came in and threw him out."

"Good for Julian."

"But before he did, I got a couple of names out of him. Wyatt and Shane."

Veronica set her coffee aside to peel the wrapper off the muffin. "So?"

"So, what's the story?"

"No story." Veronica shrugged. "I was having lunch with them when Derek showed up, acting like a maniac. The hotel asked me to come down, to see if I could get him to leave without calling the cops. Shane and Wyatt insisted on coming with me."

"Good for them." Delia nodded. "Then what?"

"Then, nothing. We went up to the hotel and told Derek to leave."

Delia's eyes narrowed as Veronica bit into the muffin. "And that's it? I don't buy it. Why does Derek think that the three of you were fucking?"

Veronica swallowed. "He kept insisting we could work things out—"

Delia snorted.

"—and I figured the easiest way to get him to scoot was to hit him in the ego. So, the three of us pretended we were fucking, and he got mad and left."

"Pretended?"

"Yes, pretended. It worked, too. You should've seen his face turn purple."

"I saw it when he came to my house. Frankly, I could've lived without the experience."

"Join the club."

"So, you didn't sleep with Wyatt and Shane?"

"Nope."

"Then why are you wearing a man's T-shirt?"

Veronica chewed her muffin and tried to look nonchalant. "What?"

"That's not your shirt." Delia pointed to the black T-shirt, now decorated with blueberry muffin crumbs.

"It's a sleep shirt, Delia," Veronica said, trying to brazen it out.

"It's a man's T-shirt, Veronica," Delia countered.

"So?" Veronica bit into the muffin again and took her time chewing. "I buy men's T-shirts for sleep shirts. You know this."

"I do know this. I also know you buy V-neck shirts because you think they make your boobs look good."

"They do make my boobs look good," Veronica said smugly.

"And that is a crew neck," Delia went on, undeterred. "It's also black, and you always buy white."

"When did you get so interested in my T-shirt buying habits?" Veronica wondered out loud.

"Girl, I have known you since we were eighteen, and I am your best friend. You can't lie to me." Delia arched one eyebrow so far up her forehead it almost disappeared into her hairline. "Spill it."

"You're such a pain in the ass." Veronica huffed out a breath. "If I tell you what happened, will you go away and leave me to enjoy my coffee and muffin in peace?"

"I make no promises." Delia folded her legs under her and leaned forward. "Dish."

"Okay. I did not sleep with Wyatt."

"Too bad. He looks frisky."

Veronica paused to give her friend an incredulous look. "Frisky?"

Delia nodded, a lascivious gleam in her eyes. "Leather and chains kind of frisky. Also, I hear he and Shane like to tag team."

"Where did you hear that?" Veronica demanded.

"From Wyatt."

"Of course, from Wyatt." Veronica shook her head. "Are you high right now?"

"Mildly self-medicated," Delia admitted. "So, you didn't sleep with Wyatt. Does that mean you did sleep with Shane?"

Veronica gave up and reached for her coffee. "Yes, I slept with Shane."

"Thank God. How was it?"

"Yum," Veronica said after a moment of thought. "Very much yum."

"Multiple yums?"

"Multiple yums, multiple times."

"Cheers to that," Delia declared and tapped her paper to-go cup against Veronica's in a Starbucks toast. "Are you going to sleep with him again?"

"I don't know."

Delia dug into the bag and came up with a second muffin. "How come?"

"Well, it was kind of a vacation thing." Veronica shrugged. "And now that we're home..."

"Oh." Delia nodded sagely. "What happens in Bermuda stays in Bermuda?"

"Something like that. Maybe. We never really talked about it, which is weird, because we talked about everything else."

"He talked?" Delia's eyes widened. "Shane talked? In more than grunts?"

Veronica laughed. "He talked a lot. Sex makes him chatty."

"Well, who'd have thought." Delia took a bite of muffin and chewed, a thoughtful look on her face. "Do you want to bang him again?"

"Jesus, Delia. Who says bang?"

"I say bang," Delia declared around a mouthful of food. "Bang is a perfectly good word. Succinct, unambiguous, and flavorful."

"Flavorful." Veronica shook her head. "Stop coming over here when you're medicated, will you?"

"You'd never see me again," Delia pointed out.

"I know."

"Ha. Anyway, back to the banging. Do you want to?"

Veronica sipped her coffee. "Yeah, I do."

"Then I say go for it. What've you got to lose?"

"I don't know. I liked him, Dee."

Delia paused. "You mean you liked him as in you liked his dick and the multiple yums, or as in you'd bake him his favorite cookies for no reason on a Tuesday?"

Veronica sighed. "The second one."

"Aw. That's great, sweetie."

"I don't know. His life is kind of complicated."

"You mean the poly thing or the bisexual thing?"

"I don't care that he's bisexual. That's not a deal-breaker at all."

"But being poly is?"

"Honestly?" She thought about it for a minute. "I don't know. Would you date a guy who was in a relationship with someone else?"

"No." Delia nibbled on her muffin, looking thoughtful. "I'd fuck him, especially if a threesome was on the table. But date? I don't think I could handle it."

She picked up her coffee cup. "But we're not talking about me. The question is, can you handle it?"

"I don't know." Veronica frowned. "I like Wyatt. And it's clear they love each other."

"How do you feel about that?"

"Happy," Veronica decided. "It makes me happy that Shane has someone who loves him that much."

"Well." Delia popped the last bite of muffin into her mouth. "I don't know much about this stuff, but that at least feels like a step in the right direction."

"I guess. Maybe I should get some books or something. There are books for every other relationship problem, right? There have to be some for this one."

"Sure. Wyatt can probably recommend some."

Veronica shook her head. "No, I don't want to ask him. Or Shane," she said before Delia could suggest it.

"Why not?"

"Because if I get into it and realize it's not for me, I don't want to have to explain." She winced. "Cowardly?"

Delia shook her head. "Cautious. And smart."

"Thanks." Veronica leaned back, but she couldn't quite see the clock on the microwave. "Do you know what time it is?"

Delia slipped her phone out of her pocket. "Seven fifteen."

"Shit. I'm going to be late, and I still have to shower." Veronica gulped the last of her coffee, then rose from the sofa and hurried to the bathroom, dragging the T-shirt over her head as she went. "You can let yourself out."

"I thought we could go to breakfast," Delia called.

"No time," Veronica yelled back and jumped in the shower.

By the time she emerged and had scrambled into some clothes, Delia was gone and she had just enough time to get to work.

Figuring out her suddenly very complicated love life would just have to wait until later.

THE NEXT FEW days gave Veronica very little time to worry about Shane. Work was even busier than usual—summer meant they'd taken on some clients that normally would be served by the public school system, so already busy schedules became overloaded. By the time she got home, she barely had the energy to shove something resembling dinner into her mouth before falling into bed until the alarm went off the next morning.

She was sorting laundry on Saturday afternoon when she came across the black T-shirt again. She'd been wearing it to bed all week and it desperately needed a wash, but then it would smell like laundry detergent and fabric softener instead of Shane. She'd grown used to his scent surrounding her when she fell asleep.

She missed him, she realized. Missed his scent and his body in bed next to hers, missed his grunts and his laugh and the way he'd roll his eyes and glare at the same time whenever Wyatt said something inappropriate.

She just missed Shane.

She set the shirt aside, then reached for her phone and scrolled through her contact list until she came to his name. They'd exchanged numbers on their last day on the island, after a bout of shower sex that had made full use of the hand-held shower wand and had left her in a satisfied heap on the tile. He'd scooped her up, carried her to the bed, and picked up her phone.

"Call this number before you crash," he'd said, handing it to her, and recited a number with a Detroit area code.

She'd already been half asleep, barely keeping her eyes open to punch in the numbers. When she'd hit send and heard a buzzing across the room, she'd clued in. "Why do you have a Detroit number?"

He'd taken the phone away from her to disconnect the call. "I used to live there, didn't see the point in changing it."

"Makes sense," she'd said on a yawn, and had fallen asleep before he could say anything else. When she'd opened her eyes an hour later, he'd already left to catch his flight.

She'd added his information to her contact list, and even assigned it one of the few photos she'd taken on her trip. They'd been in the hammock, curled together to watch the sunset, and when she'd snapped a picture of the blazing pinks and oranges of the sky, she'd inadvertently included his feet.

Before she could change her mind, she quickly tapped her screen to bring up a new text. She attached the picture, typed "wish we were here" and hit send.

Then she shoved the phone into her pocket, picked up her hamper, and trudged down to the basement laundry room. She was pouring soap into the first machine when her phone rang.

She made herself finish pouring, closed the lid, and hit the button to start the wash before she answered. "Hello?"

"Hey," he answered. "Thanks for the picture."

His voice was rough, a low, throaty rumble. He sounded that way first thing in the morning, she remembered, and during sex. Especially during sex.

"You're welcome," she said, her own voice husky with memories.

"I didn't know you'd taken it."

"I wanted something to remind me of my awesome vacation."

"My big feet fit that bill, huh?"

She had to smile at the amusement in his voice. "Well, I was aiming for the sunset. Your big feet got in the way."

He chuckled and had goosebumps breaking out over her skin. "How was your first week back?"

"Hectic," she said baldly. "Today's the first chance I've had to breathe all week. You?"

"Same. Finished up a couple of commissions, got a couple more."

"That's nice."

"It is. I like paying my bills." There was a brief pause, then, "What are you doing right now?"

"My laundry."

"You hungry?"

"A little. Why?"

"Because I'm picking up a calzone at Mama Luke's, and I'm willing to share."

"What's Mama Luke's?"

"You've never had a Mama Luke's calzone?"

"No," she said, smiling at his exaggerated shock. "Are they good?"

"Good isn't a strong enough word. What's your address?"

She rattled it off, chewing on her bottom lip. "Are you coming over?"

"If you want to share my calzone."

"Sure." She managed to say it almost casually, like she wasn't currently dancing a gleeful jig in the laundry room. "There's no visitor parking, but there should be plenty of room on the street."

"Sounds good. See you in about half an hour."

"Okay," she said, then hung up and stood there grinning like an idiot until she realized that she was wearing her oldest pair of yoga pants—the ones with the hole in the crotch—and a tank top with a spaghetti sauce stain.

Dashing back to her apartment, she switched out the yoga pants for a pair of jeans and the tank for a soft sweater in pale green that brought out the color of her eyes. Her hair got a quick taming with a brush, her mouth a quick swipe of her favorite lip balm. She debated whether or not to do something more with her face, then decided to just let it be.

She left the bathroom and did a quick scan of the apartment. The kitchen was fairly clean, mainly because she'd been too busy to mess it up, and the living room was at least presentable. She snatched up a pair of pink panties that must have fallen out of the laundry basket and carried them to the bedroom to toss them into the hamper. She was running back when she heard the knock on her front door.

She took a deep breath to steady her nerves and answered it.

God, he looked good. He was wearing the cargo pants and T-shirt she'd come to think of as his uniform, both in black, and black lace-up boots covered his feet. His hair was pulled back in its usual low tail, his beard sleek and a little shorter than she remembered. He had one hand tucked into his front pocket, and the other held an enormous foil-wrapped package, and when he smiled, his beard twitched.

"Hi."

She smiled back. "Hi. You trimmed your beard."

"Oh. Yeah." He lifted a hand to rub along his jaw. "It was getting annoying."

"Beards get annoying?"

"They very much do."

"Well, the things you learn." She stepped back. "Come on in."

"Thanks." He stepped over the threshold, his arm brushing against hers as he moved past her into the room. "I like your place."

"Thanks." She closed the door behind him and tried to breathe normally. "Make yourself at home."

"You like books."

She looked at the living room, every wall lined with shelves, and laughed. "Yeah. I like books."

"Me, too. I outfitted part of my basement as a library."

"Really?"

He nodded. "Took me months to get the shelves done, working on them in between projects."

"I just went to Ikea," she confessed and stifled a smile when he stared at her in mock horror.

"I don't think I should share my calzone with you anymore."

"You can't withhold food just because I like cheap Swedish furniture," she began, then her eyes lit on the foil-wrapped package in his hand. It was the size of a whole large pizza. "Wait, that's *one* calzone?"

"Ridiculous, isn't it?" He smiled. "I can usually make lunch for a week out of one of these."

"No kidding." She turned for the kitchen. "I'll get some plates."

"Mind if I look at your books?" he asked, his voice trailing her into the tiny space even.

"Go ahead," she called back. She pulled two plates from the dishwasher she still hadn't bothered to empty, then dug knives and forks out of the drawer.

When she walked back into the living room, he was reading the back of a book he'd pulled off the shelf, still holding the calzone.

"Do you mind eating in here?" she asked, nodding toward the only slightly cluttered coffee table. "My dining table has been taken over by work stuff."

"No problem." He slid the book he held back into place and stepped over to set the calzone on the coffee table. He took the plates from her. "Do you have napkins?"

"I'll get them. What do you want to drink?"

"Whatever you're having is fine."

"Wine?"

"Sure."

She dug some napkins out of her things-that-came-with-takeout-food-that-might-someday-be-useful drawer and grabbed the half a bottle of red wine from the counter. She found two wine glasses in the dishwasher and carried everything to the living room.

He was peeling the aluminum foil off the calzone, and fragrant steam filled the air.

She took a deep, appreciative sniff. "That smells amazing."

"Wait until you taste it," he replied and picked up a knife. She settled cross-legged on the floor and uncorked the wine, pouring them each a glass while he worked. When he'd slid a sizeable chunk onto each place, he lowered himself to the floor beside her. "Dig in."

She picked up her knife and fork, cut a piece, and popped it into her mouth. "Oh, *yum*."

"Right?" He ignored the utensils and picked up his section with his fingers, biting in with obvious relish.

"That's good." Veronica picked up her wine for a sip, then went back to her food. "Where did you get this again?"

"Mama Luke's" he told her and picked up his wine.

She shook her head. "Never heard of it."

"Technically, it's called Mama Luciano's, but everybody just calls it Mama Luke's." He set down his wine. "I order from them at least once a week. I think I put Mama's grandson through college."

"So there really is a Mama?"

He nodded. "Her son is technically the owner, but she runs the kitchen. And everything else, now that I think about it."

"Well, thanks for sharing this. It's amazing."

"Thanks for having me over," he replied. "I wondered if I was going to see you again."

She paused with her fork halfway to her mouth. "What do you mean?"

He shrugged. "I told you to call me if you wanted to. After a week, I figured it wasn't happening."

"When was this?"

He looked at her. "The last day, just before I left. When I had you call my phone so you'd have my number."

"You mean right after you fucked me into a coma?" She rolled her eyes. "Shane, I didn't hear you."

His brows snapped together in a frown. "What?"

"I didn't hear you," she repeated. "I was barely awake enough to dial the phone. The last thing I remember you saying was you used to live in Detroit."

Amusement lightened his eyes. "Those post-sex sleepies."

"Wait." She set down her fork. "You were waiting for me to call you?"

"Yeah."

"So, if I hadn't texted you today...?"

He shrugged. "I would've assumed you weren't interested in seeing me again."

"You wouldn't have contacted me? At all?"

"Nope." He picked up his wine. "The ball was in your court. Or, it would've been, if you'd been listening."

"I can't believe you thought I was listening." She sent him a chiding look and picked up her fork to resume eating.

"You know, most women don't go comatose after an orgasm."

"Well, I do. Which you should've known, you gave me enough of them."

"Good point. Thanks for texting, by the way."

"You're welcome." She smiled at him. "I'm happy to see you."

He smiled back. "I'm happy to see you too. So, what'd you do this week?"

"Not much. I saw Delia on Monday, but other than that it's just been work."

"Have you heard from Derek?"

"No, but get this. After he got booted out of the resort

and flew back here? He went to Delia's house and told her I'd been captured by a sex cult."

Shane choked his wine, his eyes watering as he stared at her. He grabbed a napkin. "Are you kidding?"

"Nope. He wanted Delia to fly down there and rescue me."

"What an ass." He mopped the table, his eyes on hers. "Do you think he'll take you to small claims court?"

"I sent back the money he gave me for the trip, so if he does, it'll just be for the stuff I gave away. Which I think he knows will make him look small and petty, so I doubt it."

"Good."

"I was thinking of sending him a thank you card."

"What? Why?"

"Because if he hadn't pulled that stunt in Bermuda, I'd never have slept with you."

His brows rose. "Really?"

"Yeah. I thought you were gay."

"You did? Wait." His eyes narrowed slightly. "What does that have to do with Derek?"

"Wyatt told me you're bisexual while you were tossing Derek out," she said, pausing when he cursed. "He didn't tell you?"

"No. What did he say?"

"Just that it might be relevant to my interests to know that you were not gay. Then he apologized for shoving his hardon into my ass. Well, apologize is a strong word," she mused. "It was more of an explanation with an open invitation."

Shane groaned. "For fuck's sake."

"It was actually kind of sweet, and it helped me feel like less of an idiot about getting so turned on by the whole situation."

"I dreamed about you that night," he admitted.

She bit her lower lip, her cheeks heating as she stared into his eyes. "You did?"

He nodded. "About you, me, and Wyatt in the shower at the cottage."

"It was a pretty big shower," she recalled, "but I don't know if it was big enough for that."

"In my dreams it was," he told her. "In my dreams it was just big enough to pin you between us and fuck you until you came screaming."

She had to clear her throat before the words would come out. "Not each other?"

His already hooded eyes darkened. "You liked seeing us kiss."

She nodded, her belly clenching at the look in his eyes. "Yes."

"Did you fantasize about it, Veronica?" His voice was low and thick, sending shivers down her spine. "Did you fantasize about the things Wyatt and I do to each other in the dark?"

"Yes," she whispered.

"Did you touch yourself when you did?"

"Yes."

"Tell me," he said softly. "Tell me what you thought about when you were stroking your pretty pussy. Tell me what got it wet and hot and ready."

Oh, God. "I thought about Wyatt sucking your cock," she whispered, the words barely audible in the thrumming silence. "I thought about you sucking his."

He moved suddenly, shoving the coffee table to the side so there was nothing between them but heated air. "What else?"

"About...about you lubing your cock."

"So, I could fuck him, or you?" Shane asked, his voice raw on the blunt words.

"Him."

"Hmm. Do you think I'm a top, Veronica?"

"I don't know." She licked her lips. "Are you?"

"Sometimes." He shifted to his knees and scooted forward. "Sometimes I want to pin him down and drive into him so hard he can't breathe, so hard he can't help but surrender to it."

He edged closer. "Then other times I want to lie back and take what he gives me, to watch him take his pleasure in my body."

He stopped in front of her, towering over her on his knees, his hands loose at his sides. "Which would you rather watch, Veronica? My surrender or his?"

Her body felt tight and swollen, her breasts aching and her pussy throbbing in time with the frantic beating of her heart. "Both. Either. I don't care."

"And where are you while all this is going on? Are you watching, stroking your pussy until you come?" He lifted a hand, trailing his long, artist's fingers along the seam of her jeans on her inner thigh. "Or are you participating?"

Participating! her brain screamed, but she couldn't make the word come out of her mouth.

His brow arched, the gleam in his eye intensifying. "Can't decide?"

"Hypothetically speaking?" she asked, her voice a husky rasp.

"Sure." His fingertips inched up her thigh, his eyes steady on hers. "Hypothetically, do you want to watch, or participate?"

Ohmigod. "Participate," she whispered.

"I knew that would be your answer," he murmured, his mouth so close to hers she could feel his breath on her lips, all but taste the spices and wine. "For all your talk about not having a sexual bucket list, the idea of you, me, and Wyatt together really gets you going, doesn't it?"

"Yes," she admitted, the air whooshing out of her lungs with the word. "I want it."

"Hypothetically?"

She swallowed. "I don't know yet."

"Fair enough." He leaned in and took her lower lip between his teeth, tugging gently once, twice, before releasing it. "I have a non-hypothetical question for you."

Her mouth was tingling, her heart racing. "What is it?"

"Can I stay the night?"

"Yes," she said and kissed him.

His tongue slid past hers, his familiar taste flooding her mouth. She wrapped her arms around his neck, then squeaked when he rose with her in his arms, her feet dangling off the floor.

He broke the kiss to nibble at her jaw, her neck, her ear. "Damn, that got you going."

She managed a half laugh. "I missed this." *I missed you.*

"Me, too." He returned to her mouth, devouring her with deep kisses and stinging nibbles until she wanted to climb him like a tree.

She reached up and yanked the tie from his hair, her fingers gliding through the silky fall of it. "Shane?"

He nipped at her bottom lip again. "Yeah?"

"Fuck my brains out."

He laughed, the sound muffled against her mouth, then hitched her higher so she could wrap her legs around his waist. "Where's the bed?"

She waved a hand in the vague direction of the bedroom. "That way. Hall. Bedroom."

"Okay," he said and carried her off while she attacked his ear. He headed down the hall, crashed into the wall once, then made it to the bedroom, where he tossed her on the bed and proceeded to fuck her brains out. Twice.

FOURTEEN

Veronica opened her eyes the next morning to find Shane propped up on one elbow, looking down at her. He wasn't exactly smiling, but he looked pretty damn happy.

"Hi," she said softly and curled on her side so she could bury her nose in the curve of his neck. "What're you doing?"

"Just watching you snore," he replied.

She jerked back with a frown. "I don't snore."

"Right, I forgot." His beard twitched once, his eyes warm. "I was watching you...what was it? Breathe with emphasis?"

She sniffed and snuggled close once again. "Don't think I don't know you're mocking me."

"I would never," he said so seriously she almost believed him.

"Do you want some breakfast?" she mumbled, already half asleep again.

His low chuckle rumbled under her ear. "Thanks, but I should get moving. And you're already going back to sleep."

"Mmm," she managed, her eyes already sliding closed.

When she opened them again, he was standing beside the bed, pulling on his pants. "Oh. You're dressed."

He fastened his pants, then swept his hair back. "I have to finish a couple of things up today. Did you see where my hair tie went?"

"Um." She sat up and struggled to engage her brain. "I think I yanked it out when we were still in the living room. But there are some on my dresser. Help yourself."

"Thanks."

He walked over to her dresser while she struggled to wake up. "How can you be this awake this early before coffee?" she asked around a huge yawn.

"It's after ten." He pulled his hair back into a low tail and reached for his shirt. "And I don't like coffee."

"I remember," she said with another yawn. "It's after ten?"

He nodded to the clock on the wall. "Ten-twenty, to be exact."

"Oh." She sank back down to snuggle into her pillow. "Okay."

He pulled his shirt over his head and sent her a beard-quirking smile. "You going back to sleep again?"

She stuck her tongue out at him. "You're just jealous."

He sat on the edge of the bed to pull on his boots. "Can't argue that. What are your plans for today? Assuming you manage to get out of bed at some point."

"I brought some work home, so I'll probably tackle that." She grimaced. "And I have to finish my laundry."

"What's the face for?"

"I just remembered I left a load in the washer last night." She sighed. "That's going to be gross."

The beard quirked again. "Sorry I distracted you."

"It was worth the mildew," she told him soberly.

"Good to know. What work?"

She blinked. "Huh?"

"You said you brought home some work." He finished tying his boots and stood. "I just realized I don't know what you do."

"Oh. I'm a speech pathologist. Or I will be, when I finish my CF."

He yanked on his boots, then stood. "CF?"

"Clinical fellowship," she explained. "I have to work for a while under supervision before they let me off the leash."

"Ah. Speech pathology, huh? That anything like speech therapy?"

"Exactly like that."

"You work with kids?"

"Yeah. I used to be a teacher," she explained, stretching as she watched him check his pockets for keys, phone, and pocket watch. "Why do you carry a pocket watch?"

"Because wearing a wristwatch when you're working with power tools is a terrible idea. Plus, it was my grandfather's."

"Aw." Her heart, already soft, went mushy. "That's sweet."

"And it's sexy as hell," he added with a wink.

She giggled. "It kind of is."

"I know. Why used to be?"

She was still vibrating from that wink. "Huh?"

"You said you used to be a teacher," he prompted. "Why used to be?"

"Oh. I loved teaching, but I felt more like a classroom manager than an educator. I wanted to spend more individual time with students. I feel like I have more of an impact this way."

"That's nice."

"It is." She dragged at her hair, grimacing when her fingers got caught in the snarls. "Ugh, I need a shower."

He leaned down. "I'd offer to wash your back, but I need to get going."

She pouted. "Aw."

He chuckled and kissed her, a brief peck on the lips that nonetheless sent her heart racing. "Want to get together later this week?"

She blinked. "Like, a date?"

That got her a full smile. "Yeah. Like a date."

"I'd like that."

"Great. When?"

"Um." She frowned, mentally flipping through her calendar. "I have late nights at work on Tuesdays and Fridays right now. We're open later so parents who work can still bring their kids in for therapy. I don't usually leave the office until after eight, sometimes later."

"I have a client meeting on Monday and a standing date with Wyatt on Wednesdays."

"I guess that leaves Thursday," she began, then she remembered. "Oh, hell."

He raised a brow as she reached for her phone on the nightstand. "Problem with Thursday?"

Tapping the screen, she brought up her tracking app and stifled a sigh. "Yes. My period is due to start that day." She looked up with a wince. "Sorry. Was that too much information?"

He was watching her with a thoughtful look on his face. "No. Are your periods really awful or something? Do they make you sick?"

"No. I mean, I don't feel great, but they're not debilitating. Just the usual: cramps, cravings, blood, and crabbiness."

"Cravings for what?"

"Chocolate, of course," she said with a little laugh. "And salty foods, like pretzels or salt and vinegar chips."

"How about we do movies in, then?" he suggested. "I'll bring chocolate and salty snacks."

"That sounds great, but I don't like having sex on my peri-

od," she told him bluntly. "So, if that's what you're thinking
…"

"I'm thinking about bringing snacks and watching a movie with you." He cocked his head when she stared at him. "What?"

"Derek would barely kiss me when I was on my period."

He sat on the bed, disgust twisting his face. "That should've been your first clue he was a fucking tool. And do me a favor."

"What?"

He lifted his hands to frame her face. "Don't compare me to Derek."

"Okay," she managed before his lips claimed hers, soft and sweet. She rose to deepen the contact, gripping his wrists as she opened her mouth for his tongue.

He chuckled, muffled against her mouth, and lifted his head to whisper, "You have to redo your laundry."

"I'll buy new clothes," she whispered back and was reaching for him again when a shrill whistle split the air.

She jerked back, startled. "What the hell was that?"

"Sorry." He pulled his phone out of his pocket. "It's the only ringtone I can hear over some of the machines in the shop."

"Jesus." She rubbed her hand over her racing heart. "It's a good thing I don't have a heart condition."

"It's Wyatt." He tapped the screen to answer and spoke into the phone. "Hang on a minute, Wy."

He lowered the phone and dropped a quick kiss on her mouth. "I'll see you Thursday."

"Okay," she said and raised her voice to be heard through the phone. "Hi, Wyatt. Thanks for the cock block."

Shane raised the phone to his ear, chuckling as he walked toward the bedroom door. "Yeah, that was Veronica. Uh-huh. No. Not happening, Wyatt."

"What's not happening?" she called after him.

"He wanted me to tell you that he'd be happy to come over and be my stand-in."

"Oh my God, he's worse than Delia."

"See you later." He shot her a wink, then walked out the door.

She laid back against her pillow, sighing when she heard the front door shut behind him. She was all worked up now, that kiss having lit a fire in her belly, and the next time she saw him she'd be on her period and in no mood to be touched.

"At least he's bringing snacks," she muttered and rose to go deal with her stinky, mildewed laundry.

"So, let me get this straight," Delia said. "You sent him a picture, he brought dinner, you told him you thought having a threesome with he and Wyatt would be hot, then you fucked like bunnies."

Veronica turned to pull a glass from the cabinet. "That's pretty much the gist, yeah."

"Then he asked you on a date, and when you told him you'd be on your period, he not only didn't cancel but offered to bring your go-to period snacks."

"Yes."

Delia reached for the plate of brownies on the counter. "That might be the most romantic thing I've ever heard."

"I know." Veronica opened the refrigerator. "Is this freshly squeezed orange juice?"

"Uh-huh. Cora made it this morning."

Veronica pulled the pitcher out. "I love your cook."

"Me, too. She made these brownies, and they're so good. You sure you don't want one?"

"If you had any non-THC ones, I would." Veronica

returned the pitcher to the fridge and resumed her seat at the breakfast bar. "I thought she always made a straight batch for Julian."

"He took them to work."

Veronica pursed her lips. "You ever wonder what would happen if he took your plate into the office by mistake and accidentally drugged all his interns?"

Delia pointed a finger at her. "Don't even think it. Julian's paranoid enough as it is."

Veronica snorted into her juice. "And he's the sober one."

Delia broke off another bite of brownie and popped it in her mouth. "Go back to the threesome. Was that just sexy talk, or are you going to do it?"

"It might not be just sexy talk." Veronica bit her lip. "Is it a terrible idea?"

"Are you kidding? It's a fantastic idea."

"What if it screws things up?"

"Like what?"

"I don't even know what Shane and I are doing at this point," Veronica pointed out. "Are we dating? Still just fucking? And there's Shane and Wyatt's relationship to consider, too."

"Shane and Wyatt have been together a long time, I'm sure they've survived bigger trials than your pussy."

"Thank you so much."

"I'm guessing," Delia said with a small grin. "I mean, I've never personally experienced your pussy. Maybe it's a huge trial."

"Why am I even friends with you?" Veronica wondered out loud.

"Look, if you want to do this," Delia began, then paused. "Do you want to do this, or is it just a hot fantasy?"

"I think I want to do it."

"I'm so jealous of your life," Delia sighed.

"Delia. Be helpful."

"Okay, fine. I think the first thing you do is talk to Shane," Delia said. "Tell him you're worried about how it will impact all of you, get his take on that, and go from there. He's the one who's done it before, right?"

"Yeah."

"Then, start there. If he's on board, and so is Wyatt—" She paused. "I assume Wyatt is on board?"

"He's made it clear he'd be happy to be naked with me at some point, yes."

"Okay, then talk to Shane. Preferably when you're unlikely to wind up screwing like rabbits again."

"You mean like when I'm on my period and already said I don't want to fuck?"

"Exactly. Then call me after and tell me how it goes."

"This is all very complicated," Veronica sighed.

"Agreed." Delia nodded soberly. "It makes me sort of glad I had my threesome in my drunken college days. Way less talking."

"But more vomiting," Veronica reminded her.

"Yeah. That was a definite drawback." Delia shuddered at the memory, then dug out her phone. "Let's order food. My brownies are kicking in, and I want something with a lot of bacon. And maybe cheese curds."

"Oh, goodie," Veronica muttered and made a mental note to pick up some antacids on the way home.

Veronica got home from work Thursday night ten minutes before Shane was due to arrive. He showed up right on time with a grocery back full of pretzels, three kinds of salt and vinegar chips, and the biggest chocolate bar she'd ever seen. He greeted her with a kiss—this one with less *hey, wanna get naked* than she was used to from him, but she figured that was due to her sex moratorium.

He cued up a movie—she let him pick since he had far more limits than she—while she changed into yoga pants and her favorite comfy sweatshirt. They settled on her sofa surrounded by snacks and watched what she was sure was going to be a dud of a movie.

Three hours later, her sides hurt from laughing so hard.

"That was funny," she said, digging in the bottom of the bag of chips.

"I thought you'd like it."

She smiled at him. "Who knew a movie with Bad Moms as a title would be so awesome?"

"There's a sequel," he told her. "Bad Moms Christmas."

"Oh, awesome. Cue it up, I'll be right back. Do you want anything?"

"A glass of water would be great, thanks."

She made a quick trip to the bathroom, taking a moment to freshen her lip gloss, then headed back out. She detoured to the kitchen for a glass of water, intrigued when she heard the low murmur of his voice. When she emerged a few minutes later with a glass of water, he was just slipping his phone back into his pocket.

"Everything okay?" she asked, handing him the water.

"Yeah. That was Wyatt."

"Oh." She curled up next to him on the couch. "How is he?"

"He's good. He says hi."

"He's sweet." She settled against the pillows and reached for the bag of chips. "So listen, speaking of Wyatt…"

He frowned when she trailed off. "Is something wrong?"

"Oh, no, nothing's wrong," she assured him, her fingers clenching on the chip bag and making it crinkle.

He leaned forward to set his glass on the table, then turned to face her. "Then what's up?"

"Well, it's like this." She blew out a breath, sucked in another, and pushed the words out. "I think I want to have a threesome with you and Wyatt."

The rest of her breath left in a whoosh, leaving her feeling lightheaded and a little nauseated. But that was probably because he was looking at her like her head had turned into cabbage. Which was sort of what it felt like.

"This is the part where you say something," she finally told him.

"It's not inspiring me with a lot of confidence that you had to say that like you were chugging cough medicine."

Her cheeks went hot. "I know. Sorry. Nervous."

"Why are you nervous?"

She forced herself not to get defensive. He wasn't mocking her, or even mad. He was just asking. She sucked in another deep breath. "I'm not sure."

"I know the idea is a turn-on, but it's okay to let it stay a fantasy, you know."

He said it gently and with such a lack of judgment that she relaxed. Whatever she told him would be okay, she realized, and just like that her nerves disappeared.

"I know," she said, her voice considerably calmer. "But I think I want to do it. I mean, if you guys do."

SHANE BIT BACK A SMILE—HE didn't want her to think he was laughing at her. But she was so damn cute, all wide-eyed and earnest, her lower lip caught between her teeth and her cheeks still pink with embarrassment.

She'd spat out the words "I want to have a threesome" like they were poison, but now that she'd gotten them out, she was much calmer. Oh, there were still nerves, but they were mostly the good kind. Anticipation, excitement, a hint of uncertainty.

He had nerves of his own—and some complicated feelings he didn't care to examine at the moment—so he shoved them aside to focus on the topic at hand.

"Were you nervous to tell me you wanted a threesome, or are you nervous about having it?" he asked.

"Um. Both?"

"Why are you nervous about having it?"

She sucked in another deep breath, pushing her tits against the front of her sweatshirt. She wasn't wearing a bra, and whatever she had under her sweatshirt wasn't nearly restrictive enough to disguise that fact. It took a disconcerting amount of effort to keep his eyes on her face.

"Because I've never done anything like this before," she told him. "I have no idea how to go about it. And…"

"And?" he prompted.

"I don't want to screw things up."

Ah. "Screw things up how?"

"With you and me," she elaborated, nerves tightening in her voice. "I mean, we just started doing…whatever it is we're doing…"

He bit back a smile.

"…and I still don't fully understand how your particular brand of non-monogamy works, and I don't want to get between you and Wyatt either. I know how important he is to you, and I don't want to accidentally cross a line—"

He held up a hand, and she closed her mouth with a snap. "Okay, let me see if I've got this right. You don't know the etiquette, and you want to make sure you don't mess anything up for anyone. Is that right?"

She nodded so hard her hair flew in her face and stuck to her lip gloss. "Yes."

He reached out to gently pull her hair away from her lips.

"Okay, then. First, there is no threesome etiquette, not like you're thinking. It's whatever the three of us want, and anything we don't want is out. Clear?"

"Okay."

"Second. Wyatt and I have been together for a long time. You're not going to screw us up."

"But—"

He laid a gentle finger against her lips. "You're not. Trust me, okay?"

"Okay," she said, her lips moving against his finger.

He dropped his hand so he wouldn't get distracted. "I have some questions for you."

She nodded. "Okay."

"Are you attracted to Wyatt?"

Her blush came roaring back, but she answered easily enough. "Yes."

"How attracted?"

"Um. I don't know how to answer that."

"Does he make your pussy wet?" he asked bluntly.

"Oh. Yeah. He did."

Her blush had taken over her entire face, turning it tomato red, and he found it both endearing and charming. "When?"

"When you were throwing Derek out of the hotel. And later that night, on the beach."

His brows rose slightly. "Did he kiss you?"

"Yes. Just a little one." She blew out a breath. "That time."

"There was more than one?"

"Well, we had a talk on our last day, about maybe doing the threesome thing, and that kiss was not a little one."

He should've known. "Mind if I call him?"

Her eyes bugged out. "Now?"

He reached into his pocket for his phone. "I feel like he needs to be in on the rest of this conversation."

"Okay." She wiped her palms on her thighs, her eyes still

wide as saucers. "If I pass out from lack of oxygen, just throw a glass of water on my face."

He pulled up Wyatt's number and put the phone on speaker. "How about you just remember to breathe?"

"Easier said than done," she muttered as the phone began to ring.

He was chuckling when the ringing cut off and Wyatt's voice boomed out of the phone. "Hey, lover. Is your date over already?"

"Nope. It has taken an interesting turn, though. You're on speaker, Wyatt, so say hi to Veronica."

"Hi, Veronica," Wyatt parroted, and his voice went distinctly flirty. "How's your evening going? Is our guy taking care of you?"

"He is," she said, and though she jolted a bit when Wyatt said "our guy", she met Shane's eyes with a smile. "He brought me chocolate and potato chips and he's letting me use him as a pillow."

"Good," came the reply. "If he's not treating you right, tell me and I'll kick his ass."

"Um. Okay."

"Now, what can I do for you two love birds this evening? Need a movie recommendation?"

"No, we've got that covered," Shane put in. "I thought we should have a conversation, though, since Veronica's decided she'd like to have a threesome."

"Did she now?" Wyatt's voice had dropped to a low purr, and Shane was fascinated by Veronica's reaction to it.

Her pupils dilated, her upper chest flushed, and she squirmed like her panties were on fire.

"She has some reservations, so I thought we should all talk it out."

"He's such a planner," Wyatt said with a chuckle. "Veronica, you been fantasizing again?"

Again? Shane lifted a brow, and Veronica flushed darker.

"I don't think I ever stopped," she replied, her eyes locked on Shane as Wyatt's low laugh filled the room.

"I was hoping you'd say that. I've been fantasizing, too. About all the beautiful, filthy things the three of us can do to each other."

Shane chuckled as Veronica's eyes went hazy. "She's kind of gun-shy, Wyatt. She's never done anything like this before."

"God, I love virgins," Wyatt sighed. "What's the big fear, darling?"

"Other than making a fool of myself?" she said drily, and Shane was relieved to see the humor in her eyes.

"Not possible, sweetness," Wyatt promptly returned.

"I guess I'm mostly afraid of doing something wrong, or somehow messing us all up."

"Also not possible," Wyatt said, his voice deadly serious. "There's no wrong, here, Veronica. Shane and I, we're there to make you feel good. If something doesn't feel good, then we stop. It's as simple as that."

Her wide hazel eyes met Shane's. "What about making each other feel good?"

"Oh, yeah, we can do that," Wyatt said, back to purring. "If that's what you want to happen."

"I think that's what I want to happen most of all," she confessed.

"Shane, I think I love this woman," Wyatt declared, and Veronica laughed.

"Wyatt, I'm going to hang up so I can work out some details with Veronica," Shane said, his eyes on hers. "I'll call you later."

"Aw, you're kicking me out?" There was a heavy sigh, then, "All right, love. Keep me posted. Veronica?"

"Yes?"

"I'm looking forward to seeing you again."

She was blushing again. "Me, too."

"Night, darling."

Shane kept his eyes on hers as he pocketed the phone. "Was that okay?"

She blew out a breath. "Yeah, but now I have cramps *and* I'm horny."

He burst out laughing. "Sorry. You brought it up."

"I know. I thought I'd be safe." She sent him a tentative smile. "We have to work out the details?"

"Not now," he said and chuckled when her face fell. "What I want you to do is think about all the things you think you might like, and make a list. Then think about all the things you might not like, and make another list. Then email them to me."

Her brows rose. "Email them to you?"

"With our schedules, it'll be faster. And you might find some things easier to say in writing."

"Good point," she muttered, going pink again, and he laughed.

"Come here," he said, dragging her to his side. He pressed a soft kiss to her mouth. "Thank you."

Her eyes were soft again, and she was smiling up at him dreamily. "For what?"

"For trusting me." He kissed her again, breaking the contact far sooner than he'd have liked, and picked up the remote. "Ready for the movie?"

He felt her disappointed sigh in his bones. "Sure."

He pressed 'play' and she curled up next to him. She was adorable and sexy and if she hadn't already taken sex off the table, he would've pointed out that he didn't mind period sex at all. But she had, so he ignored his unruly libido and hugged her to his side, laughing at the movie with her. When it was over, he kissed her goodnight and walked out the door, then went home to take a very cold shower.

"So tell me." Delia sucked noisily at her straw, slurping up the milkshake in the bottom of the glass. "When is this threesome happening?"

"I'm not sure," Veronica said. "I think next Saturday, but that's if Wyatt can find someone to cover his shift at the hospital. Sunday might also work, but Shane has an art fair he's supposed to vend at in Mt. Pleasant."

"Who knew scheduling an orgy would be so complicated?" Delia set her empty glass aside and looked around the diner. "Where's our waitress? I'm hungry."

"We ordered less than ten minutes ago," Veronica reminded her.

"Right. Hey, did you ask them if you could film it?"

"No," Veronica said firmly and stifled a laugh at Delia's crestfallen face. "And don't you ask, either."

Delia gave an exaggerated sigh. "You're such a buzz kill."

"I have enough on my mind about without factoring your buzz into the equation," Veronica muttered.

"Are you nervous?"

"Yeah, but it's an excited kind of nervous. And Shane's been really reassuring."

"You two have been seeing each other a lot."

"When our schedules mesh. Which isn't often," Veronica continued. "He works most weekends, going to fairs and festivals, and I've been putting in a lot of long hours."

"It's good, though?"

"Work? It's great. I'm hoping they're going to offer me a job when my CF is done."

"That's nice, but I meant you and Shane."

"Oh." Veronica smiled. "Yeah, it's good."

"Look at that dreamy smile," Delia chortled. "You're falling in love with him, aren't you?"

"I don't know," Veronica replied and did her best to erase the dreamy smile. "It's barely been a month."

"More than, if you count Bermuda."

"Bermuda was just sex," Veronica began, and Delia snorted. "It *was*. It wasn't until we got back that things started getting...complicated."

"With *feeeeeelings*," Delia sang.

"You're such a pain in the ass."

"Tell me I'm wrong."

Veronica sighed. "You're not wrong."

Delia nodded sagely. "Yep. Feelings complicate everything. How're you doing with the poly stuff?"

Veronica frowned. "I hate it when you say it that way. I can't put my finger on why, but it just sounds wrong."

"Forgive me, I'm high. And seriously, where is the waitress? I'm *starving*."

"Here." Veronica shoved her glass across the table. "Drink my milkshake, and try to act right."

Delia peered into the glass with a frown. "Why'd you get cherry?"

Veronica sighed. "I can't remember why we're friends."

"It's okay. I can live with the cherry." There was a loud slurp as Delia demonstrated her flexibility. "Where were we?"

"Feelings."

"Right." Lips pursed around the straw, Delia nodded thoughtfully. "You said before that Shane having another partner didn't bother you. Still true?"

"I think so. I don't feel jealous when he has plans with Wyatt, or talks about him."

"You got a bunch of books on polyamory, right?" Delia swirled the straw in the milkshake. "Have they been helpful?"

"Yeah." Veronica propped her chin on her hand. "A lot of the advice doesn't apply to me, at least right now, but I can see it being helpful down the line. Oh, and I found a support group."

Delia blinked. "A support group? For polyamorous couples? Thrupples? Foursomes and moresomes?"

"How about 'people'?"

Delia's brow furrowed in thought, then she shook her head. "Not as catchy."

"Anyway," Veronica said with exaggerated patience. "I went to my first meeting last night."

"Was it like AA, but for monogamy?"

"For God's sake, Delia."

"I thought that was funny," Delia protested, then shrugged. "Anyway, how'd it go? Did you share?"

"It was good, and yeah. I explained that I was just starting to see someone who is poly and has a current partner, and everybody was super supportive. They gave me some blogs and podcasts to check out, and a couple more books."

"Awesome. Did you mention the threesome?"

"No." Veronica winced. "The focus is really on relationships, so I felt weird bringing up sex. Besides, a lot of people seem to have kind of a trigger about it."

"What? Why?"

"Because that's always where everybody's mind goes whenever polyamory comes up. 'Ooh, you get to have orgies'. I get the feeling it rubs them the wrong way."

"Rub. Heh."

"Delia."

"Oh, come on. That was funny."

"You're a disaster," Veronica told her, then looked up as the waitress arrived, her tray overflowing with seven plates of food for Delia and Veronica's cheeseburger.

"Oh yay, food!" Delia cried, clapping her hands as the waitress began to unload.

"Thank God," Veronica said. "Quick, shove something in your mouth and stop talking."

Delia grinned and popped a tater tot into her mouth. "You love me."

"I do, but you're still a fucking disaster."

"Are you sure you can't film this?" Delia asked, swiping a finger through the whipped cream on a slice of key lime pie.

"I really need a new best friend," Veronica sighed and bit into her cheeseburger.

Fifteen

The following Saturday Veronica found herself in Shane's house with a glass of wine, two sexy men, and a big fat case of nerves.

She listened to Shane talk about the technique he used for the bookshelves he'd added to his basement library, not really hearing any of it, sipping her wine and wishing they could just move past the chit-chat and get on with it so she could stop freaking out. Then she realized he'd stopped talking a while ago, and both men were staring at her.

"Sorry." She winced. "Shit. Um."

Wyatt's lips were curled up in a smile, but his eyes were kind. "You're just about ready to jump out of your skin, aren't you?"

"Is it that obvious?"

"Yeah," he said bluntly.

It surprised a laugh out of her, and she felt herself relax just a little. "Sorry."

Shane shook his head, sending his hair dancing. He'd left it down, and it had grown a bit, almost past his shoulders. "I'm sorry. I thought taking it slow would help you relax."

"I know. And I appreciate it." Screwing up her courage, she sucked in a deep breath. "But I'm too nervous and too horny to wait any longer, so if you don't want to explain to the paramedics why some woman collapsed from a hormone-induced panic attack, you'll take me to bed and fuck my brains out."

Both men stared at her, their faces frozen, and for one horrible moment she was afraid she'd wrecked the whole thing. Then Wyatt began to laugh, and a slow grin split Shane's beard.

"Shane, I really love this woman," Wyatt said, his blue eyes dancing as he reached out to grab her hand. "Come on, beautiful. You haven't seen the bedroom yet."

Shane took her wine glass. "Go on. I'll be right there."

"Okay," she said and allowed Wyatt to tow her out of the room.

"You're going to love this room," Wyatt told her, leading her down the hall. "Shane made the bed himself, and it's awesome."

"I'm sure it is," she began, then they turned the corner into the room and she stopped dead. "Oh, wow."

"I know, right?"

She stared at it, momentarily struck speechless. "He did all of this himself?"

Wyatt nodded, his hand resting lightly on her waist. "He used a standard bed frame for the base, but the rest of it is all him."

"I knew he was talented." She lifted a hand to stroke the bedpost, the finish smooth as glass under her fingertips. "I've seen Delia's sideboard. But this is...wow."

It was art. The light streaming in the windows bounced off the gleaming wood, making it glow a deep reddish-brown. The headboard was high and intricately carved, as was the footboard. The posts at the four corners were nearly as thick as her thigh at the base, then grew progressively narrower as they rose up. They stopped a few inches from the ceiling, narrow and impossibly delicate, and each topped with a small carving.

She squinted at the one in front of her. "Is that...a frog?"

"Yeah." Wyatt chuckled. "There's a frog, a piglet, an otter, and a hedgehog."

"Oh my god, this is *amazing*," she breathed and walked toward the headboard to see the hedgehog better.

Shane walked into the room. "What's awesome?"

"She likes the bed," Wyatt said.

"That's good," Shane said mildly, and she glanced over her shoulder at him. "She's going to be spending a lot of time in it."

Nerves, forgotten while she'd been absorbed with the carvings, came roaring back. She nibbled on her lower lip as Shane walked towards her. "Am I?"

He stopped in front of her. "If that's what you still want."

She smiled, some of the knots in her belly smoothing away. Of course, he would ask. He would *need* to ask, when so many men in his position would assume or cajole or ignore her trepidation outright. He always checked in with her, always made sure she was okay and comfortable whenever they did something new, and she hadn't realized until just this moment how much she treasured that.

"It is," she told him. "I want you. I want this."

"I'm over here," Wyatt called out lightly, waving his hand as though to get her attention, and the last of her nerves died in laughter.

"Well, why are you over there when we're over here?" she asked, and giggled when he hurried over to stand behind her.

Shane smiled down at her, dark eyes reassuring. "We've been here before, haven't we?"

They were in the same positions they'd been in the little

hotel conference room in Bermuda she realized. Shane in front of her, Wyatt behind. "Minus the shitty ex-boyfriend."

"Thank God," Wyatt rumbled out, his chest brushing against her back and making her shiver.

"I wanted to kiss you then," Shane told her.

"I know," she whispered.

"I wanted to fuck you then," Wyatt said and Shane rolled his eyes.

"Let's start with a kiss," he said and lowered his head.

Veronica let her eyes drift shut as his mouth brushed over hers gently, once, twice, then trailed down to her jaw.

"That's where you wanted to kiss me?" she sighed.

"I wanted to kiss you everywhere." His teeth scraped along her jawline, making her shiver again, then drifted lower.

Veronica let her head fall back as desire swam lazily through her blood. "Mmm, there."

"Here?" Shane murmured, his teeth nibbling down the cord in her neck.

"Or here?" Wyatt asked, his mouth trailing down her neck on the other side.

"Yes," Veronica sighed, and Wyatt gave a low laugh.

"She likes it," he said to Shane, and Shane's lips curved against her neck.

"I know." He lifted his head to pin her with those dark, dangerous eyes. "Tell Wyatt what else you like, Veronica."

"What do you mean?" she asked, then gasped when Wyatt used his teeth on her neck.

"I want to know what makes you feel good," Wyatt explained, his voice a low murmur in her ear. "I want you to tell me what makes you hot."

"Um." She kept her eyes on Shane, the anchor in her shaky world. "You're doing just fine."

Wyatt chuckled. "Not good enough, sweet stuff. You know how chatty Shane is in bed?"

"Yeah."

"That's what I want." His tongue danced over the shell of her ear. "Tell me how it feels, what it does to you, when you want more, when you want less. I want to hear everything you're feeling."

She gave a breathless moan and reached up and back to thread her fingers through his hair, tilting her head to give him better access. "Keep doing that."

"Just like that, beautiful," he murmured. "Can I touch you, Veronica?"

"Yes, please." She held her breath when he slipped his hands around her from behind. They closed gently over her breasts, his thumbs scraping over her nipples through her dress. She pushed herself into his hands, her eyes still locked on Shane as pleasure bloomed. "Harder," she told Wyatt, her voice thick with lust. "Squeeze them harder."

"Like this?" he asked, his hands tightening.

"Harder," she said again, and her guttural groan as he obeyed reverberated throughout the room.

"Fuck, I love these tits," he told her, squeezing and kneading with a firm, almost harsh touch that had her fingers tightening in his hair. "I've been fantasizing about getting my dick between them for weeks."

"Really?" she gasped, her eyes drifting shut as pleasure swirled.

"Oh yeah." He shifted his hands to push her breasts together. "Look at that. That's prime titty fucking territory right there. Don't you agree, Shane?"

"Yeah," Shane rumbled, and Veronica forced her eyes open.

He stood in front of her, his hands light on her hips. His body was relaxed, his breathing even, but the blazing fire in his gaze made her pussy clench.

"Come closer," she said and hooked her free hand in his waistband and yanked him into her.

He pressed his body against hers, trapping Wyatt's hands on her breasts and grinding his erection into her belly. "Oh," she said breathlessly, pushing against that delightful ridge of flesh. "You're so hard."

"You're so hot," he replied and kissed her again.

She moaned into his mouth, heat pooling in her belly as Wyatt squeezed her breasts, licked her ear, and pushed his hips into her from behind. She had hard cocks against her belly and ass, and the sheer carnal delight of it all was nearly overwhelming.

She tore her mouth from Shane's, her breath coming in pants, and stared at him. "Shane."

"What, baby?" His hands tightened on her hips, a delicious little pinch of pain nearly lost in the sea of pleasure.

"Will you kiss Wyatt?" she asked.

Wyatt lifted his head, his groan of approval sounding in her ear. "You want to see him kiss me, Veronica? You want to watch?"

"Yes." She said it as clearly as she could, looking right at Shane so he wouldn't have any doubt. His gaze held hers for a heartbeat, blazing heat in his velvety eyes, then they shifted to look over her shoulder.

"Come here, love," he commanded, one of his big hands reaching out to tangle with hers in Wyatt's sun-streaked hair. Veronica watched, fascinated and aroused, as they came together.

Twin moans filled the air, and Veronica caught her breath at the sheer beauty of it.

She was close enough to see Shane glide his tongue along Wyatt's lower lip, as he so often did with her. Close enough to hear the guttural groan that rumbled up in Shane's chest, to feel Wyatt's hands tighten on her breasts.

It was the hottest thing she'd ever seen.

Wyatt broke free with a soft laugh and turned to her, heat simmering in his blue eyes. "We're just getting started, sweetheart," he said and she realized she'd said it out loud.

Shane rumbled an agreement, one hand still curled in Wyatt's hair, the other clamped onto her hip. "Tell us what you want, Veronica. Tell us, and we'll do it."

She licked her lips. "I want the two of you naked."

Shane's beard twitched with his smile. "You first."

He reached for the hem of her dress, lifting it slowly, his eyes locked on hers. Wyatt's hands slid down to her waist as the dress moved up, his fingertips tracing the line of lace across her belly as Shane pulled the dress over her head.

"So pretty," he murmured, tracing the soft skin of her breast above the white lace of the bra.

"You should see this angle," Wyatt told him. His hands stroked up her thighs to the cheeks of her ass, bared by the thong that matched the bra. "Fuck, this ass."

Shane's mouth curved in a smile. "Wyatt's an ass man," he told Veronica, his fingers continuing to glide over skin now peppered with goosebumps.

"So, it's a good thing I let Delia talk me into the thong?" she asked, shivering, and Wyatt laughed.

"Remind me to send her a thank you note." His hands squeezed her cheeks, and she gasped. "Oh, you like a rough squeeze here, too, don't you?"

"Grab her cheeks hard and pull them apart," Shane told him, his eyes still locked on Veronica's, his hands on her breasts. "She likes that."

"Yeah?" Wyatt shifted his grip slightly and squeezed again, pulling her buttocks apart this time, stretching all those delicate tissues in between. She shuddered between them, desire rising like the tide.

Wyatt's soft laugh tickled her neck. "You smell that?"

He leaned forward so his mouth brushed her ear. "I can smell your pussy, Veronica," he whispered. "I can smell how hot you are."

She swallowed hard. "You guys are so good at this."

Shane's grin was a wicked slash. "Baby, you ain't seen nothing yet. Let's get her naked, Wyatt."

He deftly unhooked her bra, sliding it down her arms and tossing it aside. Her breasts bounced free into his hands, calloused fingers scraping as he squeezed, lighting a thousand little fires. Cool air washed against her wet, heated sex as her panties slid down her legs, and then Wyatt's hand was there, cupping her, one smooth finger slipping boldly through her slick lips to slide deep inside her.

She wrapped her hands around Shane's forearm, her nails digging into firm muscle as pleasure sang through her. "Oh, God."

"What's he doing, Veronica?" Shane asked. His eyes were dark, his mouth wet from hers and Wyatt's. "Tell me what he's doing to you."

"He's fucking me with his finger," she managed as Wyatt's finger slid slowly outward before pushing back in again.

"She wet, Wy?"

"Oh, yeah." He pumped once, twice more, then pulled his hand free and held it up between them for Shane to see. "Look at all that honey."

"Mmm," Shane rumbled, and keeping his eyes on hers, leaned forward and sucked Wyatt's finger, gleaming wet from her pussy, into his mouth.

"How's she taste?" Wyatt asked as Shane sucked and Veronica's knees slowly turned to water.

Shane released Wyatt's finger with a long, languorous lick. "Delicious. You should try it."

Gentle fingers, one of them still wet, grasped her chin and turned her to face Wyatt. She had to blink the haze of lust from her eyes to bring him into focus, that pretty face with its halo of tawny hair and piercing blue eyes.

"I want to bury my face in your pussy, Veronica," he said, caressing her face. She could smell herself on him. "Slide my tongue in there and lap you up like dessert."

"Okay," she said faintly, and both men laughed, rumbles of delight that made her feel aglow with pleasure.

"How do you want her?" Shane asked.

Wyatt released her and stepped back. "On my face."

Veronica's eyes widened, lust tightening her core as Wyatt stripped out of his clothes and tossed them to the side. Then he was climbing up onto the big bed to lie across it, parallel to the headboard. His golden skin gleamed, his hard penis curving toward his abdomen. He beckoned her closer, licking his lips in anticipation. "Come here, beautiful."

She glanced at Shane. He was naked too, one big hand wrapped around his dick, the piercings bright against the ruddy flesh. He cocked a brow and stepped closer, his arm sliding around her waist as he bent to whisper in her ear. "Still with us?"

She sank against him, his body warm and hard and comforting even as it aroused. She twisted her head around so she could see his eyes, the heat and the lust and the softness deep within. "I'm with you."

He kissed her, sweetly at first then deeper, making her moan when he curled his tongue around hers and stroked the way she liked, the way she knew he'd stroke with his dick, sure and steady and with utter delight.

She was panting when he broke the kiss and smiled at her. "Go sit on my boyfriend's face, Veronica."

She laughed and he nudged her toward the bed, where Wyatt waited with a fist around his dick and a sexy grin.

"You guys are hot when you make out," he observed, stroking himself lazily. "I could watch that all day."

"I know the feeling," she quipped, remembering how she felt watching the two men kiss.

"I like to watch, too," Shane said, and they both looked at him. He jerked his chin at the bed, a wicked grin curling his lips. "And right now, I want to watch you fuck Wyatt's face."

She climbed onto the bed by Wyatt's hip, then bit her lip when she realized with the way he was positioned, she'd have nothing to hold onto. "Can you move so your head is by the headboard?"

"Uh-uh." Shane took her hand and gave a tug, holding onto her as she knee-walked her way toward the edge of the mattress, and Wyatt's head. "I like this position."

"I won't have anything to hold onto," she protested.

"I'll hold you up," he promised. He slid his hands to her hips and lifted, positioning her so she faced away from him, her knees on either side of Wyatt's head.

"Fuck, yeah," Wyatt rumbled, his breath washing over the needy, greedy flesh between her thighs. He reached for her, long arms and big hands enabling him to reach back to palm her ass as he pulled her down.

"I've got you," Shane said from behind her and wrapped an arm around her ribs just as Wyatt's tongue slithered over her pussy.

Her sharp gasp mingled with Wyatt's muttered, "Oh, hell yeah."

"Feel good?" Shane asked, his voice low and wicked.

"Yes," she panted.

"Tell him." Shane stepped closer, his hard chest against her back keeping her upright. "Tell him how it feels. He wants to hear, remember? Tell him."

"It feels so good," she groaned, grinding herself against Wyatt's face. She was so aroused, so primed that she knew it wouldn't take much to shove her over the edge.

"Tell him."

"Lick my pussy, Wyatt," she panted, getting into the dirty talk as the pleasure built. "Fuck it with your tongue, suck on it, fucking make me come."

Wyatt growled, his hands tightening on the cheeks of her ass and spreading them out, and she moaned.

"Oh yes, spread my ass. Pull it hard," she commanded, jerking when he complied, only Shane's hard arms around her keeping her from toppling forward. "Just like that, yes, just like that."

She closed her eyes and pumped her hips, the pressure building in her belly, tightening her thighs. He licked and nipped and sucked and fucked her with his tongue, almost frantic as she rode him harder, faster. Seeking more pressure, more contact, she angled her hips, and the action pulled her slightly away from Shane.

"What do you need, baby?"

"I gotta lean forward," she gasped, straining against his hold, relieved when he eased her down so she could plant her hands on the mattress on either side of Wyatt. The new angle put his tongue exactly where she needed it, and she rode it shamelessly.

"Yes, just like that," she chanted, breathless now as she chased the orgasm. "Don't move, don't move, don't move."

"Fuck, you look hot," Shane grunted, and she dimly heard the crinkle of plastic behind her, the snap of latex. She jolted when he brushed against her, firm and hot even through the barrier of the condom.

"Yes, yes, yes," she hissed spreading her thighs wider and grinding against Wyatt's tongue. "Fuck me, Shane."

"Spread her wide for me, Wyatt," Shane grunted, and Wyatt's hands clamped down on her ass and pulled, stretching and opening her up and it brought the orgasm rushing toward her like a freight train that hit just as Shane pushed deep.

Her scream filled the air and she convulsed, her pussy

clenching around Shane's cock and against Wyatt's mouth, incredible pleasure flowing through her like an electrical current, burning and bright. She shook so hard her arms threatened to collapse, only Shane's hands and Wyatt's mouth keeping her in place.

"Oh god, oh fuck, oh god," she chanted. Her orgasm was fading, the familiar lethargy stealing through her, but Wyatt was still licking and Shane was still fucking and incredibly, she felt the tension begin to gather again.

"You going to come again, baby?" Shane rumbled. His hand stroked up her back to tangle in her hair and tug her head up. "You got another one in you?"

"I don't...I don't know." Wyatt flicked his tongue against her clit and she flinched, overly sensitive now, and Shane felt it.

He stilled for a moment, holding himself inside her, then wrapped an arm around her torso. "Wy. Back out."

Wyatt wiggled out from underneath her, emerging disheveled and glassy-eyed, his face wet from his hair to his chin and a giddy grin on his face.

"That was fucking hot," he declared, and not bothering to wipe his face, leaned forward to kiss her as Shane resumed thrusting.

She tasted herself on his tongue, musky and sweet. He was laughing when he kissed her, happiness and joy radiating from him so strongly that when he pulled away, she couldn't help but grin in return.

"Shit." Breathing hard, he sat back on his haunches in front of her, his dick hard and his eyes locked on her swaying breasts as Shane continued to push into her from behind. "I gotta catch my breath."

"Sorry," she managed, shaking as Shane picked up speed and the pleasure began to wind through her again. "I got kind of...carried away...at the end."

"Baby, you can sit on my face anytime," he told her.

"Eating that beautiful pussy while Shane fucked you was the hottest thing I've ever done."

Shane's laugh rumbled in her ear. "That's high praise, babe."

Veronica's eyes were locked onto Wyatt's dick. He'd wrapped a hand around it, stroking almost absently. "I'd offer to take care of that for you," she panted, "but I'm afraid I might bite you."

"I have another idea, if you're game."

"Okay," she said, willing to play.

"Atta girl," he praised, then glanced around. "Where'd that bag go?"

"Fell on the floor," Shane answered, and Wyatt slipped off the bed.

"How're you doing, baby?" Shane asked.

"I'm good," she sighed. She reached back, wanting to touch. Her arms wrapped around his legs to sink her nails into his ass. "You feel so good inside me."

"You feel so good around me." He nipped at the side of her neck, making her shiver and clench around his slowly thrusting dick. "Hot and tight and so goddamn wet."

He picked up speed, stealing her breath and making her breasts bounce. He lifted them, squeezing and kneading hard so she arched into his hands. She closed her eyes, wanting to concentrate on the feelings coursing through her, then opened again when the mattress shifted.

Wyatt knelt in front of her, the bottle of lubricant in one hand and his slick and shiny cock in the other.

"Give me some," Shane said, holding out a hand, and Wyatt extended the bottle and pumped some into his hand.

"Pump bottle lube?" she asked, shuddering as Shane pulled free. "That's convenient."

Wyatt grinned. "Handy, isn't it?"

Shane slipped back into her, the lube allowing him to glide

easily through swollen tissues, and she sighed happily. "I love lube."

Shane chuckled again. "Good thing, 'cause I see where Wyatt's going with that thing."

She blinked, refocusing on Wyatt's now very slick cock. "I thought that was for you."

"Uh-uh," Wyatt said with a wink. "This is for you."

"You remember I said no butt stuff, right?"

"We remember," Wyatt said cheerfully as Shane pulled her closer. "That's not where this is going."

"Then what...?" she began, then Wyatt laid down on the mattress in front of her, his feet sliding between her spread legs as he wiggled into place.

"Bend back down," Wyatt instructed, and she obeyed, Shane's hands holding her steady until she could brace herself on her hands. "Keep coming down."

"I'm going to be lying on you if I come down any further," she said, confused. He wasn't positioned right for her to take him in her mouth, and she wouldn't have needed lube for that, anyway.

"That's the point," he told her, urging her down onto her elbows, and she began to laugh when she realized where he was leading her.

"You seriously want to do this?" she asked, her breasts plumped against his thighs.

"Fuck, yes." He scooted down a little further. "There, that's good. Oh, yeah."

She stifled a giggle when he reached for her breasts, lifting them slightly and squishing them together around his shaft. He was slick with the lube, but he must not have thought he'd gotten enough, because he picked up the bottle and pumped a couple of shots directly into her cleavage.

"Cold," she gasped.

"Sorry." He shifted his grip so he held the sides of her

breasts, pressing them around his slick length. She looked down and realized she could see the ruddy tip peeking out from between her breasts, and this time the giggle burst free.

"Okay." Wyatt nodded at Shane, who'd remained still while they'd been getting into position. "I think we're set."

"What am I supposed to do?" Veronica asked, confused as to how this was supposed to work.

"Just relax," Shane advised. "We'll do the work."

He tightened his grip on her hips, pushing her so she rocked forward on her elbows. Wyatt's cock disappeared completely when he did, buried in the valley between her breasts, held snugly around him by Wyatt's hands.

"Yeah, that's good," Wyatt muttered. She glanced down again as Shane dragged her back, watching with fascinated eyes as the head of his cock reappeared.

"Do you need more lube?" Wyatt ground out, and after a moment she realized he was talking to her.

"No, it's fine," she breathed, rocking back and forth with Shane's thrusts, watching Wyatt's cock disappear and reappear each time. She could feel him as well, that firm column of flesh tucked between the soft globes of her breasts, and it was shockingly, surprisingly erotic. "Wow."

"I told you they were perfect for this," Wyatt said, his brilliant eyes dark now with pleasure.

"It feels good," she admitted.

"It feels great," Wyatt corrected, his voice deep with rising lust. "Fuck her faster, Shane."

Shane sped up, driving into her hard enough to make her gasp. The pleasure built, but it was slow this time, and she wasn't sure she could come again.

"Don't worry about me," she told them, her voice breathless from the power of Shane's movements.

Wyatt's eyes gleamed into hers from below, his abdomen

rippling as he curled up. "Oh, we can't have that. Can we, Shane?"

Shane grunted, his hands sliding away from her hips. "Keep moving, Veronica," he said, so she kept rocking, back and forth, Shane gliding in and out of her pussy as Wyatt slid smoothly between her breasts. Shane gripped her ass from behind, strong hands pulling her cheeks apart, and she tightened on him.

His low laugh danced up her spine. "I love when your cunt clamps down like that," he told her and pulled her cheeks apart harder so she did it again.

"Oh, God."

"What do you need, Veronica?" Wyatt asked.

She shook her head. "I don't know."

"How about this?" Shane draped himself over her back, wrapped one arm around her hips, and reached for her clit.

"Too much," she groaned, flinching away from his touch. "Too sensitive."

"Make a V with your fingers, Shane," Wyatt suggested, "and put them on either side of her clit."

Veronica frowned. "That's not going to—ohhhh!"

Shane grunted in her ear as his hips drove into hers, the motion pushing her clit back and forth between his fingers, working her clit without touching it directly, and it was remarkably effective.

"God, you're so fucking hot," Wyatt panted, his cheeks flushed red as he pumped his dick between her tits.

He was close, she realized, and the knowledge that she was taking him there pushed her the rest of the way.

She came with a short cry, convulsing in Shane's hold.

"Fuck, she's coming, isn't she?" Wyatt gasped, his hips speeding up. "Tell me how it feels, Shane."

"Her cunt is clamping down on my dick," Shane ground

out, fucking her through the orgasm. "Little flutters, like a fist squeezing and releasing over and over again."

"Fuck," Wyatt ground out, his hips lifting so high Veronica's elbows came off the bed, then he was shuddering and shaking and coming all over her breasts and neck in hot, hard spurts.

Shane's thrusts slowed and he peered over Veronica's shoulder to watch Wyatt paint her breasts. "She looks good wearing your come."

Veronica was mesmerized by the sight. In a minute she was sure she'd be grimacing and reaching for a washcloth, but right now, with it warm and slick and the haze of passion still hovering over them, wearing Wyatt's come was the sexiest thing she could think of.

Well, almost.

"Goddamn, that was awesome," Wyatt rasped.

"Yeah," Veronica agreed, woozy coming down from the orgasm. "Shane?"

He dropped a gentle kiss on her shoulder. "What, baby?"

She twisted her head to look at him. "You didn't come."

"Not yet."

"Oh, good." Veronica arched her head back to skim her tongue down his neck. "Because I want to watch you fuck Wyatt."

She felt him jerk inside her, a small spasm that made her smile. She looked at Wyatt. "Will you let him fuck you for me, Wyatt? Will you let me see that?"

"Beautiful, in this moment I'd do just about anything for you," Wyatt said, his blue eyes blazing. He sat up to kiss her, hard this time, and they were both panting when he pulled back.

"Pull out, Shane," he said, his normally smooth voice ragged, and Shane did.

Veronica scooted up to the head of the bed, arranging

herself on the mountain of pillows as the two men watched. She sent them a sultry, sleepy smile. "Don't mind me."

"You want to watch, beautiful?" Wyatt asked.

She nodded. "Oh, yeah."

Wyatt smiled, devilish and sweet, then turned to Shane. "Think we should give her what she wants?"

Veronica caught her breath at the look on Shane's face. Color rode high on his cheekbones, lust glittering in his eyes when he looked first at her, then at Wyatt. "I won't be able to wait for you," he warned.

"I know." Wyatt's voice was surprisingly tender. "It's okay, love. Let's give your girl what she wants."

Shane leaned forward and captured Wyatt's mouth while Veronica watched, enthralled. They kissed for what seemed like forever, deep sensuous kisses that they both clearly loved. Hard hands roaming over hard bodies, hips grinding together.

Shane broke free and flicked a glance her way. "Oh, she likes it."

Wyatt turned to look, his eyes lighting on the rapid rise and fall of her breasts. "Yeah, she does. Let's give what she wants, love."

Shane turned away, reaching for another condom, and Wyatt crawled up the mattress towards Veronica. "Sure you're okay with this, V?"

"Of course," she said, a little startled by the question.

His mouth quirked up into a half smile. "Just making sure before we get in too deep."

She grinned. "Before he gets in too deep, you mean."

He snorted out a laugh and glanced up at Shane, who'd come to stand at the side of the bed. "I like your girl, Shane. She's funny."

"I like her, too," he said, smiling down at both of them with the bottle of lube in one hand and a condom in the other. "How do you want us, Veronica?"

"Oh." She chewed her lower lip in indecision. "Um."

"What do you want to see?" Wyatt asked.

"Everything?" she ventured.

"Well, that makes it easy." Shane looked at Wyatt. "On your back, babe."

Wyatt grinned and laid back, scooting down so his legs extended past the edge of the bed. He lifted his feet and planted them on the mattress, and Shane stepped between them. He ripped open the condom package, squirted a drop of lube onto the tip of his cock, then rolled it on.

Breathless and fascinated and aroused despite the two orgasms she'd already had, Veronica watched Shane pump lube into his palm and stroke it over his covered dick until it was glistening.

"Get me, too," Wyatt said and Shane picked up the lube again. He squirted a blob on two fingers, then lowered them between his lover's spread legs. Veronica's gaze flew to Wyatt's face when he let out a hiss at the contact, and the sheer carnal delight in his expression sent a shiver through her.

"Does it feel good, Wyatt?" she whispered, and he opened his eyes to look at her.

"So good," he told her, humming as Shane's fingers moved slowly in and out. "He's stretching me, getting me ready for that fat cock."

Veronica looked up at Shane, shocked to find him watching her with that little half smile on his face, mostly hidden in his beard. He pulled his fingers free from Wyatt's ass, wrapped a hand around his cock, and leaned forward.

Veronica leaned down, her face next to Wyatt's as she kept her eyes trained on Shane's dick. "Tell me what it feels like, Wyatt. I want to know how he feels."

Wyatt laughed, low and gruff. "He feels big, beautiful. Big and hard. Fuck, Shane, go slow."

Veronica's gaze darted to Shane's face, then back to his

cock as it slowly disappeared inside Wyatt. She held her breath, watching him inch forward, pull back and add more lube, then slide forward again. When he finally pressed hard against Wyatt's ass, fully embedded, the three of them moaned together.

"Fuck, you feel good." Shane drew back slowly, then slid back in. "Not going to last, babe."

"It's okay," Wyatt said, his expression one of blissful agony. He reached down to fist his dick, getting harder now as Shane fucked him steadily. "You can go harder."

Shane shook his head, his hair dancing over his shoulders. His eyes were screwed shut, his teeth clenched, the muscles in his neck standing out. "If I go hard, I'm going to come."

"I know," Wyatt breathed. "Do it, babe. I want to feel it. Want to feel you come in me."

Veronica watched them in awe. They weren't looking at her now, weren't looking anywhere but at each other. Their connection was tangible, nearly a living thing between them, and it was beautiful.

"Fuck, I can't stop it," Shane ground out, his hips moving faster. He slapped into Wyatt, the bed shaking with the impact. Wyatt's hand moved faster on his dick, stroking harder as Shane fucked him, his breathing changing with it.

"Yes, baby." Wyatt lifted his feet off the bed to plant them on Shane's shoulders, a strangled groan slipping out as Shane went deeper. "Come on, fuck me. Fuck me like I know you want to, hard and fast. Fuck me so your girl can see how much you love it, how much you need to come. Come on, baby. Come for me. Come for us."

Shane leaned over Wyatt, coming down on top of him and forcing Wyatt's knees back and his hips up, his feet still on Shane's shoulders, and both men groaned at the change in angle.

"Gonna come," Shane rasped, his hips jerking, his smooth, steady rhythm gone now as he raced to the finish.

"Yes." Wyatt buried his free hand in Shane's hair, yanking him up so they were face to face, staring into each other's eyes, and Veronica could see the exact moment when Shane began to come.

The groan that burst out of him was harsh and guttural, but there was a keening note to it, a wail of surrender buried under the pleasure that Wyatt swallowed in a fierce kiss. She watched Wyatt wrap his arms around his lover, holding him through the tremors and spasms of pleasure that shook his body, fierce and tender all at once. His hand stroked over Shane's back, slick with sweat, soothing him now as his shudders tapered off, and when he slumped, spent, Wyatt's arms came around him in an embrace that brought tears to Veronica's eyes.

So much love, she thought, and her heart swelled with joy for them.

She shifted, intending to slip off the bed and give them some privacy, and both men turned to look at her.

"Hey, beautiful," Wyatt murmured.

"Hey," she said back, her tight with emotion.

Shane frowned through the haze of pleasure still clouding his eyes. "You okay?"

"Yes, oh yeah." She nodded frantically and, not wanting to worry him, worked up a smile. "That was just...wow."

Wyatt's grin flashed, though there was a quiet kind of understanding in his bright eyes. "Get your money's worth, then?"

"And then some," she assured him and sent him a sassy wink to lighten the mood.

Shane's gaze flicked down her body, and a lazy grin curled his lips. "Need some help there, babe?"

She looked down, surprised to find her hand buried

between her legs. She let out a snort and wiggled her fingers, then laughed again at the wet squelch the action produced. "I guess that turned me on."

"I guess so," Wyatt chuckled. He reached out to trail a finger along the inside of her thigh, chuckling when she shivered. "Want some help?"

"Oh, that's okay," she said even as her cunt clenched at the thought. Now that she wasn't so focused on watching them, her own needs were making themselves known.

"I know that voice," Shane rumbled, and pushed himself off Wyatt. "That's her 'wanna fuck' voice."

Wyatt grimaced slightly as Shane pulled free, then rolled over to his hands and knees. He grinned at Veronica, the look he gave her so strikingly sexy she lost her breath for a moment, and by the time she got it back again she was flat on her back and he was hovering over her.

"Hey, there," he murmured.

"Hi," she whispered back.

"So, I know this has been a lot," he said casually, like she wasn't lying there with his come drying on her tits. "You've done a lot of new stuff today."

And how she thought. She'd sat on Wyatt's face while Shane fucked her, let Wyatt fuck her tits—also while Shane fucked her, and watched Shane fuck Wyatt in what was surely the hottest sexual moment of her life. And she hadn't even been a part of it.

"And I understand completely if the answer to this next question is no."

That got her attention. "What question?"

"Can I fuck you?"

Her breath caught in her throat, her gaze trapped in his. "You want to?"

"Oh, yeah, I want to." His smile was devilish as his eyes

raked down her torso, down her come-covered breasts and back again. "The question is, do you?"

"I do, but..." She looked around, her chest going tight when she couldn't see Shane. Then he stepped out of the bathroom and walked to the side of the bed.

"Babe?" He sat down and reached for her, his hand smoothing over her hair, his dark eyes filled with concern. "What's wrong?"

"Nothing," she said, her breath sighing out with pleasure and relief. "I just wanted you here."

He smiled, his fingers brushing over her cheek. "What, did you think I was going to go watch a baseball game?"

She shook her head, desire streaming back in a flood. "No, it's just...Wyatt wants to fuck me. Is that okay with you?"

"Is it okay with *you*?" he countered.

"I want to," she admitted. "But only if you're okay with it."

"Yeah, babe." He leaned down to kiss her, nipping at her bottom lip the way she liked. "I'm okay with it."

"Okay," she said again and turned back to Wyatt, who was watching her with tender amusement. "Yes, Wyatt. You can fuck me."

"Thank fuck," he groaned dramatically, making Shane laugh, and leaned down to kiss her. He nibbled his way down her neck, lighting little fires everywhere he touched. "Shane, will you get me a condom?"

"Way ahead of you," Shane said and held up a foil packet. Wyatt stopped kissing her and took it, sitting back on his haunches to tear it open and roll it on, then took the bottle of lube Shane passed him.

"She likes a lot of it," Shane told him, and both he and Veronica watched Wyatt stroke himself until he gleamed.

He lowered himself back down, his knees nudging between hers. "Spread your legs, beautiful," he told her and she did, opening them wide and watching, breath held, as he brought his cock to her cunt.

"Oh my God," she whispered and felt Shane's hand in her hair tighten.

"Look," he said in her ear, his voice like gravel. "See how hard his cock is, how hot it looks pushing into you?"

She whimpered, his words affecting her as much as the stretch and pressure of Wyatt driving into her. She was close, much closer than she'd thought.

"Fuck, you're tight." Wyatt pulled back a little, then pushed forward again. "Hot, too."

"Oh, God." Veronica's head went back, pushing into Shane's cradling hand. Wyatt pulled out again, driving back in just as slowly, swiveling his hips when he bottomed out inside her. "Oh yes, like that, just like that."

"Yeah?" Wyatt hung over her, sweat dripping off the end of his nose to splash onto her breasts, her legs spread wide around his hips. "Like that?"

"Yes." She picked up her head to look at him. "Just like that," she told him, and he took her at her word.

Over and over again he drove into her with that little hip swivel at the end. It made his dick bump up against the sweet spot inside her pussy and his pubic bone grind against her clit, and if he'd gone any faster, she'd have gone off like a rocket in minutes. But he kept it slow, with careful, measured thrusts that made her whimper and writhe but weren't enough to push her over.

Sweat trickled down her temples to seep in her hair, slicked her torso. Wyatt pulled out once completely to add more lube, leaving her feeling empty and needy until he plunged back in. She shuddered under him, tension coiling and pleasure climbing, but it wasn't enough. It wasn't nearly enough, and she thought wildly if she didn't come soon, she'd pass out.

"Shane," she moaned, his name a plea for help, for relief.

"What, baby?" he murmured, his lips at her ear. "What do you need?"

"I need your hands," she told him, reaching up to grab onto him. "Please, I need your hands on me."

"Yeah?" He leaned over her, eyes glittering like dark fire, his cheeks flushed as he watched her get fucked. "Where do you want them?"

"On my breasts," she moaned, and in desperation grabbed them herself.

"Grab her tits, Shane," Wyatt said, his hips still grinding out that slow and deliberate beat.

Shane shifted to sit beside Veronica's head, then leaned over to place his big hands on her breasts. "Like this?" he asked, and squeezed.

She arched up into his touch, her broken moan mixing with Wyatt's. "More," she begged, her hands covering his and pressing down, and he obeyed, flexing his hands harder.

"Fuck, her pussy's squeezing me." Wyatt shuddered above her, sweat rolling down his body. "I'm not going to last."

"Grab her ass," Shane told him. "Grab it and spread it."

Wyatt shifted his weight to free his hands, then reached down and grabbed her ass, spreading and pulling as Shane had directed, and the added stretch and strain on those delicate tissues shoved her right over the edge.

"Oh *fuck*." Veronica groaned and came, her body jerking between the two men, held down and held up as the spasms went on and on, rolling through her in waves that dimmed her vision and stole her breath.

She heard Wyatt shout, felt him stiffen against her and pulse inside her, and knew he'd found his release.

She lay quiet, her eyes closed. Wyatt dropped a gentle kiss on her belly before pulling free, and she felt the bed shift. "I'll get a washcloth," he said quietly, and Shane's answering murmur, so close to her, had her eyes fluttering open.

"Hi," she whispered.

"Hi back," he said with a gentle smile. "How're you doing?"

"Wow," was all she could say, and Shane laughed softly.

"I see your 'wow', and I raise you a 'holy shit'." He slid down to lie beside her. "You're amazing, you know that?"

She offered him a sleepy smile. "I think you're the amazing one," she said with a sigh. "You and the blond bombshell over there."

"Do I hear my name being spoken in vain?" Wyatt said, walking back into the room with a washcloth in hand, and she smiled at him.

"Not vain, reverence," she assured him and sighed when he began to gently clean her off. "Thanks."

"No, thank you," he said, and he sounded so serious she looked up. He smiled, his dimples flashing, and leaned down to place a gentle kiss on her mouth. She lifted a hand to his face, then let it fall limply to the bed.

Wyatt laughed and stood, shooting a look at Shane. "You weren't kidding about the post-sex sleepies."

"Yep." Shane's voice was amused. "We managed to keep her awake for three orgasms, though. I think that's a record."

"Remind me to kick both your asses when I wake up," she told them and snuggled into Shane, her eyes already drifting closed.

"Sure thing, beautiful," she heard Wyatt say, then she didn't hear anything at all.

Shane shook his head and scooped her up. She was already asleep, those cute little snores rumbling out. "Pull down the sheets, will you?"

Wyatt complied with a soft laugh. "When she drops out, she drops *out*."

"I know." Shane laid her down and pulled the covers up, smoothing them over her bare shoulders. He smiled when she snuffle-snorted, then burrowed into the blankets. He grabbed his shorts and jerked his head at Wyatt. "Let's go out to the living room."

Wyatt scooped up his clothes and followed Shane out the door, closing it gently behind him. "How long will she sleep?"

"An hour, maybe two." Shane tugged his shorts on. "You going to stick around?"

Wyatt tugged on his shirt. "Seth's got plans for tonight, so I'm free, but if you guys want to be alone, I can find something else to do."

Shane walked into the kitchen. "I think you should stay."

"More sex?" Wyatt wanted to know, and Shane shrugged.

"Maybe. Dinner and a movie is more likely," he said, heading for the fridge. "If I order from Mama Luke's, can you go pick it up?"

"Sure." Wyatt slid onto one of the wood and leather bar stools Shane had made himself. "I think you've found a primary partner, love."

Shane straightened, a Coke in his hand. He tossed it to Wyatt, then got a Mountain Dew for himself. "That's jumping the gun, don't you think?"

"No." Wyatt drank deeply, his eyes on Shane's over the can. "Do you?"

"She doesn't have any experience with polyamory."

"Neither did you when we met," Wyatt pointed out. "She seems to be navigating it pretty well."

Shane popped open his drink. "It was one threesome, Wyatt."

"You know that's not what I meant."

Shane thought as he drank. They'd been together for almost two months now, longer if he included the time in Bermuda, and she was handling the ins and outs of poly dating better than he'd expected. "She's doing okay," he admitted. "But so was Beth, at the beginning. And Julia, and Savanah."

"Don't you think it's a little unfair to compare Veronica to the ghosts of girlfriends past?" Wyatt asked. "Especially Beth. Her problem wasn't polyamory, it was that she was a controlling, conniving bitch."

"I'm not comparing, exactly," Shane said, bypassing Wyatt's all too accurate assessment of his former girlfriend. "But I've been here before, where it's new and hopeful and threesomes galore, and had it all blow up in my face."

"Is that what you're afraid of?" Wyatt asked. "That she's only here for the threesome?"

Shane reached for a takeout menu he didn't need. "It's happened before."

"If that's all she wanted, she could've had it in Bermuda," Wyatt pointed out.

"I'm just being cautious," Shane said, hedging. "Taking it slow."

"Then I'm guessing you haven't mentioned the pesky little fact that you're in love with her."

Dammit. "No."

"You're scared shitless," Wyatt said bluntly.

"Yeah, well." Shane tossed the menu aside. "It's scary."

"I know." Wyatt's voice softened in sympathy. "She loves you, too, you know."

Shane's head came up. "She told you that?"

"No," Wyatt said, and the little flare of hope died. "But I can see it. And you would, too, if you weren't so busy holding back."

"Making sure we're both on the same page isn't holding back," Shane told him, fighting to keep the resentment out of his voice. *Easy for you to say,* he wanted to shout. *You already have everything you want.*

He took a deep breath and consciously loosened his muscles. "Like I said, I'm just taking it slow."

"Okay. But you have a chance to have everything you ever wanted right in front of you. Don't go looking for reasons not to have it, okay?"

"I'm not," Shane insisted, and to ward off any further argument, reached for his phone. "What do you want to eat?"

Sixteen

"Veronica, wait up."

Veronica shouldered her bag and turned, smiling at the woman hurrying down the narrow hallway as fast as her hugely pregnant belly would let her. "How can you be this pregnant and have this much energy? Aren't you supposed to be tired all the time?"

"The benefits of poly." Cheerful and pretty with glowing olive skin and dark, laughing eyes, Lucy grinned and patted her burgeoning belly. "Jack does all the cooking, and Glory took over the cleaning since I'm not supposed to be around chemicals. All I have to do is sit with my feet up and gestate."

"Well, you look like you're doing a stellar job." Veronica slowed her pace to match Lucy's waddling gait as they headed for the exit. "When's the big day?"

"Two weeks." Lucy pushed through the glass door of the community center where the weekly More to Love support group meetings were held. "If I don't go into labor naturally by then, my doctor wants to induce me."

Veronica followed her out into the parking lot, squinting in the bright sunlight. "How do you feel about that?"

"Stabby," Lucy said bluntly. "I have a birth plan, and it does not include Pitocin. God, it's hot."

"I know." Veronica slipped her sunglasses out of her bag and onto her face. "Michigan in July, mosquitos and all. What can you do?"

"Find air conditioning whenever possible," Lucy replied. "Speaking of which, are you headed somewhere, or do you have time for a cup of coffee?"

"I've got time." Veronica pointed to the diner across the street. "How do you feel about diner coffee?"

Lucy's eyes rounded with delight. "A diner sounds perfect. I bet they have milkshakes."

"I believe they do," Veronica said with a laugh. "Let's go get you one, mama."

They settled in at a table by the window, Veronica with a cup of coffee and Lucy with a peanut butter and cherry milkshake. Veronica watched with amusement as Lucy sucked half of it down in one go.

"Do you always combine peanut butter and cherries, or is this a pregnancy thing?" Veronica wanted to know.

"I don't even like ice cream," Lucy told her with an eye roll. "Jack loves it though, and clearly, so does his spawn."

"Do you know what you're having?"

Lucy sat back, her belly bumping the edge of the table as she shifted in her seat. "We wanted to be surprised, so no."

"That's fun," Veronica commented.

"I think so, and so do Jack and Glory, but it confuses people. You know, we spent an entire weekend creating a baby registry so people would know what we needed, but apparently, they have to know the kid's genital configuration before they can buy anything."

Veronica choked on her coffee as Lucy shook her head, her curly black hair bouncing in its ponytail. "And when you tell them you don't know, they get hostile. When I told my sister we weren't going to find out the baby's sex? She called me an idiot and hung up on me."

Veronica started laughing. "You're kidding."

"Nope. Jack's mom called me the other day from Target, in a total panic because she wanted to buy some infant pajamas with giraffes on them, but the giraffes were pink and she was worried they'd be too girly for a boy." Lucy slurped up more of her milkshake. "Like they'll repossess his penis if he wears pink giraffes."

"I should really introduce you to my friend Delia," Veronica said once she'd stopped laughing. "Do you have any moral or ethical objection to marijuana consumption?"

"Well, it smells gross," Lucy said with a grimace, "and I don't want the smoke around the baby."

"She's an edibles girl, so that's not a problem," Veronica said. "Maybe after you have the kiddo there and are ready to socialize, we can all get together for lunch or something."

"That's a date." Lucy set her milkshake aside and laid her hands on her belly. "So, how are you?"

"I'm good. Busy at work, but I like it."

"And how're things with Shane?"

She knew her smile was dreamy, but she couldn't help it. "Things are good."

"Yeah?"

"Yeah. Why do you ask?"

Lucy shrugged. "You haven't talked about him in group since that first time, so I wondered if maybe you were having second thoughts about getting involved with him."

"I'm mostly in listening mode when I'm there," Veronica said. "I have so much to learn, and everybody has such good insight."

"It's a good group," Lucy agreed. "So, everything's fine? No problems?"

"No, not really." Veronica sipped her coffee. "I mean, the schedule is sometimes a pain in the ass."

Lucy grinned. "Ah, the poly lament."

Veronica laughed. "But other than that, there haven't been any big hitches."

"You really like him," Lucy said.

"Yeah." Veronica didn't even try to wipe the dopey smile from her face. "I do."

"Aw." Lucy grinned. "No big issues with his other relationship?"

Veronica shook her head. "I think it helps that I met them together, you know? I knew them as partners before I even thought of being with Shane romantically, so Wyatt's always been in the picture."

"Do you spend a lot of time with him?" Lucy asked. "Other than the threesome, that is."

"I can't believe I told you about that," Veronica muttered, her cheeks heating.

"It's okay," Lucy said and patted Veronica's hand. "I have threesomes, too."

Veronica laughed. "God, my life has gotten weird."

Lucy beamed. "Great, isn't it?"

"To answer the question, yes and no. No more naked time, but we've all had dinner together a few times."

"All of you meaning...?"

"Shane, Wyatt, Seth and me."

"And how's that?"

"It's fine. Fun."

"It doesn't get weird?"

"I thought it would, but no." Veronica toyed absently with the handle of her coffee cup. "The boundaries are pretty well established."

"Good boundaries are a poly must," Lucy agreed.

"It does help," Veronica admitted. "The first time we all got together after the threesome was…"

"Awkward?" Lucy guessed when Veronica trailed off.

"God, so awkward. We were meeting for dinner at this upscale restaurant downtown, and I came right from work so they were already at the table when I got there. I'm walking across this crowded restaurant, and they're all looking at me, and I almost had a panic attack."

"You thought sex was going to be the main topic of conversation."

"Yes!" Relieved Lucy understood, she blew out a breath. "I wasn't worried about Shane, because he's all about those boundaries. But Wyatt's default is sexual innuendo, so I was sure it would come up. But he just kissed me on the cheek and asked how work was going, and that was it."

"Sounds like things are clicking along, then."

"Yeah." Veronica frowned. "Except…"

"Except what?"

"Well, I don't know what Shane wants. Long term, I mean."

"You haven't talked about that?"

"Not really. Don't get me wrong, we talk about a lot. But he's never had a girlfriend for more than six months, and I don't even know if he wants a long-term relationship with someone other than Wyatt."

Lucy reached for her milkshake again. "You haven't asked him?"

Veronica winced. "I'm afraid of the answer."

"Veronica."

"I know, I know."

"You have to ask him, honey." Lucy's brown eyes were soft with reproach. "Wouldn't you rather know?"

"In theory? Yes."

Lucy shook her head sharply. "No. Don't do that. Don't

do the 'well, if I don't ask then it's not real' thing. It will bite you in the ass, I promise."

"Easy for you to say," Veronica muttered. "Sitting there all preggo with your husband and your girlfriend waiting for you to come home so they can pamper you."

Lucy snorted. "You think we started out that way? There were plenty of bumps, believe me."

Veronica set her chin in her hands, curiosity getting the better of her. "What was your biggest hiccup?"

"When I wanted Glory to move in with Jack and me," she replied promptly.

"Jack wasn't ready for it?"

"He had no clue I was even thinking about it." Lucy rolled her eyes. "When we first opened up our relationship, back when we were dating, I said something like, 'Hey, wouldn't it be great if we both fell in love with the same person and then we could all live together?' and he said, 'That would be amazing'. Then six years later we met Glory, and we both fell in love with her, and I thought, well, we've already had the conversation so she'll obviously be moving in at some point."

Lucy's gaze turned sardonic. "Except Jack didn't even remember having that talk. So, when Glory's lease was coming up for renewal and I asked her to move in without even talking to Jack about it first, the shit hit the fan."

Veronica winced in sympathy. "What happened?"

"We had such a big fight." Lucy sighed. "He ended up going to his mom's for the weekend, and I drowned my sorrows in about four bottles of wine."

"What did Glory do?"

"Being a wise and logical woman, she stayed out of it. Which of course made me mad, because I wanted her to agree with me that Jack was the asshole." Lucy's lips quirked with amusement. "She told me not to call her until we'd worked it out, that she wasn't going to put herself in the middle. And she was right.

"After I sobered up and Jack got sick of being at his mother's, we talked," Lucy went on, fiddling with the straw in her nearly empty milkshake glass. "There was yelling and crying and more yelling, and eventually Jack forgave me for being so eager to have it all that I forgot the rules. Because he loves Glory and he did want her to live with us, it all worked out, though she didn't move in for another year. But I didn't do us any favors by assuming that six-year-old conversation was all we needed, and you're not doing yourself any by not asking Shane what he wants."

Veronica nodded. "I know. I do. I'm just...I feel like I need to figure out what I want, too. And I want to do that without what he wants factoring in."

"That's fair," Lucy said with a nod. "Except I think you already know what you want. You're just trying to figure out if you can handle all the complications that come with it."

"How'd you get so wise?"

"Years of fucking up," Lucy said promptly and smiled when Veronica groaned. "Seriously. If you're going to be polyamorous, you need to realize that you will fuck up. It's what you do after that makes or breaks you."

"Right." Veronica lifted her coffee to her lips, discovered it was cold, and set it down. "Thanks."

"For what?"

Veronica shrugged. "For listening. For not telling me I'm being ridiculous."

"Honey, we're all ridiculous. Some of us just have more experience at it."

Veronica laughed. "Right."

"Now, I have a very important question to ask you," Lucy said.

"What is it?"

"Does this place have French fries, and can we get some?"

Veronica raised a hand to hail the waitress. "They do, and we can."

Lucy licked her lips. "Excellent. Can we get some pie, too? I could go for some pie. Cherry pie. Do you think they'd put peanut butter on it if I asked?"

While Veronica was eating French fries and cherry pie, Shane was dealing with his very pushy boyfriend.

"Tell me again why you haven't told her you love her yet?" Wyatt asked from his perch on the stool he'd dragged into Shane's workshop.

Shane focused on the varnish he was applying to the gently curved lid of the cedar chest that would pay his mortgage next month. "Taking it slow, remember?"

"You go any slower, you're going to go back in time," Wyatt warned.

Satisfied with the first coat, Shane set his brush aside and tapped the lid back on the jar of varnish. "Did you come over to crawl up my ass or fuck it?"

"I can do both," Wyatt said cheerfully.

"Lucky me," Shane drawled and brush in hand, walked past Wyatt to the workroom sink.

Wyatt pivoted on the stool. "You can't still be thinking she was only in it for the threesome."

Shane began to clean the brush with mineral spirits. "No, I don't think that. But it's still new, Wy. I just...want to be careful."

"There's a fine line between careful and fearful. You sure you're not crossing it?"

Shane snorted. "I seem to recall a certain someone freaking out the night before his wedding and having to be talked out of taking a red-eye flight to Alaska." He shot a look over his shoulder. "With the wedding gifts."

"Just the Egyptian cotton sheets," Wyatt reminded him, unbothered. "And the wine glasses. I do love those wine glasses."

"I know. I bought them."

"Anyway, I came to my senses."

"Because I stole your wallet and hid your keys," Shane pointed out.

"And reminded me that I love Seth and wanted to be married to him," Wyatt finished. "Consider this me returning the favor."

The mineral spirits were running clear, so Shane reached for the soap. "You're going to steal my wallet and hide my keys?"

"Metaphorically speaking, yes."

Shane focused on soaping up the brush with a care it didn't require. "I know we're overdue for a conversation."

"A conversation in which you tell her you love her?"

"In which we talk about the future," Shane said, unwilling to commit to specifics.

Wyatt's sigh was so heavy it stirred Shane's hair from three feet away. "I don't want to have to use the C word."

Shane paused to frown. "Cunt?"

"Coward."

Shane rolled his eyes and turned on the water to rinse the brush. "This isn't your business, you know."

"Technically that's true," Wyatt conceded. "Except I love you, and you're making yourself unnecessarily miserable over this."

"I'm not miserable," Shane protested. The brush was clean, so he carefully squeezed the water from it and hung it to dry. "I'm proceeding with caution."

"Another C word," Wyatt muttered.

Shane turned the water off and wiped his hands on his jeans. "What's it going to take for you to let this go?"

"Admit to me that you love her."

Shane spread his hands, then let them fall. "I love her."

"Good." Wyatt nodded. "Now go admit it to her."

Shane shook his head. "I'm not ready, Wy. Not yet."

Wyatt slipped off the stool and crossed to stand in front of Shane, the mutinous look on his face fading into understanding. He wrapped his arm around him in a hug. "Okay. I get that."

Shane's sigh ruffled Wyatt's hair. "Thanks,"

"But you might want to work on it," Wyatt continued, not unkindly. "She deserves honesty, Shane."

"I know." Shane buried his face in Wyatt's neck. "I don't remember this being so hard with us."

"That's because I said I love you first," Wyatt reminded him.

"Oh, yeah," Shane murmured, smiling at the memory.

"And I already had a partner, so there was less pressure on you."

"I guess." Shane took another moment to bask in his lover's embrace, then eased back. "Thanks, Wy."

"You're welcome." Wyatt pressed his lips to Shane's in a soft, sweet kiss. "Are you done in here?"

"Yeah."

"Good." Wyatt kissed him again, and this time there was nothing soft or sweet about it.

"Does this mean you're done crawling up my ass?" Shane mumbled when Wyatt shifted to nip at his ear.

"For now," Wyatt allowed and slipped a hand between them to cradle Shane's dick.

Shane shuddered at his touch, the quick transition from emotional rawness to comfort to arousal making his head spin. "Then can you fuck it now?"

"I thought you'd never ask,"

Both Shane and Veronica were so busy over the next few weeks that Veronica told herself she didn't have time to talk to Shane. He was putting in long hours during the week, working on commissions and orders from souvenir shops, and spending his weekends at the fairs and bazaars that made up a fair amount of his income in the summer months. He was at a different one almost every weekend, traveling all over the state. She'd gone with him to the Maple Syrup Festival in Shepherd one weekend, eaten her weight in pancakes, and marveled at the fact that her grumpy boyfriend's very limited communication style didn't seem to hurt his sales at all.

As July slid into August, she got extra busy herself. With school starting in a month, there were reports to write out and recommendations to make to the various school districts for the kids under her care, and the paperwork seemed never-ending. Her time with Shane grew even more limited, and she told herself she didn't want to ruin the time they did have with hard conversations. Which seemed to her like an incredibly valid course of action, though she seemed to be the only one who thought so.

She was saved from Lucy's opinion only because when she stopped by to see her after the baby was born, the new mom was so caught up in her son that the subject never came up.

Delia wasn't so easily distracted.

"You're being a pussy."

Veronica looked up from her cross-legged position on the floor, and the report she was trying to finish on the coffee table in front of her. Delia sat on the couch, nibbling on THC-infused chocolates and wearing a decidedly judgmental frown.

Veronica scowled back. "It's so weird, but I don't remember asking you."

Delia just snorted. "We've been friends for a couple of decades—"

"Thirteen years is not a couple of decades," Veronica injected drily.

"—and that means I don't have to wait for you to ask me. If I see you being a pussy, I can just call it out. It's like when people are married, so they assume the other person will want to have sex with them on a semi-regular basis."

"It is not like that."

Delia shrugged. "I don't make the rules."

Veronica stifled her impatience. It was Saturday afternoon, and she'd been trying to work for most of the morning. But it was hot, and her single window air conditioning unit had fried itself earlier in the week. A new one wasn't in her budget, so she figured she could tough out the rest of the summer without it. She'd managed reasonably well until yesterday when the temperature had risen to the high nineties. Her apartment building was old and poorly insulated, so she was currently sweating through a pair of shorts and a tank top and glaring at her best friend.

"Don't you have anything better to do than to harass me?" she demanded. "And aren't you hot? You're wearing yoga pants and a hoodie, for God's sake."

Delia looked down. "Oh, yeah. Julian keeps the a/c at home set to 'frozen side of beef', so I'm used to layering up in defense against possible frostbite."

"Well, take the damn hoodie off at least," Veronica said. "I'm sweating just looking at you."

"You're sweating anyway," Delia pointed out and nibbled on her chocolate. "Honestly, the heat isn't bothering me."

"I can see that, and I hate you for it." Veronica swiped at

the hair clinging to her sweaty face. "Go away, Delia. I'm trying to work."

Delia leaned over and scooped up the papers. "Work's over."

"Hey! Those are important."

"Relax, they're fine." Delia set them on the couch, out of reach. "I want to hear how things are going with Shane."

"Things are fine with Shane," Veronica said through gritted teeth. "You and I, however, are about to have a big fight."

"Veronica. Come on. This is me you're talking to. I've seen you make some bad decisions in the past thirteen years—"

"Do not throw your cousin Joel in my face again," Veronica warned.

"—and I have to say, I think burying your head in the sand on this might be the worst," Delia finished. She leaned across the table to lay her hand on Veronica's. "Talk to me."

"Shit." Veronica let her forehead drop to the table with a thud. "I don't know what to do, Dee."

"Well, giving yourself a concussion isn't going to help," Delia admonished, and Veronica picked up her head. "Um. You've got something..." She reached across and plucked a sticky note off Veronica's forehead.

"Thanks."

"You're welcome." Delia tossed the note onto the table. "Now talk."

Veronica sighed, defeated. "I don't know where to begin."

"Are you in love with him?"

"I think so."

"You think or you know?"

"I think." Veronica bit her lip. "I'm ninety percent sure."

"And the other ten percent is fear of what?" Delia asked.

Veronica smiled in spite of her inner turmoil. It was

comforting to be so well understood, even if it was uncomfortable. "I don't know if he wants to be with me."

"Bullshit."

Veronica blinked. "Excuse me?"

"I said, that's bullshit." Delia shook her head, exasperation and annoyance stamped on her features. "Clearly he does want to be with you. You've been dating since you got back from Bermuda, you see each other at least twice a week. He took you with him to that maple sugar circle jerk—"

"Maple Syrup Festival," Veronica corrected.

Delia waved a hand. "You say potato. My point is, he likes being with you. He fucks you regularly, he brings you salt and vinegar potato chips when you have your period, for God's sake, and for the record, I can't even get Julian to go pick up tampons or a fucking bottle of Midol."

"Pathetic," Veronica muttered.

"Tell me about it." Delia scowled. "I had one more thing, what was—oh yeah. He calls your snoring 'breathing with emphasis'."

"It is breathing with emphasis."

"I roomed with you for three years in college, and trust me, you fucking snore. The fact that he's willing to indulge your delusion about it is about as pure an act of love as I've ever seen."

Veronica sighed. "What if we don't want the same things? Long term, I mean."

"Then better to find out now."

"It's not that simple, Dee."

"It's exactly that simple. Which doesn't mean it's easy." Delia's voice gentled. "What do you want?"

"What do you mean?"

"Your future with Shane, if you could have it exactly how you wanted it, what would it look like?"

"I guess a lot like our relationship looks now," Veronica said slowly. "Just, I don't know, further along."

"Are you living together?"

Veronica considered the question. "Yes. At his place, probably. He has his shop set up there, and it's a nice house. Mid-century modern, very cool."

"Are you married?"

"I'd like to be," Veronica admitted. "I don't need a big wedding, and I'm not in a rush, but I'd like to get married one day."

"Kids?"

Veronica thought about a little girl with Shane's dark eyes, or a little boy with his rare smile. "Yeah."

Delia's brows rose. "Okay, then. Is Shane still with Wyatt?"

"Of course." Veronica frowned. "Why wouldn't he be?"

"I'm just asking," Delia said. "So that's not part of your problem?"

"No," Veronica said, then hesitated.

"I hear a 'but'."

"There's no 'but'," Veronica insisted, then relented at Delia's bland stare. "Okay, there's a little but. I don't know if he wants anything long term outside of Wyatt."

"Girl. That's not a little 'but'. That's a huge 'but'. A giant 'but'. That's a Macy's Thanksgiving Day Parade balloon sized 'but'."

"Are you finished?" Veronica asked drily.

"This is because none of the other girlfriends lasted?" Delia frowned. "I thought you said that was because they thought he'd ditch Wyatt for them."

"It was." Veronica reached for the bag of candy on the coffee table. "But maybe he likes it that way. Maybe he doesn't want two permanent partners."

"Maybe not. Guess you'll have to stop being a pussy and ask him."

"You're such a comfort to me."

"That's my job," Delia said cheerfully. "What about other women?"

"What other women?"

"Other women. Women other than you." Delia rolled her eyes when Veronica just stared blankly. "Does he plan to date women other than you?"

Veronica focused on unwrapping the chocolate. "We've never talked about that, either."

"For fuck's sake." Delia threw up her hands. "I thought the first commandment of poly was 'Communicate until you're sick of communicating, then communicate some more'."

Veronica scowled. "Yeah, well, I'm new."

"Do you at least know how you feel about him dating women other than you?"

Veronica popped the chocolate into her mouth. "Right now, it would probably wig me out, but I think that's mostly because I feel so uncertain about all of this. If I felt more stable, it might be fine."

Then she sighed. "And it might not be fine. Fuck a duck, this is hard."

"Add that to the list of topics to bring up when you stop—"

"Being a pussy, I got it." Veronica huffed out a sigh. "You're a pain in the ass, you know that?"

"So I've been told," Delia said. "By the way, you know you're eating my edibles, right?"

"Oh, hell." Veronica stared at the bag on the table, then at Delia. "How many did I eat?"

"Just one. Where's Shane tonight?"

"He's in Ionia until Monday. Hippie Fest."

"Right. Well, that's probably a good thing, because in about an hour you're going to be high as balls."

"Oh, hell." Veronica let her head fall forward onto the coffee table again. "Have I mentioned I hate you?"

Delia patted her on the head. "Don't worry. We can go to my house and swim in the pool and order takeout. Then in the morning, Cora will make sour cream pancakes and all will be right with the world."

"I'm willing to believe it," Veronica mumbled into the table. "Delia?"

"Yeah?"

"I love him."

"I know, sweetie."

"Fuck it." Veronica picked up her head. "Let's get high."

"That's kind of out of your hands at this point, but I like your enthusiasm," Delia said. "Don't worry about bringing a swimming suit. Julian's on overnight at the hospital, so it'll just be you and me. We can skinny dip."

"Fine, but if we drown and end up splashed on the front page with the headline "Nudist Pot Heads Drown in Local Doctor's Pool" I'll never forgive you."

"That's fair." Delia pushed off the couch and reached down to haul Veronica to her feet. "What kind of takeout food do you want?"

"All of it," Veronica decided, and followed her friend out the door.

Seventeen

S hane let himself into his house on Monday morning with a groan. Hippie Fest had been a hoot, and he'd sold enough stock to put him well into the black through the end of the year, but he was beat. All he wanted was a shower, a nap, and a sandwich. And he could probably skip the shower and the sandwich.

He dropped his gear inside the garage, too tired to unroll the tent so it could dry. He needed to, since it had rained off and on during the weekend and a mildewed tent was a headache he didn't want, but at the moment he just didn't care. He'd been thinking of buying a camper anyway, a pop-up that he could easily store during the winter. Sleeping in a tent was getting old, especially when it rained, or when his air mattress sprang a leak and he ended up lying directly on the bumpy ground. Both of which had happened this weekend, so he was muddy, sore, and ready to tap into his savings for a camper.

He toed off his boots and left them next to the tent before stepping into the house. He shuffled forward on stocking feet, grateful he'd put down hardwoods last year because it meant he could just glide along without expending the effort to lift his knees.

He made it to the bedroom and glide-walked into the bath. He felt a burst of renewed energy at the thought of a long, hot shower, but by the time he'd emptied his bladder and washed his hands it was gone, and all he wanted was bed.

He shucked his clothes and left them where they fell, barely having the presence of mind to pull his phone and watch from his pocket before his jeans hit the floor. He set the phone on the bedside table to charge, thumbed the switch to turn off the ringer, then climbed into bed with a heavy sigh. His body relaxed into the mattress as he floated toward sleep, but just before his eyes closed, he saw the phone screen light up.

He considered ignoring it, but it was Veronica. He'd talked to her via text over the weekend, but the only time they'd managed to connect by phone had been Saturday night, and she'd been busy with Delia.

He grabbed the phone, thumbed the screen to answer it, and closed his eyes. "Hey."

"Hey, handsome." Her voice was cheerful, with a lilting quality that made him think she'd been laughing only moments before. "How was your drive?"

"Not bad," he mumbled. He opened his eyes enough to put the phone on speaker, then laid it on the pillow and closed them again. "I missed rush hour, anyway."

"Did you have a good weekend?"

"Great. Lots of sales. Rained, though."

"You sound tired," she said, her voice softening.

"Didn't sleep much." He was fading fast, and the effort to speak felt herculean. "Air mattress leaked."

"Oh, damn, that sucks. You're home now, right? You're not still driving?"

"No, I'm home."

"Good. You going to get some sleep?"

"In bed already," he mumbled.

"I'll let you go, then. Talk to you later?"

"Okay." He fumbled for the phone, forcing one eye open so he could see the screen to disconnect. "Love you. Bye."

He managed to end the call, then sank back into his pillow with a sigh. By the time he took his next breath, he was out.

Veronica stared at her phone, her heart hammering. Had he just said *love you*? That's what he'd said, she wasn't losing her mind, right? Sure, he was tired, and maybe he didn't realize he was saying it. And maybe he hadn't meant to say it, and being tired had allowed the words to slip past his defenses, but still, he'd said it.

He'd told her he loved her.

"Oh, my God."

"Oh my God, what?" someone asked, and Veronica swiveled in her chair to blink at her supervisor.

"What?"

"You said, oh my God," Phoebe said. A tall, lean Black woman with short curly hair, angular features, and impeccable style, she nodded at the case file open on the desk in front of Veronica. "Are you having issues with Jerrod Thompson?"

"What? Oh, no. Nothing outside of the usual, that is." Veronica said, thinking of the four-year-old who had yet to say a word. "He's coming in this morning, so I was just reviewing the file. The 'oh my God' was about my boyfriend. I just got off the phone with him."

"Ah." Phoebe's frown eased into a smile. "Hot date tonight?"

"No, he's got other plans tonight." They'd moved Shane's

weekly date with Wyatt to tonight to accommodate a switch in Wyatt's work schedule. "I'll see him tomorrow."

Phoebe leaned a hip on the edge of Veronica's desk, her gold hoop earrings swinging gently against her jaw. They were the size of bracelets and gleamed against her ebony skin. "You've been seeing him for most of the summer."

"Since May," Veronica confirmed.

Phoebe arched one elegant eyebrow. "Getting serious?"

"Pretty serious," Veronica admitted, while her brain silently screamed, *he said he loves me!*

"I thought I recognized that dreamy look in your eyes," Phoebe chuckled. "You'll have to bring him around so we can get a look at him."

"Summer is his busy time, so he's pretty swamped."

"Speaking of swamped." Phoebe flipped open the folder in her hands and withdrew an envelope. "I meant to do this Friday, but my meetings ran late."

Veronica took the envelope. "What is this?"

"A formal offer for a permanent position," Phoebe said and laughed when Veronica's mouth dropped open in shock. "Contingent on you obtaining your unrestricted license, of course."

Veronica had to force the words out of her mouth. "I...I don't know what to say?"

"Say yes," Phoebe said. "I know you wanted to work in the school system, and the kids here can be a bit more of a challenge because of their age, but we're hoping you'll consider us."

"I'd love to stay here," Veronica said faintly, staring at the letter. "I just wasn't sure it was a possibility."

"You've been a huge asset," Phoebe said, her brown eyes turning serious. "The clients you've worked with have all loved you. You've got a real knack for getting to know these kids, and finding the key to working with them. We don't want to lose that."

Veronica had to blink back tears. She'd known she'd done a good job, but to hear it said out loud was…everything. "I love working here. Of course, I'll take the job."

Phoebe patted her hand. "You don't have to decide right this minute. Take the letter home and read through it. It's got all the details on salary and benefits, and a detailed job description. Make sure it's going to work for you, on every level. Then come back and say yes."

"Okay." Veronica set the letter on her desk next to her phone, feeling like she was operating on autopilot. "Thank you, Phoebe."

"You more than earned it," Phoebe assured her. "Now, about Jarred Thompson. He's got an appointment today?"

"In about half an hour," Veronica confirmed with a glance at the clock. "I was just going over his evaluation, and the last therapist's notes to see if I can find a new angle."

Phoebe pushed off the desk. "Let's find a room and talk about it. I think I have a couple of ideas that might help you."

***

"Sweetie, that's fantastic!" Delia squealed. "I'm so happy for you. We have to celebrate. Dinner party, my house, Friday night."

Veronica nudged her empty salad bowl aside. Her session with Jarred had run long, so she was taking her lunch later than usual, and the normally full courtyard was empty. She leaned back on the metal bench and tilted her face up to the sun. "As long as you promise the dessert won't have any THC in it. I'm barely recovered from Saturday."

"Lightweight. Have you told Shane yet?"

"Not yet. I talked to him just before I got the offer, and he was going to bed. It sounded like he had a hard weekend. I'll tell him tomorrow."

"Why not later tonight? I thought you had a standing Monday date."

"We do, but Wyatt's work schedule got changed again, so we switched my Monday for his Wednesday."

"You can still call him, right?"

"Yeah, but I'd rather tell him in person. Anyway, he was so beat when I talked to him, I'm surprised he had the energy to answer the phone. He was practically talking in his sleep."

"I love it when Julian talks in his sleep," Delia said with a giggle. "It's always nonsense like 'the elephants need a pedicure before they can do ballet!' or something like that."

"Shane didn't say anything about elephants," Veronica said. "He just said he loved me."

"He what?" Delia's shriek had Veronica yanking the phone away from her ear.

"He said he loved me," Veronica repeated, a laugh bubbling up in her throat. "He said it as he was saying good-bye, and he was half asleep. But he said it."

"Holy crap! Did you say it back?"

"He hung up right after, so I didn't have time."

"Would you have said it back?"

"Probably?" Veronica chewed her bottom lip, wincing as Delia's disappointed moan reverberated in her ear. "I know, that's pitiful. But it caught me by surprise. And also, I don't even know if he knows he said it."

"How can you not know you said something?" Delia scoffed.

"Because he was half asleep. Maybe it was just a reflex."

"What do you mean, a reflex?"

"You know, like 'okay, bye, love you'. Like that."

"How is that a reflex?"

Veronica huffed out a breath. "I don't know, it just is. You say it so often it becomes habit, so you say it even when you don't mean to. I accidentally said 'I love you' to the guy who called to set up an appointment to fix my cable last week."

"Slut."

Veronica snorted out a laugh. "My point is, maybe he didn't mean it."

"Oh, he meant it. Maybe he didn't mean to *say* it, but he meant it. Are you going to tell him?"

"What, that he said he loves me, or that I love him?"

"Both."

"Probably not. Even if he did mean it, he might not have meant to say it, which means he didn't mean for me to hear it. Right?"

"Fuck, you're stressing me out," Delia muttered. "Can we go back to the part where we're celebrating you getting a job? That was way easier than this angsty emo mess you've dragged me into."

Veronica opened her mouth to reply, but a beep in her ear stopped her. She checked the screen. "Hey Dee, that's Wyatt calling me. I'll talk to you later."

"If he's calling to talk about another threesome, ask if you can film it this time."

"Goodbye, Delia," Veronica said with a laugh, then switched the call. "Wyatt?"

"Hey, beautiful," Wyatt said. "Listen, have you talked to Shane today? I just tried to call him and he didn't pick up, and I know he was driving back from Ionia this morning."

"I talked to him a couple of hours ago," Veronica said. "He was home, but he was really tired. He said he was going right to bed."

"He probably put the phone on silent," Wyatt sighed. "Okay, thanks."

"No problem." She frowned. He didn't sound distressed, exactly, but he wasn't happy. "Is everything okay?"

"Yeah, it's fine. I was just going to talk to him about our plans for tonight. We have tickets to see a play, but this new schedule is kicking my ass. I was hoping to convince him to stay in."

"Considering how hammered he sounded when I talked to him, I don't think he'd have a problem with it."

"The staying in part, no. Shane would stay in every night if I let him, you know?"

"I know," she replied with a laugh.

"I was hoping to convince him to cook dinner. I'm going to have to head for his place right after work, and I won't get there till after seven. And if he's so tired he's not answering the phone, there's no way he's going to be up for putting a meal together."

"You could order takeout," Veronica said. "There's that Italian place he loves, Mama Luke's?"

"That would be perfect, but they don't do any kind of delivery, and it's on the other side of town."

"I'll do it."

"What?"

"I'll do it," she repeated. "Tell me what you want from Mama Luke's, and I'll pick it up and bring it over."

"You don't have to do that, V," he began.

"I know, but I want to. Consider it a thank you."

"For what?"

"For fixing me up with your boyfriend," she said, grinning when he laughed. "And for being so sweet to me since I started dating him."

"You know that's no hardship for me, Veronica. I like you. And I like you with Shane. You're good for him."

"Aw." She said it lightly, but she had to blink back tears. "See? So sweet."

"If you're sure…"

"I'm sure," she said firmly. "I already know what Shane

wants, one of those obnoxiously huge calzones. Do you want to split it with him, or get something else?"

"I love their Fettucine alfredo," he told her. "With chicken. You're sure this is okay?"

"Absolutely," she told him. "What about a salad?"

"We can split one of their large Caesars," he said. "How about I call in the order? I'll put it on my credit card, and then you just have to play delivery girl."

"No," she told him firmly. "It's my treat."

"V," he began.

"Wy," she shot back. "Let me do this. Anything else? Breadsticks?"

"We don't need breadsticks," he said, but tone clearly said *mmm, breadsticks*, so she mentally added them to the list. "This is really great of you, Veronica."

"I'm happy to do it. What time are you going to get to his place?"

"I was supposed to pick him up at seven. It'll be at least that before I get there."

"Okay. I'll plan to get there by seven, then I'll be out of your hair."

"Since we're not going to the play, you could stay and hang out with us. We'll probably just watch a movie and zone out."

"No, this is your time together," she told him. "I'll just pop in, play food fairy godmother, then pop back out."

"You sure? I don't mind, and I know Shane wouldn't." His voice turned seductive. "Maybe we could hang out naked."

She burst out laughing. "You're such a pervert."

"I know. That's why you like me."

"True," she conceded, still laughing. "But no. I'm not going to crash your date, even if you're naked."

"Bummer," Wyatt said with an exaggerated sigh, but she

could hear the smile in his voice. "I was kind of hoping for a repeat of our threesome."

"Well." Veronica cleared her throat. "We'll have to talk about that, won't we?"

"I guess we will," he replied, still amused.

"But not tonight."

"Okay, then. I'll text him and let him know the play is off, and dinner is handled."

"Good idea. If he gets himself all cleaned up to go out then finds out he didn't have to, he'll crab about it for days."

Wyatt's laughter rang in her ear. "That's our grumpy fucker. Thank you, Veronica. Really."

"It's nothing," she began.

"It's very much something, and it takes a lot of the pressure off tonight. Now we can just relax. So, thanks."

"Anytime," she told him, and she meant it. "I have to go, my lunch break is about over. I'll see you tonight."

"If I miss you tonight, save a kiss for me."

"Always," she quipped and hung up.

She gathered up her lunch debris and trooped back inside. She had a few more clients to see in the afternoon, and the accompanying paperwork to handle. But she'd be done before five, giving her plenty of time to skip home, change her clothes, and pick up dinner for her boyfriend and his boyfriend.

She shook her head and headed back to her desk. Four months ago, she was dating Derek and finishing up school to leap into a whole new career. Now she had her first job in that career, a new boyfriend who also had a boyfriend, and there was a distinct possibility of more threesomes in her future.

Life could be wonderfully, beautifully weird, she thought and went back to work.

EIGHTEEN

Shane stepped out of the bedroom feeling mostly human. He'd slept for six hours straight, then spent an hour in the jetted tub soaking out the kinks from two nights on the hard ground. By the time he strolled into the kitchen, dressed in jeans and a Henley the color of raspberries, he was feeling almost human, and desperately hungry. He hadn't gone grocery shopping in a week, so there was nothing in the fridge but a half pint of cream that he kept on hand for when Wyatt simply had to have a morning cup of coffee, a couple of very sad looking apples, and a container of the yogurt Veronica liked.

"Thank God Wyatt's bringing food," he muttered to himself.

He wandered into the living room, intending to stretch out on the couch and peruse the options for movies while he was waiting. He'd barely sat down and picked up the remote when the doorbell rang.

Assuming Wyatt had forgotten his key, he padded over to open the door.

When he saw Veronica, dressed in a flippy little skirt and a clingy tank top with a smile on her face, his heart sank.

"Hi," she chirped and stepping over the threshold, rose on her toes to kiss his cheek. "Whew, that drive over. Traffic is murder this time of day, isn't it?"

He watched, nonplused, as she brushed past him. "Veronica? What're you doing here?"

"I brought dinner," she said and lifted the bags in her hands. He recognized the logo before she said, "Mama Luke's."

"I see that." He followed her into his kitchen. "Why did you bring Mama Luke's?"

"You were so tired when I talked to you this morning, I thought you'd appreciate not having to cook," she said, plunking the bags on the counter. She peeled back the Velcro flap on the insulated hot bag, wincing as steam came pouring out. "Shit, that's hot. Where's a—oh, there it is."

She snagged the dishtowel from the counter and, using it as an oven mitt, slid out a foil-wrapped calzone. "I'm just going to put this in the oven on warm until you're ready to eat, okay?"

"Did you forget that we switched nights?"

She was pulling a foil-topped container of the bag, the escaping steam making her face pink. "What?"

He waited until she'd put the container next to the calzone and turned the oven on low before repeating himself. "I said, did you forget that we switched nights."

"Oh." She laughed, shoving her hair out of her face. She was sweating a bit, her hair damp at the edges and clinging to her face. She was so pretty, flushed and smiling and wearing a tank top thin enough for him to see how the air conditioning had caused her nipples to pucker, and he almost reached for her before he remembered she wasn't supposed to be here.

"No, I didn't forget," she said, moving on to the paper sack on the counter. Another foil tray came out, then a six-pack of Mountain Dew. "But after I talked to Wyatt this afternoon—"

"You talked to Wyatt?"

"Yeah." She pulled a stack of napkins out of the sack, set them aside, then began opening cabinets. "He called me when he couldn't reach you."

He watched her pull down plates and glasses, dig silverware out of the drawer. "I was asleep."

"I know." She carried everything to his small dining table with a smile. "I told him you'd sounded beat when I talked to you, so you probably didn't hear it."

She was laying out place settings, plates and glasses, knives and forks. She came back for the foil tray on the counter, then paused. "Are you hungry now, or are you going to wait to eat?"

"I'm hungry now," he replied. "But I don't understand what's going on."

"I told Wyatt you probably weren't going to be up for going out," she explained. She peeled back the lid on the foil tray, revealing a large Caesar salad. "I think I'll just leave this in the container. No sense dirtying up another dish."

"Veronica, stop."

Her head came up, surprise in her hazel eyes, and he took a deep breath. His temper was beginning to simmer, and he knew if he didn't watch himself, it would boil over. "You told Wyatt I wasn't going to be up for our date tonight?"

She blinked. "Well, after we talked, I thought—"

"You had no right to do that."

"What?"

"You had no right to do that," he repeated, his voice getting sharper as his temper grew. "Veronica, Wyatt is my partner."

"I know that," she began, and though her voice was normal, her eyes had gone wide with shock.

"Do you?" He asked and waved a hand at the kitchen. "Because you're not showing a lot of respect for that relationship."

"Shane, I only wanted—"

"That's right, *you* wanted," he said. "You wanted to come over, bring dinner, see me, and to hell with the plans I already had, is that it?"

"Of course not."

"How many times have I told you how important it is for me to keep clear boundaries?" he demanded. "How many times have I told you, that's the only way this works? Boundaries, communication, respect."

She was silent, watching him with wide, wounded eyes. He hardened his heart to them. She had to hear this, she had to *understand* this. If they were going to have any sort of a chance at a future together, she had to.

"You had no right to call off my date with Wyatt."

"That's not what this is."

He didn't believe her. "It's not."

"Of course not," she said. "Wyatt's still coming over, I didn't tell him not to."

"So then this is what, you horning your way into being included?" He shook his head while she blinked at him with fresh shock. "That's not okay either, Veronica."

She shook her head and drew in a deep breath. "You don't understand," she began, then stopped when he held up a hand.

"No, you don't understand. My time with Wyatt is important. You don't get to just poke your way in whenever you're feeling lonely or horny or whatever this is."

"I'm not lonely or horny," she protested, a hint of anger

breaking through the shock. "You think this is me angling for another threesome or something?"

"Is it?" he asked. "Or is it you trying to edge Wyatt out?"

"I would never do that," she said, and the utter conviction in her voice gave him pause. "I know how important Wyatt is to you, and I'm not trying to interfere with that."

"You can't prove it by me," he said bluntly, and she drew back as though he'd slapped her. "He's a permanent part of my life, and if you can't accept that, then we have a real problem."

"I've already accepted that," she said, the words tight with anger, her eyes glittering with hurt. "And the problem is, you don't believe me."

She turned on her heel and walked out of the kitchen, and seconds later he heard the front door slam.

He planted his hands on the counter, cursing under his breath and talking himself out of going after her. Dammit, he was right, and if she couldn't respect his relationship with Wyatt, he needed to know now. He was already in love with her, and if he let her in, let himself believe they could have a future together only to find out later that she couldn't handle it, he'd never be able to put the pieces of his heart back together again.

He heard the front door open and close again, and his head snapped up, eyes narrowed on the kitchen doorway. Then Wyatt walked in.

"Hey, baby," he said, leaning in for a kiss. "What's up with Veronica?"

"Nothing," Shane muttered, not wanting to get into it. He kissed Wyatt back, letting it soothe some of the ragged edges. "Hi. Missed you."

"I missed you, too." Wyatt smiled at him, curiosity in his blue eyes. "Are you sure Veronica's okay?"

"She'll be fine," Shane said and wrapped his arms around Wyatt. "How was your day?"

"Chaos," Wyatt said with a sigh. "They switched over to the new computer system over the weekend, so of course nothing is working right. Things that should take two seconds to chart are taking ten minutes, and the pharmacy was backed up to hell and gone because the automatic med dispensers went on lockdown, and nobody could figure out how to fix them."

"Sorry, babe."

"It's okay. They'll get it worked out. But right now, thank God, it's not my problem. You hungry?"

"Starving," Shane admitted. His stomach had been rumbling ever since Veronica had unpacked the calzone. "I don't know what you have planned for dinner, but I've got a calzone from Mama Luke's I'm happy to split with you."

Wyatt shot him a confused look. "What do you mean, you don't know what I have planned for dinner?"

"You said in your text that I shouldn't cook."

"Yeah, because I didn't want you to start making something before Veronica could get here."

Shane jerked back, his eyes flying to Wyatt's face. "What did you say?"

"I didn't want you to start making something before Veronica could get here," Wyatt repeated. "I wasn't sure what time she'd make it over. What's wrong with you?"

Shane stared at him. "You knew she was coming by?"

"Yeah, we talked about it when I called her."

"You called her."

"What are you, a myna bird?" Wyatt asked with a laugh.

Shane rubbed a shaky hand over his face, a sick feeling curling in his gut. "Maybe you better start from the beginning."

Wyatt shrugged. "I called her when you didn't answer your phone this afternoon. She told me she'd talked to you, that you were beat from the drive and probably still sleeping."

"Keep going," Shane urged when he stopped.

"There's not much else," Wyatt said, clearly confused. "I told her we had theater tickets, but with the craziness at work and you so tired, I'd rather bail on the play and stay in. She offered to pick up dinner."

"She did?"

"Yeah. She said she'd swing by Mama Luke's, pick up a calzone for you and Fettucine alfredo for me, then bring it by."

Shane closed his eyes as Wyatt continued talking. "I told her she didn't have to, but she insisted. Wouldn't even let me pay for it."

Shane opened his eyes again to find Wyatt watching him carefully. "Anything else?"

"Yeah. I told her she could stay for dinner, hang out and watch a movie with us, but she wouldn't. Said she wanted us to have the time alone since we haven't been able to grab much lately."

"Fuck," Shane muttered. "Fuck, fuck, fuck."

"Shane?" Wyatt asked, confused, but Shane shook his head and walked into the living room. Wyatt followed, frowning as Shane sank into the couch and laid his head back, still cursing under his breath. "What's going on?"

Shane sighed. "I thought she was crashing."

The cushion shifted as Wyatt sat down beside him. "What?"

He turned his head to meet Wyatt's confused eyes. "I thought she was crashing our date."

"Why would you think that?"

Shane muttered something under his breath, and Wyatt frowned. "What? I didn't hear that."

"Because Beth did it that one time," he said more clearly.

Wyatt stared at him. "Tell me you didn't accuse her of doing what Beth did."

"Not in so many words," Shane began.

"That means you did," Wyatt groaned. "Jesus Christ, Shane. What did you say?"

"I implied she was trying to edge you out," Shane told him, and remembering the rest, winced. "Then I suggested she was horny and lonely and might possibly have been angling for another threesome."

Wyatt stared at him, aghast. "Have you lost your fucking mind?"

"I panicked, okay? I got...scared."

"Well, at least you admit it," Wyatt said. "Of what?"

"That she won't want to be with me if I'm not monogamous."

"Huh?"

"Look, I know she *says* she's fine with it," Shane began. "And she seems okay now. But what happens if she figures out down the road that she's not? If she starts to resent me, or hate me for loving you, too?"

"What if she falls in love with someone else?"

Shane frowned. "What?"

"What if she falls in love with someone else?" Wyatt repeated. "It's just as plausible a scenario. You've never thought about it?"

"Well, no."

Wyatt shrugged. "We've both seen it happen. Are you going to be okay with it if it does?"

"I don't...I don't know." Shane looked at Wyatt, a ball of misery in his gut. "I'd probably need some time to get used to it."

"You don't think she deserves time to get used to this?"

"Of course, she does," Shane sighed. "Shit, Wyatt. I panicked."

"Yeah, I get that. I still don't understand why."

"Because I'm in love with her," he said quietly and looked up into Wyatt's knowing eyes. "I love her, Wyatt."

"I know," Wyatt said quietly.

"I never loved Beth, or any of the others. I couldn't, or I didn't let myself, I don't know which it was. And that was fine because they couldn't love me either."

"Couldn't love you while you loved me, you mean."

"Yeah. But I think she can, Wy. And it scares the crap out of me."

"Why?"

"Because if it all goes to hell, it'll break me." He took a deep breath and forced the words out. "I want everything with her. A home, babies, a life. I want what you have with Seth."

"Well, Seth and I aren't having any babies anytime soon," Wyatt teased gently.

"You know what I mean."

Wyatt sobered. "Yeah, I do. What are you going to do about it?"

"I don't know." Shane dragged a hand through his hair. "Do you think she can forgive me?"

"How's your groveling game?" Wyatt wanted to know.

"Rusty."

"Well, brush up on it," Wyatt said briskly and slapped him on the shoulder. "You're going to need it."

Veronica pulled her car to a stop and switched off the engine. She dug out her phone, scrolling through the contacts until she found the one she wanted. Opening up a new text, she typed *Hey. Are you available to chat, or are you busy with the little one?*

Almost as soon as she sent it, the little dots appeared that told her Lucy was typing out a reply. *Baby's napping,*

Jack's at work, and Glory's making dinner. I'm supposed to be folding laundry, but I can do that and talk. What's up?

It's complicated, Veronica sent back. *Would be better if we could talk in person.*

Sure. You can come over if you like. How long will it take you to get here? Feeding time is in an hour.

I'm in your driveway, she wrote back.

This time the little dots didn't appear, but in less than a minute the front door of the tidy little bungalow opened, and Lucy stood in the doorway in shorts and a loose tank top. She held a hand over her eyes to shade it from the glare of the sun, then gave a beckoning wave.

Veronica climbed out of the car, slamming the door behind her, and made her way up the flower-lined walk. "Pretty," she said, keeping her eyes on the flowers. "Who's the gardener?"

"That's all Jack," Lucy said. "I hate working outside, and Glory has a black thumb."

Veronica nodded. "Me, too. I tend to overwater or give them too much sun."

"Uh-huh. Are you going to look at me, or mope at the daisies?" Lucy wanted to know, and Veronica raised miserable eyes to hers.

"Oh, honey." Lucy's face filled with sympathy as she drew Veronica inside. "Let's go find something cold to drink and you can tell me what happened."

Ten minutes later, she sat in Lucy's living room, a bottle of beer going warm on the table next to her, pouring her heart out. "And that's when I left," she finished.

"Wow. He really hit you with both barrels, didn't he?"

Veronica nodded, blinking back tears. She'd gone past angry to devastated, and she knew if she gave in, she'd just start bawling. "It just felt like it came out of nowhere, you know? I thought I was doing something nice for him, for *them*, and somehow, I screwed it up."

"I don't think you screwed it up, but I can see how you feel that way." Lucy rocked in the glider across from her, a bottle of water in her hand. "Tell me again why you brought them dinner?"

Veronica shrugged. "When I was talking to Wyatt, he said he didn't want to make Shane handle dinner since he was so tired from his trip. But Wyatt doesn't cook, and the takeout he wanted was on the other side of town. I offered to pick it up."

"You didn't have any ulterior motive?" Lucy asked, her soft eyes steady on Veronica's. "No secret wish for a quickie in the bathroom, no desire to wiggle your way into their evening?"

"No," Veronica said, taken aback. "I mean, I thought it would be nice to see them both, maybe chat for a minute, but that's it. Wyatt invited me to stick around and watch a movie with them, but I said no."

"Why?"

"Because it was their date, not *our* date. I didn't want to interrupt their time together."

Lucy nodded thoughtfully. "Okay. Do you want my opinion?"

Veronica rolled her eyes. "No, I came over here to disrupt your maternity leave because I'm just that big of a bitch."

Lucy waited a beat. "That was sarcasm, right?"

"Yes, it was sarcasm, and yes, I desperately want your opinion. I need to know if my instincts are right on this, or if I screwed up."

"I don't think you screwed up, at least not big," Lucy said. "Maybe you stepped on Shane's toes a little by not checking with him directly, but considering the circumstances, it's completely reasonable for you to think checking with Wyatt was enough."

Lucy took a sip of her water. "Wyatt also may have stepped on Shane's toes a little, but again, considering the circumstances, I think he had every reason to expect that this would be fine with Shane."

"So, I didn't screw up, and Wyatt didn't screw up."

"Right. Which leaves Shane. And boy, did he screw up."

Veronica sighed, feeling unbearably tired. "That's what I thought, but I'm so new at this, and right now, I don't know which end is up."

"Look." Lucy leaned forward. "He was entitled to get mad because you showed up unannounced. And he's entitled to be mad that you and Wyatt had a conversation about him behind his back. Both of these reactions make him a bit of a jerk, in my opinion, but he's entitled. What he wasn't entitled to do was jump to conclusions, then not give you a chance to explain yourself."

"That's what I thought, but I then thought maybe I was missing something."

"Nope. Big fat entitled jerk."

Veronica sighed. "I'm so mad at him. How can I love somebody this much and still be so mad at him?"

"Just one of those things," Lucy said cheerfully.

"What should I do, Lucy?"

"Well," Lucy began, then turned at the sound of a faint cry.

"Sorry to interrupt." A woman with warm brown skin, a round face, and sparkling eyes walked into the room with a squirming bundle in her arms. "But somebody woke up hungry."

"I'll take him," Lucy said, her face going soft at the sight of her son. "Hey there, little man. You ready to eat?"

The other woman settled the baby in Lucy's arms, then straightened to smile at Veronica. "I'm Glory, by the way."

"Veronica," Veronica replied and managed a smile. "It's nice to meet you. I've heard a lot about you."

"All good," Lucy put in, lifting the hem of her tank top.

Glory perched on the arm of Lucy's chair. "Can I get you anything?"

"I'm good, thanks." Veronica watched as Lucy guided the baby's avid mouth to her breast, his squeaks and grunts fading when he latched on.

"Fuck, that stings," Lucy muttered, but the look on her face as she looked at the baby was one of tender indulgence. "Good thing we only do this a few times a day, huh buddy?"

She glanced up at Veronica. "The pump isn't great, but at least it doesn't hurt like this."

"I didn't know it hurt to breastfeed," Veronica said.

"Believe me, neither did I," Lucy said and Glory laughed. Lucy tilted her head back to grin at her partner. "We all learned pretty quickly though, didn't we?"

"The whole floor of the hospital learned," Glory reminded her. "The nurses said you were scaring the other patients."

"Pish. Knowledge is power, isn't it, little man?" she cooed to the baby.

Glory smiled at Veronica. "It's a good thing we'd already decided on the breastfeeding, bottle-feeding combination."

"We wanted Glory and Jack to be able to feed him as well," Lucy explained. "That way everyone gets to bond with him, and I don't lose as much sleep."

"Makes sense. Did you guys finally settle on a name?"

"We went with Graham, in the end." Lucy smiled. "It's Glory's father's name, and we wanted him to have something of hers."

"That's lovely," Veronica managed.

Glory was watching the baby feed, her eyes shining with emotion. "I think I only got my way on that because Lucy wants to keep the other name we were considering in case we ever have a girl."

"Rory," Lucy supplied. "I just think it makes a more interesting girl's name. Besides, you don't look like a Rory, do you? No, you're definitely a Graham."

Veronica watched Lucy nuzzle her son with a little spasm of envy. "I should go, let you guys get some rest."

She rose to her feet, gathering her purse. "Thanks for listening, Luce."

"What are you going to do?" Lucy wanted to know.

"I don't know." Veronica shrugged. "Let things cool down, I guess. Then, if he doesn't call me, I'll call him, and we'll have it out."

"My advice? If you love him, work it out. But don't let him off the hook." Lucy smiled. "At least not right away. Good luck."

"Thanks."

"I'll show you out," Glory said and started to stand.

"No, stay." Veronica waved her down. "I can find the way. Enjoy your family."

Glory settled back on the arm of Lucy's chair with a smile. "It was nice to meet you."

"You, too." Veronica paused in the doorway, looking one last time at the pair of them, heads together as they watched their child nurse, love and contentment like a glow around them.

She wanted that, she realized. Not the baby, necessarily, at least not right away, but the intimacy that was so bright and strong she could almost see it. She wanted that with Shane.

She turned away, closing the door gently behind her, and walked back to her car.

She drove home on autopilot, thankful that the streets were mostly clear of traffic now. Her mind felt muddled, her body weighed down, all the emotional upheaval of the last few hours drained away to leave her hollow. She knew she'd have to think about all of this again—Shane's accusations, what it meant for their relationship that he so clearly didn't trust her. Did they even have a future anymore?

Maybe he'd never wanted a future with her. She had only that one mumbled, accidental 'love you' to indicate he felt anything more for her than sexual attraction and basic affection. The truth was, they'd never talked about the future, and she was going to have to face that maybe she'd built castles in the air, dreaming up a future with a man who never wanted it.

She parked her car with a sigh and switched off the engine. Her stomach rumbled as she climbed out, reminding her that she hadn't eaten. She climbed the steps to her apartment with a sad little laugh. She'd fed her boyfriend and his lover but hadn't bothered to get herself any nourishment. "Thanks, universe, for the on-the-nose metaphor," she muttered.

She'd order a pizza, or maybe Chinese since any sort of Italian food was just going to remind her of Shane tonight. Of course, she was going to be thinking about him no matter what she had for dinner unless what she had for dinner was a fifth of vodka, and that wasn't possible because she was all out and the liquor store didn't deliver.

She was making a mental pro/con list on the merits of a liquid dinner and calculating exactly how long it would take her to get to the liquor store and back when she turned the corner and froze.

Shane was sitting on the floor in front of her apartment, his back to her door. His head was tilted back, his eyes closed, and her first thought was that he looked so tired. Lines that weren't normally there were carved deep into his face, dark circles under his eyes. Even his posture looked tired, his shoulders slumped and forearms draped over his updrawn knees.

Her second thought was that he'd been such a jerk, and it was a goddamn crime that he still looked so fucking good.

She opened her mouth to ask him what he was doing here when he spoke.

"I don't blame you for not talking to me," he said, turning his head so his cheek was pressed against the door. "You tried to do something nice, and I jumped to all the wrong conclusions."

He was talking to her door, she realized. He thought she was in there, not answering, so he'd parked himself outside her door.

"I'd like to explain," he went on, his eyes still closed. "If you want me to go, I will. You don't owe me anything, and what I have to say doesn't excuse what I did. But I'd like to tell you why."

Veronica took a careful step back, then another, biting her lip and praying he wouldn't open his eyes until she'd managed to get out of sight. She let out a soundless breath of relief when she stepped back around the corner to the top of the stairwell and leaned against the wall.

"Since you're not telling me to go," he went on, his voice carrying clearly to where she stood, "I'll take that as an okay to keep talking. But if you want me to stop, or leave, just tell me."

There was a moment of silence, as though he was waiting for a response. When none came, he began speaking again.

"I know I've told you before, about some of the other women. Julia, Beth, Savanah. I know I've been comparing you to them, and that's not fair. You're not them. But I didn't think they were them at first, either."

Veronica lowered herself to the top step carefully, all her attention on the man on the other side of the wall, pouring his heart out.

"I was never unclear with them about Wyatt, about how important he is to me. And they all seemed to accept that, at first. They loved the idea of having him join us in bed, anyway, and knew that I needed time of my own with him. But after a while, they started to resent it."

He was silent for a moment, as though he was giving her time to respond. When she didn't, he went on.

"It was little things, at first. Pouting when I couldn't do something with them because Wyatt and I had plans, or trying to get me to bring them along. Then it got to be more than just pouting, or trying to tag along. Beth ambushed a date once."

There was a scuffling noise, like he was moving around, then a thump. "Sorry. Didn't mean to bang on the door, I'm just getting more comfortable."

Veronica smiled at that, her heart aching to go pull him off the floor and hug him. But he wasn't done talking, and she wasn't done listening.

"Anyway, I was telling you about Beth. Beth was fun. She was kind of shy, didn't like big crowds or going to events with a lot of people, so we mostly stayed in. She liked Wyatt, too. The idea of having him in bed with us was scandalous for her. She grew up in a small town in Wisconsin and came to Lansing for school, and until then she'd never really thought of things like threesomes or non-monogamy.

"She was all for it, but I think looking back she viewed it as a sort of sexual adventure — something wild she'd do while she was young and could look back on years later. I don't think she ever thought of it as a viable long-term option, and I guess she assumed I felt the same way. That Wyatt was a phase I was going through, and I'd grow out of it."

There was a heavy sigh. "When I didn't, she started to get manipulative. Little things, like forgetting to give me phone messages from him, switching dates on the calendar. It took me a while to see she was doing it on purpose. Wyatt tried to tell me, but I loved her, you know?"

Veronica bit her lip, a little pang under her heart at the hurt in his voice.

"At least I thought I did," he went on, so softly she had to strain to hear. "I ignored most of the signs, made excuses or believed hers."

He was quiet so long she almost went to him. She was rising to her feet when he spoke again. "Anyway, Wyatt and I had a date coming up. It was our anniversary, and we'd planned a short trip. A cabin on the lake, just the two of us for the whole weekend. And she crashed it."

Veronica's mouth dropped open, and she slapped a hand over it to keep the gasp from escaping.

"She just...showed up," he went on. "Strolled in with a couple of bags of groceries and the Lord of the Rings box set, because we'd talked about all getting together for a marathon viewing one day."

Oh my God, Veronica mouthed to the wall, and mentally sent Beth the finger.

"She got angry when I asked her to leave," he said, and the bone-deep weariness in his voice tugged at her heart. "Started shouting, throwing things. Wyatt went for a walk so we could talk it out, and that's when she asked me when I was going to grow up. That's how she put it—grow up and get rid of my boyfriend and the silly, immature need to have my cake and eat it too. She wanted to get married and have babies, she said, and she couldn't do that with me if I was going to insist on playing house with Wyatt."

Veronica's stomach dropped, a feeling of dread coming over her.

"She never even asked me if I wanted kids."

Do you? she asked silently, her palm pressed to the wall while she waited for him to answer the unspoken question.

"I do want them," he said quietly, and Veronica's sigh of relief almost drowned out his next words. "But I want Wyatt, too. She said that was ridiculous, and she gave me an ultimatum, right there in our little rented cabin. Her or Wyatt."

I hate this bitch, Veronica thought.

"Since she's not here and Wyatt is, you can probably guess which way I went," he said with a sad little laugh that broke her heart all over again. "And it wasn't a hard choice to make. When she gave me that ultimatum, I knew she didn't love me. It was for the best, but it still hurt."

He drew in a deep breath. "Anyway. That's why I blew up today. When you showed up with dinner I just...reacted, without stopping to think. I was an asshole, and I'm sorry. I hope you can forgive me for jumping to conclusions."

Veronica had to blink back tears as she pushed to her feet. She started to step out into the hallway when his next words froze her in her tracks.

"The thing is, I love you so much more than I ever thought I loved Beth. And I want it all."

What? she silently implored. *What do you want? Tell me.*

"I want to love you, and have babies with you. I want to love Wyatt, and make him babysit."

Veronica clapped her hands over her mouth to hold back the laugh, and barely noticed the tears streaming down her face.

"I want Wyatt to be the best man at our wedding, if we decide to do that someday. But even if you don't want babies, and you don't want to get married, I still want to be with you. For as long I can, I just want to love you."

Veronica could barely see through the tears, both hands over her mouth to hold in the sobs. She stepped around the corner to see Shane rising to his feet, the look of defeat and sadness on his face making her cry harder, then he lifted his head and saw her.

"Veronica?" He glanced back at her door, then at her. "You're not in there."

She shook her head, swiping at tears. "No, I'm not."

"You heard that?" he whispered, cautious hope lighting his face.

She nodded, coming to a stop in front of him. "I think all my neighbors heard it, too."

He winced. "Sorry. I didn't think about that."

"Don't you dare be sorry," she said on a fierce sob. "That was the best thing I've ever heard in my life."

"Does that mean you forgive me for being a dick?" he asked cautiously.

"Yes," she assured him with a watery laugh. "But if you do it again, I reserve the right to kick your ass."

"Fair enough," he said, a cautious smile making his beard twitch in that way that she loved so much.

"I've been going to a support group," she blurted out.

He blinked. "What?"

"A support group," she repeated. "It's called More to Love, it's for polyamorous and non-monogamous people."

"Since when?"

"Pretty much since we got back from Bermuda. I've been reading too, blogs and books, and listening to podcasts on polyamory."

"Why didn't you say anything?"

She shrugged, feeling a little foolish. "I wanted to make sure it was something I could do. That it was the right choice for me, not just something I was putting up with for you."

"And is it?" he asked, cautious hope in his teddy bear eyes.

"I think so," she said slowly. "I'm still working out some of the details, but I think we can make it work. I want to try. Because I love you."

He stared at her. "What?"

"I love you," she repeated.

His arms came around her, bands of steel that squeezed hard and cut off her air, but she didn't care.

"Really?" he asked, and she realized he was crying too.

"Yes." She kissed his cheek. "Yes." His other cheek. "Yes." His mouth.

When she broke free, she pressed her forehead to his. "We still have to talk, you know."

"I know."

"Want to come inside?"

He nodded.

"Want to spend the night?"

He nodded again.

"Okay." She dug out her keys, then stopped. "Wait. What about your date? Where's Wyatt?"

His smile went bright as the sun. "He's at my place. He told me if I didn't get my ass over here and beg for your forgiveness, he was going to make me go to one of Seth's lawyer dinners."

She blinked. "Good threat."

"Yeah. He said to tell you, if you forgave me, welcome to the family."

"Aw." She slipped her key into the lock and opened the door. "Maybe he can meet us for breakfast."

Shane smiled. "I think he'd like that."

Epilogue
Thanksgiving, One Year Later

S hane tried to slip out of bed without waking his sleeping lover, but his pocket watch banged against the nightstand, and he felt the mattress shift behind him. "Shane? You going?"

He turned to Wyatt. "Yeah. I promised Veronica I'd help her with the cooking today. Go back to sleep."

Wyatt yawned hugely, shivering in the cool morning air. "What time is it?"

"Just after four."

"Fuck." He blinked rapidly. "Why do people start cooking so early on Thanksgiving?"

"According to Veronica, because big ass turkeys take forever to cook, and so dinner is ready to eat at halftime of the Lions game." Shane tugged his jeans on, then reached for the cashmere sweater Veronica had given him for Christmas the year before.

"Good reason," Wyatt said with a sleepy smile. "It's nice, you guys having everybody over today."

"Yeah. She's jazzed about it."

"Her friends from the support group are coming?"

"Far as I know." Shane stepped into his boots, careful to do it quietly. Seth was asleep down the hall, and he didn't want to wake him. "They're bringing the kid, too, so that should be interesting with the puppy."

"I love how you call him a puppy when he already outweighs you."

"He doesn't outweigh me. He might outweigh Veronica before long, though."

Wyatt sat up against the headboard, the covers falling to his waist. "What time are we supposed to be there?"

"Game's on at noon, dinner at halftime." Shane picked up his keys and shrugged into his jacket. "If you want to come early, you can."

"Seth probably won't be up for a few hours, but we'll be there by kickoff. Do you need us to bring anything? Maybe a pie?"

Shane lifted his hands to tie his hair back. "You're going to bring a pie?"

Wyatt shrugged. "If you need a pie, we'll bring a pie."

"You're going to make a pie."

"I'm not going to make a pie, I'll buy a pie. Do I look like Betty Crocker to you?"

"It's Thanksgiving Day, Wy." Shane finished tying his hair back.

"So? Meijer is open."

"Thanks for the thought, but we're covered for pie. Could use some beer, though."

"Meijer has that, too."

"Great. Get some beer." Shane leaned over the bed, lingering over the kiss just long enough to wish he had time to climb back in. "See you later."

"You and your woman. Speaking of Veronica, you think she might be up for another get-together soon?" Wyatt's grin turned impish. "I've had this hankering for peaches lately."

Shane straightened, amused. "We'll talk about it. But not today. Don't make Thanksgiving weird."

"I'm the soul of discretion," Wyatt said soberly.

"Uh-huh. By kickoff," Shane said. "If you're late, we're making you do the dishes."

Wyatt grinned. "I'll just put all the plates on the floor for the dog to lick. That's why you got him, right?"

"Gross, Wy." Shane headed for the door. "Very gross."

"I've seen you do it," Wyatt told him.

"Don't tell Veronica or you'll never taste peaches again," Shane warned.

"Damn, that's cold." Wyatt clutched his chest as though wounded, then laughed. "Love you."

Shane paused at the door to smile at Wyatt, all tousled blond hair and sleepy blue eyes. "Love you, too. See you in a couple of hours."

He let himself out of the house and climbed into his truck, the radio on low as he made his way through town. The city felt nearly deserted in the dark of pre-dawn, and he was pulling into his driveway in less than half the time it normally took. But the lights of home were already lit, and he could hear music when he let himself in the back door.

Dolly Parton, he realized, heading for the kitchen as the opening strains of 9 to 5 rang through the house.

"If you so much as lick this bird, I swear you'll never sleep on the bed again," he heard Veronica say over the music, and rounding the corner, came to a stop. She stood at the wide island in one of his dress shirts, the sleeves rolled to her elbows, the tails flirting with her bare thighs. Her hand was halfway up a turkey's ass while she lectured the gangly mutt who sat patiently at her feet, his head nearly level with her waist.

"I'm not kidding," she told the dog and crammed another handful of stuffing into the bird. "You'll have to sleep on the floor like a..." She paused, frowning. "I was going to say like a dog, but you are a dog."

The dog merely licked his chops and eyed the turkey, clearly calculating how far he'd have to jump to gain access to the countertop.

"I don't think he knows he's a dog," Shane said, smiling when she jumped. The dog never took his eyes off the turkey. "He doesn't act like one, anyway."

"What do you mean?" she asked as he crossed the room to greet her with a kiss. "He knows he's a dog."

He kissed her again, inhaling the scent of peaches and Veronica and whatever was already simmering on the stove. "He sleeps on the bed, tries to climb in the shower with me every morning, and sticks his tongue in every wine glass he finds."

She giggled. "So? Dogs do that."

"Uh-huh. And I don't know if you noticed, but he's a shit watchdog. He's so focused on the turkey he didn't even hear me come in."

"Sure, he did. But he knew it was you, and he's hungry."

"Right." He eyed the dog. The vet thought he had some Great Dane in him, and Shane thought she was probably right. "Are we sticking with George for his name?"

"You don't think he looks like a George?" Veronica asked, her head tilted to the side. Her hair was longer now, and she'd pulled it back into a cute little tail that bounced when she moved.

He reached out to tug it. "I think he looks ridiculous."

She elbowed him in the ribs. "Stop that. You'll give him a complex."

He looked at George again, who hadn't stopped staring at the bird. "Right. You need help with this?"

"In a minute. How was your date?"

"It was good. We hit a comedy club downtown."

She resumed stuffing the bird. "It was fun?"

"Yeah. You'd like it. We'll go sometime."

"Okay. And how's Wyatt?"

"He's good. He says he's been missing you."

She glanced up, a look of confusion in her pretty hazel eyes. "I see him all the time."

"Not that kind of missing you," he replied and cocked an eyebrow.

"Oh." Her cheeks turned pink, and her teeth came out to nibble on her lower lip. "That kind of missing."

"Yeah." Unable to resist, he slipped an arm around her and leaned down to nuzzle into her neck. "What do you think?"

"I wouldn't be opposed to that," she said, tilting her head to give him better access. "Maybe this time I'll try taking you both on."

He growled against her neck. "Now you're just teasing me," he told her, loving the way her breasts jiggled against his arm when she laughed. "I told him we'd talk about it later."

She jerked back, alarmed. "Not at dinner, right? Because I'm already going to have enough trouble keeping Delia in line."

He chuckled. "No, not at dinner, and not today."

"Okay." She smiled up at him, her cheeks rosy and her eyes bright. "By the way, George slept on your side of the bed last night. You might have to fight him for it tonight."

"You're not supposed to let him do that," he reminded her and glared at the dog. George kept staring at the turkey.

"Hey, he started out at the foot of the bed, but after I was asleep, he migrated up." She shoved the last little bit of stuffing in the turkey and nudged Shane aside to walk to the sink. "He's a pretty good cuddler, but he pokes me with his feet and he snores."

"You snore," Shane reminded her, and grinned when she glared at him.

"Don't start with that." She washed her hands briskly, jerking her chin at the turkey. "Can you put that in the oven for me?"

"Sure." He lowered the door of the oven, spilling heat into the room, and hefted the roasting pan. "Damn, how much does this thing weigh?"

"Only twenty-five pounds."

He bobbled the pan, nearly making George's day, but caught it at the last second. "Twenty-five pounds? Babe, there are ten people. And one of them is a year old."

"So? This way everyone can take home leftovers."

He shook his head and slid it into the oven, then shut the door. "You don't think you're going overboard?"

"It's our first Thanksgiving," she reminded him. "It's a big deal."

"Last year was our first Thanksgiving," he told her, and now that she wasn't covered in salmonella, pulled her into his arms.

She snuggled in. "Last year was our first Thanksgiving together, but we were just dating. Now we're living together, and hosting all our friends. It's a big deal."

He smiled at her earnestness. "You're very cute."

"Flattery, sir, will get you everywhere."

"Everywhere, huh?"

She wiggled closer to nip at his collarbone. "Everywhere."

"Will it get me a shower buddy? I didn't take the time to clean up at Wyatt's."

"Hmm. I could be persuaded to wash your back."

He started backing her down the hall. "Just my back?"

"Maybe a few other things." Her eyes laughed up at him as he maneuvered her down the hall, through the bedroom to the bath. "Your feet get kind of stinky."

He choked on a laugh. "Good to know."

"Make sure you shut the door, or George is going to follow us in," she reminded him.

He kicked it shut, then toed off his boots. "If you're going to wash my feet, you're going to need to be naked."

"Well, if I have to," she sighed and began unbuttoning the borrowed shirt.

He stopped to watch, enthralled as always by the contrast between the curves and dips of her body and the straight lines of the shirt, and by the time he remembered to take off his clothes she was already naked and in the shower. She ducked under the spray, her eyes laughing at him as steam fogged up the glass wall. "Come on, slowpoke. I have a lot to do before everyone gets here."

"Yeah?" He got naked in short order and joined her. "Well, I have you to do before everyone gets here."

She snorted with laughter. "That's terrible."

"You love it," he told her.

"I love you," she replied, her voice softening.

"I love you, too." He leaned down to kiss her, loving the slide of her soft lips on his, the taste of her as she opened up to him. "Thanks for taking a chance on me."

"You're welcome. Thanks for dicking me down so good in Bermuda I had to come back for more."

He buried his face in her neck, shaking with laughter. "If we ever get married, you should put that in your wedding vows."

She snorted. "Yeah, my mother would love that."

"Maybe not exactly those words," he reconsidered, thinking of Veronica's mother. Humorless was a good description. "But the sentiment."

"I'll see what I can do." She pulled back to look at him. "Are you asking me to marry you?"

"Do you want me to?" he countered.

She smiled at him, her fingers toying with his hair. "Maybe in another year."

"That's what you said last year," he pointed out.

"I know." She shrugged. "I'm not in a hurry. I like where we are now."

"So do I."

"Speaking of which, are we just in this shower for hygienic purposes, or can I get a Thanksgiving dicking?"

He heaved a sigh. "If I must."

"Hey, you don't want to get it on, I'll just make love to the showerhead," she said and reached over to grab the massage wand. "It has more settings than you anyway."

"You keep threatening to do that, and one of these days I'm going to make you do it while I watch," he warned her.

"Yeah, yeah, yeah," she said, clearly unimpressed with the threat. "Hurry it up, will you? I have pies to bake."

He scooped her up in his arms, laughing. "Fuck, I love you."

"I know." She curled her arms around his neck, a smug smile on her pretty, pretty mouth. "I love you too. Now prove it."

He did.

And they lived happily ever after.

The End

For Readers

Thank you for reading ***Sharing Shane***! I hope you enjoyed Shane and Veronica's journey as much as I enjoyed writing it.

Authors love reviews, and I'm no different. If you have thoughts on ***Sharing Shane*** you'd like to share with other readers, you can do so on Goodreads, BookBub, or your favorite bookseller's website. Please also feel free to post your thoughts on your blog or social media accounts, and know that your review—be it 1 star or 5—is welcome and valued.

Hannah

Thank You

To Lexie Eldridge for her keen editing eye and for believing so strongly in this project.

To Christine Warren for always being willing to listen to me talk out my plot problems—even when I don't actually have a plot problem.

To my husband for his love and support and for being my biggest cheerleader. I love you, babe.

And finally, to my beautiful child, for putting up with Mom writing "those yucky romances".

About the Author

Hannah has been reading romance novels since she was young enough to have to hide them from her mother. She lives in the Pacific Northwest with her husband—former Special Forces and an OR nurse who writes sci-fi fantasy and acts as In-House Expert on matters pertaining to weapons, tactics, the military, medical conditions, and physics—their daughter, who takes after her father, her best friend Christine Warren, and a ridiculous dog named Agatha.

ALSO BY HANNAH MURRAY

Single Titles

Their Perfect Fit

Honey and the Hitman

Sun, Sea & Satisfaction Guaranteed

Just A Little Crush

Goldie & The Bears

F.I.L.T.H Series

Stuffed

Starved

Feast

Perfect Taboo Series

Book No. 1 – Santa Daddy

Book No. 2 – The Shame Game

Book No. 3 – Sharing His Submissive

Book No. 4 – Show Me Something Good

Book No. 5 – In His Hands

Book No. 6 – The Sadist and the Brat

Previously Published by Ellora's Cave
Now Available in KU!

Jane and the Sneaky Dom

The Devil & Ms. Johnson

Knockout

Tooth and Nailed

One Hit Wonderful

A Toy Story

scan for the full book list